TOO SOON?

Marcus looked up her, at her hair shining in the firelight; he watched the thoughts flicker across her green-gold eyes. Then he rose and walked around the table, taking her hand and lifting it up. "Make yourself comfortable for the night," he said. "I will sleep outside."

She started to protest, then pressed her lips together. She could hardly invite him to share the tent with her. So she gave a little nod. Marcus gathered a blanket and prepared to leave while his servant cleared the table. They were left alone again.

"Sleep well," he said. "We will break camp early." He gazed at her for a long moment, and then he raised his hand to her face and did what he had said he would not do. He leaned down and kissed her.

His warm lips found hers, and one arm drifted across her soft shoulders. At once his body responded to her softness. She stretched her arms around his neck and returned the kiss, her body betraying her desire. Suddenly, the longing she had held suppressed for so long spilled over, and her mouth parted to receive his deepening kiss.

"Come with me," he whispered. "I will make you mine."

His touch was gentle now, like music from a lyre. He moved slowly, dropping kisses on her throat and shoulder, pushing her mantle aside. Then he wrapped her in his arms again and held her as if he would never let her go. . . .

PATRICIA WERNER

THE FALCON AND THE SWORD

ZEBRA BOOKS
KENSINGTON PUBLISHING CORP.

ZEBRA BOOKS are published by

Kensington Publishing Corp.
475 Park Avenue South
New York, NY 10016

Quotations from the poetry of Fortunatus are from *A Basket of Chestnuts: From the Miscellanea of Venantius Fortunatus,* translated by Geoffrey Cook. Cherry Valley Editions, Cherry Valley, New York, 1981

Quotations from Gregory of Tours are from *The History of the Franks,* translated by Lewis Thorpe, Penguin Books, New York, 1974

Zebra, the Z logo, Heartfire Romance, and the Heartfire Romance logo are trademarks of Kensington Publishing Corp.

First Printing: August, 1993

Printed in the United States of America

Sixth Century Gaul

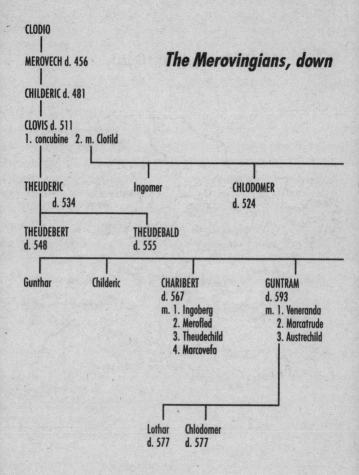

The Merovingians, down

CLODIO
|
MEROVECH d. 456
|
CHILDERIC d. 481
|
CLOVIS d. 511
1. concubine 2. m. Clotild

THEUDERIC   Ingomer   CHLODOMER
    d. 534   d. 524

THEUDEBERT   THEUDEBALD
d. 548   d. 555

Gunthar   Childeric   CHARIBERT   GUNTRAM
                        d. 567   d. 593
                        m. 1. Ingoberg   m. 1. Veneranda
                           2. Merofled   2. Marcatrude
                           3. Theudechild   3. Austrechild
                           4. Marcovefa

                        Lothar   Chlodomer
                        d. 577   d. 577

to Dagobert (not complete)

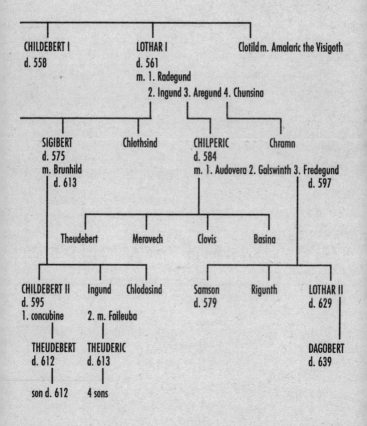

CHILDEBERT I
d. 558

LOTHAR I
d. 561
m. 1. Radegund
2. Ingund 3. Aregund 4. Chunsina

Clotild m. Amalaric the Visigoth

SIGIBERT
d. 575
m. Brunhild
d. 613

Chlothsind

CHILPERIC
d. 584
m. 1. Audovera 2. Galswinth 3. Fredegund
d. 597

Chramn

Theudebert   Merovech   Clovis   Basina

CHILDEBERT II
d. 595
1. concubine

Ingund

Chlodosind

Samson
d. 579

Rigunth

LOTHAR II
d. 629

THEUDEBERT
d. 612

THEUDERIC
d. 613
2. m. Faileuba

DAGOBERT
d. 639

son d. 612

4 sons

Prologue

The priest Gregory of Tours scratched away with reed stylus on a sheet of parchment. *A great many things keep happening, some of them good, some of them bad,* he wrote. *The inhabitants of different countries keep quarreling fiercely and kings go on losing their temper in the most furious way.*

He paused and stared at his words. Not very literary, he was well aware, but it said what he observed. And after all, this was to be a chronicle of his own times. He lamented the fact that his Latin was faulty, even though he'd had the best education Roman Gaul could offer. But he was determined not to let a grammatical error here or there stand in the way of his narrative, the story of events as they unraveled before him, slotted into the history of the world.

He had already dealt briskly with the creation of the world, galloped through the Old and New Testaments, and dovetailed into the invasions of various tribes into Gaul, their conflict with Rome, and in not too many pages, got to the rise of the Franks. But it was his own times he was most concerned with, for this book was a project he planned to work on most of his life.

He was about to apply the stylus to another sentence

when the outer door opened, and he heard his host speak to a servant. Gregory put down his work and rose, glad to see his friend returned home.

"Ah, Gregory," said Bishop Salvius, who entered the room where Gregory had his parchment spread on a sloping writing desk. "I see you have been at work."

Gregory came around the desk to greet the bishop. "It whiles away the time until I set out on my return journey."

The servant noiselessly entered the room carrying a silver tray which held a blue glass carafe and two drinking glasses. The bishop gestured for the servant to leave the tray on the marble table. Then he poured both glasses full of deep red wine, which turned black in the heavy blue glass. He handed Gregory his, and they raised their glasses to each other's health.

"And how is the chronicle going?" asked the bishop, seating himself in the chair opposite the desk where Gregory had been working.

"I've nearly reached our own times."

"That is quite an accomplishment if you began at the beginning as is traditional in such a work."

"I cannot take too much credit," said Gregory. "The creation of the earth and the Biblical stories took up the first book. I am only just a few pages into Book Two."

Salvius smiled. "A pity I won't be here at the end of your life to read what you have written. Surely by then you will have filled a great many books."

"Perhaps," mused Gregory.

Their conversation turned for a while to the upcoming council in Paris, the reason Gregory had stayed on at Rouen. But already he was chafing to return to Tours where he was deacon and there was so much work to do. Finally both men rose and donned their cloaks, brought by the servant, for they had been invited to dine at the house of a wealthy Gallo-Roman merchant who was a generous contributor to the church. The parchment upon which Gregory wrote waited for his return:

In 486 A.D. King Clovis led the Frankish tribes in Gaul to overthrow the Roman power, thus beginning the rule of the Merovingian kings, so called because they traced their ancestry to the hero Merovech, an earlier Germanic leader of the Franks. The Frankish people attempted to imitate Rome in culture and politics, thus melding their more Teutonic habits with the remnants of Roman Gaul.

When the Romans withdrew their forces, the Church remained in place. In a pitched battle with the neighboring Teutons, King Clovis recalled that his wife had been urging him to accept Christianity. He raised his eyes to heaven and called on the Christian God, promising that if aid were granted he would believe and be baptized.

The battle was won and on Christmas Day, 496 A.D., King Clovis and 3,000 of his followers became Christians. When he was told of Christ's crucifixion, he clutched his battle axe and cried, "If I had been there with my Franks, I would have avenged His wrongs!"

The Merovingian dynasty ruled for 265 years until Pepin the Short was made king in 751 and so established the Carolingian dynasty which followed.

This manuscript is about Clovis's sons' sons. . . .

Chapter One

Venantius Fortunatus drank from a cup of the abbey's best hot-spiced wine, then wiped his sleeve across his lips. He looked up into the noble face of Queen Radegund, foundress of the Abbey of the Holy Cross.

"You always indulge me in the pleasures of the table, my holy mother. Is this fair, when you and Sister Agnes cannot share these dishes with me? At least come sit at the table with me. I cannot bear it when you wait on me hand and foot and yet take nothing but bread and herbs yourself."

Radegund smiled lovingly at her guest and did as she was bid. She sat on the wooden bench at the long trestle table and arranged her fine unbleached woolen robe about her as if it were the silken finery she used to wear when she was queen. She never forgot that she was once a queen, though she did everything in her power to forget that she was ever wife to a Frankish king.

Even then she had devoted her time to Christian charity, eschewing the Frankish court with its boisterous banquets, dangerous hunts, uncultured and rough-spoken vassals. After six years, she had finally obtained the king's permission to renounce the world and establish the Abbey of the Holy Cross on this plot of land at the gates of the city of Poitiers in Roman Gaul.

Fortunatus sat in an ornately carved high-backed armchair at the head of the table so that Radegund and the abbess, Sister Agnes, could better serve him. He spilled a drop of wine on his wide blue linen sleeve, and Sister Agnes handed him a damp cloth and a bowl of water with which to sponge the stain.

"How clumsy of me," he said. "And I do not want to waste a drop of this fine wine."

"It gives us more pleasure to please you, for you are a most agreeable guest," said the Mother Superior. "The wine does not go to waste."

Radegund always lavished attention on such devout and cultivated men, for they were a rarity in the land now. And since the Italian poet, Venantius Fortunatus, had stopped at the abbey on his excursion of piety and pleasure across Gaul, she had welcomed the literary discussions and listened avidly to his news.

For himself, he was charmed by the devout queen, who was much older than he. He rarely saw the ash-colored hair she kept hidden under her wimple, but he adored her noble beauty, even in her advanced years, and found but a few character lines in her long oval face. He felt it a shame that she had to wear the un-bleached cream linen and wool of her order, for he wanted to see her in vibrant tones complementing the tint of olive in her complexion, the opaque gray-green eyes with small dark flecks.

"But you do too much," Fortunatus continued to insist.

He brushed his fingertips across the rose petals that covered the table and gazed at the garlands of fragrant blossoms that mantled the limestone and plaster walls.

14

Though he protested, hadn't he found himself in Poitiers longer than he had planned to be? For him, these meals with his dear friends, Radegund and Sister Agnes, recalled the elegance that had been the Roman empire at its zenith, a Rome of which he had read much in the writings that had survived—a Rome that was close to his heart. For he was perhaps more of that time than this.

Wine flowed from his cup and warmed his veins. Herbs grown in the convent garden seasoned his food. And he was becoming aware that his friendship with the two women had deepened.

"Ah, Agnes," he said, as the young sister reentered, carrying a platter of roast goose. "What have your lovely, capable hands prepared for my ever greedy stomach?"

"A goose, fattened on corn grown in our own fields," she answered.

Her eyes, at first hidden by her wimple, smiled merrily as she set down the goose, then placed before him bread still warm from the embers in the hearth. Then she sat, her back straight, on the bench opposite Radegund. Agnes served, Radegund poured more wine from a ewer, and Fortunatus ate and drank.

Finally, he sat back, his hunger mollified. "I do not see how I can tear myself away from here," he said. "But tomorrow I leave for Tours, three days' journey."

"But you will return, will you not?" said Radegund. "You had promised to tutor Judith, and I have granted her permission. She is a bright girl, and she has stretched our capabilities."

They spoke of the novice who had come to them eight years ago at the age of eight, captured in a border skirmish when the Frankish King Chilperic had fought the Visigoths who now ruled Spain. Radegund had taken a special interest in Judith's upbringing and had given her the best education she could, including Greek and Latin literature, the poets as well as religious writing. It was a similar upbringing to Radegund's own, though she had been raised to be a queen.

"I'm afraid she has not been content with her domestic skills, though she does them well enough. She has read all the pious books, and her Greek and Latin are good enough that when she takes her vows, I shall use her in the scriptorium. We have many books that need transcribing so as to make more copies available."

"Then what can a poor poet like me offer her?" asked Fortunatus. "It seems you have done your job well, my noble mother." He tilted his winecup. Seeing it was empty, Agnes quickly refilled it.

Radegund smiled one of her angelic smiles at her friend, and then looked down at the table as if aware that she was enjoying herself too much. When she had replaced exhilaration with compassion, she raised her eyes again, more appropriate expressions of her feelings now forthcoming.

"Though a Visigoth by birth, there is something in Judith that longs for the glory of antiquity. Shall we say I simply believe you to be kindred spirits? No harm would come of it. She believes she could learn from you. I do not think she is wrong."

Pride shone in Radegund's eyes as she thought of her plans for Judith. It was not too much to hope that should she prove worthy, she might one day become abbess and run the abbey when Radegund and Agnes were too old to do so and would wish to retire to solitary contemplation.

Fortunatus had been half listening to Radegund while his thoughts drifted to the younger, fairer Sister Agnes. She was exceedingly pretty tonight, though her wimple covered all but her smooth brow, her downcast eyes, her lovely proportioned nose, and delicate pink lips. Her loveliness stirred him.

She glanced up just once to catch his gaze and return his smile. Then she went to fetch the sweet — strawberry pudding with pomegranate seeds. When he had finished the tasty pudding made by the nuns, Fortunatus sat back in the chair. Truly, he was comfortable here, warmed by the food, the wine, the company. And in another month it would be very cold for travel.

"Ah, but you tempt me sorely with each new task you find for me to make myself useful to you. Is it not because all excuses for staying are used up, and I truly must set out again?"

Radegund and Agnes exchanged glances across the trestle table. Then Agnes turned her whole body toward him.

"Why leave? Why not stay with us?"

The air escaped his lungs, and he felt dizzied by the expression of sisterly love he saw on both women's faces. At that moment a decree of destiny rang in his ears, and he knew as he looked at them that he would not recross the Alps to his homeland in Italy.

Fortunatus had spent most of his life traveling from villa to court to basilica, composing for the kings and the nobility of the semibarbarian Franks who had conquered Roman Gaul. His Latin poems, if not always perfectly understood, were well received and well paid for in coin, gifts, and hospitality. But he had never been so happy as at this holy abbey with Radegund and Agnes, whom he loved as a mother and a sister.

"I must admit the idea pleases me," he said.

"I had prayed for this," said Radegund, bringing her hands upward and folding them together on the table. She leaned forward. "There are matters that call for immediate attention and firmness. You are aware of the abbey's considerable landholdings. Unfortunately there are those who threaten with encroachment. We need a man to help us."

"We felt your skill at negotiations and worldly knowledge would be beneficial," said Agnes, her cheeks again taking on a rosy flush, her dove's voice floating mellifluously to Fortunatus's ears as she took up the argument. He thought she had leaned on the word "worldly."

He saw his role immediately. Advisor, ambassador, confidential secretary to the former queen and the abbess. He had no trouble with the moral pliancy that would allow him to continue some of his softer, more sensuous habits. But Fortunatus never forgot to pay homage to the principles his conduct sometimes betrayed.

He cleared his throat. "If you wish, then I shall take holy orders."

All three smiled warmly at each other. "Let it be done," said Radegund.

When they first fought their way into Gaul, the Frankish tribes were allotted lands to live on in return for military assistance they agreed to provide the Roman emperors. Roman Gaul was now divided into three Frankish kingdoms, which had been ruled by the Merovingian dynasty ever since Clovis united the Franks in Gaul in 486 and carved himself a kingdom upon Rome's retreat.

It was the Frankish custom to divide the kingdom equally among all male heirs, and so the sons of Clovis had divided it. When Lothar, the last of Clovis's sons, died, his four sons in turn repartitioned Gaul among themselves.

Now Lothar's eldest son had died, bringing about a new territorial upheaval in the empire of the Franks. King Chilperic ruled over the kingdom of Neustria to the northwest. His older brother, King Guntram held all of the territory of Orléans and Burgundy as far as the Alps. The kingdom of Austrasia, to the northeast, belonged to their other brother, King Sigibert, who combined his share of the Auvergne with the entire northeast of Gaul and Germany as far as the Saxon and Slav frontiers.

North of Paris, at Soissons, an immense estate sprawled on the edge of a great forest. The royal villa was a vast building surrounded by Roman-style porticoes made of limestone and highly polished wood and decorated with ornate carvings. Behind the main villa were arranged the quarters of the palace officials. Other, more humble, timber-frame houses were occupied by the artisans and craftsmen needed to support the royal residence. Goldsmiths, armorers, weavers, and curriers were for the most part natives of Gaul. Cow sheds, sheep pens, barns, huts of the farm laborers and the serfs of the estate completed the village.

Inside the villa, in the large hall used for interviews, King Chilperic clenched his fist and brought it down hard on the marble table before him. The ambassador who stood opposite him stepped back a pace, his long robe swinging out of the way of the royal seal, which tumbled to his feet as if animating Chilperic's displeasure. A palace administrator, who was one of the king's many hands and eyes, scrambled to pick the royal image off the mosaic floor.

"I have promised to forsake my queen and concubines so long as I obtain a wife worthy of me, and I will live with my new wife according to the law of God," said Chilperic irritably. "Must I suffer these further negotiations?"

He pointed a heavily beringed finger at the ambassador, his long hair and moustache giving him a fierce visage.

"You were responsible for making the King of the Goths understand that I will present his daughter with a morrow-gift worthy of her nobility."

He spoke of the Teutonic custom for the groom to give the bride a valuable present when she awoke from her marriage night as the price of her virginity. Chilperic was prepared to present to Galswinth, the Gothic princess for whom he was negotiating, five cities together with the lands adjacent to them and all their populations. She would collect tributes and taxes from them all.

"Yes, my lord."

The ambassador was patient, even though his long journey from Spain had tired him enormously. He longed to retreat to his chambers and rest his sore body on his feather mattress, but this inevitable meeting with the king had to be concluded first. He shuffled words in his head and opened his mouth to speak.

"King Athanagild has found that such an alliance with you offers so many political advantages that he wishes to hesitate no longer, but on receiving the guarantee of these final arrangements written in the marriage contract, he will sign it."

The ambassador's words placated Chilperic somewhat. "Indeed, it is most fortunate that my brother Charibert died so recently. Because of that I have gained Limoges, Cahors, Bordeaux, Bigorre, Bearn, and the cantons of the Upper Pyrenees. I am the nearest neighbor of the king of the Goths, my future father-in-law." His lip curled under his blond moustache, and he gave a satisfied grunt.

Color returned to the ambassador's face. "And you have accepted the amount offered for the dowry in money and valuables. Surely King Athanagild will agree now."

"I have accepted the amount of the dowry?" asked Chilperic.

"You were about to accept." The ambassador gave a sympathetic smile, for he trod the narrow line between cajolery and persuasion. The latter was far more dangerous.

"Very well," boomed Chiperic. "Let us get on with it. Enough months have passed. I am anxious for my wedding. Then no one can say that I am living a less noble, less kingly life than my brother, Sigibert."

"Surely no one can say that, my lord, especially since you will be wed to the eldest princess, whereas Sigibert settled for the younger, less experienced daughter. Surely the older daughter will bring you more grace."

He bowed his head as if to emphasize the advantage of the match with Princess Galswinth.

It rankled Chilperic that when Sigibert had brought his bride from Spain she had at once become noted for her beauty and charm. Chilperic knew his brother doted on her, lived without any concubines, and that everyone said Sigibert's queen, Brunhild, was discreet and intelligent. It further rankled Chilperic that he, himself, might be less respected than Sigibert, even in his own realm.

The height of insult came when he had decided to ask for Athanagild's eldest daughter. His envoys had met with difficulty, returning with the message that the king of the Goths believed the rumors that Chilperic, though a Christian, was leading a heathen life. They referred to his excesses in drink and the many women he kept. Not to be outdone by the reputation his brother earned when he took a high-born wife, Chilperic had agreed to Athanagild's terms. It had become an obsession to marry the Gothic princess Galswinth.

A sound rumbled from Chilperic's throat. "Give it to me." He reached for the document the ambassador held in his hands in front of him. The ambassador untied the leather thong and unrolled the document, copied in the best Latin hand. He placed the parchment on the table, and handed Chilperic a stylus, which the king dipped into a jar of ink and used to scratch his signature in the place provided.

The administrator who had earlier rescued the royal seal from the floor now dipped it in hot wax and stamped it on the document, making it official. For the seal represented the king's authority, showing him front faced, long haired and eyes staring, as if about to speak for himself.

"My congratulations, sir," said the ambassador in a low, serious tone.

Chilperic tossed the stylus on the table. "Tell her to hurry here to enjoy the honors at my side. Athanagild will not regret his decision."

Neither king, ambassador nor retainers in the king's royal chambers noticed the wooden door at the side of the room move shut a fraction of an inch. It was the door that led down a private passage and eventually to Chilperic's bedchamber.

The woman in the passage now was no stranger to it, and so had the convenience of overhearing the king's business whenever she wanted. As his favorite concubine, her movements about the royal residence were not restricted.

Fredegund shut the wooden door carefully and ran

along the flagstone floor to the bedchamber when she heard Chilperic dismiss the ambassador, for she suspected that the king might come into his private apartment to relax after his interview.

Once in the bedchamber, she quickly loosened the girdle knotted at her waist and lowered herself to the gold-balustered feather bed, turning herself on the side so that one breast hung heavily against the opening of her sleeveless yellow tunic. Then she lifted the material up over one leg, which she bent. She half shut her eyes, her golden hair splayed across embroidered cushions, a gold-spiraled armlet coiling tightly across the flesh of the arm that was flung across an ermine rug covering the bed.

No sooner had she arranged herself than Chilperic came through the door. Seeing her thus, he stopped and stared at her.

"Fredegund. What are you about? You'll get fat if you do nothing but lie about in my chambers all day."

But even in his admonishment, she could see that he was teasing her, for his words had turned throaty, the way they always did when he saw her thus.

She feigned sleepiness. "I was with the other women, my lord. But I longed for a rest. My fingers are pricked from the needles used to embroider your robes, and the spinning can be exhausting. I was in hopes that you would conclude your business for the morning and seek some relaxation here yourself."

She curved fingers and hand in a gesture for him to join her and moved slightly, smiling knowingly and wetting her lips. Chilperic laughed, a pleased light in his eye, feeling his erection start. He took his time, however, first pouring himself a goblet of wine from the silver ewer on the small table beside the bed.

He drank it down, poured another and brought it to

where Fredegund had moved to lie on her back, her robe pulled up to reveal both thighs. He drank while gazing at her fine translucent skin, her tousled hair, the color of ripe grain, her sleepy eyes under sand-colored lashes. He handed the goblet to her while he unclasped the buckle that fastened his vermilion mantle.

Then he raised his cream-colored tunic and unfastened the tight-fitting breeches beneath, exposing his erection for her to toy with. She rose to her knees, clasping him about the waist, leaning forward slightly, so that her breasts fit heavily into his hands. He leaned over and opened her mouth with his lips and tongue, while with one hand she began to work her magic on his groin. She sucked the wine from his lips and blond moustache.

When he was ready to enter her, he pushed her back on the bed, her tunic thrown up about her waist, her legs splayed. Then he plunged into her as she rolled her head back and forth in pleasure.

When he was done, he rolled beside her, his tunic only half covering his manhood, while she lay with her eyes closed, her hair caught under his head. The sexual hunger in Fredegund's body was beginning to recede, replaced by her resolve to use all her wiles to save her place with the king. She was determined that no Gothic princess was going to stand in her way. Contract or no contract, she would see that the licentious ruler of the western Frankish kingdom would not be able to live without his concubine's indulgences. She would stimulate his appetite so that there was no danger of its being satisfied by some frigid Goth.

Chapter Two

Judith approached the brass-spigoted marble pillar in the corner of the stone courtyard where the kitchen met the refectory. The marble pillar, about five feet high, was carved all around with fish and birds. The brass spigots bent outward, each with a stopcock. A catch basin circled the pillar, and drains took the water away.

She reached for the jar of slippery, pastelike soap that sat on top of the pillar and turned on a spigot to dabble her hands in the stream of water. How good it felt on hands that were ink-stained and dry from helping the sisters in the scriptorium.

She pushed up the sleeves of her spun hemp tunic to wash up to her elbows and then splashed the cool water on her face, the tingle refreshing her. She had been up since dawn, and as usual at this time of day, she had started to drowse. But the water made her blink her eyes and think of the interview ahead.

She replaced the linen towel on the wall hook, picked up the rolled parchment she had left leaning against the wall, tucked it in her sleeve and hurried along the flagstones to the rose garden where she was to meet Father Fortunatus.

It was only a few weeks since he had taken holy orders and become a priest. He had no real time to tutor her at present because of his many administrative duties, but he enjoyed their literary discussions as much as she did. A rapport had formed between them.

Judith had not been unhappy at the abbey, for Radegund's rule was not severe. Sister Agnes liked to say it was gentle as a linen robe. At least in the closed community, Judith had received an education and a taste for culture lacking in the world outside. It had become Judith's joy to assist the nuns as they transcribed books, and she had even taken to writing down her own thoughts at the end of the day on spare sheets of parchment she had obtained to practice copying.

Since Father Fortunatus was instructing her in classical literature, she had asked him to instruct her in the writing of verse as well, though she had not yet shown her efforts to anyone. But perhaps she would today, since she had brought the parchment with her.

She saw him at the end of the garden in his plain linen robe with tapered sleeves and white rope knotted at the waist. He was bending over a rosebush, and she slowed her pace, not wanting to startle him. But he sensed her coming and straightened to meet her.

Venantius Fortunatus was a vigorous and handsome man, despite the recently acquired tonsure which ringed his head and left his crown unshaven. The ample sleeves of his gown did not hide his long elegant fingers, now bejeweled with only a few of the gold and silver rings he so loved.

"Ah, Judith, it is time for our lesson," he said when he saw her. "What have you brought?"

She extracted the scroll from her sleeve and held it shyly behind her. He glanced at the supple young figure in the plain, unbleached garment touching her shoulders.

She smiled back at his welcome look, her green eyes sparkling against a lightly tanned complexion. She brought the scroll in front of her, still holding it with both hands.

"I have taken to heart your instructions in meter, Father. I hope you do not think it vain of me, but I have tried to put some of my own words in verse."

Fortunatus opened his eyes wider with interest. "Very ambitious. May I see?"

Even though she wanted his appraisal, still her hand shook as she surrendered the scroll to him.

"I'm sure it's nothing," she rushed on. "I've done much copying of verse. It seemed so natural to try my hand."

He unrolled the parchment and murmured some of the Latin words.

"It's very good," he said. He continued reading, frowning in places, but then a look of pride filled his eyes as he reached the end. He handed it back to her.

"Radegund was not wrong when she told me you showed much promise. You must continue your efforts."

The praise stunned her. "Surely, you find fault . . ."

He waved a hand to the side. "There is a line here or there that needs work. Some of the words do not flow naturally into one another. But you will learn by practicing. You already have a grasp on the Latin poets. Fortunately you were brought here"—he gestured to the abbey buildings surrounding them—"where Radegund's propensity for learning has rubbed off on you."

Judith lowered her gaze. "I have been grateful."

Fortunatus glanced at the downturned eyes, the brush of color in the golden complexion, and he saw the way she held her mouth in a straight line. He knew the expression, and he stretched his fingers to lift her chin so he could see into her eyes.

"What trouble lies in your heart, Judith? Would you not like to share your thoughts with me?"

The streaks of color in her cheeks flared across the rest of her face. "I . . ." She held herself in check.

How could she tell him the embarrassment she felt in confessing her thoughts to him now that he had taken holy orders? When he had first come to the abbey, a man of the world, a poet who had traveled far, she longed to talk to him, not only to learn all she could of the culture he represented, a rare light in these times of change, but of the news he always brought to the abbey. And she was fascinated to hear of the affairs of the world, the battles and squabbles of kings, the marriages of nobles, and the miracles that occurred at the tombs of saints. Yes, abbey life had been happy enough, but she knew now she was not cut out to be a nun. Dare she tell him that? The poet would have understood. The priest might not.

Fortunatus held her gaze, looking behind the transparent green eyes into her mind, a fertile mind, and one he would not want the wrong tutors to tamper with. Most of the minds he had met with had become rusty since the time of the barbarian invasions. Of course it was in monasteries and convents such as this where a sharp mind or two was most likely to be nourished. While the rest of the world either fought or struggled for survival, those who took religious vows had the leisure to learn. The religious life did have its advantages, something he was aware of when he had agreed to remain here.

He dropped his fingers and gestured to the flagstone path before them. "Come, walk with me. I enjoy the view from the walls. We can talk there."

Her heart hammered at the invitation to walk on the rampart. Usually they had their lessons in the garden.

They passed two nuns on hands and knees, pulling weeds out of the black dirt of a rose bed. Fortunatus was discreet. If this young woman had some problem to air, she could better unburden her thoughts in private. They passed under a stone archway and ascended the narrow steps that twisted upward. From atop the wall, where the sun shone brightly and a temperate autumn breeze touched their faces, they could see the garden on the other side and the countryside beyond.

The abbey grounds and outbuildings were arranged partly within and partly without the eastern wall of the city of Poitiers, which stood on a tiny acropolis rising out of the plain. Here the River Clain and a winding brook, the Boivre, met, nearly encircling the promontory, leaving it connected to the shore with only a small fortified isthmus.

The wall made of squared stones and mortar rising to a height of some thirty feet, served as the cloister's façade, with the main gate opening outward onto the garden where the nuns grew vegetables and herbs. Beyond, on the plains, were the farms with fields just harvested that comprised the abbey's landed estate.

Walking now along the high wall, they approached one of the stone turrets that gave the peaceful convent a peculiar martial appearance. They paused next to the stone turret, from where they could look down on the abbey, built like a Roman-style villa, with porticoes extending toward the courtyard. To the right the dormitory and the refectory. Behind these were the spinning, weaving, and drying rooms, the book room and the baths. To the left, connected by a colonnaded walkway, lay the chapel, built of stone with timbered roof.

On the other side of the far wall was Radegund's separate cell of limestone and brick, which she recently had built so that she could retire in seclusion for a good part of the year, leaving the running of the convent to Agnes and Fortunatus.

They walked for some moments in silence, gazing out over the thick masonry wall to the field and vineyard strips, edged by the river Clain and the forest beyond that. A road wound down the slope that led toward the river, then rose again on the other side. It was what Judith had been thinking of—life beyond the wall.

She gazed at the road cutting through the fields and felt her spirit lift out of her body and float toward the trees that lined the Clain. Her feet were solidly rooted where she stood, but she felt for a moment as if she could see farther than the low horizon, oddly displaced, as if she did not belong to her own time and place.

She turned to face Fortunatus, looking into the blue eyes. She stood so close she could see the heavy white webbing in the iris, the tiny veins under his skin. She knew that if she did not speak now, it would become more difficult later.

"I shall not take the veil," she said.

She stood facing him, her brows raised in defiance, wondering if he would make her defend her decision. But she had no other choice. She loved the abbey, but she did not feel God's call as the other sisters did. In some indefinable way she sensed that she was not meant for the religious life. At age sixteen, she was just beginning to taste the possibilities of her existence, even if she could not explain it. There was a feeling of ripeness about the coming days, a feeling that she wanted to use her talents for some new purpose, though she did not know what it was.

Fortunatus blinked, then relaxed his features into easy acceptance of the confidences with which people had always entrusted him. He smiled, turned again to watch the peasants, moving like specks in the distant fields.

"When this abbey was being built," he said slowly, "people watched from afar, deeply impressed by the preparations such a royal personage as Queen Radegund was making for retiring from the world. 'See the ark being built near us against the flood of passions and the storms of the world,' they said. For such a world it is."

He turned to Judith, whose face was tilted upward as she watched him, feeling less need to defend herself than a moment before.

"If you do not intend to take the veil," he said, "you will live in that bloody world? What will you do? Will you marry?"

Her words faltered at first, but then picked up speed, for this, too, she had thought out.

"I have no family to negotiate a marriage for me, and no dowry. Surely it is too much to hope, but I had thought that you could advise me."

She looked again at the fields that rolled across the plains in the distance. Here and there were the huts of the tenants.

"I would not ask for much, and I have learned how to cook and make clothing. I could make someone a good wife. Perhaps I could marry one of the abbey's tenants and remain nearby."

Fortunatus hid his smile. To her intelligence, charm, and unmarred beauty, he would add guilelessness. Surely any other young woman with a mind that had been trained as hers had been would have ambitions beyond being the wife of a peasant tenant. But he saw her point. She was officially only a freedwoman, and could marry either up or down the social scale. Judith had been captured at the age of eight with her mother in a raid when the Franks attacked the Visigothic capital in Spain. She was sent northward into the Frankish kingdom where her mother was made a slave of one of the king's warriors. When her mother had died of abuse and homesickness, the nuns at the Holy Cross bought her freedom and took her in.

He glanced at her sidelong. His last thought was not fitting to his new office of cleric. She would be very agreeable as a concubine. But he pushed the thought aside. That would not be practical here.

"Will you help me?" she asked.

He cleared his throat. "I will speak to Mother Radegund."

"Thank you, Father." Then she wrinkled her brow doubtfully. "Do you think she will find me ungrateful?"

Fortunatus smiled benevolently. "Though both Sister Agnes and our foundress Radegund rejected the married state, they would not withhold that blessing from another who sees that as her proper role. I am sure they would not want you to take holy vows unless you were very sure. A bride of Christ who breaks her vows is condemned to an eternity of hell."

Judith could see how the holy state of matrimony was preferable to that.

Thus agreed, they stood together for a moment, contemplating their own thoughts. Then Fortunatus paced back the way they had come, going on to other things. For days now he had experienced a need to air news of events that would affect the entire kingdom, and the abbey in particular. He had discussed it with Radegund, but she had been too caught up in abbey affairs to spare him much time.

And he had been keeping himself away from Agnes, struggling with passions that his holy vows had not yet quelled and knowing that the day would come when discipline might not be enough to withhold them from one another. But that was a private matter. Judith appealed to him as a companion because of the brightness of her mind and the openness of her expression. He felt a momentary regret that she had elected not to remain part of his little flock.

"We'll be very busy these next weeks," he said. "Have you heard of the wedding procession that will be coming here from Spain?"

"From Spain?" she said, following his slow, contemplative steps. "My own country." Though in truth she had few memories of her early childhood beyond the Pyrenees.

"Yes. King Chilperic has set his first wife aside. Sent her with her children to a convent. He will marry the Gothic princess, Galswinth."

Judith stopped and stared into the air before her. "Galswinth."

Though the abbey was sheltered from much of the news of the outside world, still she had heard of the goings-on of the Merovingian kings who ruled Gaul. But she hadn't imagined that her fate might ever be linked with theirs.

Fortunatus took her contemplative look and the repetition of the princess's name to be one of fascination with news and went on with his gossip about how Radegund was after all like an aunt to Chilperic, who respected her greatly. And how she always extended herself to counsel the king when asked, as well as trying to keep the peace between Chilperic and his brothers. But for Judith the name Galswinth suddenly conjured up a series of images, vague at first, but clearer as she considered them. She and Fortunatus had stopped and were gazing beyond the river at fields divided by hedge.

"I knew Galswinth," she murmured to herself, not minding that Fortunatus did not hear.

Judith and Galswinth had played together as children at the royal residence where Judith's father had forged weapons for the king of the Goths. The two girls, being nearly the same age, took a liking to each other. Eventually the small princess had sought excuses to visit Judith so that they could play games together. The two girls would even sit in her father's armour workshop and watch the sweating artisans at the laborious process of making mail shirts and welding swords out of case-hardened iron. Judith shook herself. Of course that was many years ago. She wondered how much the princess might have changed, or if she would remember her old friend.

"When will the royal procession pass by?" she asked, hoping Fortunatus had taken no notice of her daydreaming.

"Three weeks hence, by my calculations. From here they will go on to Tours and then to Rouen for the wedding."

Fortunatus sighed. He knew Chilperic's reputation and was somewhat familiar with the arrangements for this royal marriage. Gossip traveled quickly across Gaul, even on roads that were no longer kept up as efficiently as they had been in Roman times.

Indeed, sometimes Fortunatus himself was amazed at the celerity with which news traveled by word of mouth. He was musing on the phenomenon and paying no attention to Judith who had dropped a pace behind him as he moved on.

She murmured the princess Galwinth's name, turning it over and over on her tongue like an incantation. But then she shook her head, the breeze lifting a strand of hair that fell across her face. She raised her hand to comb the hair back in place with her fingers, the silent thought imprinting itself across her mind.

Galswinth must think me dead.

Chapter Three

The bells rang for matins, and the nuns in their white woolen robes filed sleepily into the narrow stone chapel. The novices followed in pairs, heads bowed respectfully. From the small window in the novice's dormitory, Judith could hear the plain song, led by Father Fortunatus, but by the time they missed her, it would be too late.

She turned from the window and hurried across the wooden floorboards between the rows of plain beds. At the door, she paused long enough to open it quietly and shut it behind her, then ran along the corridor to the stone steps leading to the courtyard below.

The midnight chill seeped into her bones as she opened the heavy oak door a crack and looked out into the quadrangle lit by a hunter's moon that eased the darkness. Her heart thumped against the coarse brown woolen cloak. From here she could see through the glazed windows of the chapel into the nave where the sisters worshipped in the wavering lamplight.

Judith pulled her cloak closer around her, the loose hood covering her head against the autumn cold. The chanting floated across the dark courtyard, filling her with a mixture of guilt and a small wave of uncertainty as she thought of Sister Agnes's lovely face and of

Queen Radegund. She loved them both as mothers, but she must not let her misgivings stop her now.

After giving it much thought the last few weeks, she had decided to leave the abbey, and she had to do it at this moment; otherwise, the rest of her plans, dangerous as they might be, would never materialize.

Although Father Fortunatus had promised to help her marry, she could not leave her future in his hands. Though a few weeks ago, she might have settled for a suitable husband found by him, her new plan was better, though riskier.

From the arched doorway, Judith gazed at the dark shapes of the limestone, and timber-framed buildings surrounding the inner courtyard. There had been many times when she thought that Radegund might have understood some of her feelings, for she, too, had been brought to Gaul, captured at the age of six by the Franks in dispute with the Goths over their outer borders.

Judith shut the door, the scrape of wood on stone vibrating along her spine. As she ran along the cloistered walk, she hugged the inside wall against the threat of open space between each column on the opposite side opening onto the quadrangle. When she came to the junction with the buildings on the west side of the quadrangle, she felt safer. The buildings on this side of the cloister were unoccupied at this hour, except for the kitchens. Matins was a long midnight service, giving her ample time for her escape.

She felt guilty thinking of it in those terms, but had she waited for permission to see the royal procession today, she was afraid that Sister Agnes would have asked too many questions.

She gained confidence as she felt her way along the rough masonry walls, coming to a passage that led to the atrium directly in front of the chapel. She had thought over the many passages between all the buildings of the abbey, but this was the best way, if the most dangerous. True there was a side door that led from the central kitchen, and it would soon be unlocked by Sister Mathilde, awaiting the peasants who trudged up every morning bringing grains, poultry, and cheese from their farms. But that would let her outside of the city walls, and for her purposes, she needed to remain within them.

She went along the narrow passage, holding her cloak out of the mud as much as possible. Then she quietly slipped along the covered walk of the atrium as she had done the inner cloister, hoping no one left their prayers before she got to the stone steps that led to the turret. She hurried up the steps and along the rampart. From the turret at the corner, a small window let down a few feet to the roof of a house outside the abbey, but within the city walls. She would have to climb over, using the many vines and branches for footholds on the other side to scramble down.

Then she would have to skirt the part of the abbey that was within the city to get back to the city gates, but there would be time for that. Covered by her woolen cloak and fleece-lined boots, she would look like one of the townspeople.

Once in the tower, she crouched to catch her breath. Her heart pounded, and she shook from head to toe, wondering if her plan would succeed or if she would be forced to return, shamefaced, to the nuns in the light of day.

She gathered her robe and cloak and hoisted herself onto the window ledge, each pebble and piece of rock that dropped to the floor resounding like thunder in her ears. Then using toeholds in the rough stone wall, she dropped to the timber roof of the house next to the abbey. Again, thick vines came to her rescue and she scrambled down to the muddy street below. Now she crept along slowly, trying to avoid the piles of garbage left in front of houses for the pigs to eat.

Finally she found what she was looking for. A set of windows in a low shed revealed blacksmith tools. She tried the door and found it unlocked, slipped in and closed it behind her. There was fresh straw on the floor, and she knelt down, wrapping her cloak around her to try to get a bit of sleep, for it was still some hours till dawn.

As she lay there, she wondered if she would sleep. Thoughts and images floated round in her head, but she finally dozed fitfully, her dreams full of guilt at what she had done battling with fear that her plan would not work.

As the gray light of morning cast its pall over the city, Judith awoke, stiff and cramped. She was hungry, but she daren't think of food. She slipped out of the shed and made her way through the narrow winding streets to the city gates to await the procession that would pass through today. For the hundredth time, Judith went over what Fortunatus had told her. King Chilperic had promised to dismiss his other wife and concubines to marry the princess Galswinth.

Judith knew it was a bold plan, but she would try to approach Galswinth as she passed by to ask that she take her into the royal household—if only she could make Galswinth remember her. But eight years had passed. How could she expect her to?

The sky began to get lighter now, and the merchants came out of their clay and wattle houses to go about their work. Housewives came out to shake mats and cushions on the street.

As the gatekeeper lumbered up to open the city gates, Judith found a place among the other towns-people beginning to gather on the road just inside the gates to await the Gothic train. Hens foraging beside a rivulet that ran down the center of the street pecked at Judith's robe, and she had to shoo them away. Artisans carrying their goods on their backs were about, crying their wares. Anticipation seemed to fill the people around her who murmured expectantly to one another and began to look toward the gates, squinting their eyes to look beyond.

Finding a vantage point between a brawny workman and a woman carrying a baby, Judith finally saw the train in the distance, winding slowly over the plain like a coiled serpent.

When the train was nearer, she could discern the long file of horsemen, carriages, and baggage wagons, and the traveling cart that carried her friend from Spain, following one of the old Roman roads through Gaul. Peasants in their fields stopped their work and watched as the procession marched toward the walled town, and townspeople now spilled through the gates where Judith waited.

She could have fought her way through the dirty, smelly crowd to await Galswinth's retinue outside the gates, but Judith knew she would have little chance of approaching her there. But here, where the streets were narrow, she might be able to break through the line of guards to get the princess's attention.

Some distance away, the caravan halted. The escort was composed of nobles and warriors of both Gothic and Frankish kingdoms, and outside the gate the horsemen got down to uncover their horse's harnesses and cast off their riding cloaks. Then they armed themselves with the brightly embossed shields that were slung at their saddle bows.

Judith saw Galswinth step down from her heavy traveling cart, her full-length, red-silk mantle sweeping behind her, while a tall, tower-shaped, silver-sheathed chariot was drawn up. A wave of awe swept through the crowd, for even at this distance, the sight of such royal splendor was a marvel to behold for the struggling peasants.

For the same reason churches were decorated with flashing gems, brilliant mosaics, and burning incense to lift the ordinary peasant out of the filth and misery of his everyday life, so too was the pomp of royal ceremonies with the barbarian rulers' love of gold, colored glass, and valuable gems.

Now the procession was ready for a ceremonial entry. It was apparent that the appearance of the Gothic princess delighted the Frankish peasants, whose yells and cheers increased. Judith pressed into the crowd, but was pushed back as the mounted escort shouted at the people gathered to watch. As the first horsemen passed by, she began to panic. She had to get near enough to Galswinth's chariot so that she could call to her. Seeing an opening between a ragman and a housewife, Judith slipped through, stumbling in the way of the train.

"You there, get back," yelled a fur-cloaked and helmeted Goth.

From his gold-inlaid sword fittings and decorations on his helmet and breastplate, he appeared to be one of Galswinth's personal retainers. Judith was near enough to smell the horse's breath as the Goth jerked on the harness. A second Goth, covered in fur vest with metal-studded cross garters on his strong legs, his helmet covering his eyes, appeared at her side and grasped her arm.

41

"Let go of me," she shouted. "I, too, am a Goth and a friend of the princess Galswinth."

"Ha, ha, ha." The mounted guard seemed to think that quite funny. He pointed his lance at Judith and she ducked to avoid the sharp point. The man who had seized her dragged her away from the horse's hooves and tried to force her back into the crowd, as the peasants reached out to touch the ornate saddles and weapons of the royal escort.

The chariot was slowly moving by and would soon be lost around the bend of the street inside the gates. Seeing that the guards would not believe her, Judith opened her mouth and gave the loudest piercing yell she could muster.

"Galswinth, Galswinth, it is I, Judith. Help me."

A jeweled hand flashed out the side of the chariot and gestured for the caravan to stop, causing the carts behind it to jostle forward. The confusion about the train increased, but the young princess leaned out of the chariot as the guards fought off the people kneeling by the side of the train to beg.

Long dark hair fell loose about graceful shoulders, tresses held by a crown of gold that surrounded her head, holding in place the bangs cut straight across her forehead. The tight long sleeves of her tunic were embroidered with silver and gold threads. Her crown reflected the sunlight as did the gold brooch set with red garnets that fastened her mantle.

But Judith succeeded in attracting Galswinth's attention just as some of the townspeople were seizing her by the clothing to drag her away from the guard.

"Look at her robe," said the housewife who had been standing behind. The woman pulled aside Judith's cloak to reveal the fine unbleached spun hemp garment underneath.

A toothless old crone beside her clawed at the material. "Why they weave them that way at the abbey, she's from the abbey then."

The brown eyes in the chariot were staring at the goings-on, and a Frankish lord rode up to reassure Galswinth and to apologize for the commotion, but the princess gestured to him.

"Galswinth," screamed Judith just as the ragman began to drag her away, and the old crone began to pluck at her robe with long knotty fingers. "Are you one of the nuns, girlie?"

Finally recognition dawned in the princess's eye. "Who is it?" she said to the Frankish noble, who was attempting to keep his horse from shying at the crowd. "She says she knows me. What is the name she says?"

And after another cry from the street below, Galswinth recognized the name at last.

"Judith!" She was nearly out of the chariot herself, but the guard at her side prevented her. "Quickly," she said to him. "Bring her to me."

Judith had not heard Galswinth's order, but she was set down roughly, nearly losing her balance. Already her clothing was stained with mud from the street, and her face streaked with dirt. She stood there confused, trying to get her bearings when a strong hand gripped her arm, causing her to cry out again.

"This way," the voice said, and the guard beside her shoved her before him.

She started to struggle, but then saw through her tangled hair that Galswinth was leaning out of the chariot, beckoning to her.

At first, Galswinth seemed uncertain, but as she looked into the face with mud-streaked cheeks, at the sand-colored hair, the green eyes with dark brows above them, doubt fled.

"Judith, is it really you? I thought never to see you again."

Small tears formed at the corners of the obsidian lashes and brightened the brown eyes as the princess reached for her childhood friend.

Judith grabbed the hands that clutched the air before her, relief sweeping through her. "It is I, Judith, your old friend."

"Come." Galswinth moved aside and made room for Judith to scramble into the chariot beside her. Then she leaned out again and spoke to the Frankish noble and the barbarian guards who awaited her orders.

"It's all right," she told them. "This is a friend from my childhood. She will ride with me."

She pulled aside another curtain and crawled into the space behind the front seat, pulling Judith with her. Ignoring the crowd outside, Galswinth turned her attention to making her friend comfortable on the fur robes that lined the inside of the chariot. She dropped the outer curtain, and they stared at each other, each examining the other face, looking for changes the years had wrought and yet knowing instantly that the spirit within remained the same. And so, a tiny flame of hope sparked within Judith's breast.

Then they were in each other's arms, hugging and laughing, Galswinth's tears rubbing off on Judith's dirty cheek. "I cannot believe it," said Galswinth. Then she held the disheveled Judith at arm's length.

Judith's joy at having found her friend had made her forget her own appearance, but now she looked down at her soiled robe and muddy boots and self-consciously brushed her tangled hair from her face.

By contrast Galswinth was dressed in a fine-woven tunic with an intricate geometric design embroidered with gold and varicolored threads. Judith could only

44

stare at the gleaming gold collar about her throat and the gold brooch set with red garnets that closed her mantle at the shoulder. The design was a cross within a cross, a sign that the princess was a Christian. On her feet were leather sandals trimmed with gold threads.

Suddenly their positions in life seemed a huge gap between them, and Judith looked down in embarrassment. Only Galswinth's ingenuity put Judith at ease.

"I still cannot believe it," said Galswinth again. "How did you come here? Were you dropped from heaven? How did you know I was passing this way?" She did not wait for answers, her own words tumbling out in their stead.

"But, of course, you know I am on my way to . . ." Her eyes rounded, losing some of their luster, and she glanced at the corners of the litter, then back at Judith. "I've come from Spain to be married to King Chilperic."

"I know. It is what gave me the courage to seek you out," said Judith.

"You live in Poitiers then?"

Judith nodded. "At the Abbey of the Holy Cross."

"The abbey? Then you—"

"No, not a nun. The sisters took me in after my mother and I were captured. I suppose you didn't know that, thinking us dead."

"Yes. I didn't see the battle, but there have been many reports of it. So many tales . . ."

Grief afresh seemed to threaten them both, but Judith impulsively reached out and grasped her friend's hand. "Let us not speak of that now."

But Galswinth had turned eyes inward, lost in thoughts that had plagued her these many months. "I remember what they said then. How the women were dragged with bound hands and disheveled hair, cov-

45

ered with their husbands' blood. I wept for them as I wept then for you." She turned large eyes toward Judith, tightening their handclasp.

"Such is warfare, Galswinth," said Judith, looking deeply into her old friend's eyes and attempting to help steady her. She knew what Galswinth was thinking: that she was about to marry one of the very men who had attacked their own people.

Judith saw the expression of fear, then of repulsion that swam in Galswinth's eyes, and compassion flooded her. But another feeling was beginning to take root in Judith. She knew she had done the right thing in seeking Galswinth. She had thought she had done it for herself, but she saw now how she could best serve her friend.

"Do not worry, Galswinth. I will stay with you if you will have me."

"Oh yes! You will be my confidante and live with me in the royal household."

Those words would have meant everything to Judith only a few days ago. Indeed, she had not dared to hope to go from abbey ward to royal confidante in so short a time, but now other concerns mingled with the success she had achieved.

As the chariot turned, they heard shouts outside, and Galswinth parted the curtain to see what was going on. A donkey-driven fish cart had broken an axle, and the driver was bemoaning his fate from his place in the middle of the street. But the Frankish and Gothic guards soon had the cart moved aside, and the procession was on its way again. They had left the crowds behind and were now passing through the other side of the city where it was mostly deserted.

They were not far from the basilica, and many of the robed figures they passed on the street looked to be part of the clergy. Judith gazed at the faded, peeling stone, painted by the Romans, the figures in the murals like ghosts themselves from a century ago. Above them empty stone buildings with gaping windows watched the train pass with hollow eyes.

The Franks had only ruled here for three generations. Before that, Roman legions had given Gaul four hundred years of stability. Queen Radegund had told Judith that Poitiers was much larger two centuries ago, and these buildings had been filled with residents and government officials. But now Galswinth dropped the curtain, as there was little to see.

They took another turn. Ahead, an order was shouted and the chariot halted, sending the two girls off balance. The paving stones resounded with the clatter of hooves on the street. Harness metal clanked, and horses and riders moved about outside. Then the curtain of the litter was jerked back by one of Galswinth's guards and the girls stared out at a stocky man with muscular arms and a broad chest. His purple mantle was fastened at the shoulder with an amethyst clasp. His hair came below his ears, as was the Frankish custom among noblemen, and his fingers rested on a gilt bronze dagger hilt. But it was the eyes Judith most noticed.

He stood rigid, the eyes in his squarish face flicking from the princess to Judith and then back again. Hazy gray eyes with ghostly shapes in them. He bowed low once. When he rose, he stepped up close to the litter. He spoke to Galswinth, who had drawn her mantle around her and now sat up straight. Judith could see her royal upbringing in the way she posed, realizing that this man, whoever he might be, was about to deliver a formal address. Only the quiver of Galswinth's coal-colored eyelids betrayed her fear.

47

"I am Epoald of the house of the Arnulfings and mayor of the palace," the man said. "I come from King Chilperic to greet you and to escort you on the remainder of your journey. I am instructed to make sure you are comfortable in your lodgings here."

Galswinth nodded her head. "Thank you. We place ourselves in your hands, Epoald, for I know that the mayor of the palace speaks for the king."

He bowed again, then said, "I will lead your party to the villa where your welcome has been prepared."

Galswinth raised a sinuous arm and gestured to her retainers to follow Epoald. Then the curtain dropped around the two girls, and they were left inside their protective cocoon. The affairs outside would be taken care of by others.

Judith huddled closer to Galswinth in an unconscious gesture of protection. Galswinth did not need to speak of her apprehension about becoming Chilperic's bride, for Judith could easily see through the murky brown eyes into the troubled soul.

"I begged my father not to send me away," Galswinth said almost in a whisper, as if needing to speak of the events that had brought her to this point. "My mother traveled with me from Toledo as far as the mountains. I could not bear to leave her there.

"Is it true what I've heard about him? Is he a crude and lascivious man as they say he is?"

Judith's face reddened. Despite being cloistered at the abbey for several years, she had heard of the lives of the kings that ruled over the provinces of Gaul.

"It is true that King Chilperic is a vigorous man. I've heard he can be ruthless when others stand in his way."

Galswinth's red lips hardened into a straight line, but she did not look away.

"But he is driven to convert all the Jews to Christianity," Judith added, as if trying to find some mitigating qualities about the man whose debauchery, even though he considered himself an amateur theologian and poet, seemed repugnant to the more civilized Gothic princess.

"My sister . . ." Galswinth began.

"Yes, I know. She married Chilperic's older brother, Sigibert," said Judith.

"I know King Chilperic sought me out of envy of his brother."

"And Sigibert has been good to your sister, Brunhild. She is revered everywhere. It is a most holy marriage."

King Sigibert, the ruler of the Frankish kingdom of Austrasia to the east, married Brunhild in the year 566 and, unlike Chilperic, had been satisfied with one wife.

"Chilperic's first wife, Audovera, has been confined to a nunnery," Galswinth said.

Judith wondered if Galswinth did not fear the same fate, should Chilperic tire of her. Suddenly a sense of resolve arose in Judith. Galswinth herself had qualities that Chilperic would surely find desirable. If Judith were there to bolster her friend, and if Galswinth used her nobility and femininity on the Frankish king, perhaps the marriage had hope. Perhaps the Gothic princess could civilize Chilperic's taste.

"He has also set his other concubines aside," said Galswinth matter-of-factly.

Judith could see that the concubines did not concern Galswinth much. If Chilperic had concubines to take his attentions from Galswinth it might make Galswinth's life easier. But to Judith's way of thinking, that could be dangerous as well. Galswinth's only hope would be to remain in Chilperic's favor.

The chariot jolted to a stop, and in a moment the

curtains slid back and a stool was brought for them to step down. The mounted guard had formed a pathway leading toward the marble steps to the porticoed façade of the villa ahead, where mail-shirted Frankish soldiers stood with spears erect, guarding the door. Epoald waited for them in the sun on the steps.

Fredegund sat on a hassock beside Chilperic's bed, combing her thick hair as he tightened the belt around his linen tunic. The fire in the stone fireplace had burned down and Chilperic picked up the blackened poker to coax the flames. It had been a week since Fredegund had been in his bed. Their lovemaking had been especially demanding, and she had sensed his reluctance when he had asked her this time.

"Sire," she spoke in a low, throaty voice, "I am aware that you are soon making a royal liaison which will no doubt increase your dignity and political favor. May I offer my most deeply felt congratulations."

"You may, Fredegund."

He took a swig of wine, then burped loudly. He walked toward her, and she knelt to tie the thongs of his cross-gartered, leather sandals.

"I am afraid my new liaison changes things between us," he said. "That was the last time you will be asked to my bed. I have made a promise. I must live with this new wife exclusively."

He took Fredegund's narrow chin in his hand, tilting her face upward. "I will not forget you, however. You may take the many presents I have given you, and you may have your choice of several households I have thought to send you to."

"And what of my daughter?" She spoke of the four-teen-year-old she had borne from her early induction into the profession of concubine, before she learned how to prevent unwanted pregnancies and births. Rigunthis was the bastard daughter of a Frankish count who had been killed in battle.

"She has done well with her instruction in the convent these late years," Chilperic said. "I have written an agreement to dower her in marriage even though she is not my own flesh and blood."

"You are generous, sire."

She ran a braceleted arm about his waist. Already he could feel the tingle at the base of his groin again. His hand dipped to cup the breast that hung invitingly against the folds of her tunic. He would miss their copulating, for Fredegund had sexual gifts that few other concubines had. It would be hard to give her up.

Already the thought was forming that even though he had given his word, perhaps in a year or so, if his new wife did not satisfy his appetites, and he doubted she would, he could find an excuse to summon Fredegund again. Best, in that case, to send her where he had little fear of losing her loyalty, though he did not expect her to remain untouched by another man. That would be impossible once he had released her from his service.

She caught his hand in hers and ran her tongue over the base of his palm, then glanced upward through her sand-colored lashes, pleading humbly, her cool blue eyes invading his resolve.

"Must I leave the palace, sire? I will bequeath my place in your bed to this new wife because you ask me to do so. But I could not bear to suffer being sent away from your very presence. Allow me to work at a lowly post, in the kitchens where I was born." She lowered her eyes submissively. "In honor of my mother."

Rarely did Fredegund find a reason to remind anyone of her humble birth—that she had risen from kitchen slave to royal favorite, a formidable feat. But now was a moment when such a reminder would only help her scheme. She continued with her reasoning, her eyes cast downward.

"If I may no longer be your mistress, allow me to remain in some humble post to at least harvest and wash the vegetables that will be set on your table. To serve you in even this humble manner would be a way of repaying you for all you have given me."

She turned her beautiful, calculating eyes toward him, eyes like icy crystal globes, but he felt his heart twist around her conniving soul, a soul not unlike his own.

She dropped his hand. "Of course," she added, "If you send me away to serve another . . ."

She left the sentence unfinished, but he knew what she was suggesting. That she could easily turn her gifts of intelligence and beauty to her advantage within another household. The household of a noble, who might then become more powerful than Chilperic wanted? For Frankish rulers must always be wary of the threat of noblemen on whom the king relied to bring out their armies when there was a war to be fought.

Such noblemen had whole armies loyal to no one but themselves or at least loyal to the money they would be paid to fight. Keeping them in their places was always a delicate balance. Should Fredegund become involved with such a man . . .

The thought frightened him. He suddenly realized how much she must know about him, about the rule of the kingdom just from spending time in this very room. No, he suddenly saw, he must not let that happen. And the alternative was equally abhorrent to him; to strip her of all means, send her far away into the hands of some lowly serf who could not appreciate her. To see that lovely hair matted with straw and crawling creatures, hands cracked, dry, red from work in the fields — no he could not do that.

He knew it would be dangerous to allow this beautiful concubine to remain among the women in the royal service, but looking at her, even knowing she had wits to match his own, he could not say no.

Chapter Four

The royal procession rested at Poitiers for three days. Galswinth insisted on presenting her friend with many fine gifts, including a pair of tiny inlaid brooches and bracelets of twisted gold and silver from the extensive mines of Spain.

At first Judith tried to refuse all but the most practical gifts, such as a clean tunic with long sleeves, but it became evident that Galswinth received much joy in giving the gifts. She would gaze tenderly at her friend as she showed her how to wind pearls through hair now combed and coiled, and she would drape the folds of her robes made of silk, imported from Byzantium. No longer was Judith a handmaiden of Christ dressed like a slave.

"I'm afraid I haven't much practice with this kind of finery," Judith told Galswinth as they sat in a bedchamber in an old Roman villa on the edge of the city. "I came to Gaul with nothing, and though I never wanted for anything at the abbey, our clothing was of plainer cloth than these."

The soft finery flowed over her figure in quite a different fashion from the loose robes worn as a novice. But better than the finery that clothed her was the food that filled her stomach. Though the meals at the abbey were healthy, and though guests at the abbey were fed royally, Judith found that she had an appetite greater than the nuns, who tended to eat sparingly.

Here, seated with Galswinth and her attendants at a long banquet table, Judith feasted on chicken blancmange, young peapods quick-fried in butter, crisp lettuce from the villa's garden, and roast venison with a cinnamon-pepper sauce. At every meal she stuffed herself until she thought she would burst.

Galswinth teased her. "Judith, if you eat like that for a year, you'll be too fat to ride in my litter."

In the evening, when the fire in the brazier had burned low, the two girls sat on feather mattresses covered with furs. They watched the moon rise against a dark sky outside the arched windows of Galswinth's chambers. Somewhere in the night, a peacock screeched. Galswinth had dismissed her attendants, feeling calmed by Judith's company, as if when Judith spoke, some sort of wisdom conveyed itself to the incumbent queen.

In return, Galswinth told Judith much about Spain. As she spoke of her homeland, tears came to her dark eyes, and she would gaze distantly out the window of the villa. Judith held her hand as they pondered the land across the Pyrenees. And Galswinth's descriptions helped Judith's memories fall into place.

Still, she had not the ties to break that Galswinth had, and when she thought of the refined princess preparing to become Chilperic's bride, she had to swallow her own fears. Galswinth made Judith tell all she knew of Chilperic, and of the queen he had set aside, for Galswinth still feared her reception at the royal villa in Rouen. Even though she had been raised to be a queen, she was not ready.

Judith strove to inspire her friend and to please her

ear by reading poetry and telling her tales of miracles performed at the many saints' tombs, tales she had heard at the abbey when the nuns read at mealtimes. Such distraction entertained Galswinth, and, Judith hoped, gave her courage to face the future. It was even possible that life with Chilperic would not be the horror that Galswinth feared. And Judith never failed to remind her that she might be able to civilize him.

In order to distract her, Judith had begun to tell Galswinth of the time when four suns appeared in the heavens and a comet blazed like a flaming sword after the great plague.

"And was it a good sign, that four suns appeared in the sky?" asked Galswinth.

"It was good," Judith said. Though she herself had heard many interpretations of these signs, she knew that she must not say anything at all to disturb Galswinth lest she take it to mean that her own marriage was doomed.

"There is another tale," she said quickly. "A lovely one. Venantius Fortunatus told me of it. There was a married couple who lived their lives in purity and were buried in the same church. But their tombs were originally at opposite sides of the church. One morning, the tombs were found lying side by side because the couple did not wish to be parted even in death."

Galswinth sighed deeply. "I know nothing of love." She looked at her hands, which were resting on her lap. "What am I to do if I cannot love my husband?"

"You must pray," said Judith quickly. "You must fast and keep a vigil all night before your wedding. I will guard your door that night so you will not be disturbed."

Galswinth raised imploring eyes to her friend. "Is there not something else we can do?" Her face became animated and she leaned forward, her voice hoarse as she grasped Judith's hand. "Can we not seek an omen?"

Judith's pulse quickened. She was afraid of what her friend was suggesting. "I told you. The omens have already been read. Your marriage will bring good fortune to the kingdom."

Galswinth's grasp on Judith's arm tightened and her whisper rasped. "But what will it bring to me? What of my life? Judith, I must know."

Judith's eyes were drawn to the princess even though the tremor that crept up her spine warned her against what was about to happen.

"If you mean the *Sortes Biblicae*, it is forbidden." The trial of the Sortes, an attempt to discover the future by a random opening of the Sacred Books, had been condemned by the Church, though many still attempted it in secret. "Galswinth, don't be foolish. Do you want to be excommunicated?"

But Galswinth persisted. "No one would know," she said in a hushed voice. "Besides, it isn't a mortal sin."

She had slid closer to Judith, so close, that as Judith looked into the dark eyes even by the flickering of the wax tapers, she could see the passage to the princess's soul. She loved her friend and would do anything to relieve the anguish that lay in that soul, but could she do something that was so dangerous? Not only had she left the abbey without telling anyone, but now to seek the future in this forbidden manner? She must find a way to deny Galswinth's request.

"Let me think about it," said Judith, trying to stall her friend.

"There is a chapel that opens off the courtyard," Galswinth said. "I saw it as we passed. Surely the Sacred Books are there."

Already in her mind, Judith saw the books of the

Prophets, the Apostles, and the Evangelists lying on an altar. They would have to sneak in, say a quick prayer that God would thus reveal what was ahead for Galswinth.

But the omens had been read. Fortunatus had told Judith that everything pointed toward the consummation of this marriage. It was only Galswinth's own revulsion at having to give up everything she loved and marry a man known for his excesses that frightened her so, Judith tried to tell herself. Silently she prayed that what Fortunatus had told her was true.

She exhaled deeply. The royal princess had just rescued Judith from a life she felt she was not fit for, asking nothing in return. Surely, she owed Galswinth this much.

"Very well," Judith relented. "But we must do it tonight, when everyone is sleeping. Lie down now and close your eyes. I will wake you when all is quiet."

The strained look disappeared from Galswinth's face, and in her eyes Judith read the look of faith. Surely now the princess would sleep.

"Stay here then. Sleep beside me," murmured Galswinth.

Judith extinguished the candles and they lay on the feather mattress under fur rugs. She thought that perhaps they would both fall asleep, and that when morning came, the whole thing would be forgotten. She gazed at the princess's reclining form and saw that the obsidian lashes now lay heavily against her milky skin, and her breathing evened.

Judith began to doze, images of Mother Radegund, Fortunatus, the Holy Books, mingling in her dreams, but something began to shake her, and she awoke to see Galswinth's face hovering near hers. Though most of the princess's pale face was in shadow, her dark eyes were bold with expectancy.

"Judith, wake up. We must go."

Judith rose sleepily, limbs protesting, but she got to her feet, seeing that Galswinth was determined. They wrapped fur-lined cloaks around themselves; then, in soft boots, they tiptoed across the cold tile floor.

Judith opened the door slowly. At each creak of the hinges, the guard outside snorted, but did not waken. His spear lay on the floor beside him and his head rested on his wooden shield. Other guards sprawled on the floor nearby, snoring loudly.

Awake now, the blood moving more quickly in her veins, Judith pointed silently and mouthed, "Follow me." Then she began to run along the gallery overlooking the open court below, the cold air making her shiver in spite of her cloak.

When she turned a corner, she halted, giving Galswinth a chance to catch up. For a moment she was reminded of the games they used to play in Toledo, running from Galswinth's nurse. But this was not a game. This was a princess who was about to marry a king.

Once down the stone steps, they hurried along the covered walkway and then turned into the arched opening to the chapel. Inside, Judith gasped for air, choking on the incense and the smoke from two oil lamps that hung above the altar.

They stood on a marble floor in the small chapel. On the altar was a gold crucifix studded with colored gems that flashed in the light from the flickering oil lamp. Judith was drawn to the side, to where the sacred books lay on carved wooden lecterns. She shut her eyes and let out a breath. She had hoped the books would not be here, though she knew that would be unusual.

Galswinth had already knelt before the altar to pray,

and Judith did likewise, but her prayer was more a jumble of thoughts than anything else. When she opened her eyes, she saw that Galswinth had approached the first lectern and was opening the fine vellum cover of the Book of the Prophets. She was mumbling some words that Judith couldn't hear. Then, her eyes still shut, she opened the parchment pages with leather thongs.

Judith rose as Galswinth's eye fell on the verse that would give her a sign, her hands trembling as she touched the illuminated lettering and mouthed the Latin words from the Book of Job.

"Have the gates of death been opened unto thee? or hast thou seen the doors of the shadow of death?"

Quickly, she closed the heavy book and moved to the Book of the Apostles, letting her trembling finger drift over its gem-encrusted cover. She opened the book and drew in a sharp breath as she read from the Revelation of St. John.

"Neither repented they of their murders, nor of their sorceries, nor of their fornications, nor of their thefts."

They mustn't go further, Judith thought. Surely whatever the third book said would not outweigh these two. But Galswinth had already turned to the Book of the Evangelists with hands outstretched, her eyes closed. Then she stopped and looked down, where the stiff pages fell open.

Judith did not have time to see what the verse said, for Galswinth knelt on the marble steps and shrieked, her hands on her face, fingers splayed. She swayed toward the altar, grasped the gold cloth, and for a moment Judith feared she would topple the vessels that rested there, cross and all. Then she froze, stared into the air in front of her, certain she at last knew her fate. "I shall die."

She stared at Judith, who had frozen watching her, expecting Galswinth to faint or cry. Instead, the frightened princess rose rigidly and stepped forward, as if a ghost of herself were now facing the future, as if her royal breeding took over where she herself could no longer carry on. She walked away from the altar, her cloak trailing her soundless steps.

Judith hastily straightened the altar cloth, her eye falling on the verse from St. Matthew that Galswinth must have read, ". . . after the tribulation of those days shall the sun be darkened, and the moon shall not give her light, and the stars shall fall from heaven, and the powers of the heavens shall be shaken."

She mumbled a quick prayer and hurried after her friend.

After that night, Judith and Galswinth spoke little. Galswinth withdrew into herself in an effort to blot out her new life, and spent the last few days of preparations for the marriage in silent resignation. There was nothing else to do. The contracts had been sighed. She would not be allowed to return to Spain, no matter how much she wanted to.

On the day of the royal wedding ceremony, clothed in rich muslin and green silk, gold bracelets on her arms and her hair braided with pearls, Judith stood with the crowd in the basilica at Rouen, staring at the many colored marbles, the blaze of mosaics, the sanctuary gleaming with the radiant jewels on the gold cross. Clouds of incense rose as the procession of white-robed churchmen passed down the center aisle to the chanting of the choir.

The splendor of the basilica with its row of marble pillars lining the sides, the rich tapestries, and the high-timbered roof decorated with tracery and carved figures of angels was a blaze of glory, almost overwhelming to Judith, who stood stiffly, her eyes beginning to tear from the incense.

She had not been able to shake the feeling of unease she'd had ever since the night they had resorted to the *Sortes Biblicae*. She had cursed herself again and again for not preventing Galswinth from going to the chapel that night. Whether or not the prophecies would prove true, they had pushed Galswinth further and further into herself.

Judith stood now with the odd feeling that she was part of a dream. Events had moved so far and fast since that day only a few weeks ago when she stood with Fortunatus looking over the abbey walls. She experienced a pang of nostalgia for the simple life of the abbey. But she had been right to leave there; she was not cut out to be a nun.

And that decision had led her swiftly to the royal court of Neustria by an odd twist of fate. She wondered sometimes, when she lay down at night, if she might not wake up suddenly to find herself in the austere surroundings of the novices' dormitory again. But instead, each day she rose to garb herself in fine weaves, silks and jewelry, all gifts from a royal princess.

More churchmen filed by in stately procession, adorned with varicolored vestments, advancing to the sound of the rhythmic chants. Finally the bishop appeared with a crook-shaped ornamented staff, the symbol of his office, being carried before him. His vestments flowed behind him, richly embroidered with wide bands and jewels, and the tall mitre on his head like a low cloth crown with high peaks.

Finally came Galswinth, bedecked in a fine linen tunic with embroidered girdle and weighted down with heavy gold jewelry and precious stones ornamenting her hem. Her plaits were wound around her head under her crown and veil as befitted a married woman. But Judith perceived the effort with which she moved down the aisle, as if the splendor of becoming a Frankish queen was draining the life from her.

Watching from her place next to the colannaded aisle, Judith looked closely at King Chilperic, who waited on the steps of the altar, dressed in a white robe and a brocaded cloak. His flaxen hair, sprinkled with gold, was parted on the forehead and fell in long braids over his shoulders as was the tradition. He wore a crown of gold.

The Merovingian dynasty had a magical hold on the allegiance and imagination of the people of Gaul, Frank, and Gallo-Roman alike. In hushed tones at the abbey some of the nuns had spoken to Judith of a secret spell that guarded the Merovingian kings, assuring their permanence over any usurpers, because their blood was divine, despite their very human appetites. And it was said that their power resided in their long hair.

The bishop finished his sermon. The vows were exchanged. With a cry, all the Franks of the kingdom of Neustria, lords and ordinary warriors alike, drew their swords in a clatter of metal scraping on metal and brandished them in the air, uttering an ancient pagan formula, swearing allegiance to the new queen. Chilperic placed his hand on a gold box containing sacred relics and vowed never to repudiate the daughter of the king of the Goths and never to take another wife, so long as she lived.

Judith was pressed into the crowd with the others as they filed out the massive wooden doors of the church. Outside, she paused on the steps, readjusting her eyes to the sunlight as the crowd moved past her into the noisy street where beggars reached toward the noble men and women, begging for alms. Invalids propped against the stone walls of the basilica awaited blessings. Judith moved on, skirting the outstretched hands, trying not to look into the faces, having no coins with her to give them. She felt a tug on her hem and turned, catching at her tunic and nearly losing her balance.

"Alms, alms," cried the wavering voice of a beggar sitting on the stump of a leg at the bottom of the steps. Out of the corner of her eye, she saw a tanned, muscled arm hold a coin above the rheumy eyes. The beggar released her hem to catch the coin that fell within his grasp.

Judith turned to thank her rescuer and looked into the eyes of a tall, broad-shouldered nobleman she had seen in the basilica. His curled, dark coppery hair lay across a high, noble brow, and she could see by his dress that he was Gallo-Roman, for he wore a wide-sleeved, knee-length white tunic trimmed with a wide band of gold.

His deep blue mantle was fastened by a gilt bronze clasp. His hair, which curled around his ears, was clipped short, as the Gallo-Romans did not follow the Frankish custom of wearing their hair long. On his right hand was a gold and silver ring set with a large square garnet, its brilliance in the sunlight nearly blinding her.

The glance of his brown eyes was followed by lips raised in a curious smile. She nodded her thanks and prepared to hurry on, but his hand, steadying her by the elbow, assisted her down the steps.

"Marcus Petronius, count of the Austrasian Palace, at your service."

His voice was rich and direct, and she took note of

the worthiness of his title. "Thank you, Count Marcus Petronius."

He continued staring at her, his mouth relaxed, appraisal still in his intelligent eyes.

"Come," he said, his fingers still touching her elbow. "Let me escort you to the palace. You wouldn't want the hands of these beggars to soil your finery. I'm on my way to the wedding festivities, and so are you."

She responded to the light in his eye. "How —" she began.

But he glanced at her attire, smiled again, then without waiting for her answer, guided her through the stone-paved street.

Marcus led her to a two-wheeled chariot, and she stepped up behind him as he took the reins from a servant. She hung onto the sides as the vehicle jerked forward into the throng of people following the wedding party. She was glad for the ride through the crowded streets to the palace. When they reached their destination, Marcus left the chariot in the charge of his servant, who had run behind, and they climbed the wide marble steps, crossed an open, mosaicked hall and entered the banquet hall. Counts of the cities, governors of the northern provinces of Gaul, fur-clad patriarchal chiefs of the old Frankish tribes from beyond the Rhine — all had arrived with their retinues for the festivities.

Gallic nobles, polished and ingratiating, mingled with the brusque, Frankish lords, the vassals of the king. Wine and beer flowed from bejeweled goblets or Teutonic drinking horns to the healths and challenges hailed by the drinkers.

Marcus handed Judith a silver goblet of wine and after he had taken a sip from his own, he looked over the crowd indulging in the nuptial banquet. When he turned to her, she again noticed the brown eyes with gold flecks around the irises like a sunburst. He said nothing as he watched her, and they both drank, the honeyed-wine tasting sweet on Judith's tongue and making her blood run faster.

"Tell me," he said, fingering the gilt copper hilt of a dagger that hung from his girdle, "How does life in the land of the Franks compare with Gothic Spain?"

He must have thought she had arrived with Galswinth's retinue. She smiled slowly as she replied, "Though I, too, am Visigothic by birth, I cannot answer your question, because I have spent the last eight years in the Abbey of the Holy Cross with the holy Mother Radegund." She spoke seriously, and could not understand the look of curiosity that came into Marcus's eyes.

He gazed at the thick light brown hair, the green-brown-gold eyes, the soft figure under the folds of her tunic and tried to imagine her in cloistered surroundings. Lately a novice?

But then raising his eyes to her intelligent face, he nodded to himself. Yes there was a refinement about her that could only come from a royal household or the training of a convent. She had certainly not been raised among the common rabble.

"I am an emissary from the kingdom of Austrasia," he said, "and have come with gifts from Chilperic's brother, King Sigibert, for the new queen. I return to the eastern province tonight." He wasn't very happy about leaving because he would have liked to converse further with this novice-turned-royal companion.

"You are Gallo-Roman then?"

Her sandy brows raised. She could see that his manners were far more refined than those of Chilperic's barbarous warriors and the Franks who administered the king's affairs. This Marcus Petronius was a cultured man, far more appealing than most of the men in Galswinth's retinue.

He smiled. "I am descended from an old family of Gallo-Roman landholders who became vassals of the Frank kings after Chilperic's grandfather, Clovis, conquered Gaul in the year 486."

He sipped from his goblet. The Frankish kings had retained many of the members of the old Gallo-Roman aristocracy in order to make use of their experience and their influence over the Gallo-Roman sections of the population.

"But tell me about life at the cloister," he said.

"It was," she hesitated, glancing a little shyly at the revelry that was taking place around them. "It was very quiet." She shrugged. "One fell into the pattern established by the Order. The entire community devoted two hours every day to literary studies. The rest of the time was spent on spiritual exercises, reading religious books, and other domestic chores, depending on one's ability and willingness."

A glint of amusement crept into Marcus's eye. "And your willingness for these domestic chores?"

Her eyes snapped in defense, but as she opened her mouth to speak of how she had carried out all her novice duties perfectly, she saw the humor in his gentle eyes, and her flash of anger died.

"I suppose," she admitted, "that I was more willing to perform some duties than others."

"Ah, I see."

A camaraderie of mutual understanding began to grow between them. "But I was fortunate that the sisters of the Holy Cross were such good teachers. And my tutor was Father Fortunatus."

"Venantius Fortunatus?"

She nodded.

"I did not know he had taken holy vows. He is renowned for his poetry across the length and breadth of Gaul."

As they wandered along the arcaded gallery, she could see that Marcus's attention, which had been all hers for many moments, was drawn to a crowd gathered around the king and queen, who now approached.

Marcus set his goblet on the tray carried by a passing servant. Then he lowered his head toward Judith's.

"I would like to hear more of this cloistered existence of yours and learn of the nuns' teachings, but I must pay my respects to the king and queen."

Judith had consumed more wine than she was used to, which she decided explained the weakness in her knees. But she smiled at him, not wanting to keep him from his obligations.

"Yes, you must."

He lifted her hand and kissed the knuckles, his gaze wandering to where the folds of her tunic crossed beneath her breasts, the gesture and glance taking her breath away. If only such a man resided at the Neustrian court. She had met none such among the Frankish nobles and while Mother Radegund had entertained a few Gallo-Roman nobles at the abbey, Judith had not met them herself.

She slowly withdrew her hand. Marcus was a count of the Austrasian palace and had no cause to remain here. She watched him as he strode across the mosaicked floor to where Chilperic and Galswinth stood. His dignity and grace were a contrast to the drunken Franks now slavering kisses on some of the women. She saw Marcus bow before Chilperic and Galswinth, saw Galswinth engage him in brief conversation, and then after a few moments he bowed once more and allowed himself to be led away to the banqueting table by Epoald. He did not look back.

Judith drifted around the edge of the room. She had begun to make friends with two of the women, Mosella and Clothild, and talked with them for a while. She sat for a time with the other women at the banquet tables, but after filling herself with rabbit in wine syrup, cheeses and fruit pastry, she left the festivities. She reached a side door and slipped through, then walked along the tiled portico where the cool evening air refreshed her. She stopped where the low stone wall offered a view of the gravel drive below.

Looking down, she saw Marcus Petronius cross the drive to a waiting party of cloaked horsemen. He drew on gloves, then mounted, donned his helmet, took the shield his servant handed him, and with a lift of his hand, signaled the guard who traveled with him. Hooves scraped on gravel and the horsemen galloped into the evening, cloaks billowing behind. Judith was moved, watching them go, and regretted she had not had more time with the noble Roman.

"A pleasant evening," said a voice behind her. "Do you mind if I take the evening air with you?"

She jumped, all other thoughts having been dismissed as she watched Marcus's departure. A young priest stood beside her, white-robed with a gold crucifix on a chain about his neck. He was clean shaven and tonsured, the fringe of hair ringing his bald crown. His nose was long and slender, his eyes inquisitive and friendly.

She stood up from where she had been leaning against a stone pillar. "I'm sorry, Father. I did not hear your approach."

"Father Gregory from Tours," said the priest, inclining his head. "Have you been enjoying the wedding festivities?"

"I—"

Her sidelong glance toward the inner chambers must have given away her thoughts, and she saw that the astute-looking priest did not miss it. His smile was understanding.

"Yes," he said, following her gaze.

Through the doors could be seen drinking horns and goblets tipped as their contents spilled down chins. Some of the Goth roared in laughter.

"I'm afraid pagan instincts are still strong in this part of Gaul," said Gregory. "But then unfortunately, debauchery is not uncommon, even among the priesthood."

He surprised her with his candor.

"I know who you are," Gregory said, smiling at her once again. "You were Radegund's protégé."

She blushed in embarrassment. "I was. She expected much of me, but I'm afraid I was not meant to take the veil."

"It is just as well if you've not been called to take it. Marriage and motherhood are also blessed states."

"Yes, Father."

She did not say that at the moment she was thinking more of immediate survival than about marriage and motherhood.

"Walk with me," he said. "I've a need to clear my head of the wine and company within."

It had started to mist, the gauzy effect of the moist air softening the outlines of the buildings surrounding the palace. The evening and the odor of wet leaves reminded her of the garden where she used to walk with Fortunatus, and she spoke of him to Gregory.

"Yes. I know Venantius Fortunatus. Indeed I was

present at Sigibert's court when he eulogized Queen Brunhild. He is a very good poet. One of the few who knows classical literature as well." He sighed as if he missed such a rare companion.

Gregory's presence made her feel a need to unburden herself after the many events of the past week, to seek reassurance. Here was a man who was used to hearing confessions and who might give her that reassurance.

"Father Gregory, can you work miracles?"

He smiled gently. Miracles were important to sustain people through the drudgeries of life, and he sensed the anxiety in this young woman, in spite of the finery she wore. But whether she worried for herself or for another, he could not tell.

"Priests do not work miracles, my dear," he said. His voice was soothing. "God works miracles. We must remember that the most urgent interest of this brief life is to ensure the soul's safety from the terrors of the next life."

She stopped walking, and he turned to her, so that they confronted each other as rain began to slant down.

"There are terrors in this life, too, if rumors be true," she said to him.

He looked into the bright clear eyes, surmising her thoughts. "And am I to understand that as a member of this royal household, you are in fear?"

She glanced away. "Yes. Perhaps not so much for myself, but . . ."

He raised a hand to stop her. "Ah, it is as I thought. You fear for the safety of another."

"Yes." She looked down quickly.

"Then I will pray for you and for . . ." He let the last word rise as in a question.

71

She looked at him. "For the new queen."

His eyes flickered as he read her thoughts.

"Yes, for Galswinth. Rest assured I will pray for her."

He reached for Judith's hand and folded it in his own. Judith felt the assurance and compassion that emanated from him, and she smiled in appreciation.

She had made two noble friends this night, men who carried their heritage proudly, embers that smoldered from the old Roman fire amidst the barbarian imitators.

"Thank you, Father." Her expression relaxed a trace. "I feel much better."

They turned to watch the water drip from the balcony above, forming puddles in the stone courtyard. Then Judith took her leave. She did not return to the festivities. Rather, hugging the inside walls of the colonnaded walkway, she made her way around the courtyard and up the stairs toward the chambers in the gallery above.

She knew that Galswinth would not need her tonight. She sought the women's quarters, and lay down on her feathered mattress, staring out at the rain slashing across the black sky. A jagged streak of lightning crossed her window, followed by a crack of thunder, and Judith huddled deeper in her fur rugs.

Outside, Gregory covered his head with his hood and hurried out into the wet away from the palace, making his way through the streets toward the house where he was a guest of a fellow churchman. His heart was troubled, though he had not let it show to the fair lady Judith. He considered himself a keen observer of life, and read much into Judith's intimations.

Lightning and thunder crashed in the skies above him, and as he turned back toward the royal palace, a jagged streak of lightning seemed to twist itself into coils of serpents falling from the clouds. His heart contracted; the sign foretold the death of kings. He pulled his hood farther forward and ducked under a balcony to protect himself from the rain, thanking Providence that he had not far to go.

Chapter Five

As it was a mild winter day, Judith accompanied Galswinth and the other ladies, Mosella, Clothild, and Adelais outside to sit at the edge of the woods to pick dried currants. In the distance Judith heard the bells at a nearby monastery ring for sext, and her mind began to recite the prayers required at midday before she could stop herself. She shook her head but said nothing. The other ladies might not see the humor in it, chattering as they picked their way through the high grass and brambles.

Most of Galswinth's companions had come with her from Spain and none had spent time in an abbey. Rather, they had been trained to serve royalty in the Visigothic court where splendor and the cultivation they had copied from Rome was the rule.

While the attendants from the household spread the rugs on a plot of grass at the edge of the woods, the ladies wandered into the trees, searching for the prickly shrubs of the tasty fruit. Judith stayed close to Galswinth.

"I think the king will be pleased if we bring back many baskets of currants," said Galswinth. "I have discovered he has a taste for fruit."

Judith glanced sideways at her friend. "Then you

will surely be able to please him today. The dried currants are abundant this late in the year. See there, our friends have found bunches and are greedily tasting them as well as filling their baskets."

Galswinth allowed herself a smile and Judith noticed that her eyes looked calm today. At first when Galswinth had insisted Judith become her companion, she could not help but notice Galswinth's agitation at the thought of marriage to Chilperic. Then followed the period of adjustment that being thrust into a strange life with a strange man brought. But of late Chilperic and Galswinth seemed to have learned to live with each other, and Judith sensed that her friend had relaxed.

It should bode well, but still it did not. Perhaps it was the uncertainty of life at the Frankish court. In the three months she had been here, she had become more and more aware of the friction between Chilperic and his brother in the Austrasian kingdom. At the Frankish court there was always talk of war. And within Chilperic's own court, Judith observed the king's love of power. From the conversations she overheard on her way to and from the villa, she also learned that the lords who served the king were jealous of one another and that some secretly backed others in authority who might oppose the king.

But why dwell on such thoughts on such a fine day as this? Galswinth's cheeks were rosy, her smile a sign that she was enjoying herself. Why not let her?

Judith led her to a bush where dried currants grew in profusion. She pulled one off and popped it onto her tongue. The fruity taste made her reach for another.

"Try one of these," she said. "Currants grew in the

woods behind the abbey. It was one of the abbess's favorite pastimes to gather them and . . ."

She stopped herself before she mentioned just who it was that she had seen Sister Agnes gather them with. It had been no secret at the abbey that Fortunatus had spent an inordinate amount of time gathering berries, flowers, and other kinds of plants with Radegund and Agnes. Especially with Agnes before he had become a priest. Judith had seen them set out together more than once and return quite late.

But Galswinth was in a mood to be entertained and pressed her friend. "And what?"

"Oh." Judith shrugged. Who was she trying to protect? She was no longer a ward of the Abbey of the Holy Cross. "She often went to the woods with Mother Radegund and Father Fortunatus before he became a priest."

Galswinth saw nothing in that. "I suppose they would want to go beyond the cloister walls on fine days."

Judith thought of one particular time she had followed, and something of it must have shown on her face, because Galswinth studied her carefully while eating a berry.

"It seems there's more to the story," said Galswinth. "Just who else went to these woods?"

Judith could not resist a smile. It was good to be sharing secrets with her friend just as they had done as children, and it encouraged her to see Galswinth interested in something besides her own circumstances.

"Well," said Judith, moving on to another bush and grasping several currants to drop into her basket, "the foundress of the abbey, Radegund, and the abbess, Agnes, were great friends with the poet Venantius Fortunatus before he took holy orders. If you ask me, he did that partly so he could stay at the abbey, because he'd been a guest so many times before."

Galswinth smiled, following Judith to take currants off the shrub. "And so?"

"Well. He composed poems to them both. I . . . well I happened to hear him reading some of them to his two friends after they had supped."

"You were eavesdropping?" Galswinth looked at her in mock horror.

Judith shrugged a shoulder. "When I was younger I used to look for all sorts of ways to entertain myself at the abbey. I liked to . . . learn things."

She stopped in her currant picking to look at Galswinth directly in order to make her point. "I did not know where I fit into worldly life. But I was not meant to spend the rest of my days in a religious order. Something else called to me."

She brought herself back to her story. "So I used to sneak about the abbey. It wasn't too hard to miss vespers or compline. They were not so hard on those who hadn't yet taken their vows."

She smiled at the recollection of her pranks, warming up to her tale. "There was a crack in the wall where Radegund and Agnes used to take Fortunatus to dine, especially when he would first arrive from one of his long journeys to the courts where he composed poems for royalty. Though the sisters ate only bread and herbs themselves, they served Fortunatus with all sorts of delicacies. And he would read his poems to them."

She blushed as she recalled some of the more sensuous ones and recited one of them for Galswinth:

"If the breezy rain
   would not prevent me
without your knowledge
your lover would visit you.
I do not wish an hour's absence
When I see light
there is my love!"

Galswinth chewed her currants slowly. Then she said, "He composed that for the foundress and the abbess?" Her eyes were dark and round with curiosity.

Judith nodded gravely. "And this one:

'You, the life of your sisters
your mind in God
you ignite your body
   to nourish your soul
   tending your annual vows
today
   have incarcerated yourself . . .
You forget time
   as if you were not desired by a lover
(Momentarily
   as I behold you
   I imagine
   myself
   in that role)
But
   Let us marry your vow
and here
   in the spirit

78

        I accompany you
            in your cell
            where it is forbidden to go.' "

"But that is not poetry to brides of Christ," said Galswinth.

Judith raised a mischievous brow. "Well, at the time he was not a priest."

Galswinth was drawn into the gossip. "It's shocking."

Judith continued picking currants. "I think there might have been more to his friendship with Agnes than met the eye," she said.

"Do tell. What did you find out?"

"Well," said Judith, setting her basket down. "I followed them to the woods one day. That is, when Fortunatus and Agnes went without the Mother Radegund. I was curious, so I followed. They didn't know it, of course."

Then she broke off her narrative, feeling suddenly that she was betraying old friends by describing their private lives. She changed her description to general terms. "They walked along a certain path, mostly talking."

"And?" pressed Galswinth.

Judith tried to find a way out of what she was about to reveal. "Well, they sat for a while on a log. He recited more of his poetry to her, and she seemed . . . well, enraptured."

Galswinth's face was flushed with interest. "Is that all?"

That was not all, but Judith was too embarrassed to go further. She could not bring herself to tell Galswinth what she had witnessed. Indeed, at the time, she had the barest minimum of knowledge about the sins of the flesh that took place between a man and a woman.

But the picture of Fortunatus lifting off Agnes's wimple and brushing her cheeks with his fingers that day had stayed with Judith. And there had been other times when she had followed them.

Her own thoughts and thankfully their conversation was interrupted by the gay laughter of the other ladies making their way toward Galswinth and Judith.

"See how heavy are our burdens, mistress," called Mosella, an attractive young woman with curly dark blond hair and laughing eyes who held up a very full basket.

"We beg to rest," said the pretty brown-haired Adelais.

"My companions have eaten as many currants as would fill a hogshead with wine. They need to lie down lest they become ill," teased Clothild. Her red hair glinted in the sun.

They all laughed and Galswinth turned to lead them out of the woods. Judith followed, but more slowly, for she had no desire to hurry back to the rugs and chat with the other women. She longed for more time with Galswinth alone, feeling as if she still needed to make up for the years that had separated them.

And she wanted to hear words from Galswinth's own mouth, from her own heart. Was she happy? Would she ever get over her homesickness? What was Chilperic really like when they were alone? Was he kind to her? Such questions she could not ask as long as they were surrounded with the frivolous women assigned to keep Galswinth occupied.

So Judith paused and reached to gather more dried fruit for her basket. In the distance she heard the other ladies chatter as they spread themselves out on the rugs. It was surprisingly sunny for a midwinter day, though the nights got cold.

Judith turned and passed from one tree to the next, not concerned about wandering into the woods. Fingers of bright sunlight penetrated the trees, and the women were within hearing distance. As her footsteps took her across the pine-needled floor, her mind wandered back to the abbey. She decided she would write a letter to her friends. Father Gregory's words had encouraged her, and she thought that maybe they would forgive her if they understood that she had joined Chilperic's household in order to serve her long lost friend, the new queen.

The crack of twigs brought her out of her reverie and she turned, wondering if someone was there. At first she did not see the outlines of the animal facing her, because his grayish black hair blended with the black thicket in which he stood. But the protruding teeth and great tusks extending from his lower jaw showed white, and a ray of sun caught a gleam of the eyes. Judith was paralyzed with fear; she knew the boar would charge if provoked.

Her voice caught in her throat. She knew she was safer if she stood still than if she screamed and ran, but the basket slipped from her hand, and the boar lowered his snout as if following the smell of the dried fruit. Judith backed into the sharp needles of a low shrub.

Her mind belatedly functioning, she wondered how near were Galswinth's guards with their spears. If she ran to the edge of the forest and shouted warnings for the ladies to flee, would there be a guard close enough to avert the danger? Not daring to breathe, she watched as the boar pawed the ground and knew that in the next minute the choice would be made for her. She began to edge around the bush she had backed into, and then she was running.

From her left she heard the crash of hooves, and though they did not sound like the direction the boar would come from, she ran for her life. The jingle of a harness sounded at the same time the whoosh of a spear passed near her head. Then the horrifying squeal of the wounded animal made her turn her head and she saw the boar fall, eyes in a rage of pain.

Her own heart in her mouth, she still ran, but then brought her feet to a stop before she reached the edge of the trees. And as her lungs heaved from the short run, she saw the blond horseman draw his horse to a stop and dismount. Only then did she realize she had been saved. She slumped against the scratchy bark of a tree.

The man moved closer to his kill and leaned down to investigate the wound. He tried to dislodge the spear, but it had gone clear through and would come out only when the animal was butchered. He stood up, hands on hips, and turned his head toward her.

Their eyes met, and she tried to catch her breath to thank him, willing her feet to move. She recognized the Frankish warrior as one of the counts of the palace, though she didn't know his name. She approached man and beast cautiously, as if afraid that the boar would get up even now and charge her. She would never forget the look in the animal's eyes on the instant of death: unforgiving, as if knowing she was the cause.

She forced her eyes away from the awful sight and raised them to the man looking at her.

"Thank you," she said. "I owe you my life."

He smiled, liking the sight of the girl, who he saw was one of the queen's ladies.

"Fortunate for you I was already on the beast's heels in the woods."

"I did not see a hunting party," said Judith. "But perhaps I was distracted. I should not have gone so far into the woods alone."

"No you shouldn't have," he said, coming closer to her.

She saw now that he was indeed a powerfully built man under his knee-length tunic with short fur-covered vest and loose, cross-gartered leggings. His face was rugged, but not unpleasing, for he was young and clean shaven with the exception of a long blond moustache, and his hair came almost to his shoulders. Proud blue eyes questioned her. He was not as young as she was, but not more than ten years her senior, she judged.

"You are one of the queen's ladies," he said.

She nodded. "My name is Judith. Galswinth and I were friends in Spain a long time ago."

He pivoted on his heel and walked with her away from the slain boar. "I am Count Ivar, servant of the king."

"Again, I thank you, Count Ivar, for saving my life."

He grunted. "I was chasing the boar, myself, and I did not know the queen was on this side of the woods with her ladies. Perhaps it was lucky for us both.

When I saw you, I doubled my efforts to kill the boar before he charged anyone nearby. Let us offer thanks to Ardhuina."

Judith's eyes widened. "Are you not a Christian?"

Ivar looked amused. "Of course. All Chilpcric's men are Christians. He would have it no other way. Surely you know of his efforts to convert Jews and pagans."

"Then why . . . ?" She closed her mouth, fearing she was meddling, but his statement had surprised her.

He looked at her more closely. "Perhaps in Spain, Christianity has a firmer hold. We hunters, though Christians, are not unaware of the power some of the old gods still have." He chose his words carefully. "Though I would not be pleased if my words reached the king's ears." He frowned down at her. "Women gossip. I should not have said anything."

She turned round eyes at him. "Your secret is safe with me, Count Ivar."

His blue eyes examined hers, and satisfied, he smiled. "Yes, you do owe me your life, it is true. I might see fit to take it if I am betrayed."

Judith nodded solemnly at him. They turned back to where his horse waited. He stood on a nearby stump and hoisted himself onto his mount. Turning the horse, he looked down at her.

"Come, I will lead you back to your queen and then send my attendants for the boar."

She glanced back at the dead animal with revulsion. "Yes, you must retrieve your spear."

Ivar grinned. "Perhaps I will send the spear head to you as a trophy."

She glanced up at him. "As a reminder of the

incident? I'm not sure I want to remember."

But it occurred to her that it would not do to offend this count. His manner was not unpleasing, and she did owe him her life. "However, I will accept your trophy gladly."

Satisfied, Ivar smiled again and turned his horse. She followed him out of the woods.

The next day Judith emerged from the stables where she had visited the horse that would be hers. Such noble steeds were a joy to behold, unlike the draft animals that pulled carts with goods to the abbey. She had never actually ridden those horses, but the peasants had let her sit on them while they did business with the abbess.

As she crossed the quadrangle, she spied Ivar coming toward her. He was dressed in knee-length tunic with fur covering, his leggings cross-gartered with leather bands up to the knee. His belt was adorned with precious stones and metal studs, and from the belt was suspended his sheathed scramasax, the double-edged dagger favored by Frankish warriors. He saw her at the same time and halted.

"I hope you've stayed out of the woods since we last met," he said.

She could not resist his smile. "I have, sir. I have vowed never to venture into them without a host of guards around me."

He threw back his head and laughed, the sun glinting off his shoulder-length hair and adding a luster to his blue eyes. "I hope I am fortunate enough to be one of that guard," he said.

When she looked into his eyes she could see golden

streaks that radiated from the black pupil all the way to the edge of the iris like spokes of a wheel. She told him where she had been, and the excitement of owning the wonderful steed she had left in the stables showed in her eyes as she spoke.

"Well, I shall have to examine this horse for myself," he said. "But at the moment I am on my way to the mews." He paused, then said, "Have you seen the king's hawks?"

She glanced in the direction he was headed. Though she knew Chilperic had a passion for falconry, she had never ventured near the birds. Now Ivar's question piqued her curiosity, and she met his gaze.

"No, I haven't, but I would like to. Are you offering to show them to me?"

He observed the girl before him, interested in her. Since the day he had rescued her from the boar, he had seen her whisk about the royal villa and the sight of her had arrested him. Ivar was more given to following his instincts than to worrying about the results of his actions, and like the other Franks he was hedonistic and ambitious. And he had a fair share of intelligence. His ancestors had fought beside Merovech against Attila the Hun in 451, as it had been handed down in the songs that had been recited for a hundred years by the bards.

More than anything Ivar was a warrior and loyal to the king. He seldom wasted time on women. Only when debauching with his comrades did he use the opportunity for physical release. While not unaware of Judith's female charms, he already felt connected to her in some way. He was also very superstitious, and the boar may have been an omen. Crossing her path again must be fate. So he took her along to the mews.

They passed many outbuildings where the agricultural tasks were accomplished, and finally came to a large cleared space where several trainers were working with the falcons.

Judith gasped in delight. To the left, twenty or thirty falcons were put out to weather on blocks of wood cut from logs with the bark on them, leather straps secured to one leg and tied to a curved iron perch bent into the wood at both ends. Here the birds plumed and preened their beautiful feathers of hues from brown and white to rusty red and blue-black. Trainers moved among them, carrying birds on their left hand, where powerful talons clutched a thick buckskin glove.

Judith watched, fascinated, as one trainer in the field swung a heavy feathered object tied with red cloth and bits of string. The bird, which had left the trainer's wrist moments before, now dove at the bait tied at the end of the rope.

"See how she dives at the lure," said Ivar, following Judith's gaze. "He is training an eyess, one taken from the nest."

The man walked to where his bird was feeding and petted and talked to it as it ate its reward.

"The eyess, taken young, has no fear or hatred of man and requires simply to be led to do the will of its master. But she is not so bold as the haggard."

She looked at him questioningly. "The haggard? You must forgive me. I know little of hawking." Now she felt she had to explain. "I did not grow up in Galswinth's court in Spain. I have lived in Gaul for half of my life, in the Abbey of the Holy Cross. Most of our meat was provided by the hunters around Poitiers."

"Ah," he said. "Then you've never been around the hawks that hunt small game for the king's table."

"No."

"They are noble birds," he said, not looking at her. "The merlins and the sparrowhawks are fit for ladies. For a falcon can amuse as well as earn its living by hunting."

His words aroused her interest and she examined the birds and trainers more closely.

Ivar went on to explain. "The haggard is one taken as an adult after several seasons of flying in the wild and killing for her own food. Such a bird must be won by patience and turned from thinking of man as her enemy. She must unlearn all her instincts and be taught submission until she obeys the will of her master. It takes many weeks more to train a haggard, but the results are worth it. No bird flies like the haggard."

Ivar gestured for her to follow, and he led the way to a fine, large bird he called by name and petted.

"Isault is a fine gyrfalcon," he said, running his hands over her shiny black and rust feathers as she danced under his touch. Her sharp claws were large and powerful, and Ivar donned his own glove before holding out his hand so she could mount his wrist.

"Come," said Ivar to Judith, and they took to the field.

They walked past the area where the other birds were training, to the end of the clearing. Isault perched quietly as Ivar scanned the skies. Judith waited, not sure what she was going to see, but aware that in a moment the noble bird would perform for her.

Before she saw what Ivar saw, he had murmured words of encouragement and flung the bird from his wrist. Now she spread her graceful wings and climbed upward in long, spiral curves. Ring after ring she made until Judith saw the prey Ivar had sent her after, a small rook coming slowly from the direction of the sheepfold on the hill beyond. Rising with each stroke of her powerful wings, Isault still shot upward.

The rook was coming on nicely until he must have sensed something suspicious and took a sudden swerve. He saw his enemy and made upward at no mean rate, but the pace of the falcon was too much for him and soon she was above him. Poising herself for a moment, she dove. Judith tensed, waiting for talons to grasp their prey, but with a clever shift, the rook escaped her. Judith breathed again.

Now the trainers in the field had stopped and everyone watched the chase. Isault shot up again like an arrow from a bow, while the rook made for a nearby copse. But on reaching the covert, he found that his enemy, man, had reached it first and drove him upward with shouts and beating of sticks in the bushes, forcing him into the open. Meanwhile, Isault began to ring upward into the clouds above for another attack.

Up went the rook, mounting nearly as fast as the falcon, becoming smaller and smaller until Judith feared she would lose sight of the two birds. Still, Isault soared steadily into the wind. She completed her mighty circle while the rook turned downwind. In another moment Isault turned, far above the rook, and descended like an arrow. No chance, thought Judith, watching as if under a spell.

Suddenly the rook dropped like a stone toward a clump of trees, but now Isault was on him and with a mighty blow, just before the rook reached the trees, she pounced, knocking him to the ground. From behind Judith came cheers, and she glanced at Ivar, whose face registered his pride and pleasure as he whistled and called to Isault at the same time they set off at a run for the trees.

In no time they reached the clearing where the rook had landed and Isault was depluming her kill. Ivar praised her and petted her; then, after fastening the leather strap to her leg again, he dropped a soft leather hood over her eyes and lifted her to his wrist.

"A good kill," he said to Judith. "She will be rewarded and fed from the board."

The other trainers stood around discussing the fight as they made their way back. Judith felt her heart beginning to settle after the exciting battle.

"She is a noble bird," said Judith when Ivar had replaced Isault on her perch, and fed her a freshly killed pigeon.

"Indeed."

His bird taken care of, he turned his attention to the girl beside him. "Perhaps you will accompany me on a ride with the falcon one day," he said. "If your new horse is accustomed to the birds."

"Oh yes," she said without stopping to think whether her horse was trained for falconry or not. "That would be wonderful." Judith had not thought much past her encounters with this man, but she liked the fact that he had shown her the hawks. Surely it would not hurt to have such a man as a friend. The Frankish court was still a strange place to her, and she had not made many friends. The women in Galswinth's entourage were kind enough to her, but she was still an outsider, and perhaps because she was Galswinth's favorite friend, the other women did not take her into their confidence.

Judith followed Ivar to the edge of the field where she turned to bid him goodbye.

"I must return to the queen," she said, raising her eyes slowly to his, not minding his standing so close to her. "I thank you for showing me your noble bird in flight."

He nodded, his eyes traveling over her face and glancing off the rest of her figure. "You must convey my compliments to the queen."

"I shall do so," she said, feeling a tremble course through her. Then she turned and hastened across the quadrangle of buildings toward the villa.

Her thoughts were full of Ivar and the falcon as she made her way along the arcade to the wing where Galswinth had her apartments. She joined the ladies who were spinning and carding wool in a large room where they sat on stools.

"Oh, there you are, Judith," said Mosella. "We were wondering where you'd gone."

Judith took a seat and picked up some wool to card. "I was in the mews. Count Ivar showed me one of the falcons and she made a great kill."

All the women murmured excitedly. "Do tell us about it," said Clothild.

"Yes, do," said Mosella. "I've been to the mews, but no one explained anything to me. And you say the bird made a kill?"

Judith did not at all mind recounting the morning's adventure, careful as she described Ivar not to include her own responses, which she was unsure of.

Naturally, she was fascinated by him; her exposure to men had been limited to bishops and peasants who came to the abbey. She found herself ignoring the Frankish nobles, most of whom looked at her lewdly when they had been consuming wine. And the nobles in administrative positions, such as Epoald, seemed too involved in their own business to notice her.

And while Ivar exhibited the same fierce qualities as the other Frankish warriors, there was a brightness in his eyes and a gentle sensuousness in his voice when he talked to the falcon that Judith could not help but find pleasing. Still not quite free of the restrained habits the nuns had tried to instill in her, she found it necessary to keep these feelings secret. Except for the yearning looks she saw in some of the other young women at the abbey when they stole a glance at a strong man, and the strange relationship that existed between Fortunatus and Agnes, Judith was a complete innocent. Only her instincts and the responses she felt as her womanhood bloomed told her there were many mysterious things yet to be known, secrets to be careful of, no doubt. Pleasures of the flesh, obliquely referred to in the holy books, which were considered sins.

Chapter Six

In the kitchens, where slaves toiled endlessly from dawn to dusk, Fredegund kneaded dough. She had chosen working in the pastry kitchen because the soft dough would not ruin her hands as long as she was careful not to burn herself when reaching into an oven with tongs or removing a tray. But long gloves and thick pads protected her.

Fredegund detested the kitchens, her own revulsion the worse because her mother had been a kitchen slave. But she did not think her banishment from the king's quarters would last long. Aware of the political situation, she accepted her temporary fate while Chilperic nursed his pride with a bride as cultivated as that of his rival brother, Sigibert, in Austrasia. Chilperic prided himself on ruling a population in Neustria comprised of more civilized Gallo-Romans than the Teutons who made up a large part of the northwest where Sigibert ruled.

Seizing on this influence of civilization, Chilperic had educated himself, studied the Christian scriptures, and debated with visiting bishops, who never failed to encourage him in his determination to convert the Jews. Thus, the chance to ally himself with the king of the Visigoths and obtain a queen who would gain him further admiration from his populace was not to be overlooked. For his new bride's rumored grace and intelligence were greatly admired.

This much Fredegund knew, because she knew her king well. And she had no choice but to watch him satisfy himself with this despised Gothic princess. But Fredegund had fought too hard to become the king's favorite to lose her position so quickly. She was used to the mild power it had brought her in the court, the comforts and luxury a king's concubine enjoyed, and the security of knowing she could rule a king's heart. In a word, Fredegund craved power, and if she now flung around large clumps of dough that would become bread for the king's table, and spent the larger part of the day covered in flour where her simple muslin tunic did not drape her pampered skin, it was because she knew she could work her way upward in palace circles again.

If there was one thing Fredegund understood, it was intrigue. She had learned it from listening when she had become a slave at Chilperic's court in the first place. She heard the whispers of counts and dukes who favored and who opposed the king's plans; she observed the movements of the mayors of the palace and the confidences exchanged in hushed tones between emissaries from the courts of Burgundy or Austrasia. She had learned her lessons well.

On her way to the bedroom of the king, she had made friends and kept them. She had favored many a count with jewels, coin from the treasury when she could steal it, and the pleasures of her body, which she made sure kept its beauty. She applied oils from the east and tried and true enhancements for the hair and the skin, and though she delighted in sensuous tastes afforded at the king's banquet, she was careful not to eat too much and to keep to an active life so as never to become fat.

The smallest trace of flabby tissue was starved, massaged, and worked away. Her instinct for the art of lovemaking did the rest. She caught many a man in her snare and then learned enough about him to threaten to blackmail him if he should not do her bidding. Nor did she overuse the favors owed her. She knew that in building power, one did not abuse one's friends or they would turn on you. No, the loyalty she had sought and had retained was won by her wiles in such a way that she could be sure of the nobles she had bound to her.

At the moment no one would go against the king, not as long as he favored his new queen, but Fredegund was patient, willing to work slowly, to wait until Chilperic's passion for Galswinth waned. Then she would be there to remind him of her loyalty to him, even of her willingness to serve him in the hated kitchens.

As she worked, Fredegund happened to glance out a window at the quadrangle where the kitchens faced storehouses and the wash house. She saw two slaves drag a large wooden tub out of the shed. Peering closely at the slaves, she thought she recognized them as those who served the queen. At once she realized where the tub must be going, and she quickly straightened and seized a rag to dust off the flour from her arms and chest. Then, before the slaves had the tub across the space of the yard, Fredegund met them.

Picking up one side of the tub, which they were about to set down for a rest, she said, "If you're going to the queen, I will help you. I have a message for her, so I must go there myself."

The two slaves, young girls from a border tribe given as part of the tribute owed Chilperic, stared suspiciously at Fredegund. But they shrugged, said nothing and picked up the tub again. Fredegund assisted them until they got the tub to the tiled arcade of the villa where they could roll it. She had only seen Galswinth from a distance as she roamed about the estate with her ladies, or at meals the few times she found an excuse to serve in the large banquet hall. Now it was time to get close to the queen so that she could observe her. One must find the weakness in one's rivals, and that could be done in only two ways: by bribing servants and by observing for oneself. Fredegund used both measures, but favored the latter.

The villa was equipped with a lavatory and running water piped in from the river. Roman ingenuity had not been lost on the Frankish nobles who tried to make use of everything the Romans had left behind and plumbing was a great convenience for those who could afford it. But baths were still brought to the king and queen. They did not bathe with the other noble men and women in the lavatory.

The two slaves got the tub up the steps leading to Galswinth's apartment with only slight assistance from Fredegund, who did not want to run the risk of splinters in her smooth hands. But as they entered the queen's chambers, she assumed the proper expression of humility. Her eyes downcast, she darted glances about the room, taking in the queen's ladies at their needlework.

A fire had been built up in an open hearth in the

center of the room where a chimney led upward. The tub was placed on a straw mat near it. Water was heating in a large pot with handles on either side, which the two slaves now lifted and poured into the tub. A second and third pot of water were also emptied into the tub and then one of the queen's ladies brought soap, sponges, and towels.

"Is there anything else your ladyships need?" asked one of the slaves meekly.

"Thank you, no," said Mosella, overseeing the activity.

Fredegund glanced up to see the queen approach. In a swift glance, Fredegund took in her fine, dark hair, unbound about her shoulders, her clear, porcelain skin, dark lashes and brown eyes. In her brief glance she paid special attention to the eyes, and it took only a moment for Fredegund to strengthen her resolve.

The woman before her, holding out her arms so her women could undress her for the bath, was no formidable rival. Everything about Galswinth spoke of weakness to Fredegund. And she felt an instant resentment when she saw the fine clothes the queen wore. The rich silk tunic embroidered with gold was the sort of thing Fredegund had worn when she was the king's favorite. The itchy hemp garment she now wore stiffened her resolve to regain her place as concubine, and she had to grind her teeth together to keep from showing her sudden anger.

To give herself something to do, Fredegund reached for one of the pots, which she assumed the slaves intended to take away. She was right, for the other two girls took the other pots. Again, Fredegund let her sly glance slide over the princess as she tested the water with her foot. There was no confidence in her movements, little determination in her face.

She looked at the soft, slim body and felt a wave of jealous revulsion. This was the woman Chilperic slept with. Fredegund's hands tightened around the wooden handle of the iron pot. She mustn't show her hatred. Patience, patience, she forced herself to remember, as she and the slaves took their leave.

An attractive girl with green eyes and thick, wavy light hair watched Fredegund, and the former concubine caught the curious gaze. For the blink of an instant they stared at each other, then Fredegund lowered her eyes and hastened after her companions. One of the queen's friends, Fredegund thought; she had seen her about the villa and remembered hearing her name.

This girl had something in her face to make Fredegund wary. A good judge of character, she noticed at once the intelligence in Judith's eyes and also saw that the girl was intensely loyal to Galswinth. Something about her conveyed her protectiveness of the queen. If Fredegund had to outwit anyone in order to get to the queen, it would be this girl with green eyes.

Since there were no wars to be fought, Chilperic's mind turned more and more to the hunt. This morning, the king, queen, and their retinue prepared to hunt a stag that had been seen in the woods. Rising well before dawn, Judith and the other women dressed in linen undertunics, fine leather boots, and cloaks dyed bright colors with borders of varicolored hues.

Trudulf, the count of the stables, had the horses

ready, and the nobles swarmed about the stable yard as dawn tinted the eastern sky. The nobles who surrounded the king were boisterous as they prepared to set out after the stag, hoping to chase any fierce animals that might also get in the way. Drinking horns were passed around; wine stimulated the men for the chase.

Trudulf approached Galswinth's retinue and assisted the queen on to her mount, a pure white courser of good blood lines. Judith had met Trudulf many times on her visits to the stables and under his watchful eye she had improved her riding skills. Judith rubbed the smooth muzzle of her own horse, which she had named Black Lady, as Trudulf approached.

Black Lady's ears perked forward and she stamped the ground as if she, too, anticipated the hunt. Trudulf patted her flank and then led the horse to a mounting block to help Judith up into the saddle.

"A fine morning for a hunt," he remarked to Judith as the other stablemen assisted the rest of the court into their saddles. His eyes surveyed the assembly.

"The omens were read last night, and they are good." He smiled easily at Judith who sat proudly on her horse.

"Do you mean the astrologers read the stars last night in anticipation of today's hunt?" she asked as Trudulf continued to stroke Black Lady's flank.

"Most assuredly. A portent of any evil must be warded off before the king sets out."

At that moment, Judith caught Ivar's eye where he gazed at her from across the quadrangle. Her lips curved upward in a smile and he raised his drinking horn in a salute to her. Then he tossed the empty horn to an attendant and nudged his horse forward, following the king, who had set out.

The men would of course lead in the hunt, followed by the women and then the retainers who would bring food to spread out for the company in the middle of the day. She noticed the slaves loading their bundles and crockery onto a cart for the day's repast. The woman who had come into Galswinth's chambers the other day with the bath arrested Judith's attention.

Perhaps it was the look on the woman's face as she narrowed her eyes, watching the queen's retinue. Judith had become accustomed to the usual downcast looks of the servants, too overworked to gaze speculatively at anything except the task they were immediately absorbed in. But this woman stood straight, hands on hips until someone handed her a jug, which she set upon the cart. Her eyes flicked past Galswinth and grazed over Judith, who felt a sudden disquiet.

She leaned down to Trudulf, who still stood, surveying the horses. "Who is that woman with the yellow hair?" she asked him, moving her head in the direction of the refreshment cart.

He glanced in the direction Judith meant and then up at Judith. A wary look came into his soft brown eyes. "Her name is Fredegund," he said in a low voice. "She was the king's mistress."

At once Judith understood the malevolent looks that came from the former concubine. This must be one of the women who had been set aside when Chilperic married Galswinth. And Judith could tell the woman wasn't pleased. As Judith urged her horse forward, she looked again at the place where Fredegund stood. She bent to her task, but without the submission characteristic of the rest of the slaves. Then, as if she felt Judith's eyes on her, she raised her own and the look in them gave Judith a shiver. Her eyes seemed the color of cracked glass.

"Good hunting," said Trudulf.

"Thank you," Judith replied.

With no more time to consider Fredegund, Judith followed the women from the compound along the road that wound beside the forest. It was a fine winter day, and as the sun climbed higher, exhilaration spread through the nobles intent on the hunt. The woods were thick to their right, but the king's warriors led them toward gentle slopes where they could ride without risk of entanglement in undergrowth.

For a while the group strung out in one long and colorfully winding line, and Judith found her spirits lifting as she felt the sure strides of her horse under her. Now and then she caught glimpses of Ivar, riding far ahead near the king. Then a shout went up from the huntsman; the stag had been sighted, and they were off.

The men rode hard, their horses seeming to leap over rivulets, fallen logs and rises in the ground, nothing keeping them from following the stag into the copse where it darted for shelter. The women heard the horns and felt the thunder of the men's horses galloping ahead, but since they weren't involved in the kill, they made their way more slowly across the countryside. For an hour they rode, wandering far from the villa, and Judith enjoyed viewing unfamiliar countryside.

Finally, a great shout went up. By the time the women's group came out on a rise where they could see down into a small valley, the men were off their horses. The beast had been killed and the king was clapping the noble on the back who had first speared the stag. Judith caught sight of the slain animal and turned away. Although she knew there would be meat for their table that night, she rued the death of so fine an animal, and she could see that the men enjoyed the bloodletting as much for sport as for the necessity of getting game.

The butchers were left to carve the animal and the hunters remounted, off to seek other prey. But Galswinth was inclined to rest. Not wanting to watch the butchering process, she picked a grassy slope a little distance away and gave orders.

"Have the servants spread our rugs here. We will wait for the men to return for their midday meal," she told Epoald, whose duty it was to coordinate the efforts of the household and send word to the hunting party as to where the queen had chosen to gather for refreshment. He bowed and turned to his stewards to issue orders. One young man mounted his horse and set out after the hunt to bring them back when the time came.

Judith was glad to have the chance to dismount. Galswinth had chosen well, for there was a stream nearby where Judith led her own horse to drink. She did not turn Black Lady over to servants because she wanted to care for the fine mare herself so that a bond would form between them.

She knelt to bathe her face from the cold stream, as Black Lady drank. When she returned to the rise, she watched as the servants coaxed their mule to bring the refreshment cart up the little hill so that they would be ready to serve when commanded.

The servants built a fire to warm the mulled wine,

which they ladled into goblets for the ladies. By the time the men returned, the party was in a feasting mood.

Judith took her place with Mosella, Clothild, and the other women and watched Galswinth with Chilperic, who had joined her on a white fur rug set aside for the royal couple. Around them the lords tipped back the drinking cups and boasted about this and other hunts while the servants unfolded a trestle table upon which they set the food. The king and queen were served first and from Chilperic's attention to Galswinth, Judith judged that he was enjoying his wife's company.

"What a fine day," said Clothild, watching the noblemen in their revelry. "Indeed," said Mosella, running a hand over her shiny curls, in case a certain young lord looked her way.

"I wouldn't like to throw the spear," said Clothild, "but I would surely like to race across the grass on a fast steed the way the men do."

Judith eased her breathing. She had not gotten over her uneasiness about the marriage, perhaps because of the unlucky verses they had read the night they had resorted to the *Sortes Biblicae,* perhaps because of Galswinth's own premonitions about marrying the Frankish king. Judith could not put aside the worry that her friend was not entirely happy in the Frankish court, though she could not put her finger on any particular danger.

Her mind traveled back to her conversation with Father Gregory, when she asked him to pray for the new queen, and she found herself wondering when and where she might see him again. She was well aware of the comfort that talking to those of spiritual

103

awareness could bring. When she had been troubled in the convent, she had gone to Mother Radegund, who had never failed to offer her solace. Even Fortunatus, with all his worldly experience, had been a man whose counsel she could always listen to. Father Gregory had been such a person, and she wished he did not live so far away in Tours, because she would have liked to talk to him again and seek advice.

She gazed again at Chilperic as he gnawed on a thick turkey leg and talked and gestured to his lords who lounged on rugs nearby. Then she saw the source of Chilperic's pleasure: He was proud of his wife; Chilperic thought her a prize. Rumor had it that he had married her to best his brother Sigibert, who had married Galswinth's sister, Brunhild, and now that he had done it, he must be satisfied.

"Judith, you seem so thoughtful," said Clothild, reaching for a piece of cheese on a tray a servant brought. "Aren't you enjoying yourself?"

Judith turned and put a smile on her face. "Yes, of course. I'm sorry. My mind was wandering."

"You are always thinking," chimed Mosella. She laughed without embarrassment. "I suppose you learned about thinking in the abbey."

Judith shrugged and tried to join the conversation. She handed her empty goblet to a passing slave and accepted a piece of fruit from the tray another slave offered. Chilperic spoke a few words to his wife, then turned away from her to address his lords. Galswinth in turn rose to move to the rug where her ladies sat, and the women moved to make room for her. The company mixed freely now, and several of the lords stopped to speak to the queen's ladies, entertaining them with their deeds of the hunt, leaving Galswinth and Judith to converse in a relative island of privacy.

Ivar passed nearby, his gaze drifting to the queen and Judith and then away to where he spoke to his companions. Galswinth noticed Judith's attempt to bring her eyes back from the handsome lord, and studied her friend.

"Count Ivar seems to notice you, Judith. I believe it is not the first time. Isn't he the one who rescued you from the boar?"

Judith blushed. "It is true. He showed me the king's mews the other day as well."

Galswinth was silent for a moment, then whispered, "You could do worse."

Judith's eyes widened. Having no experience with men, she did not know how to defend herself. Finally, she allowed herself to speak to Galswinth about him. For it was true, she had noticed his glances on more than one occasion, and was growing more curious about him.

"What do you know about him?" she asked the queen.

Galswinth shrugged. "I do not know him well, but my husband seems to favor him. He has said that Ivar is brave in battle and has been quite useful in the border wars when the tributary tribes threaten rebellion." Galswinth leaned closer and whispered, "It is said he has a great scar below his hip where a Saxon tried to leave his spear."

The image made Judith shudder. She did not really know what to think of Ivar, but his interest in her stirred an idea that had begun to form at the back of her mind. As she had tried to learn about Chilperic's court and had heard much from both rumor and snatches of conversation overheard, she had sensed that power was balanced on the basis of loyalty. And Chilperic's attempt to best his brother Sigibert with a royal wife did not stop there. Judith had become aware of the frequent disagreements between the two brothers over territory. Though no one said so, it was not unlikely that there were Austrasian spics in the Neustrian court.

None of this affected Judith or Galswinth directly, except in Judith's constant alertness to danger in any quarter. She began to realize that the queen needed to acquire the loyalty of nobles herself, and as one of the queen's women it was Judith's responsibility to help garner such loyalty. In Ivar, Judith sensed a Frankish lord who might be depended upon in time of need. Her thoughts had barely formed the idea of protector in her mind when from Galswinth's look over Judith's shoulder she became aware of the long muscular legs standing beside her at the edge of the rug.

She looked up to see Ivar, whose eyes flicked over her before he bowed to the queen.

"My ladies," he said, "I hope you are enjoying the day."

Judith glanced at Galswinth, who smiled comfortably, then addressed Ivar.

"We are, Count Ivar."

"Then I hope you will tell me if I can serve you today in any way."

The queen gestured to Judith and said, "I understand that my lady Judith has taken an interest in the falcons. Such an education is good for her. She has spent much time in a convent and has not acquired any skills of the outdoors. Perhaps you can also instruct her in the finer points of becoming an excellent horsewoman."

Ivar looked pleased. "I would be most glad to do so."

He extended a hand to Judith, who rose from the rug. She started to ask permission from Galswinth to go, but the queen had already become distracted by another of Chilperic's nobles who handed her a fresh goblet of wine.

Chapter Seven

"Walk with me," he said to Judith. "Perhaps you would like to see where the stag was killed."

Blood on the ground was not one of Judith's favorite sights, but she did not want to offend Ivar and so followed him through the boisterous crowd.

They walked down the rise, past the place where slaves had tethered the horses, then followed the line of trees. But once that far, Ivar did not seem interested in the spot where the stag had been killed. Instead, he veered into the trees, careful to step where undergrowth had been trampled down, helping Judith over fallen logs.

The revelry was left behind as the quiet forest closed in on them. But this time she felt no danger for Ivar wore his scramasax on one side and a sword sheathed on the other. Both hung from a wide leather belt encrusted with precious stones and gold studs. He seemed certain of his direction, but after a while he slowed. They came to a cleared space, so she could walk beside him.

She saw that his face was relaxed, and sensed that he liked the woods, perhaps better than the court. As he took her hand to help her over tangled brambles she found his touch sinfully pleasurable, and avoided meeting his eyes. Once, he paused and examined the ground.

"Bear tracks," he said. "But old ones. The bear will be in his winter sleep by now."

They went on through, then suddenly she heard Ivar make a sound of surprise and she looked up. She drew in a quick breath at the sight. They were in a place deep in the shade of interlacing boughs. Standing beside an old oak, a stone figure was hung with animal skins and horns. Ivar placed his hand on her shoulder as if in surprise—and to keep her from going closer.

Then he exhaled a breath and spoke. "The goddess Ardhuina. I should have remembered this was a sacred grove. I should have guessed it when the stag fell so easily."

"What are the skins and horns for?" asked Judith with a little shiver.

"Huntsmen hang them there to propitiate her."

He gestured that they could move forward and they walked closer, though Judith stopped a good distance from the idol.

"It's true that Saint Martin has replaced her as protector of Christian huntsmen, but some of us . . ." He glanced over his shoulder as if afraid of being heard, though there was no one there but themselves. He spoke in a lower voice. "Some still honor the pagan goddess as well."

She remembered his comment the day she had been saved from the boar. The coolness of the forest began to chill her and she longed for the sun. She turned, not wanting to look at the stone idol anymore, and Ivar followed her. They heard the crackling of twigs, and Ivar grasped the handle of his scramasax.

But as a doe scampered into the clearing behind them and then leapt gracefully away, Ivar relaxed his grip. Judith was thankful that he had not decided to kill it. Perhaps he felt they had enough meat for the day. Judith felt a pang of remorse for the doe, wondering if it was looking for its mate, who had been sacrificed to the hunt.

"You have an affinity for living things," Ivar said, watching Judith's expression as her face showed concern for the doe. She looked up at him.

"Yes, I suppose I do. At the abbey I was always nursing wounded animals brought to us. Mostly when they were well I returned them to their homes in the woods or fields. I helped with a few foalings, too."

He grunted. "We must respect the beasts of the woods and fields. For they sustain us, do they not? We kill them because we must eat. But they are our friends as well. In that sense we are one of them."

"Yes," she said, understanding his viewpoint.

"I will take you out with my falcon soon," he said.

"I would like that."

They had stopped some distance from where the sun spilled in at the edge of the woods. Ivar stood close to her, and she was aware of her blood racing. She liked being with him, and his obvious strength and masculinity awakened responses in her that were tempting and frightening.

Ivar looked into her eyes and saw the pattern there where the golden specks had formed a many-pointed star in the green heavens. Blood surged in his loins. He reached into his fur-covered vest and grasped a small medallion hanging on his chest. He lifted the leather thong that held it over his head and handed it to her.

"To ride in the forests and use the beasts of field and air, you will need protection."

She stared at the curving interlaced design that surrounded a small engraved figure of a bird she did not recognize. But she did realize that the symbol was the same as that which marked his belt, his saddle gear and the shield she had seen him carry. She looked at him questioningly and felt what passed between them.

His lips lifted in a half smile. "It is said that the talisman enables the wearer to understand the language of animals and ensures protection from ferocious beasts."

"I see," she said, not really knowing what to say.

"Go on, wear it. It is a gift."

She placed the thong around her neck, letting the talisman fall between her breasts. "Thank you," she said.

In a quick movement Ivar seized her and pulled her to him. His mouth descended on hers and his arms went under her cloak to enfold her against him. Judith was surprised but yielded to the mouth that claimed hers. The strength of his body was warm and reassuring and the hands that pressed against her back not unpleasing. She opened her lips to his, and as her tongue met his, the blood quickened in her veins. There arose within her a response to the man who held her, and she allowed the embrace to continue.

Sensing her release, Ivar continued his explorations, his hands grasping the curve of her buttocks.

But he moved easily, knowing that women did not like rough treatment. His tongue ploughed her mouth hungrily and one hand came up to grasp her breast. He had guessed that her flesh would be desirable, and standing with her in the woods, he now knew it for certain.

Their embrace was interrupted by the sound of the hunting horn, and though he tried to shut his ears to it, the training that was ingrained in him forced him to raise his head: The party would be leaving, and he must be with the king. Stealing one moment longer, his hand clasped her waist and he lowered his head once more to taste of her mouth.

The sound of the horn also helped Judith struggle with the sensations that overwhelmed her. Though a virgin, she had begun to guess at the activities that went on between men and women. The convent had not been completely bereft of girlish speculation, and since she'd been in the court, Galswinth's women often gossiped about the Frankish lords, commenting sometimes in a lewd manner on their endowments.

But she had been taught that these things were a sin, even though the women who spoke of them seemed not to care. Ivar moved so that he had only one arm around her shoulders and guided her toward the sunlight.

"We must go back," he said gruffly.

His arm about her helped to steady her, and by the time they reached the edge of the woods she was able to place her feet in the direction of the hunting party. After the cool depths of the forest, the sunlight seemed blinding and Ivar's nearness still had her senses swimming. She tried to replace the flush on her face with a neutral expression, but wondered if

Galswinth and the other women would be able to see right through her.

Luckily the melee where the feast had been cleared away was such that as riders mounted horses, there was little worry. She found her horse; Ivar assisted her to mount; then he disappeared among his fellows. Once on her horse, she fingered the talisman he had given her, wondering at its supposed powers. Black Lady shook her head and whinnied softly as if knowing, and Judith patted her neck.

What she did not know was that by wearing the talisman where others could see it, she was now marked as Ivar's woman.

Some distance from the activity of the court's departure from their outdoor meal, Fredegund slipped behind one of the carts and listened carefully to a conversation between Epoald and two counts of the palace. Epoald spoke in a very low voice, shielded from others by the taller men who stood with their heads bowed to his. Only the angle of the cart where Fredegund stood hunched against its corner allowed her to hear their words.

"The new queen is not yet pregnant," said Epoald, "but if she becomes so, measures must be taken. The king's son by his former wife is safe in a monastery in Ireland, where he can be protected. He will serve our purposes, gentlemen, for we can control him."

"We must protect him at all costs," said Count Bertram, the man who had killed the stag. His flinty gray eyes scanned the activity of the servants and nobles not far away.

His companion, Count Godulf, added his own

words. "The Merovingian kings have too much power. They rule by cruelty and greed alone. When they can be counseled by nobles who have the people's interest at heart, it is well enough. But it is best to put them on the throne while they are still minors and govern for them as regents. For in spite of their divine blood line, I for one do not believe the head is always so divinely endowed."

"A mayor cannot make a king," said Bertram.

"Not yet," said Epoald. "Not yet."

Epoald himself dared not voice what he secretly wished for. For several generations the Arnulfings had sat at the right hand of the king. They would continue to do so. They were a family rich in property already and the lords of the Neustrian court respected them. They looked to the Arnulfings for leadership. The other lords might bicker, but they all respected the Arnulfings who quietly, unobtrusively sowed loyalty among the Frankish nobles. Perhaps one day . . .

Fredegund listened carefully as the men discussed what might be done if Galswinth bore a son. Clearly these three were Chilperic's enemies. That knowledge was valuable to her. While she would not risk crossing Epoald openly, she might be able to render Chilperic a favor and so raise herself in his esteem. For though she was not unaware of this and similar conversations among the Frankish nobles who had been gaining in power slowly over the last decades, it was still the king who could restore Fredegund to a position of power.

She slipped away quietly and returned to her drudgery, but now she had a plan: As soon as possible she would get away from the kitchens and repair to a cave where she had taken her most valued possessions soon after Chilperic set her aside.

The party returned to the villa and dispersed for afternoon rests, which gave Fredegund the opportunity to do what she wanted. She left the villa by a side door wearing a hooded cloak so that she would not be noticed. Once in the woods, she hurried along a path that wound through thick, uncleared forest where only she knew where to step to avoid entanglement or sinking in a bog. In an hour she came to a cave and moved aside brush that cleverly concealed the entrance.

She went to the back of the cave and moved aside a flat rock that covered a deep cavity from which she removed an iron casket. Pulling it out carefully, she lifted the plain, unadorned lid that revealed her treasures. The vials that contained the substances she had been experimenting with were covered. She examined a few by smell and decided they were still in safe and serviceable condition, then she selected three and secured them in a pouch tied to her girdle.

She had learned some of the black art of poisoning from old women who were considered to be witches. But she knew that experimentation would be necessary before she set her plan in motion. A few unknowing and worthless slaves would do. Satisfied with her plans, Fredegund replaced the casket in the ground and left the cave as if no one had ever entered it.

The next morning Judith was crossing the quadrangle toward the stables when she became aware of a loud wailing coming from the slave quarters. She paused and turned in that direction just as Trudulf came out of the stables and set a pitchfork by the rough-hewn wall.

"What is it?" she said to him.

His eyes drifted toward the wattle and timber buildings behind the kitchens. "Slave girl's dying. They're taking her to a saint's tomb to pray for a miracle," he said.

Judith took a few steps in the direction of the horrible sounds of wailing and moaning; she had often helped the sick in the convent.

"Has a physician been summoned?" she asked Trudulf.

"He was roused from his bed last night but couldn't keep her from getting worse. She's bleeding from the inside."

Judith felt a shiver go down her spine. Hemorrhaging was one of the most dangerous things to deal with. She had seen Radegund and Agnes try to stop the internal bleeding, usually to no avail.

Judith felt a dryness in her throat as she moved toward the procession of slaves following a litter on which the slave girl was lying, writhing in pain. She felt helpless as she watched the party make its way toward the track that would take them to the saint's tomb and uttered a small prayer for the girl. If she had to die, let it be quickly and without any more pain.

Judith turned back toward the stables and nearly collided with Trudulf, who was watching what she had just been watching. He glanced at her with a hardened look.

"There's trouble afoot," he muttered, his eyes darting about as if to make sure no one heard them speak. Then he turned and walked with her into the stables where the smell and sounds of the horses offered them a reassuring comfort.

"What do you mean?" asked Judith as they approached Black Lady's stall.

"Bad omen the girl dying. Full moon last night."

Judith tried to swallow against the dryness of her throat. "Couldn't it have been something she ate? A poisonous mushroom perhaps?"

He grunted. "Kitchen staff would be executed for allowing poison foods into the kitchen. It's the sort of mistake they're not allowed to make. Too dangerous for the king and his nobles."

Judith took his meaning. But why would anyone want to poison a kitchen slave? Her eyes asked the question but Trudulf's did not answer. He opened Black Lady's stall and moved along her side, a dark look on his face.

"Who was the girl?" she asked Trudulf.

But he only shrugged. "No one of importance. No one who will be missed."

"What a pity," said Judith. "Perhaps she will recover in any case."

On the other side of the outbuildings that led to the slave quarters, Fredegund watched as the dying girl was carried away. She waited until the slaves had gone, then entered the dark hut where the girl had been ill. A half-wit, who was stirring up the fire to burn the clothing of the sick girl, was the only one there.

"I've come to burn the bedclothes," Fredegund said to the bent over woman who barely looked at her with her distant gaze. "It's a good thing there's already a fire started," she continued and bent over the

117

low, narrow bed to strip the woolen blankets off the straw pallet. She was relieved that the half-wit was her only witness, because the foolish slave would not notice the gloves Fredegund wore nor the long sleeves which covered them almost to her palms.

She pulled the blankets off and threw them into the fire, shoving aside the half-wit, who scuffled away to empty a pail of water and clean up after the physician's attempts to save the girl's life.

Fredegund used a long stick to poke the blankets into the flames and waited until they turned to ashes before she left the hut. No one would suspect her, for she moved from the slave quarters to the kitchens freely, but it was good that no one was there to see her with the blankets. The bedclothes impregnated with the deadly powder had worked. She knew that the slave girl had lacerated her hands and arms while using a sharp paring knife yesterday and the cuts would absorb the poison. After the convulsions started, it had not been long before the organs ruptured.

Fredegund felt a sense of satisfaction which fed her resolve. Already the heady excitement of carrying out her plans stimulated her as she hastened back to the pastry kitchens. Hemorrhaging could be a painful death, and while she did not care how her rival died, the result would be sure if the bitter powders were correctly applied. But before that deed was done, she must complete the other steps in her scheme, and already her thoughts turned toward the evening's visit she had planned to the blacksmith who must forge for her a special knife.

* * *

118

Judith came out of the stables and caught a glimpse of Fredegund hurrying from the slave's cabins toward the kitchens. Standing in the shadows of the stables, she was not seen by the former concubine, and so did not mask her expression. But Judith saw the slight tingle of flush in the blond woman's face, the excitement in the icy blue eyes, and felt a coldness shroud her heart.

It struck her that Fredegund might not be satisfied with her position as slave when she had once been the favorite of the king. Although Judith did not see what the demise of a simple slave girl might have to do with it, and she did not know what part Fredegund might have played, she did not like what she considered. She must speak to Galswinth in earnest and warn her to keep a watch on Fredegund. The queen must be sure she could trust the companions about her.

A royal feast was planned the following night for the hunters to celebrate their kills after two days of hunting. The women donned their finery and Judith accompanied Galswinth to the banquet hall. The queen took her place at the king's table which was spread with delectable food and huge portions of meat on gold platters. Chilperic and his lords had already begun the revelry, and wine flowed freely. When Judith took her place at a table directly below Galswinth's she saw Ivar, seated at the end of the king's table, and he sent her an appraising look that made her blush. She glanced quickly away and tried to occupy herself with the women's conversation and the tasty food and drink.

"What is this?" asked Clothild, picking up the talisman that dangled at Judith's breast where two embroidered crosspieces emphasized her bosom under the fine linen tunic.

"A lucky charm," said Judith, feeling satisfied with the food. "The count . . . Ivar gave it to me."

Clothild gave her a knowing look. "He must greatly admire you in that case." She herself sent a glance toward Ivar, who was engaged in conversation. "Such will make you the envy of all the women of the court."

Overhearing them, Mosella turned to admire the talisman.

"Ivar said it will help me communicate with animals," Judith explained.

Mosella looked at it with wide eyes. "Then it has magic in it." She raised a knowing brow and cocked her head. "It has not taken you very long to find an admirer."

Judith did not know what to answer. That Ivar had paid her attention was clear, and that she respected his strength and his position was a good thing. The feelings he aroused in her were another matter, and she declined any more wine, not wanting to become muddled by the distraction.

When she had left the convent, thoughts of marriage had been replaced by her new duty to Galswinth. Women who were married by capture or by purchase were nothing more than chattels of their husbands, and marriage here was out of the question because Judith had no dowry and no male relatives to negotiate for her. She had talked Fortunatus into helping her find a suitable husband before her circumstances had changed, but he would certainly not help her now. In any case, marriage did not appeal to Judith at present.

After dinner an orator was summoned and stood in the center of the hall to begin reciting a poem of the great deeds of the Franks in times past. The man had a commanding presence and his full, resonant voice arrested his audience's attention. The lords loved to hear of the great deeds of their Teutonic ancestors. He spoke the oral history in a fascinating rhythmic voice, and for a while Judith listened with interest.

His poem told of an earthborn god and his children, the heroic conflicts of the Merovingian fighting warrior chiefs of old and of their mortal conflicts with the gods, of kings slain by treachery, and of battle with the hated and feared Huns.

One thing the bard made clear: The Frankish kings had come a long way since their warrior chieftain forefathers who had wandered in bands in the forest. Clovis had thought in terms of a kingdom, and his sons had expanded it. Now his grandsons had to push out their boundaries if they were to be a credit to their heritage.

But at last Judith longed for some air and slipped away from the party. Once out of the hall, she passed through adjoining corridors and then stepped outside to the arcade that enclosed the courtyard. It was chilly, and she hugged herself. Her mantle was thin, and the cold winter night air penetrated the long sleeves of her tunic, so she could not stay outside for long.

A clink of a sword on flagstone startled her. Looking behind her, she saw no one. But the shadows could be hiding someone, and she was suddenly frightened that she might be accosted by a drunken lord or by a dirty slave who might be lurking about.

She could not risk going back the way she came, so she picked up her pace and fled down the arcade. Now the footsteps sounded more quickly behind her, and her heart raced; she was being followed. She turned into the first door she came to and found herself in the church. Pausing behind a pillar for breath, she waited to see if her assailant would discover her refuge.

Ivar's silhouette appeared in the arched doorway, his face half lit by the votary candles. She did not call out because she knew no help would come. While she did not fear harm from him, she instinctively drew back, for when he saw where she stood, looking at him from behind the pillar, he moved forward.

In an instant Judith knew what was about to happen and she trembled. She did not deny the sensations and thoughts she had harbored about this man who had given her his charm, but her virginity was dear, and she was suddenly frightened by the idea of what Ivar wanted from her.

She took to her heels again, her feet skimming the marble floor, and fled down the side aisle, past the frescoes adorning the wall, running toward the chancel.

Not saying a word, Ivar came forward.

Darkness shrouded the corners of the church beyond the flicker of light cast by oil lamps mounted at intervals along the center pillars. Ivar was some distance behind, and even though she could not see him, she heard the clink of his sword. But now that she was in the sanctuary, she realized her mistake: there was no way out but the way she had come.

She guessed Ivar's appetites, and she also knew the pleasure of his touch when he had kissed her. It was only her modesty and strict upbringing that fought within her now. He walked toward her, and though she sensed the determination in his stride, she no longer moved. Already her body tingled, and then he came close enough that she could see the lust in his eyes. She tried to speak, but her mouth was dry, and she was out of breath from running.

Ivar stared openly at her body, apparent through the material of her tunic, for her mantle had fallen from her shoulder. The fluttering light from the oil lamps outlined her shape as the embroidered edging emphasized her round breasts, nipples protruding outward toward him.

Unable to wait, he quickly loosened his belt and breeches, scabbard and sword dropping to the floor, then he pulled her linen upward and placed his hand between her thighs. And yet she did no more than struggle momentarily against his persistent fingers as he readied himself.

Lifting her against him, he held her buttocks in one hand, and while supporting her back with the other, he braced her against a marble pillar and thrust against her.

Sounds of pleasure emitted from his throat while his tongue probed her mouth. At last he was taking pleasure in the wench who had tempted him with her saucy looks as she roamed about the palace. Caring mostly for his own pleasure, he continued his assault, pausing only to pull the material of her bodice aside and lower his mouth to each breast in turn so he could taste their succulence, pulling hard on her nipples until she cried out from his roughness.

But then he covered her mouth with his own again. With one motion, he laid her on the cold marble floor and straddled her, planting himself in her for his last swift movement of hip and groin, which brought his full release.

"Ahhh," he moaned as he pushed his weight against her, feeling the last resonant throbs as his warm seed filled her. Only then did he look down at her eyes.

"So," he said, brushing his hand across her nipple roughly. "That was not so unpleasant, was it?"

She only moved her head from side to side, her silky hair splayed round her face as she attempted to get up. But he held her down. He ran his tongue across the inside of her mouth, already feeling the stirrings of his desire for her again, but he could dally no longer. He pushed his tongue into her mouth one last time and then pulled his body from her, glancing at the trail of moistness he had left between her white thighs.

He put his hand over her breast, wanting her again, for she awoke in him a fierce eroticism that left him dissatisfied even now. He had been tempted by her for too long to feel fulfilled by taking her only once. Even after joining their bodies together, his desire was only half quenched—muted until the seed of lust grew strong in his groin again.

He stood, picking up his sword from where he had dropped it. "Cover yourself," he ordered her. "We are in a holy place."

Judith struggled to her feet, her body aflame where he had thrust himself into her. Then when Ivar had readjusted his clothing, he took her arm and led her down the steps. He moved her against the wall in the shadows and leaned down to taste her mouth once more.

"Let no other man touch you," he said. "You are

my prize. You will come to me when I ask you, will you not? We will delight in these pleasures together, and I will teach you many things."

The ache of her loins had numbed only slightly, and she gazed at the broad expanse of his chest, blond fur showing through the lacings of his shirt, realizing that the sensations he had caused her were newly thrilling, if painful this first time. But she did not dislike the feeling of his strong powerful arms around her, and she longed to stroke his chest, lay her cheek against his muscular shoulders. She knew from his handling of the falcons that he could be gentle as well as rough. Most of all he could be a help to her in this court where she sensed danger.

"I will be your woman, Ivar," she said, lifting her chin to meet his gaze. "You may do with me as you wish. I want only one thing in return."

"And what is that?" he asked, a pleased look coming into his lusty eyes.

"Your protection."

Chapter Eight

In March, the court moved to the royal villa outside Tours, because it was cheaper to move the court from place to place to obtain fresh supplies for the huge household than to transport the goods to the palace. The procession of guards, ox and mule carts with supplies and treasure, litters for the ladies, the mounted nobles and all the slaves stretched in a long winding train across the countryside following the old Roman road. Judith rode in the royal chariot with Galswinth so that they could speak privately in the tentlike structure, something that was difficult in royal quarters where the queen's women slept in her chambers when she wasn't with the king.

Of late Galswinth seemed nervous and Judith was concerned to learn how her friend fared.

"Three more days until we reach Tours," said Judith, leaning against a cushion in the jostling chariot, Ivar's medallion dangling provocatively against her breast.

"Yes," said Galswinth. She was dressed in silk tunics with a girdle of intricate cloisonné design, and ruby and emerald brooches on her bodice and fastening her vermilion mantle. Heavy gold bracelets dangled from her wrists, and her hair was braided in plaits under a soft veil of gauze.

"Is it very difficult to be a queen?" asked Judith.

Galswinth turned her dark eyes to her companion. "I was raised for this; I should not complain."

"Have you had news from your sister, Brunhild?"

"Oh yes," said Galswinth. "She is greatly admired in Austrasia, and her husband treats her well." She said it with a trace of envy. "How I wish I could see her."

"Can you not plan a royal visit?"

"That would be possible, but Chilperic has advised me not to go at present. He and his brother are arguing about a border each claims. The king presented me with the city of Cahors, and it seems that Sigibert claims that as part of the territory left him when their brother Charibert died. They must meet in Paris to discuss it."

"Can you not go with the king to Paris and see your sister then?"

"Alas, no. Brunhild will remain at Metz." She cast a look of concern at Judith. "The king will not allow me to enter the limits of Paris. It is too dangerous."

Judith frowned. "But Paris is a neutral city. I learned from Mother Radegund that when Charibert died and the territories were redistributed among the remaining three brothers, Paris was declared neutral so that councils could be held there and that it would be ruled jointly by all three kings."

"Yes, and the taxes distributed equally to all three of the treasuries."

"Then why? . . ." Judith waited for the anxious shadow to pass from Galswinth's face.

Galswinth shook her head. "I fear an outbreak of fighting."

Judith opened her eyes wider in question. "Really?"

Galswinth leaned closer. "At present Sigibert is busy protecting his northern borders from the incursions of the Saxons. I fear my husband will take the opportunity to claim Cahors by force."

"Would it not be better for Chilperic to assist Sigibert against the Saxons?" said Judith feeling a little shiver run down her arms, for the Saxons controlled the North Sea and were a constant menace along the northern coast of Gaul.

Unlike the Franks who were no longer the raw barbarians their ancestors had been, the Saxons had never rubbed shoulders with the Romans and so had not learned the business of government. They continued in their piratical ways, marauding by sea. She had heard stories of their acts of atrocity and knew that they now possessed most of Britain, that faraway land that sat in the sea at the very edge of the known world.

"I've never seen the Saxons," said Galswinth, voicing some of Judith's thoughts. "But they are said to be terrible. At present they are keeping away from Neustria." She swallowed nervously. "I think they have been bribed to raid Sigibert's lands instead."

Judith said nothing. Truly she was learning just how treacherous the machinations of the Merovingian courts were. There seemed to be something in the nature of the Merovingian kings that did not let them rest with ruling the kingdoms they possessed. Rather they sought expansion at every possible opportunity, obliged to outdo their fathers from whom they had inherited Frankish Gaul.

"What do you think will happen in Paris?" asked Judith.

"I don't know," said Galswinth. "But if Sigibert turns his back, Cahors may fall."

"Can you not dissuade him?"

"Chilperic does not listen to my advice. He tells me I should not worry about politics. It is his duty to expand

and secure our kingdom. For our sons."

As she said it, she looked even more worried, and Judith knew what she was thinking.

"Are you . . . ?"

Galswinth shook her head sadly. "I must produce an heir, and quickly. Chilperic's son by his first wife, Audovera, is in a monastery in Ireland." She lowered her voice even further. "I know there are certain lords of the court who support him and would seek any excuse to put him on the throne when Chilperic dies."

If that happened, Judith knew, Galswinth would lose all power, not being the heir's mother and would at best face humiliation and be sent to reside in a convent.

"Do not worry," said Judith in an attempt to comfort her friend. "I'm sure you will produce a son for the king and all will be well."

"If I live long enough to do it," said Galswinth, her eyes turning inward. Judith knew she was thinking of the prophecies they had read that night before her marriage.

"Does the king not love you?" asked Judith, taking her hand.

"I do not know," said Galswinth. "He gives me gifts and makes sure that the nobles honor me. But I cannot say that he loves me."

While Judith knew that such was not always the case in a royal marriage, it pained her to see her friend so unhappy.

"I wish I could go back to Spain," Galswinth whispered. "I would leave him all my treasure."

"Don't say that, Galswinth. Nothing will happen to you, I promise you. And you will have a son."

The rivers they had passed were high and running

from recent rains. The procession had camped at the edge of a large landholding, the home of a Gallo Roman noble who gladly sold all the grain, meat, and dried fruits he had to the king's train. Epoald made the arrangements, and the carts that had left Rouen carrying only enough perishables to feed the court for a few days were taken to the villa where slaves loaded casks and sacks of supplies. The landowner had a fine vineyard, and a good supply of wine was also obtained.

When the train paused north of Chartres, Ivar took Judith hawking. The spring migrations of birds on their way northward provided excellent opportunities for game. Here heaths provided long stretches where they could give rein to their horses, being careful to avoid peat bogs, and the horizon stretched far and away allowing them to watch the hawks as they pursued their prey.

Ivar gave Judith a glove and showed her how to hold Isault on the side of her fist.

"Holding her for the greater part of the day tires the muscles," Ivar said. "But after a few weeks, the muscle will strengthen."

Indeed Judith felt the weight of the bird as she and Ivar sat still on their horses, watching the sky for prey.

When Ivar spotted a speck in the sky he gave the signal, and Judith unhooded the bird and slipped her by flinging her wrist toward the prey. With a whoosh of wings, Isault took to the sky.

Now Judith could see the two crows approaching; they swerved as the falcon mounted. The crows attempted to turn upwind, but Isault flew fast and hard to overtake them. The chase was on, the gyrfalcon quickly gaining on the flapping, squawking birds.

Judith watched intently as the crows tried to duck into the cover of some trees, but Isault had gained her height and spiraled downward after them. With a pounce, she stunned the crow and a burst of black feathers tumbled earthward.

Suddenly a flock of crows flew out of the trees, crying their revenge, milling around Isault, diving and darting with their jabbing beaks.

"Oh no," cried Judith, watching the horrible attack. She looked at Ivar, who squinted his eyes into the sunlight, his expression unreadable.

Then he began to whistle to her, voicing his encouragement.

"Come, Isault," called Ivar. "Here." And he urged his horse forward toward the mobbing crows.

With a graceful descent, Isault dove away from the crows and with wings spread she landed on the gloved wrist Ivar held up to her. Then he stroked her with his other hand and dropped the hood over her. She shook one leg and danced on his glove, but even Judith could see the lines of his face relax as the bird settled.

"Just in time," he said to Judith, turning his horse so they could ride away from the still noisy crows. Ivar continued to speak to the bird in a soothing, encouraging voice.

When she appeared calm he said, "Another moment, and her successful entry would have been turned into a desperate retreat. If a falcon is mobbed on her entering flight, she might never hunt crows again."

Isault had flown enough for the day, and so they handed her over to an attendant who placed her on the field cadge. Then they took out several more falcons. Judith found that the hunting flights did not follow any set pattern. There were always surprises. The quarry's behavior, the condition of the hawk, changes in wind, all affected the flight. Sometimes the birds rang up and up out of sight, and it was always with a sense of relief when they could be seen again, the falcon in her lethal dive toward prey struggling to get away. More times than not, the falcon was successful.

When the birds had all been exercised, Ivar ordered the attendant carrying the cadge to secure all the birds and bring them back to camp. Then he and Judith rode ahead.

Feeling exhilarated from the expedition, Judith tried to find words. For most of the day her attention had been on the job at hand, but now she and Ivar were riding slowly down a gentle slope, a breeze rustling in the copse beside a stream to their right.

She felt she ought to speak, and yet she didn't know what to say. Now that Ivar had agreed to be her protector, she felt bound to him in some way.

Just as the brightly dyed tents of the camp came into view, Ivar spoke. "You have heard of the two kings' argument over the city of Cahors."

"Yes," answered Judith. "Is that not what they will discuss at their coming meeting?"

"Ha. The meeting is for show only. Both kings long for a battle. Chilperic cannot expand to the north, for the sea stops him. He must seek new territories to the south, and so he must push against his borders with Guntram and Sigibert."

Judith frowned. "Why must there always be war?"

Ivar turned his blond head toward her, gazing at her with a touch of humor in his serious eyes.

"War is the way of the Franks. How else can we glorify ourselves and our king? It is our purpose to fight. Even our women know that."

She pressed her lips together, wondering how she would feel if Ivar were killed. But she said no more, taking it as a reprimand though he had not spoken curtly. Perhaps he was making allowances for her since she had been in the convent for so long.

"My ancestors were chieftains who honored themselves by fighting with Aetius against Atilla on the Catalaunian Plain," Ivar went on. "Then we were named friends of the Romans, fighting with them against the Alamans, the Goths, and the Saxons. We were awarded land by the Roman emperor in the west. And then when we repelled the Romans themselves, we took more land as booty."

He smiled broadly to Judith. "And so my family has much land near the city of Orléans."

The way he said family gave her a sudden thought. "Do you . . . have a wife?"

Ivar looked at her wide eyes and laughed. "No, I have no wife."

She lowered her eyes, embarrassed.

She shouldn't have been so forward, but she needed to know. Many Frankish nobles had concubines whether or not they had wives. When she had surrendered herself to Ivar, she had not stopped to think about whether or not he had wives. She was glad he was not married, though if he were there would be nothing she could do about it. She had allied herself with him for the purpose of gaining strength in Chilperic's court. Her own feelings about the matter were hazy, tinged with daring but fearful of what she had done.

"Come," he said. And he dug his heels into his mount. Black Lady lit out after him, though Judith did not hope to overtake him.

They entered the camp and Judith handed her horse to Trudulf, who took Black Lady to feed, water and brush her and then tie her up with the line of horses for tomorrow's march. And after describing the expedition to Trudulf, she made her way to the tent that had been raised for Galswinth and her women to spend the night.

They were busy arranging themselves on feather mattresses with fur rugs that had been laid out with enough cushions to keep them comfortable. But after the evening meal, Judith felt unable to settle down to an evening listening to the poet who came to the tent to entertain. Instead she wandered among the tents, listening to the laughter, the chatter and in the distance the hooting of owls in the woods. She decided to visit Black Lady and went along the line of horses. When she reached the mare, the horse nudged her as if looking for a treat.

"Good girl," said Judith, rubbing her nose. "Yes, I brought you a sweet." And she gave the horse the treat she had saved from supper.

Then she headed toward the silvery twist of river to bathe her feet in the stream and had just sat down on the steep grassy bank when she heard muffled laughter and saw two figures emerge from behind a tree.

She thought of rising to let them know she was there and then she heard Fredegund's low, guttural laugh. Judith shrank down the bank, somewhat protected by a bush, and when it became evident that Fredegund had met the man for the purposes of a liaison, Judith sought to creep along the bank and find a way back without being seen. But the words of the man carried along the bank to her, and she paused to listen.

"You tempt me, Fredegund," said the man. "But how do I know it's true that you seek revenge against Chilperic?"

Fredegund sat on the ground and invited the man to do the same. "Because, Godulf, how do you think I like wasting my talents in the kitchen? When I was with Chilperic I learned a great deal about matters of state.

Things that men with ability such as yourself could benefit by, don't you think?" She ended her statement in a suggestive tone and leaned toward Godulf. "Now let's pour some of that wine."

Godulf produced two goblets from a satchel, then untied a wineskin and poured dark liquid into the goblets. In the seconds that it took him to retie the wineskin, Fredegund passed her hand over his goblet. When he looked at her again, her cloak had slipped from her shoulders, and her sleeveless linen chemise crossed at the bodice revealed a deep shadow between her breasts. She leaned on her side, moving her hips seductively.

Godulf eyed her greedily and took a swig of his wine. Fredegund laughed and stared into grayish-green eyes. His hand reached out to touch her inviting breasts, but her eyes were fixed on his skin, which even in the bright moonlight she could see turn gray. He opened his mouth in an effort to speak, but Fredegund pushed him onto his back and clamped her hand over his mouth.

From where Judith crouched she saw the man's spasmodic convulsions, and the sight so paralyzed her that she forgot to cry out. She was so stunned by what she was witnessing that she did not at first understand it. The man was convulsing. At first Fredegund appeared to be trying to help him, for her hands were at his throat and then his chest as if loosening his clothing.

Only too late did Judith realize that when Fredegund rose it was not to summon help, but rather to pick up her cloak and the two goblets, leaving the wineskin where it was. She glanced about to make sure no one was about and then fled up the hill toward the camp.

"*Mea Domina,*" Judith whispered, half prayer, half

135

swearing, then she jumped up and ran to the man to see if she could help him.

But when she reached the limp figure and looked at the staring eyes and ashen face, she realized he was dead. She felt for a pulse and listened to his chest, but there was neither breathing nor heartbeat. Her throat dried, her own heart almost stopped beating. If he had been victim of a sudden seizure, surely Fredegund would have called out. But she had not.

Judith rose to her knees and then to her feet in sudden terror. The woman had murdered him. Judith looked around in panic. She must tell someone what she had witnessed. But then another thought became paramount: If someone came upon the scene, they would think she herself had murdered the man. No one would believe her.

She did not stop to examine the fact that she had higher status than Fredegund, who was at the moment no more than a kitchen slave, while Judith served the queen. In Judith's mind she was still nothing more than a slave herself, captured by these Franks in a bloody skirmish.

She found herself running up the embankment and when she reached the edge of the camp, she was out of breath. Only then did she slow herself to a walk and with head down, made her way past the small groups of men gathered around fires, gaming with dice. She could not go there. She did not want to tell anyone what happened but Galswinth, and for that she would have to wait until she was alone. And so she picked her way through the camp, ears tingling, waiting until someone raised the alarm that there was a dead man by the river.

But nothing happened. Shaking, Judith made her way back to the line of horses and found Black Lady, with whom she communicated in broken, nonsense phrases which the horse somehow seemed to understand. Running her hands along the mare's soft neck helped comfort her.

Sometime later, when most of the camp slept, Judith crept back to her tent. All the torches had been extinguished by the time she crawled into her bed.

In the morning the camp was abuzz with the talk. Godulf had been found by the river where he had evidently drunk too much and had a seizure. The physician examined him and reported that it had been a matter of the heart. Everyone said prayers and Chilperic pledged to endow a shrine at Tours, hoping to ward off any evil portent that Godulf's death might signify.

But there seemed to be no suspicion of murder. Judith had no time alone with Galswinth, and so kept her secret for the time being. By the time they reached the city of Tours, Godulf's death was relegated to the past as the royal procession entered the city. They were greeted by Bishop Salvius and Judith was glad to see Father Gregory once again.

They were settled in a palace not far from the basilica, and Chilperic hosted a banquet that evening to honor the two churchmen whom he considered among his best friends. His most trusted lords were present as were a few of the queen's ladies; the affair was rather intimate. And though the two holy men partook of wine and the rich foods offered, the nobles did not become drunk; rather, they listened attentively to Chilperic's debates with Gregory and the bishop, for Chilperic loved to show off his knowledge of theology.

Attending the banquet also was the Jew Priscus, a

merchant with whom Chilperic did much business. Chilperic counted many Jews among his friends, but he was bound and determined to convert them all to Christianity. On this evening, fortified with the two well-versed churchmen, Chilperic again launched into his argument with Priscus.

"Come, Bishop," said Chilperic. "Place your hands upon him."

Then to Priscus, "Why cannot you comprehend what has been promised to you by the words of the prophets? The mysteries of the church were foreshadowed in the sacrifices of your own race."

Unperturbed, Priscus accepted a little more meat offered to him by a servant. "God has no need of a Son, and he does not brook any consort in heaven."

Chilperic frowned. "The fact that the Son of God was made man resulted from our necessity, not His. Listen to one of your own prophets foretelling that God should be made man: 'He is both God and man, and who has known Him?' And again, 'Behold, a virgin shall conceive and bear a son, and shall call his name Immanuel.' " Chilperic continued to quote the Old Testament, clearly proud of his erudition.

The Jew replied with his own lucid arguments until Gregory and the bishop felt compelled to intervene. But in spite of all their arguments the merchant showed no signs of believing them, but continued to sip his wine and sample the fruit and pastries presented for his enjoyment.

Judith waited patiently for the catechism to end, hoping that Chilperic had planned some entertainment for his guests and that she might get a chance to speak to Father Gregory alone. When she saw him lean over to whisper a few words to the bishop and excuse himself, she knew her opportunity had come.

138

She suspected that he had gone to the lavatory, and when he returned along the balcony, she was there, waiting for him. Torches bathed the covered balcony and the courtyard below in a yellowish light, and from the banquet hall came the clash of cymbals and the drone of a panpipe which accompanied the performance of trained leopards from the east that the king found amusing.

Judith waited in the shadows of a recess, only stepping out when Gregory approached, his sandals softly scuffing the stone walkway, his simple wide-sleeved robe flowing gracefully to the floor.

"Father Gregory," she said.

He gave a start and then saw her standing in the shadows like an apparition. "Why my dear, you startled me. It's Judith, isn't it? I remember speaking with you at the wedding feast. How have you been?"

They had begun to walk past the door leading to the banquet hall as if in accord that they would enjoy some private conversation without the distraction of a leopard leaping across the floor.

"It is that I wish to speak to you about, Father," said Judith urgently, glancing about to make sure they were not overheard. "You remember that I asked you to pray for . . . for this household."

"Yes," he said, his smooth face drawing into an expression of concern. His eyes were hawklike in intensity, but warm with compassion. "And I have done so. I hope all has been well?"

She gave a small shake of the head. "Something dreadful has happened, and I wanted to tell someone only . . ." she paused, feeling the cold knot in her stomach the way she did every time she thought about what she had seen the night Godulf met his end on the riverbank.

"I think there's been a murder," she hissed.

"Ah—"

She raised a finger to his lips, preventing his surprised exclamation from leaving his throat.

Gregory gained control over himself and whispered more calmly. "What makes you think so?"

"I witnessed it. At least I think I did."

His face darkened pensively as he listened to her story. She left nothing out, from the death of the kitchen slave the day she had seen Fredegund leave the slave quarters when the girl had been taken away, to the scene at the riverbank. "Fredegund was clearly seducing Godulf," Judith said. "And when he began his convulsions she did not cry out. Rather she stayed with him, leaning over him as to make sure that he died. It was awful."

Gregory squeezed her elbow in a reassuring gesture. "I'm sure it was. And you did not report this?"

She dropped her voice even lower. "I was afraid."

"Hmmm. I know Fredegund," said Gregory as if weighing the situation. "She had a strong hold over Chilperic once. Perhaps you were wise to keep the matter to yourself."

Surprised to hear the priest say so she asked, "Why?"

Instead of answering, he raised his head. "Leave this to me. Certainly the woman needs to be made aware that her soul is in danger. I will speak to her. Do not fear, I will give no hint as to where I have gotten this information. And her powers of intrigue cannot extend to the church. She needs chastizing, and—" He looked at Judith as if thinking also of more worldly solutions. "And if she knows that I have found out the truth, perhaps she will come to her senses. She cannot commit such heinous acts without dire consequences."

"What will you do?" asked Judith.

"Speak to her first in private. If she does not confess, then a public accusation will be necessary."

"But—" Judith did not want him to do anything that would place Galswinth in danger.

"It will be all right. She will either have to swear on a saint's tomb, which is dangerous, I assure you, or she will have to have a host of witnesses who swear to her innocence. She is not in the king's favor now. I doubt very many will want to place their own souls in danger by committing perjury."

Judith was doubtful about the effect that Gregory's solutions might have, but she felt better that she had spoken to him. They walked a little ways further and then turned back.

"But what can I do, Father?"

"Does Fredegund know what you have observed?" he asked.

"No, I don't think so."

"Then see that she does not find out."

It was raining by the time Salvius and Gregory took their leave from the royal party. The night was dark, for there was no moon, and they pulled their hooded cloaks close around them as they made their way through the narrow streets toward Gregory's house. Not far from the palace, they paused to look back.

"Look at the roof of that building," said Salvius. "Do you see what I see?"

Gregory saw only the new tiling the king had put there recently. But he remembered the coiled serpents he had seen the night of the nuptials and he knew at once what Salvius was going to tell him. Nevertheless, he answered, "No, I see nothing. But if you yourself can see anything else, tell me."

Salvius gave a great sigh and said, "I see the naked sword of the wrath of God hanging over that house."

Gregory shivered, then he spoke in a distant tone, as if the voice of prophecy spoke through him. "There is a curse that haunts the house of the Merovingians, is there not? And I fear it will make their palaces reek with blood."

Gregory told Salvius what he had learned about Fredegund, and they agreed to summon the young woman to counsel her about her soul on the morrow.

It was a few moments before the two churchmen gathered their cloaks closer to them and continued down the street.

That night, as Chilperic prepared for bed, his steward brought him a folded and sealed sheet of parchment. After the steward left, he melted the seal and opened the sheet to read it. At first there appeared to be nothing on it, and so he moved his candlestick nearer the bed so he could examine the parchment more closely.

As the heat from the flame came near the parchment, writing began to appear. Chilperic gave a gasp as the brown writing appeared slowly across the page as if an unseen hand were writing it before his very eyes. His hand trembled. But the writing stopped and the sentence was incomplete. Moving the page closer, more writing appeared and then he understood.

The ink required the heat from the flame to make it visible. When he held the parchment so that the flame heated the entire page but did not burn it, all the writing finally appeared. Then Chilperic read:

My Lord and King. It was I who was responsible for Godulf's death. He and others were plotting to unseat you and gain control of your kingdom for themselves. Already they control your son, whom you believe to be safe in the Irish monastery. But your son will be the tool of the ambitious lords who are against you. As I knew this, I did the deed you needed done so that your hands would remain unsullied.

Fredegund

Chilperic's heart rattled in his chest. What treason was this she spoke of? She had murdered Godulf? Chilperic had thought him a trusted friend.

He crushed the paper and dropped it on the table, then paced across the room, a thousand thoughts flying through his head. In the past when he had suspected treason he had been quick to act. He must summon Fredegund and find out what she knew.

He made sure his door was bolted, then started to summon his steward to help him undress. But first he must burn the page upon which Fredegund had written, for he must protect her as well. He reached for the crumpled piece of parchment and pulled it apart, preparing to tear it to shreds. Then he stared at it in wonder. For the writing, which had shown itself under the heat and light of the candle, was now gone.

Chapter Nine

A single oil lamp still burned against the darkness in the chamber Judith had been given. Epoald had assigned it to her when they had arrived, saying the women's chamber was small, and the king wanted to accord Judith the honor of her own small room.

His words had made her nervous. The king? Why was she being separated from Galswinth and the others? Perhaps Chilperic had word that she had either murdered Godulf herself or had witnessed his demise. When Epoald had shut the door, she'd stared at the bolt as if expecting him to lock it from the outside. But it hadn't moved. She could leave if she wanted to. She moved to the door and threw the bolt, locking herself in.

Then she turned about to the small chamber, where shadows from oil lamps flickered against the wall hangings that moved slightly from the draft seeping in through an oilskin-covered window and under the heavy door. Judith stretched out on the divan that had been placed next to the brazier.

Images from the recent days passed through her mind, and she wondered if she would be able to fall asleep, so on edge was she. Her talk with Gregory had helped. But would his words of warning stop Fredegund? Judith doubted it. But she had hesitated to speak of what she suspected to Galswinth, only telling her to be very careful because there might be those who considered the queen their enemy.

Galswinth had been so frightened of marrying Chilperic that Judith did not want to be the herald of events that would send her friend into paroxysms of fear again. The recent smiles on her face had been too hard won. But now Judith saw that she could not let down her guard. And being away from Galswinth she worried for her safety. At the moment Chilperic seemed in accord with the queen. If only she could become pregnant, that might foil Fredegund's plans. But the king's temperament was unpredictable, and since Judith had joined the court she felt more and more sure that in this arena more so than in any other, matters did not stay the same. Change, often violent change, was the byword. Witness poor Godulf. Why had Fredegund murdered him?

Fredegund's face formed in her mind. The former concubine did not seem to Judith the type of woman to remain satisfied with her lot. Chilperic had loved her once. He might do so again. And after the incident at the riverbank, Judith had no doubt that if Chilperic were encouraged, Fredegund might very well pose a serious threat to Galswinth.

Judith shifted her position to her side, bending her knees and drawing her feet up closer, watching the glowing coals of the brazier. At that moment, she was startled to see one of the heavy wall hangings move aside. She gasped as Ivar appeared against the stone walls.

He smiled at her and then threw back his head and laughed softly. He stood with his feet spread, his hands on his hips and gazed at her where she lay with her hand on her chest, her mouth parted and her eyes wide in surprise.

"I see you did not know of that passage to this chamber," he said, taking a step closer.

She shook her head and found her voice. "I did not. I presumed I was locked safely away for the night."

He ran his hand along her ankle and calf as he came to sit on the divan with her. "You tease. Hardly locked. I'll wager that door is closed only by the latch."

"Not so," she said, not minding the touch of his hand to her skin as her chemise slid higher along her leg. "You see for yourself there is a bolt which I have thrown."

He grunted in satisfaction. "All the better. Then we are left alone."

She indicated the wall from which he had materialized. "Where does that passage lead?"

"To the courtyard eventually. All the better for the king to meet his mistress in this room."

"That is what this chamber is used for?"

He nodded, holding her eyes with his. "Indeed. Did not the mayor of the palace select this chamber for you?" he asked, still ministering to her calves, massaging them so that her muscles relaxed.

"That is so. But I thought it was because I would be close to my mistress," she said, not wanting to tell Ivar the real reason she feared she'd been put in this place. "Galswinth's chamber is next to this one."

"That is so. But it would be equally convenient for the king if he were to choose this room instead of his wife's, would it not?"

She trembled at the thought. "But surely not the king—"

He interrupted her. "No, not the king. For he has given me the privilege. Once I made my desires known, he relinquished all claims to you."

She trembled at the idea that the king was the one to give Ivar possession of her, and she attempted to sit up. But Ivar pressed her back onto the slope of the divan more with his eyes than with the hand that touched her bare shoulder, where the chemise had fallen aside.

"Stay where you are."

His glance smoldered over the curves which her linen garment outlined in its soft folds. Already he could feel the throb of his own blood under his clothing and pulled the material covering her legs further upward, revealing her supple thighs. Then he reached down and unfastened his clothing.

She obeyed his command not to move but watched as the breeches fell away and he stripped himself of his short tunic so that his muscular limbs and torso were revealed to her, embarrasing her, but at the same time sending the blood coursing through her veins.

Slowly he knelt beside the divan and she lifted her hips so he could pull her chemise over her head. She shivered as she lay before him, her naked skin on the fur-lined divan.

"I see you wear my gift," he said, lifting the talisman which lay between her breasts fastened on a silver chain. "That is good."

He looked at the pointed nipples rising from her abundant bosom and he moistened his lips. He gently grasped her shoulders and lowered his mouth to taste her skin. A thrill rippled through her, and she rolled her head to one side as he placed his lips and tongue on her throat. With his fingers he began to probe and tease her where her own throbbing had become warm.

She felt herself open up to him and wondered again at the new mysterious hunger this man seemed to awaken in her. Was it he himself who held such power over her body or was it the newness of the mysteries Ivar was showing her? Mysteries she had grown ripe for in the abbey where such knowledge was suggested but forbidden.

He swung his leg over the divan and met her breasts with his mouth and tongue. She writhed against him as his mouth pulled, sucked, teased, while his fingers probed deeper and deeper.

"Ivar," she breathed in pleasure, one hand clawing at his thick, blond hair and strong back while the other pressed his head even harder against her. She was hardly aware of the words she uttered, only the sensations that carried her away.

Ivar drank in the feminine fire he held in his hands. His pleasure took him to heights he had not imagined in such innocence. He could have done no better in choosing a concubine, for Judith's sensual responses held no artifice.

He knelt over her, his knees straddling her. With one hand under her back he bent to again taste her skin, teasing her with rapid motions of his tongue. Judith quivered harder under his ministrations, her words incoherent as she pushed her hips forward, inviting him.

Finally he raised his head, his own passion no longer controllable as he thrust himself into her tingling center. Her mouth fell against his male nipple, and she sucked him hungrily, groaning as he began his thrusts, her legs wrapped around his like a vise.

He took no concern for how hard he thrust nor for the harshness of her nips on his skin, for the harshness only roused him further and increased her own demands.

Healed from her first joining with him, Judith could now enjoy the sensual delights to their full, awakening more and more to what must be known as true passion. She cried out against his chest, dragging her fingers through his hair, digging her hands into his shoulders as her body shook. Ivar was excited beyond reason and hurried his own movements until his organ throbbed with its own releasing, the ecstasy that he had sought. It lasted and lasted as long as he could prolong it.

Then he moaned, fell hard against her, the last of his pleasure spent. They still clung together as the last glimmer of pleasure slowed, the wetness of their loins evidence of what they had taken from one another.

"Ivar," she whispered hoarsely, her hands kneading his arms and shoulders. The word had a begging sound as if she wanted him again.

He raised his head to speak to her. "Yes, my beauty. I want it again as well. I would take you for an accomplished concubine had not the blood on the chapel steps proved to me that this is not so."

There was humor in the sated look of his blue eyes. "Though we must have rest between times."

Truly she was a prize. The thought occurred to him that he must not boast too loudly about his new concubine, lest she catch the king's eye. She was his for now. But that could change on a whim. Better to make sure the king was well entertained so that he did not get any ideas about Judith.

Other men would not dare to touch her, for they would know that death would be the price. She was his woman. She wore his talisman. All knew that.

He extracted himself and rolled to one side to gaze down at her naked beauty. Would she attract too much attention from the king? He thought not. For though lovely, she seemed to keep her voluptuous secrets to herself, hidden under folds of modest garments. There was still the air of the convent about her—until her passions were unleashed in the bed. He thought perhaps his secret was safe.

Wild roses bloomed in the thickets where Fredegund explored for a new place to keep her roots and powders and concoctions. She took the unusual winter roses to be a sign of her reinstatement by the king's side, so when she was summoned to the apartments where the bishop was visiting, she was surprised.

For the interview she dressed in fine linen with bracelets of silver on her arms, for when Chilperic had demoted her to kitchen slave she had kept the gifts he had given her, keeping them locked away in a trunk, the key to which she wore about her neck. And so she appeared on the steps to the brick and plaster house in haughty grandeur, unaffected by the incense that wafted up from ceramic dishes set about the room with plain straight-back chairs and a gold statue of Christ in his agony.

The door closed softly behind her and Father Gregory entered. She had expected Bishop Salvius and did not know this tonsured, white-robed young man with a long Roman nose and a not unattractive face. The priesthood was a waste, thought Fredegund as Gregory smiled gently, crossed the room and took a seat in the chair opposite a long carved oak table.

"I am Father Gregory, newly the deacon of the district," he said, indicating that she might sit down. "Please be seated."

She sat stiffly, her eyes narrowing. What did he want with her?

"I thought it would be a good idea to have a private talk," began Gregory. "Though we do not know each other, I am aware that your position has recently changed, and as one of our flock, I am interested in your well-being."

She remained suspicious. Why should he care about her? "Yes, Father?"

"How have you taken to your new position at the palace?"

She gave a jerk of the chin. "You mean do I like shoving loaves of bread in and out of the ovens all day?"

Gregory saw that the interview was going to be difficult. "I mean that when we are not happy about our lot in life we are sometimes liable to err in an effort to put to rights what we consider we deserve. Vice sometimes insinuates itself into the heart," he paraphrased Seneca, "when we are dissatisfied with our lot."

A tingle slithered up Fredegund's spine. Did this self-effacing priest know something? She smiled, turning on her charm.

"Whatever do you mean, Father?"

"Fredegund," he said, "let me come to the point. I want to make sure that you have the opportunity for confession. The bishop tells me you have not been in church for a while. Perhaps you feel the need for confession?"

Her jaw stiffened, but she kept her smile in place. "Why Father, I have nothing to confess." She opened her hands wide. "I am innocent of any sin since my last confession. I have not had the opportunity for carnal relations since . . ." She moistened her lips, not wanting to offend the priest with the wrong language. "Since the king returned me to the kitchens."

"Ah." Gregory sat back, his finger beside his nose. Though he was young, he was a perceptive judge of character. He could see that Fredegund was lying; she was undoubtedly guilty of a great number of sins from greed, lust, covetousness, and adultery, on up to possible murder, if what Judith had told him had any weight.

However, he could not accuse her outright without endangering Judith, the only witness. He smiled. "Naturally I am interested in the welfare of your soul. Virtue in this life is rewarded in the next. The church offers sustenance in times of struggle. Be sure and avail yourself of that sustenance, Fredegund."

Her eyes hardened, and she was hard put to remain at ease. If the conniving little priest did not know anything at all, he suspected something. But she was not about to let some self-righteous little mouse best her, for all his upbringing. For she did not miss his Gallo-Roman accent. Many sons of wealthy families went into the church, and Gregory was probably one such. Most likely he thought himself better than the Franks. Well, she would show him a thing or two. But her main objective became getting out of here.

"I will take your advice, Father," she said as sweetly as the venom in her heart would allow. "You will see me in church from now on."

"That is good, my dear. And if you should feel the urge for confession . . ."

Not to a sniveling dog like you, she thought. "Thank you, I will remember."

She left Gregory showing great humility, but once in the street, she set her face for the palace and ground her teeth. Someone had whispered something in the priest's ear about her recent activities, but who? She had been careful not to be seen. Of course now she had told the king what she had done on his behalf. But he would never tell a churchman, despite his interest in theology.

No, if Chilperic were displeased, he would deal with her himself. He would not leave it to the church. He founded monasteries and donated heavily to churches because they were instruments of his political power in consolidating Gaul. He converted Jews because he hated them. But that did not mean that he would hand her over for doing him a few favors. Chilperic was not a sanctimonious man.

Fredegund cast about for who might have seen her with her vials of poison. If she had an enemy, she must find out who it was.

What Ivar told Judith about the necessity for war was true. Though the Franks had adopted many ways from the Romans, repose was still unwelcome to their Teutonic race. To them it was abhorrent to earn by sweat what they might purchase with blood.

Since their days as a wandering tribe, they fought for their chief. On the battlefield it was disgraceful for the warriors to surpass their chief in valor; disgraceful not to equal their chief; and infamous to retreat from the field surviving him if he should fall. In return, the follower required generosity from his chief. The spoils of war were necessary to supply the warriors with noble steeds, worthy arms, and a plentiful table. In earlier times the funds for these rewards had to be found in war and rapine.

The Romans had taught the Franks taxation, and so tributes were required from conquered or border tribes who considered themselves better prepared to pay a tribute than to fight the mighty Franks.

And so lately Chilperic had held many conferences with his lords, seeking advice and considering his moves. All these men came from fathers who had received land as gifts from Chilperic's father or his father's father in recognition of their service to the king. Most of the landholdings were rich, soil-producing farms, but the Frankish warriors left the running of their holdings to their wives, leased the land to vassals, or rented it to serfs.

Chilperic's tributary tribes had paid their tributes and he was hemmed in by his brother's lands. Chilperic needed a war. It was this that he had summoned the counts of the palace to discuss.

"King Sigibert is displeased with the belligerent Saxons to the northeast, is he not?" said Euphonius, a man who had seen many battles and was older than Chilperic by a decade.

"Hmmm," said Chilperic, leaning back in the tall wooden chair, his robes falling over the arms to the floor. "That is true. Most of Sigibert's attention has been on his northern border this year."

"The Saxons helped your grandfather in the destruction of the Thuringian kingdom and placed themselves under Clovis's suzerainty," said Count Bertram, voicing what everyone present already knew, "but for the last few years they have refused to hand over their annual tribute, have they not?"

"Then why not help King Sigibert?" said Lupus, a young, clever, but very trusted lord from the region of Aquitaine.

The other lords laughed and Chilperic considered. "It might be possible. We could ally ourselves with my brother to repel the Saxons, take our share of booty, and then demand a section of his lands in return."

The sounds of agreement rumbled through the assembly.

"The Saxons need to be taught a thing or two," muttered Count Fulrich. "They don't yet know who is the superior race in Gaul."

"If they retreat to the sea, we have no way of follow-

154

ing them and making them pay tribute," said Bertram.

"Then we will surround them and cut them off from retreat," said Chilperic, liking the idea immensely. Then followed a discussion of strategy, which lasted late into the night.

On nights when Ivar did not summon her, Judith spent much time reading through Chilperic's small collection of books, which he prized with all the pretensions to his own literary accomplishments. Galswinth had obtained permission for her companion to read them.

Working in a corner of the women's apartments at a small oaken reading desk, Judith also attempted to write her verse, practicing what Venantius had taught her about rhyming and meter. But she showed her work to no one. Alas, there was no one to show it to but the king himself, whom she avoided as much as possible, or Epoald, whom for some reason she did not entirely trust. And occasionally she read aloud from the books to the women as they worked.

"What else did you do in the convent?" asked Mosella as they sat over their embroidery one evening.

Judith put down the biography of St. Martin. "We studied every day, and then there was always work to do. Spinning, weaving, mixing dyes, washing vegetables, shelling peas, nothing was too humble for a ward of the convent."

"And you learned to write in a fine hand," said Clothild almost enviously. "And play music on the lyre."

"It sounds almost like an ideal life," commented Adelais, "except that there weren't any men."

"Not if you don't count the peasants who delivered

155

their goods to the abbey or the visiting priests," said Judith.

"Hardly men." Mosella laughed. "No strong, muscular warriors is what Adelais means."

"And time for prayers," murmured Galswinth, whose dark eyes lifted from her work and gazed into the space above the heads of the young women surrounding her.

"Yes, time for prayers," returned Judith. The queen's look suggested that the life of the convent appealed to her more than being a queen.

Judith felt the weight of that look in her heart and feared that Galswinth was not happy. She wished she could help her friend, but what could she do? Galswinth's happiness lay in the hands of Chilperic, a man influenced by many motives. Judith had absolutely no power to influence any of those motives; it made her feel helpless.

She thought of the secret pleasures she experienced with Ivar each time he came to her, and felt badly that Galswinth seemed not to be experiencing such ecstasy in her marriage. She wondered why—Chilperic seemed a virile enough man. Did Galswinth's fears prevent her from giving herself up to passion? Or did Chilperic not possess the skilled touch of an expert lover? It made Judith blush to think about it. Then, afraid the other women would read her thoughts, she buried her head again in the *Life of St. Martin*.

Chapter Ten

The huntsmen crashed through the forest on the trail of a deer, which they had chased for some distance. Chilperic was in the lead and as the deer leapt across fallen logs and avoided muddy bogs, the hunters followed. But too late the deer boxed itself into a covert against a smooth-faced cliff, from which there was no escape. The hunters came on mercilessly.

Having caught only a glimpse of the fleet-footed deer when their dogs had sniffed it out, they now saw the creature cowering against the dripping gray cliff where water from a spring oozed from above.

Suddenly Chilperic reined in his horse and held up a hand. "Wait, hold off," he called out, and the huntsmen behind him pulled their horses to a stop, some circling quickly, all holding their spears. Then they saw why. Sun broke through clouds and they saw that the deer was pure white against the gray rock, not fawn colored, and there were no other marks.

"The white doe," said Ivar, who had come up beside Chilperic. A sign of the goddess Ardhuina.

"That she is."

Chilperic got down from his horse slowly and the other men followed. They would never kill the white doe.

For a few moments no one spoke; they all watched the doe, who seemed to understand that her fate had been reversed. Her quivering stopped and she walked delicately forward a few steps, observing the men before her. As if becoming the goddess she signified, she stood stone still, brown eyes alert.

Many of the warriors' hearts trembled; they had never seen the white doe and they feared to look upon her.

When Chilperic observed the surroundings he realized that the doe had led them to her sacred grotto so that she could show herself. He got down on his knees and his men followed suit.

"White doe," he said in reverent tones. "You are our luck, you provide us with game, you are the sap in the trees, the dew on the grass. We revere your noble beauty. Make our hearts brave, bring rain, preserve our crops. We will bring offerings to this, our sacred grotto."

A breeze wafted through the leaves high above them and the deer lowered her head gracefully as if in acknowledgment. Then she turned and bounded away, into the forest.

The men stood, filled with awe, while at the same time relieved that the deer was gone. For though the Franks were superstitious as well as Christian, they were afraid of such omens and signs though none would admit it to his fellows. Most accepted Christianity because it was simpler. There were only two gods to worship, the one in heaven and his son who had been sacrificed. They also prayed to the saints, who were powerful in the miracles they worked. But the old ways could not always be ignored. When one of the old gods showed himself and demanded tribute, the superstitious Franks were too fearful not to comply.

After the vision of the white doe, Chilperic declared the day's hunting at an end. They had taken much game and even from here the scent of blood was strong where the slaves had been sent to butcher the kills and take the meat to the palace. The warriors headed homeward.

As Chilperic left the grove, he drew in a breath of surprise, for waiting silently next to a tall poplar on a fine chestnut mount sat Fredegund, who had waited to show herself until the group of hunters had passed.

Chilperic drew rein, but motioned for his companions to go on. "Leave me," he said, and his lords continued on their way. They had seen that a woman waited for him, though they could not tell who it was.

Their steeds trotted through the soft dirt and ground cover until the sounds faded, leaving Chilperic a short distance from Fredegund. She wore a sleeveless tunic of soft blue, a girdle of embroidered gold cloth, and at her throat a bronze torque burnished to look like gold that Chilperic himself had given her. Her mantle had been woven of silver and turquoise thread and was fastened with a clasp emblazoned with the eight-legged horse of Woden executed in enamel. From the point where the folds of her tunic crossed each other under her breasts was fastened a pin made from the carved head of a cat, small chains dangling from its mouth. Her golden hair was braided and coiled about her head, giving her a regal look. For a moment, Chilperic forgot he had relegated her to the kitchen.

"Fredegund," he said, riding his mount nearer.

"My lord," she said softly, respectfully, with only a hint of reminder about her powerful sensuality.

He got off his horse and lifted a hand to help her down. "What are you doing here?" he asked, still appraising her looks and appreciating the fact that she had not let them go. Other women who had been cast aside often wept and wailed, bemoaning their fate if cast into a nunnery, letting looks go, for if the king no longer looked at them, who would? But not Fredegund. He saw the pride in the icy blue eyes and the confidence within her that had raised her above her birth as a kitchen slave in the first place.

"My lord gave me this horse," Fredegund reminded him. "I have needed to keep it exercised."

"Ah, so."

He took her hand and led her a little way, feeling already the tingling of excitement at her presence. For all her lack of noble blood, she had regal qualities that he admired. Her determination and cleverness were akin to his own, and he found himself suddenly wishing such qualities resided in his queen. Galswinth was refined, cultured, intelligent, but meek at heart. Fredegund, on the other hand, possessed the Teutonic qualities of strength, fearlessness, and cunning.

Fredegund let her mantle fall off her shoulder, baring arms clasped in spiral silver bracelets. She gave a sigh which conveyed her appreciation of being in her lord's presence once again.

"I suppose," said Chilperic slowly, "that I have not thanked you for ridding me of Godulf. When I received your cleverly penned epistle I investigated and found that what you said was true. There was a plot afoot to undermine my decisions regarding the Aquitaine. A few of the counts were thinking of declaring the province an independent kingdom and offering it to my son Merovech. Just in time I was able to waylay their emissaries. They were made an example of.

"That is good," said Fredegund smugly. "I told you that I wanted to remain in your palace where I could best serve you, even if I were banned from the

160

royal bedchamber."

She glanced up at him through her thick lashes, her eyes working their way into his armor of conscience.

"I am glad I was not so foolish to send you far away," he said. "It is true, I owe you a reward. What would you like?"

"Nothing, my lord, save the honor of serving you."

They had stopped to face each other and Fredegund allowed her fingers to drift upward on the gold threads of his fur-lined mantle. Her lips were pouted and she stood close to him, knowing his responses would be voluntary as her knee touched his.

"And how would you serve me?" he said, his voice already throaty as he looked down into the shadowy cleft of her bosom where the cat pin fastened her garments.

She tilted her head, her eyes meeting his, but her lashes lowered. With one hand she cleverly unfastened her girdle so that her tunic unwound. "I would seek to please you, my lord, as I have turned my every effort to learning how that best be done."

Chilperic's blood pounded in his veins. How he had missed Fredegund's fire, the skill in her strong hands, the animal passion in her greedy limbs. With no more hesitation he clasped her to him, lowering his mouth to hers in a wet, hungry kiss. Quickly he unpinned her mantle, tossing it on the ground for a rug, then he folded back the rest of her tunic, pleased that she wore no shift under it. As quickly he unfastened his own cloak, adding it to the bed in the soft grass, then he got to his knees, bringing Fredegund with him, her arms entwining his neck and shoulders as his hand explored the curves he had missed these last months.

She pulled him onto the cloaks on the ground and in moments showed him the ecstasy that could be his if she were reinstated as his mistress. When she was finished with him, he was ready to grant her anything.

"I can see that your new wife must not be able to satisfy you completely, my lord."

He grunted as he rolled off of her. "It's true, she has been a disappointment."

Fredegund seized the moment and raised herself up on one elbow. "I am resourceful, my lord. Perhaps I can be useful to you in more ways than one."

He turned his head to look into the metallic blue eyes bearing down on him. "Perhaps you can." He thought of Godulf.

"But I cannot help you with such favors if I am pressed to duty in the kitchens for the rest of my life. You must raise my status so that I can be nearer the court."

"You know I cannot do that, Fredegund. I have sworn an oath to set you and my former wife aside. I cannot take a mistress or else King Athanagild will reclaim all of Galswinth's dowry. I cannot afford that."

She outlined a circle on his chest with her finger. "Perhaps there might be a way to reinstate me with status without taking me as your official concubine. Make me a serving woman to the queen."

He eyed her with wry humor. "I hardly think you have the temperament for it, Fredegund."

"Oh, I don't wish to be one of her companions. Just allow me to wait on her when she needs something. To bring her baths, serve trays of food and wine."

"And why, may I ask, do you wish to be placed in so humble a position?"

"It's better than the kitchens where I get flour in my hair and eyes and run the risk of burning myself in the ovens. I might be able to see you, my lord, if I were in the palace, somewhere that I can gain information by careful overhearing of conversations. I can bribe favors if I have access to your lords and if I hear what the queen's ladies have to say. Women are great gossips, and I have no doubt that your wife's women are no exception. Surely liaisons must have formed by now between them and the lords who claim to be your friends. Let me find out which ones are your true friends."

Chilperic could see the wisdom in what she said, still he hesitated. It was known that Fredegund had been his mistress. If word leaked out that he was sleeping with her, he would forfeit Galswinth's dowry. And he could not afford to arouse Galswinth's suspicions. He could not neglect the marriage bed because he needed to produce sons by her. But if Fredegund were accessible, perhaps he could treat himself to her charms now and then if he were careful. Chilperic was a lusty man and as king was not used to curbing his excesses.

He reached out to fondle Fredegund's luscious breasts again, thinking how his wife's small, tight breasts paled beside these ripened fruits. As he pulled her down to nibble on her full, moist lips, she extracted his promise.

Judith was surprised when Ivar announced that he wished her to accompany him on his visit to his family's demesne. The demesne was comprised of several large land parcels awarded to Ivar's father and grandfather when the Merovingian chiefs before Clovis helped the Romans push back the barbarian tribes of the Suevi, Langobards, and Thuringians.

The women in Galswinth's entourage agreed that Ivar was paying her a great honor to be taking her on such a visit. Judith herself remained confused about the reason why he wanted her. They were only three days' journey to the estate, he had told her, and he did not plan to be gone very many days. She was pleased that he wanted her because it must mean that he did not want to be away from the pleasures they had been sharing. In truth, however, she knew that if he had to be away for reasons of battle or on the king's business, he would not think anything of having to leave her behind. Perhaps he did not wish to leave her where the king might turn his eye toward her. Ivar was possessive.

Judith did not spend time wondering if he would someday take another woman. While the feelings between them were warm, they were too new for Judith to put a name to them. She felt passion and affection but she was not in love with him. She had given herself to him in return for protection, and found pleasure as well, but it was difficult to know if love would ever grow.

Ivar had said nothing of marriage, and Judith understood her position: She was his property. A sort of agreement had formed between them. That it was pleasing in addition to being expeditious was a boon.

Galswinth looked both pleased and anxious that Judith would be joining the party setting out for Orléans. She fussed over her friend as if she were going to be away for a very long time. Judith hesitated to go, but she could think of no excuse not to, and she had sent a message to Father Gregory to call on Galswinth in her absence.

Galswinth presented Judith with many gifts to take with her. Not satisfied with a new traveling cloak, and a rock crystal pendant to suspend from her belt, Galswinth presented her with a gold-handled knife, which Judith turned over carefully in her hands.

"It's beautifully carved," said Judith. "You do too much for me."

"Nothing is too much for my oldest and dearest friend," said Galswinth. "Keep it safe in the scabbard. See, it is fitted so it can hang from your belt as well."

Judith tried to make light of her preparations. "With a magic crystal and a sharp knife, surely no danger can befall me."

Galswinth's eyes flitted around the room, in which they were alone. "You cannot be too careful. You will be on the road."

"Traveling with Ivar and his servants who will be fully armed."

"Even so . . ." Galswinth's meaning was clear.

Judith pressed her hand. "Do not worry. I shall be safe, as will you be, I trust."

Galswinth gave the hollow smile that she had worn since she had lived at Chilperic's court. "Safe? I do not know."

"Galswinth, do not start worrying. You must send to Father Gregory if you need anything. He has promised to watch over you."

"You really believe I need watching over, don't you?"

Judith wished she could take back her words. "As you say, there is violence abroad at times, and while we are far from any border skirmishes, we must be vigilant. It is a time of change, Galswinth. You must be careful at all times. There might be those jealous of you, so you must guard your position. Any ruler would have to do the same. Make sure of your servants' loyalty. Promise them rewards if they discover plotting against you or the king."

She tried to make her advice sound like nothing more than common sense, but she could see by the flicker in Galswinth's eyes that her friend was afraid. For a moment Judith felt a flicker of anger. If only Galswinth were more of a fighter. She was pious and cultivated, she was gentle, but she did not know how to outsmart cunning rivals or assist her husband to do so. Those qualities were needed in a strong queen, and Judith feared that Galswinth lacked them.

"I won't be away long," she said.

Galswinth took a few steps back, shivered slightly, and sat on a hassock in front of the fireplace in the center of the room where a brick chimney rose to the roof.

"I have heard a rumor that Ivar will not be alone when he goes to see his father."

"Oh?"

Galswinth moistened her lips. "My companions have, as you suggested, already gained the confidence of some of the counts. I cannot swear it, but I believe a number of the lords have planned hunting expeditions in the coming days. The king will not be able to join them, because he will be in council with his bishops."

Judith frowned. "Ivar said nothing about that."

Galswinth lowered her voice. "Though I regret to lose your presence here, I am glad you will be with Ivar. If there is a secret meeting, and what am I to suspect but that it is secret? You must find out what it is about. My husband speaks to me a little, and he has warned that some of the nobles may seek to gain power for themselves. It is a delicate position. The counts have their own followers, whom they call out to aid the king in times of war. But the same followers are loyal only to their lord, not the king. So what is to stop the lords from forming their own army if they decide not to obey the king?"

Judith gazed thoughtfully into the fire. "I see what you mean. I have not heard any such rumor. And of course if I asked Ivar, he would deny it, knowing that I am close to you. However, I will keep my ears open and let you know anything that I learn."

166

Galswinth knew that if the king were endangered, her own position would be threatened. She would be at best sent to a convent or returned to her father's country, but without her dowry, humiliated.

Judith thought about poor Godulf, and wondered if Fredegund's act of murder might have something to do with such a plot, but she could not bring herself to worry Galswinth with the information. She had told Father Gregory, so she had someone with whom to share the burden. Perhaps, being away with Ivar, she would have a chance to question him, too. She fingered the pendant and the knife, hoping she would not have to use the knife, but promising to keep the pendant by her side for luck.

Chilperic sat on the high-backed chair in the chamber where the king's justice was dispensed. He studied the scroll before him as he rubbed his chin solemnly, more to gain time to think than to reread the case that had already been put before him. The abbott of the St. John's Monastery claimed that his neighbor, a freedman with a small landholding, had been farming a portion of the abbey lands between a stream and a rise of ground with a thick hedge on it, which the landholder claimed to be the boundaries of his land. He had showed his deed, granted to him by the Count of Auxerre, which marked off the boundaries using the natural contours of the land.

On the other hand, the monastery's land grant described boundaries in terms of distances and laid out the property in straight lines as the crow flies. The title of Count of Auxerre had now fallen on the son of the man who had granted the freedman his little plot of land and had stuck by his father's grant, but the monks were adamant, greedy, Chilperic thought, and had brought the matter to the king because Chilperic's late brother had endowed their monastery. Now Chilperic must settle it.

He rubbed his temples, not really caring who got the land.

"Sire," spoke Ado, the little landholder, desperately trying to hold onto every inch of ground. "I pay one head of cattle and a hundred bushels of corn in tribute to the count and of my own free will donate an equal amount of corn to the monastery, because such was the tradition before I was freed. I did not believe Saint John would want it otherwise, even though there is no legal requirement that I do so. If you take away the strip of land between the stream and the hill, I will not be able to afford such tribute to the monastery."

Chilperic nodded at this logic and turned gray-green eyes on the stubby little abbot. "What have you to say to that?" he asked.

"I am sure the saint would be just as satisfied if we took care of the land ourselves and raised our own corn to feed the monks and the hungry."

The two men started to squabble again, and Chilperic felt the apathy of fatigue that seized him after listening to a whole day of such squabbles on top of other administrative duties. Confirming sentences of the counts, confiscating property from outlaws, handing out grants as a reward for fidelity to his lords, making appointments to office, disciplining officials, after a while it all blurred, and he longed to get off his throne.

A further annoyance seized him. He thought to settle this last dispute quickly and then retire to his bedchamber to a goblet of wine and then summon Fredegund. But she had gone on a pilgrimage. She had promised Father Gregory a day of prayer vigil, followed by handing out alms to the poor. He wondered what had inspired her sudden bout of piety? Anyway, he could not look forward to seeing his mistress for three days.

He turned his attention back to the matter at hand. Normally he would not offend an abbot. But the Monastery of St. John was a retreat for the extremely austere, for whom he had no patience. They were loyal to no one but themselves, mortifying their flesh to an irrational degree. He smiled at the abbot, whim making him decide to uphold the farmer's grant.

"Holy Father," he began. "While my piety makes me want to grant your wish, and declare the land in question as belonging to the abbey, it appears to me that my father was in error when he laid out the monastery land grant. He obviously did not know that Ado's land already included that to the hill and the copse. It is my judgment to let the landholding stand. In exchange, Ado will continue to pay the first calf of the season as well as the bushels of corn."

He raised his hand and handed the scroll describing the dispute to Epoald, who was standing by to dispense justice once Chilperic had decided.

Epoald took the scroll, then motioned for the two disputants to follow him to a table at the side of a room where a scribe quickly wrote down the decision. Then Epoald watched as both disputants signed the agreement.

"The king's justice be upheld," said Epoald and ushered the two men out of the royal chambers.

In the anteroom, petitioners saw Epoald emerge and rose to wave their petitions in his face, all shouting to be next.

"Order," growled Epoald. "The king will see no one else today. Come back tomorrow."

He made his way through the crowd, turning to glare as a peasant reached out to touch his robe. The peasant drew his hand back, chastised. Everyone knew the mayor of the palace could advise the king, and all sought to gain his favor.

However, he did accept the gifts that were slipped to him as he passed down the row of those waiting to see the king. A carafe of wine, a loaf of fresh bread, gold pressed into his palm. Such bribes were hoped to inspire Epoald to place their case first on the next day or to whisper in the ear of the king.

Epoald accepted the gifts with a solemn acknowledgment, while not promising to be able to assist the petitioners in any way.

Chapter Eleven

Judith admired the large orchard that Ivar pointed out as soon as they got to the boundaries of his family's demesne. Row upon row of fruit trees graced the road, many already in bloom, now that spring was beginning. On the other side of the road they followed a vineyard that stretched as far as the eye could see.

Judith had elected to ride on her beloved Black Lady for most of the journey, though a cart traveled with them carrying clothing and extra weapons. The old Roman roads were mostly safe, and the group had stopped at an inn the first night. The second night they had enjoyed the hospitality of a monastery, and being entertained by the abbot had reminded Judith of Radegund and Agnes. She wondered if they had received the letter she had written them and promised herself to write another as soon as she had the opportunity.

After they had left the Roman highways, the road cut through thick, uncleared forests for great distances. Scattered in islands among the great woods were cleared lands, both free peasant holdings and larger domains that were part of the great estates. If they didn't belong to the church, these larger manorial lands belonged either to Gallo-Roman nobility who had held the lands since the Romans settled here, and who had stayed and been later appointed to royal service by the Merovingian kings, or they belonged to Frankish nobles who had taken over lands from departing Romans or who had been awarded land for helping Clovis unite Gaul under one sovereignty.

They passed a grove of trees, and a villa now came into view.

The main house spread in a large rectangle, and from this distance the red tiles shone in the sun. Around the villa were the workshops of weavers, tanners, metalsmiths, and carpenters, with brick-chimneyed kitchens in separate buildings. A low, thick hedge surrounded the entire compound. As they drew closer, Judith could see that there was a great deal of activity. A main gate led to a large central courtyard where servants held horses, and several carts were being unloaded.

Judith's interest grew as she recognized some of the nobles from Chilperic's court. Ivar drew rein and raised his hand to his friend, Count Lupus, a young blond man with a handsome face and bright, intelligent blue eyes. So, Galswinth had not been wrong. There were to be several guests at the demesne.

Just then an older man appeared from a doorway. He was dressed in tunic to the knees, fur vest, and gem-studded belt. From the lines in his tanned face, she could see that he had more years on him than Ivar and Lupus, but he wore them well.

"Father," said Ivar, when he saw him.

"Welcome home," said the older man, smiling as Ivar dismounted and embraced him, clapping him on the back.

"It is good to be here, Father. I see that several of our friends have joined us."

Father and son laughed, together with Lupus, as if the sudden gathering had been spontaneous, though they knew better. Then the older man's eyes fell on Judith, still sitting on Black Lady. His eyes lit with curiosity.

Ivar gestured to Judith. "The lady Judith agreed to accompany me," he told his father. "She is companion to the queen."

The older man exchanged a quick glance with his son as if perceiving that she was also Ivar's concubine. Then he turned his mature visage back to her.

"Judith is welcome to our house. We will do all we can to see to her pleasure."

The father took her bridle and led Black Lady to a place in the yard where Judith could easily dismount. When she reached the ground, she faced her host.

"I am pleased to be here," she said.

"Ah, such beauty will enhance our gathering. Ivar has not told you, I am sure, but several of the nobles decided to partake of my woods for hunting for the next few days. The forest is thick with game. But I am being rude. I am Ivar's father, Gararic."

He inclined his head in a manner that was more Gallo-Roman than Frankish.

He went on to elucidate. "We have held this demesne for three generations. My mother was Gallo-Roman, and my father Frankish. This villa was hers, and so passed to me when they died. My own wife passed on many seasons ago."

"I'm sorry," said Judith.

"Her spirit still dwells among us," said Gararic, looking inward for a moment of reflection. Then he motioned to a young girl to attend to Judith. "Eulalia will see to your needs."

The girl had olive skin and dark hair, hidden under

a pale yellow turban. Her long-sleeved tunic was brightly striped in yellow and brown. The garment came to her ankles and was belted at the waist with a sash of the same material.

While servants unloaded the baggage, Judith followed Eulalia across the courtyard and through a door that opened onto a small alcove. Off the alcove was a sleeping cubicle with a comfortable-looking bed with feather mattress, a hassock, and small table with oil lamp ready for use. A small, high window opened onto the courtyard.

"The latrine is across the courtyard behind the lavatory," said the girl. Ivar's big-muscled servants delivered Judith's trunk and set it at the foot of the bed.

"Would you like me to take your things out for airing?" asked Eulalia.

"Yes, thank you," said Judith. She liked the girl's bright eyes and suspected that Gararic treated his slaves well, for she saw no welts or scars on the smooth-skinned girl.

"I'll wash the mud off and change into a clean tunic," said Judith, untying her traveling cloak and letting Eulalia take it from her.

She left the girl to the unpacking and ventured forth, being careful to stay out of the way of the carts rolling off to the stables after they'd been unloaded. The lavatory was situated in its own small courtyard, spigots releasing fresh water piped in from the nearby stream. After their days of travel, it felt good to wash away the dirt. She let the water run through her hair, and rubbed her scalp briskly before wringing her hair out in the cotton towels Eulalia had given her. Then she wrapped her hair in a second towel and was recrossing the courtyard when she saw another party enter the compound.

Curious as to who the nobles were who had gathered here, she made out Count Germanus, another of Chilperic's vassals. Judith stood under the portico next to a wooden pillar, watching the party. When she caught sight of the blond woman in their company, her mouth opened in surprise. Though the party was across the large yard by the entrance, the golden hair that peeked out of the hood was unmistakable. Then the familiar face turned in Judith's direction, and she instinctively moved behind the pillar so as not to be seen. Fredegund was with Germanus's party.

A kitchen slave, traveling with Germanus? Judith's mind raced. The former concubine must be taking up her trade again. She must be Germanus's lover. Other thoughts occurred to her, and she recalled Galswinth's warnings about the meeting here. What had Fredegund to do with it?

Memories of Fredegund with Godulf came back full force, and Judith had the impulse to warn Germanus at once. But of course she could not. Surely Fredegund did not have the habit of murdering all her lovers; otherwise, Chilperic himself would be dead. No, there must be something more to it. A plot, as Galswinth suspected? Judith had thought she had accompanied Ivar to the demesne for the excitement of an outing, but now she knew her mission: She must discover what was going on here. She returned quickly to her cubicle.

Ivar sought her out after she had changed garments. "My father has planned a banquet for tonight," he said. "You will be a guest of honor, together with the other women present."

"Thank you," said Judith, looking refreshed now in golden-brown tunic with gold embroidery at the hem and edges of the sleeves. From her belt hung the crystal pendant Galswinth had given her. She had left the

175

gem-studded scabbard and the ornamental but sharp knife in her quarters. Ivar had seen the new trinkets, but had said nothing. Wearing a knife while traveling was commonplace since one never knew when one might meet with danger, but to wear the knife while at the demesne might be thought to be an insult, so Judith had decided to leave it in her baggage.

"I must meet with the lords who have honored us with their presence for a few days. There will be entertainment tonight following the banquet."

His eyes held a preoccupied expression, but before he left her, they slid over her costume, appreciating the way the material fell over breast and hip. She felt the flush from his gaze and knew that entertainment also meant a night of passion. She and Ivar had been separated while traveling, he sleeping with his men and she alone with a guard outside, but now that they were at the villa they would have privacy whenever it was desired.

"Then I will occupy myself until evening," she said, meeting his gaze. "Perhaps I will take a walk in your father's orchards."

He nodded. "Take Eulalia with you and one of the strong slaves. The territory is safe from any known threats, but I do not wish to take a chance."

She nodded her agreement. She would not ordinarily mind if servants followed her on her explorations of the surrounding countryside, but a plan was beginning to formulate in her mind, and she did not want to be hampered by anyone. As it turned out, Ivar's father took matters out of her hands.

The nobles were gathering in the great hall for discussions, but Gararic did not need to be a part of that. He was well aware of the matters important to these lords who constituted a decisive element in Neustria's success and survival, no matter who the monarch was. The nobility had always been a strong political factor among the Franks from the time of the tribal development up to the present, and among them the strong, the powerful, and the wealthy rose to the top.

But Gararic wanted his son to be the voice of their family. The older man was satisfied to provide a place for this important meeting. And he could enjoy showing his son's mistress his possessions while the men met.

As Count of Orléans, Ivar's father served as the king's mouthpiece in judicial and civil matters in the city of Orléans and the surrounding territory. Unlike the counts of the palace who almost never left the court, the counts of the districts made a circuit of their districts to hold judicial courts. They defended orphans and widows, punished robbers and murderers so that the king's subjects could live in peace and happiness. Each year the count conveyed the taxes in his jurisdiction to the royal treasury. But Gararic had set aside his provincial duties to play host to the gathering of nobles.

Judith was just starting across the courtyard when Gararic saw her and changed direction.

"I hope your quarters are comfortable?" he inquired, the creases deepening at the corners of his eyes as he smiled.

"Yes, quite."

"Perhaps you will allow me to show you around the demesne."

"Nothing would please me more," said Judith.

"Then let us go on horseback, for our lands are extensive. I will get you a fresh horse; your own animal has traveled far."

They walked through the compound to the stables where horses were saddled. Eulalia and the brawny slave were also mounted. The slave's armed presence as they began their ride toward the vineyards gave Judith her first clue as to the nature of the council taking place in the great hall. Surely Gararic would feel safe on his own lands if the meeting were not controversial.

They passed along a track and Judith could see where wild growth had been cleared to make room for the neat fields. The track led between field and woodland, and they proceeded carefully so that the thick growth of thorns and brambles did not catch at their clothing.

After circling fields and vineyards for some time, they came to a village of huts where the tenants lived. Some of the land was rented to serfs who paid a portion of what they raised in tithes and fees to the master. In spite of gathering clouds overhead and the scent of moisture in the air, the serfs were busy working out of doors; in the spring, there were a myriad of tasks. Tools to make and repair, flocks of fowl to raise, and all the endless chores demanded of those who must till the soil and keep a roof over their heads. When they saw the master ride by with his entourage, the serfs stopped their work and bowed their heads in a gesture of respect.

"My son tells me you were a ward of the Abbey of the Holy Cross in Poitiers," said Gararic, when they had passed the village and taken a track that would lead them back to the villa compound.

"That's true," answered Judith. "I am Visigothic by birth. I was captured by Frankish warriors a long time ago and brought to Gaul as a slave. Because I was so young, I was fortunate enough to be given over to the Mother Radegund, King Chilperic's aunt. In the abbey I received an education."

She said it with pride, knowing that to be able to

178

read and write was not so common among the Franks, even the nobles.

Gararic nodded, his eyes scanning his lands with pride. "Indeed fortunate. And then Queen Galswinth plucked you from the convent."

Judith gave a wry grin. "It was I who plucked myself from the abbey and threw myself on Galswinth's mercy. We had been friends as children in Spain."

"I see. And so you are a queen's lady now."

"Yes."

"But your parents are no longer living?"

"My father was killed in battle, and my mother died shortly after I was brought to Gaul. So I have no family." She sighed. "My father was a goldsmith. He wrought fine weapons and jewelry for the king. I suppose now I consider Galswinth the closest thing I have to family."

"My son needs a wife," said Gararic bluntly. "He seems to favor you."

Judith blushed. "I am honored that he brought me here."

She could think of nothing else to say. Ivar had never put forward the notion of marriage. She did not know if he even thought about it.

"Since you have no family, it would be up to the king to negotiate for you."

"Yes, I suppose."

Though she should feel honored to have Ivar's father bring up the subject of marriage, she felt guilty about the idea of leaving Galswinth's side. Though there was no reason she could not be married and still live at court, once married, she would have to obey her husband's orders and go where he went.

"We must carry this discussion further," said Gararic. "Now I have something to show you."

179

He motioned for the entourage to turn to the right and they came upon a group of buildings set in a cleared space, still a small distance from the villa, which was visible from here. Several men worked among the buildings, and Judith was intrigued by a large pen made of high, pointed stakes tightly laced together. Nearby were cages of various sizes. The group dismounted and a servant came to take their horses.

"I recently entertained a very interesting man. He was a trader who had been to Africa. He had with him a feline cub whose mother had been trained to hunt game. The man rested with me for some weeks, and left the cub in exchange for my hospitality. I had thought to give it to Ivar to train, knowing his way with animals."

Gararic stopped and turned to Judith as they approached an iron cage. "Ivar tells me he has taught you hawking."

"It is true, we have gone into the fields with the falcons."

"And you enjoy it?"

"Why yes. I have always had a fondness for beast and fowl."

The older man looked pleased. "Ivar said also that you did not panic when stalked by the boar."

Remembering their meeting in the woods, she answered, "Perhaps I did not. But fortune was with me that day."

"Yes."

Now Judith looked closer at the iron cage and saw the feline cub trotting back and forth. It was small and agile, with a tawny coat with closely set black spots.

"It's called a cheetah. It is very fast," said Gararic. "And it feeds on deer and antelope."

"I've never seen anything like it," said Judith.

"It is young, and is being accustomed to humans. Come, let us take it out of its cage."

Judith watched with fascination as a servant was summoned. He wore a thick hide shirt and leggings and put on gloves to protect himself from the cub's claws. Then he opened the cage and picked up the chain that was fastened to a ring around the cub's neck. The cub tussled with the chain, baring sharp, pointed fangs, but the servant easily handled it, bringing it out to show.

"Let us see if you have a rapport with wild animals," suggested Gararic, obviously enjoying the spectacle. "We will take the little cheetah for a walk. You can handle her."

Judith was surprised when Gararic directed another servant to hand her a pair of gloves. Then he had her replace her riding cloak with a fur jacket that offered more protection against claws and teeth, should the cheetah play rough. Excitement rippled through her. Truly Ivar's father must favor her to be letting her handle the exotic animal. Then she remembered the talisman Ivar had given her, which she wore constantly around her neck. If it did enable the wearer to communicate with wild beasts, now was the time to use its powers. When she was ready, she took the chain from the handler and knelt to let the cat get her scent.

"Does it have a name?" she asked as she held her hand out to let the cheetah sniff her.

"Perhaps you will name it."

She glanced at him wide-eyed, greatly surprised at the honor. Then she looked down at the little cat who bared its teeth. But then it crouched down and approached, sniffing her hand. She instinctively spoke in a soft, soothing tone and moved slowly.

"Good Cheetah. What shall we name you?"

"Now get up slowly," said Gararic, "and walk around the compound, leading her on the chain. Make sure she knows that you are in control. Try to see and smell as a wild animal. Try to anticipate anything that might frighten her."

Judith did as he said, greatly enjoying her walk with the cheetah. She knew the animal was not a pet, but would be trained to hunt as its parent had done. The cat could prove dangerous, but with training started so young, perhaps it would learn to obey humans.

"Why don't we call her Kahluli, since she is from the East," suggested Judith.

"Hmmm," said Gararic. "A good name. In India such animals are trained to hunt. I see no reason why this one cannot be trained to do the same. I had planned to have my animal trainer do the job. But . . ." He seemed to be thinking, then made up his mind.

"Perhaps I shall make a gift of this cheetah to you and let you take it back to court and raise it yourself. Ivar can help you train it."

Judith was stunned at the suggestion of such a gift. "Me? You would give the cheetah to me? But surely she is very rare and valuable."

"Valuable yes, especially if trained to hunt. Rare? Not where she comes from."

"I . . . I hardly know what to say. I ought not accept . . ." Judith stammered.

"Of course I would not want to burden you. If you do not feel you can take the time to care for the training, I will give her to my son."

"Oh no. I would love to. I mean, I don't know how to train a cheetah. But if you think Ivar knows . . ."

"He knows enough about taming wild beasts, and I will tell you both what the trader told me."

Judith gazed into Gararic's eyes, which had a yellow band that went from the pupil to the edge of the iris. She liked the hint of gentility mixed with the determined strength she saw in Ivar's father and felt that they were forming a friendship. She lowered her head in humility.

"I would be pleased to accept the gift. I will take care of this animal and train her to the best of my ability. I will do everything to be worthy of being Kahluli's owner."

Gararic smiled. "Good. Then walk her a little longer. Be sure to let her rest as well. Speak in soothing tones, but show her you are in control. A few simple commands to begin. And you must be patient. It will take many months before she is trained to obey you and can be allowed to hunt off the leash."

"I will be patient," she assured him.

"Then I will leave you for a while. When you are ready, return her to the cage. My man will give you food for her. Feeding an animal helps it form a bond with the feeder. I will give instructions that no one else feed her while you are here, and of course when you take her back to the palace you will be her new mistress."

Judith nodded. Gararic left them, and Eulalia and the strong slave watched with interest from the edge of the compound as Judith walked the animal around, commanding her to sit and rest at intervals. Finally, she returned Kahluli to her cage and gave her some pieces of fresh game.

When Judith left the compound she was startled to see Fredegund seated on a white horse, watching her. Judith hesitated, her first impulse being to turn away, but then she held her head up and approached the courtesan. The woman's cold eyes watched her with disinterest, and Judith tried to squelch the feeling that Fredegund knew that she had seen her with Godulf. But surely not; if she had seen her that night, she would have made it known. Judith had never spoken to Fredegund, but now that they found themselves here, she knew it was time.

Keeping her eyes on the blond woman on the horse, Judith approached neither hastily nor slowly.

"I see you dance with the leopard," said Fredegund speculatively when Judith had come near enough.

"It is a gift," said Judith rather proudly. "From Ivar's father, Gararic, our host."

Fredegund lifted her brows. "Then you are favored."

"Perhaps." Judith was wary.

What did Fredegund want with her? Surely not just idle feminine conversation. For unlike the queen's companions, Fredegund seemed a woman unto herself, with no need of female friends.

"Who did you come here with?" Judith asked boldly. If she were to find out what Fredegund was up to, she had to begin somewhere.

Fredegund gave her a sly smile. "Count Germanus has always been an admirer of mine."

"I see." Judith weighed her next words but plunged ahead. "Germanus is a very wealthy and respected vassal of the king's. Perhaps you will no longer have to work in the kitchens."

She was rewarded by a level gaze assessing her.

"You are not stupid," observed Fredegund. "For you have gained the favor of one of the strongest counts of the palace yourself." She tossed her golden hair around her and gave a throaty laugh.

Judith felt a swell of resentment at Fredegund comparing herself to her. At that moment the full force of her position as a lord's mistress hit her like a blow between the eyes. Even so, she held herself above the other woman.

She had not been a king's mistress, cast off only to throw herself on another lord as soon as was convenient.

"Ivar is my protector," Judith said, trying to sound as haughty as Fredegund.

Fredegund gave her a lascivious glance. "A good choice. I'm sure he protects you very well."

Unconsciously Judith fingered the talisman at her breast.

"There is to be a great feast tonight," said Fredegund, changing the subject. "After the lords have had a chance to talk."

"What are they talking about?" Judith asked, moving closer.

Fredegund eyed her carefully. "Don't you know?"

"No. Ivar said nothing. I did not even know the other lords were coming here. But it must be a matter of great importance."

Fredegund looked anxious. "One would think so."

"Do you not know why they have come?" Judith pressed.

Fredegund gave a quick shake of her golden hair. "No." She looked as if she were going to say something and then decided not.

At that moment Judith saw the flicker of uncertainty in the other woman's eyes. That's why she's come, Judith thought. She's come to find out what this meeting is about. And why? To inform on the lords to Chilperic? The thought chilled her. She decided to watch the wily Fredegund carefully. The woman was becoming more and more mysterious.

And then another thought seized her. Perhaps she had killed Godulf at the king's request. That was why the matter had never been brought out into the open. Judith tried to keep from trembling. Perhaps Fredegund was an assassin for the king.

New fear sprang in her breast. Fredegund was no friend of Galswinth's. What Galswinth had suspected was indeed likely to be true: Her very life might be in danger.

Chapter Twelve

After leaving Fredegund, Judith dressed carefully for the banquet. Eulalia arrayed her in a lemon-colored silk undertunic with delicate embroidery over which she draped a long-sleeved forest green serge overtunic. A gem-studded girdle encircled her waist, and strands of gold were braided through her hair, which was gathered into a single plait. A gauze veil was fastened to her head with a long cloisonné pin.

When she entered the banquet hall she spotted Fredegund at once, hanging onto Germanus's arm. She was lavishly dressed in a costume of rich gold and brown, her veil a filmy white, which drifted down her shoulders, while at the same time showing off her blond hair.

Ivar caught Judith's eye and looked approving. He took a chalice of wine from a passing servant and tipped it back. Then he crossed the room to her to show her where they would sit. The women joined the men tonight, for the king was not present and there was no high table. Gararic entered the room and held up his hands for the gathering to be silenced.

"Welcome to my house," said Gararic to the crowd. "No table is raised above the others tonight. For you are all my guests of honor."

A murmur of agreement passed through the crowd.

"Feast and drink, for there is plenty."

He then strode to a seat at one end of the far table and as he took a seat in the high-backed chair, the rest took seats along one side of the two long tables where huge platters of roast pig, arrangements of fruit, uncut loaves of fresh bread, and other tempting morsels left almost no room for the pewter bowls upon which some of the food would rest between going from knives and fingers to mouths. Slaves carved the pigs, served cheeses, and ran up and down the other side of the tables bringing in more food.

Wine and ale flowed from gold flagons into brass drinking cups, and the din increased as the guests enjoyed themselves. Judith sipped her wine slowly, watching the assembly. At the next table, Fredegund sat with her back to Judith and she watched as the courtesan imbibed from her wine cup, then poured the red liquid down her protector's throat. Several times Count Germanus leaned over to kiss her and slid a hand around her waist and down her buttocks for a squeeze.

She laughed with him, leaning toward him as did most of the other women as the revelers got drunker and drunker. From time to time a lord would stagger to his feet and offer a toast to which everyone else cheered. Out of the corner of her eye Judith watched Ivar drink as much as the other men in the room, but he did not slobber on her, although he did enter in to the bantering and jesting.

After the meat was taken away, entertainment was brought in. Female dancers dressed in scarves and male dancers in satin leggings twirled, cavorted, and leapt across the banquet hall to the delight of the guests. They were accompanied by flute and drum and a male singer with a high, thin voice.

When one drunken lord passed by and grasped Judith by the shoulders, all she did was gasp and Ivar turned on the man, throwing his hands away from Judith.

"Watch what you're doing there, my man," growled Ivar.

The man was quickly sobered by Ivar's look and raised his hands in an apologetic gesture, then made his way out of the room. Finally the dancers left. Ivar wiped his knife on the bread, which he threw to the dogs.

Count Fulrich rose and walked to the center of the room in front of both tables.

"My friends," he said, raising his wine cup high in the air until the roars of the feast settled down to murmurs as all eyes turned toward him. "Should we not now drink a pledge to the matter we have agreed on this very afternoon?"

Loud mutters and some grunts of agreement. "Those who drink together are bound by a pledge, are we not? Let anyone who does not want to join us, leave now unmolested under the rules of the protection of a guest in his host's house."

"Here, here," most of the men agreed.

Judith tensed. Was she now going to hear what had been decided at the meeting? She did not have long to wait. Count Fulrich liked the sound of his own voice, and the wine had given him eloquence.

"Chilperic quibbles too long with his brother over the cities in the Aquitaine, while he ignores a more immediate threat to the north. It is true that Saxony ought to be Austrasia's problem, but King Sigibert is also distracted and does little more than place legions of border guards to keep the Saxons at bay. They have refused to pay their tributes to either king for seven years. If they are not stopped, they will eat away at our kingdoms. It is time for Neustria, Austrasia, and Burgundy to unite in one strong Frankish kingdom and not merely defend our borders against the Saxons but cross into their marches and take as much of it for ourselves as we can."

The counts were on their feet, shouting their assent and lifting their cups in a toast. Judith trembled. *Invade Saxony!* The idea stunned her beyond belief. She had heard tales of terror about the pagan warriors to the north who had no respect for life or limb. They were said to eat human flesh and practice all manner of gruesome deeds. Whereas other tribes conquered by land, the Saxons rode the sea to the north and frightened the seacoasts with unexpected raids. Now the Franks were going to invade Saxon lands? And without the kings?

Judith happened to catch a glimpse of Fredegund, who no longer leaned on Count Germanus but sat forward, staring intently at the man speaking in the middle of the floor. Her eyes showed no signs of being bleary with drink.

All the lords were on their feet now, yelling battle cries and drinking to the coming war with the Saxons. Judith hugged herself, feeling the surge of excitement but also aware of a certain fear that came from contemplating such a confrontation. Suddenly Ivar reached for her arm and pulled her up. With a gesture of his head he motioned for her to leave the room. She made her way through the melee and pushed open the doors to the banquet hall. She passed through the anteroom and out to the arcade.

Night had fallen and stars twinkled brightly overhead. Having no mantle, she hurried along to her sleeping cubicle. No sooner had she reached it than Ivar appeared.

"Come with me," he said. And she followed him.

He led the way along the arcade to another passage and then to a larger room, this one more luxuriously furnished with fur robes across a large bed, and fire burning brightly in a brick fireplace. A wine flagon and two cups sat on a silver tray placed on a table in front of the fire. Ivar sat on a large chest of cedar while a servant removed his boots. Then he held up his arms as the servant unbuckled his belt. There was no sword, of course. To go armed to supper would be an insult to Gararic, and none of the men had worn arms, at least not arms that were unconcealed.

The servant poured the cups full of wine and then Ivar motioned for him to leave. He handed a cup to Judith, took a sip from his and sat down on the edge of the bed, beckoning for her to join him. She wanted to speak to him of the Saxons, but she saw the look in his eye and knew that his needs must be satisfied first. She unbound her hair, and when he put his hands on her waist and pulled her to him, she yielded willingly. His mouth found hers and his tongue greedily probed.

"Hmmm," he murmured, his hand coming up to her breast. Then he set her away from him and unfastened her belt and lifted the tunic, which she pulled over her head. She started to remove the undertunic, but he shook his head. "No, wait," he said.

Then he took his pleasure, caressing her. Finally he allowed her to pull the garment over her head. Then he knelt in front of her to gaze at her nakedness, desire coming into his golden-spoked blue eyes. His mouth descended on her fleshy mounds and his fingers plied their way against her. Driving her to a new thrill of wonder, Ivar stood and removed his own clothing, and she gazed with awe at the strength of his maleness, naked for her to behold. She felt a sudden great pity for the nuns at the Abbey of the Holy Cross who would never experience such a sight.

She slid back on the bed and Ivar climbed over her, arranging himself between her legs. But he took his time sampling her flesh with tongue and lips and hands, finally slipping into her and beginning the wondrous pulsing that was pure pleasure.

Ecstasy claimed them as they thrust toward each other and passion exploded between them. Judith felt herself united with the coal black sky and the diamond stars she had viewed outside before they had met here, and then she reentered the physical universe and slowly, slowly descended back into her own body and became aware of her breathing, and Ivar's, where he was sprawled on top of her.

After a time, he stood and picked up his wine to take a sip. He brought her the cup and she sat up, leaning against the bolster at the head of the bed and accepted the cup, the liquid soothing her throat. When he settled himself beside her again, she spoke.

"This plan to invade Saxony," she said. "Is it not daring?"

"Indeed," said Ivar. "But Count Fulrich is right: We must show them our spines. Too long have we been involved in the bickerings of the kings. We must think of the Frankish kingdom."

"Then you do this without the king's knowledge?"

"He will know. We will advise him first. But if he decides to go against us, we will take our army and go to Saxony without him."

She turned on her side, her hair falling over her shoulder and breast. "Would he not then punish you for treason?"

"Not if we win," he said grimly. "For if we add to his lands, he cannot but reward us. If we lose, we will be dead. He cannot punish us then."

Judith sat up and drew on her undertunic, for even with the fire, there was a spring chill in the villa. "I fear something else," she said, returning to the bed and sitting next to him.

"What is that?" he said, running his finger along the material covering her thigh.

"The concubine Fredegund," she said.

His hand stopped, frowning, and then he moved his hand along her thigh again. "Why do you fear her?"

"I believe she killed a man and she might kill again." She told Ivar what she had seen the night Godulf died. As

192

she spoke, her words poured out faster, her urgency growing.

"She made love to him and then she killed him. Oh!" Her hands flew to her face and she gave Ivar a look of horror.

"What is it?"

"She is with Count Germanus now. What if she plans to murder him, too? Who can tell? She might be in the king's employ and out to murder his enemies by gaining their confidence first. It could be true. There was no investigation of Godulf's death. Might that be because the king wanted it?"

Ivar frowned. "It might be. You were right in telling no one. You only endanger yourself until you know the truth of the matter. But I think you need not worry about Count Germanus. I believe he can take care of himself."

Nevertheless Judith felt anxious. "If Germanus is dead in the morning, will you not feel responsible?"

Ivar grunted and grasped his breeches from off the floor. "What would you have me do? Spy on the poor man?"

She did not mean to tell him what to do, but she wrung her hands. "I only wish to know what Fredegund is about."

"Come on then," he said gruffly, "put on your clothes and we shall find out for ourselves."

She dressed hastily and followed him. Rather than putting on his boots, he slipped his feet into soft tanned leather shoes. She followed him out into the passage and instead of going toward the main arcade, they went to the rear of the wing and out onto the dirt behind the building. Luckily there had been no rain, so the ground was hard. Ivar led the way as silently as a bandit, and they stopped beside a small U-shaped window.

They peered into the window, and the sight they beheld made Judith blush. It was not unlike that which she had just been indulging in with Ivar with the difference that Fredegund lay sprawled on the bed, her legs hanging off the edge, while Germanus bent over her, his trousers lowered.

Judith knelt quickly out of view. Ivar hunkered down, but in a few moments they raised their heads again and Judith peered over the edge of the window. Luckily there was no moon to light their silhouettes as they did their spying.

Now Germanus lay on the bed, his eyes closed and Fredegund rose and dressed. But she completely ignored her lover and to Judith's surprise, quietly opened the door and left the room.

Judith ducked down again whispering to Ivar. "She's left."

He gestured with his chin for her to return the way they'd come. When they gained the passage that led to his chambers, he grunted softly. "No skullduggery there," he said. "We might as well get some sleep."

"I want to make sure," she said, not budging to reenter his bedchamber.

"Hmmmph. Have it your way. But I'm done with this business." He patted her buttocks, left her there and went to his bed.

She stood for a moment, then turned and hastened along to her own sleeping cubicle. Eulalia was asleep on the mat on the floor, and Judith quietly moved to her trunk so as not to wake her. She lifted the lid and then removed the dagger with its jeweled hilt and fastened it to her belt. Then she wrapped herself in her mantle and went out into the night again.

Just what she was waiting to see she did not exactly know, but she was too anxious to sleep. And when she saw Fredegund emerge from a door that must go to her bedchamber, she was glad she had come out. Though

Fredegund was now dressed in a dark cloak, the hood revealed her hair, and Judith was sure it was she.

Judith stood in the shadows of a pillar, watching Fredegund, who pulled the wooden door shut behind her and arranged her cloak, then glancing in both directions, she started across the yard. When she reached the other side she took a passage between buildings that Judith knew led to the stables. Hurrying quietly along, Judith reached the corner in time to see Fredegund cross the space that separated the stables from the living quarters of the villa.

Luckily, the drunken party from the banquet was by now either unconscious from the wine or were indulging in more lascivious pursuits, so no one was about to call out to either of the women lurking in the shadows of the stables. Judith kept near doors and carts that offered protection, and evidently Fredegund was not suspicious that she was being followed, for she never looked behind her.

Judith waited for a few moments, her racing blood warming her in the chilly night. Then she heard the sound of a foot scuffling in the dirt and drew back. A man crossed the yard in front of the stables, but as he came nearer, she saw that he had on peasant clothing. But she saw the long sword scabbard that protruded from underneath his plain woolen cloak. Another man entered the compound and Judith perceived that these were servants. Then when Fredegund led a horse into the yard she handed the reins to one of the men and they exchanged words Judith could not hear.

It appeared that they were preparing to leave. Growing more and more curious, Judith looked for a way she could move closer and hear what they were talking about. But it was too dangerous. Her own small knife would be no protection if Fredegund should order her servants to kill her. So she crouched where she was and watched as two more horses were saddled. Then they mounted and trotted out of the stable yard. Judith followed to watch them exit the main gate of the villa. Then they kicked their steeds and were off at a gallop. Where were they going in the middle of the night?

She stared after them for as long as she could make out their dark figures, which soon blended with the night. Then she shivered in the cold and hurried back to her sleeping cubicle, entering so as not to awaken Eulalia. She slipped out of her cloak and lay on her mattress, pulling the robes around her. Even the wine she had consumed earlier did not make her sleepy now. There were too many questions.

Where was Fredegund going? And what of the plan of the nobles to invade Saxony? What would Chilperic think? Clearly the nobles were gaining power as a group. For here were nobles who did not fear the Merovingian sacred blood. What would such a move mean for the monarchy? And what would it mean for Galswinth?

Fredegund and her servants rode through the night, stopping only once to rest for a few hours and to change horses. She had left her white horse at the villa so as not to attract the attention of robbers in the woods. Count Germanus knew that she had to return to the palace because she was still a serving woman to the queen, and her absence for more than two days would be noticed. He had enjoyed her favors and took pride in having slept with the king's former mistress. He had not thought it unusual that she had offered her favors, thinking that she was simply tired of the lowly position to which she had been relegated and sought to earn a few jewels and favors by granting a rich lord her favors. Germanus took advantage of the situation with alacrity.

But he did not understand her wily mind at all. She had

wormed her way into Germanus's confidence so that he would bring her to the meeting of the Neustrian lords. And now with the information she sought, she galloped as fast as she could to Chilperic.

Arriving late the next day, she refreshed herself before sending one of her trusted servants with a message for the king to take a ride in the woods behind the palace where she would be waiting for him. Chilperic got away as soon as his official business of the day had come to a close, relegating the last few petitioners to Epoald to dispense the king's justice for him. He rode out with his guards but bid them wait for him in a copse at the top of a ridge.

He guided his horse down a path to a protected fold in the hills at the bottom of which Fredegund waited. She stood flanked by a rock that almost looked cut in the shape of a throne, and Chilperic was at once aware of the interest her presence always aroused in him.

"I have information for you, sire," she said when he had dismounted.

"And what is that, Fredegund?" he asked, coming closer and seeing the fire in her eyes as she let her mantle fall open from the neck revealing her cream-colored tunic.

She wasted no words. "The counts of the palace, many of them, are plotting against you. They plan to present you with a plan to move against the Saxons."

"And if I do not agree to this plan?"

"They are going to move anyway."

He hissed through his teeth. "Who plots against me, Fredegund? Do you have names?"

"I do, sire."

Now she moved toward him, letting her hands drift to his cloak and find their way to his embroidered hunting shirt beneath.

His hands grasped her shoulders and his eyes took in

197

her lusty beauty. "And what do I need to do to pry this information from you?" he said, his guttural tone a sign of his willingness to play her game.

She smiled seductively. "It is I who desire to serve you, my lord."

"Ah, just as I hoped."

His mouth came down on hers and his hands groped inside her mantle. He wanted the names of the treasonable counts, but that could wait until he had satisfied himself with Fredegund, who met his lust with her own fire. Their clothing was quickly unfastened so that passion could be unleashed. Fredegund led him from one pleasure to the next so quickly his head throbbed and his body responded as he took her against the thronelike rock. Then he grunted and stretched himself on the rock.

"What more could a man want," said Chilperic, "than a mistress who helps him destroy his enemies?"

Encouraged by Chilperic's praise, Fredegund let her hand trail up his chest where his hunting shirt was unlaced.

"I could better serve you, my lord, if you raised me up in your household."

"But you forget, I cannot do that," he said, matching her coaxing tone. "I promised not to take an official concubine or any other wife when I married Galswinth."

"There is one way," she said, laughing slyly. "Galswinth herself can be disposed of."

"And?"

"Make me the queen."

Chapter Thirteen

After a day of hunting and another night of feasting, the nobles began to leave the demesne. Ivar's party got underway when the sun was high the next day. Ivar bid his father goodbye and Judith thanked him again for the exotic gift.

They made a strange-looking train led by Ivar and his guards. Next came Judith, then a cart on which rode the little cheetah in its cage, followed by another body of guards and the baggage cart.

Now they were out of the boundaries of the estate and passing through thick woods, broken here and there by peasant freeholdings. They approached a market town, and Judith saw to her horror that in a clearing a hanging was about to take place. The hanging tree was being hammered together, and the luckless victim was tied to a tree under guard.

One of Ivar's servants rode over to find out what the man had done and came back to report that he had stolen three horses. As the party rode on, Judith did not watch.

The town was bustling with trade. The center of the town was an elaborate church built for St. Denis. Market stalls were set up in front of the church's façade, and the party stopped to eat at an inn on the other side of the square. Judith was served at a small table by the fireplace as befitted a lady while the men ate trenchers of meat around a large trestle table.

Not until they resumed their journey did Judith have a chance to speak with Ivar again, but she did not bring up the subject of the Saxons, knowing that their words would be heard by the servants. Instead, they spoke of training the cheetah; Ivar promised to help her.

"It will grow up to be a fine hunter," he said confidently. "See how it plays. The streak of wildness will serve you well. She will master game as easily as she now plays with a stick. But we will see that she is subservient to her mistress."

Judith felt a sense of pride that she would be mistress of such an exotic beast and could not wait to show her new possession to Galswinth.

By the time they returned to court, preparations were underway to move the court to the royal villa on the Marne River. Judith rode some of the distance in the litter with Galswinth and told her of the hunt, but she did not say anything of the plot to battle with the Saxons. She would find out soon enough since the counts of the palace planned to present the idea to Chilperic as soon as the court was settled.

The fortress on the Marne River was circuited with towering walls and battlements into which the people could flee in times of danger. Like the other royal villas, surrounding it was the community of cooks, bakers, vineyard cultivators, ploughmen, spinners, slaves, and serfs engaged in every industry demanded by the royal household. Here the king and his lords hunted in the forest of Chelles, and Judith spent every day with Kahluli, feeding the little cheetah and accustoming it to her scent, voice, and touch. She led Kahluli by the chain and made her sit on her horse, for the cheetah must be used to horses if she were going to hunt with them. Black Lady seemed not to mind the little cat, only tossing her head and whinnying when Kahluli hissed. When the cheetah was big enough, Judith would let her go after small game at her command.

When a small traveling cart arrived one day with a young girl, Judith and Galswinth hardly took notice. The fourteen-year-old was housed in the women's quarters and it was only when the gossip reached their ears that they learned the girl was Fredegund's daughter.

Fredegund was living with Germanus openly and was no longer working in the kitchens. Judith kept a wary eye on her, instinctively not trusting her. But as long as she did not threaten Galswinth, Judith could do nothing.

The lords made their move on the day Chilperic summoned his supreme council. Though the king's word was absolute, the counts deliberated with him on all matters of state. They gathered in the royal hall where Chilperic was seated on a gem-encrusted gold and ivory throne, garbed officially in purple surcoat, emerald-studded girdle, and gold diadem. The lords were assembled before him. Count Fulrich spoke first.

"My lord," he began, coming to the center of the room directly in front of Chilperic. "We have reason to propose that your dispute with Sigibert might be better settled at a council in Paris with your brother Guntram and the bishop of Paris as mediators. A more pressing matter has come to our attention, which we wish to place before your royal sovereignty."

Chilperic eyed him craftily. This was what he had been waiting for. "Go on," he said.

"Raids along the coast from the Saxons occur almost daily. We must put an end to them once and for all."

"I see," said Chilperic. "But we have competent guards on our northern borders, and my dear brother, Sigibert, guards the eastern frontier. We need not fear the Saxons, who know our power well and would not dare to launch a real invasion into our territories."

Some of the nobles exchanged looks, and Chilperic observed them carefully. Thanks to Fredegund's information, he could play the devil's advocate.

Count Bertram spoke next. "Our armies need to fight if they are not to turn to sloth," he said. "We have had a year in which to see that our agents properly farm our lands. But we cannot raise the taxes on our people anymore. The burden is already great. It is time to gather in the spoils of war."

"Here, here," shouted several voices. As usual, talk of war raised their enthusiasm to the level where agreement was felt in the room, no matter what the king said.

Chilperic, too, was not averse to planning battles, but he was itching for a fight with his brother and it galled him that his counts had taken it upon themselves to plan a battle that they intended to carry out with or without him.

"And what of the troops I need in the Aquitaine? There is the matter of the city of Cahors to settle."

"The Aquitaine can take care of itself," said Lupus. "It is the Saxons we want."

The room exploded with interjections and war cries.

"Kill the Saxons . . ."

"Show them our might . . ."

Now was the time for Chilperic to exert his power. He raised his hand in a gesture for silence, and the shouts and grumbles ceased.

"I will decide when we will invade Saxony," he said, and now the power in his voice and his countenance gave them to understand that he was not ready to be swayed by their arguments. "Other border tribes need subduing. I will not waste men on a campaign that may do us no good."

The men withheld their grumbles, but their faces tensed. Fulrich glowered directly at the king but held his tongue. Chilperic rose and walked down from the dais to stand among them.

"And if I say there will be no invasion," he challenged them. "What then?"

No one spoke, but all felt the challenge. No one would openly contradict him. The men were itching for a fight. If Chilperic would not give it to them, how many of them would take matters into their own hands? A few who had at first been in agreement with the plot to invade Saxony with or without the king began to waver. The blood that had throbbed in the temples of the counts still throbbed, but a few who were truly awed by Chilperic's divine power became afraid to counter the determined gray-green eyes and the royal bearing. But not all. Fulrich and his followers were still determined. Still, no one would speak. Chilperic broke their silence.

"I have a witness," he thundered, "to your treachery."

The lords were stunned. None of them had informed any of their servants about the meeting, and they had carried it off successfully that they had gone to the count of Orléans's demesne to hunt. Who had betrayed them? Chilperic did not miss the hands that strayed to dagger hilts, ready to kill the traitor among them.

"I, who am heir to the omnipotent Roman emperors in the West, I, whose grandfather united the tribes of Gaul into one kingdom, I decide when and where we will invade."

His bellowing stunned them all into a meek silence. Not satisfied with that, Chilperic went on, hectoring them about Merovingian greatness.

"We, who after long wars and many wanderings came to settle in Gaul, crushed the other German leaders, showing their peoples our strength. Now the people of

Gaul know who is king. But because my father divided his kingdom as is our tradition, my brother, Sigibert, is a thorn in my side that must be dealt with."

"Why not add Saxony to your glory?" came one brave voice who dared to interrupt him.

Chilperic made his way to Count Munderic and stood nose to nose with him, a fierce expression on the royal face. "It is true that the Saxons are also a thorn, to be dealt with when I say so."

The counts seemed to have recovered themselves and remembered that their function was to advise the king. "The Saxons are not as mighty as they once were," said Bertram. "They will tremble before us."

"Perhaps," said Chilperic. Then he turned slowly, letting his gaze wander to every pair of eyes. "But I do not take counsel from treasonous lords."

In the silence Chilperic raised his imperial voice. "I accuse you all of treason, participants in a conspiracy to undermine the throne. Who here denies it?"

There was a moment's hesitation which gave Chilperic his answer, but then Fulrich, quick to understand that they must stand united shouted, "Innocent."

Other voices followed. "Innocent."

When they had all made their claim, Fulrich spoke again. "As your counselors, all our actions are meant to serve you, sire. When we fight, we fight for the glory of Neustria and to gain spoils for the royal treasury."

"Then all here deny treason?"

All answered at once to deny it.

Chilperic lowered his voice, but the covert knowledge he possessed gave it a chilling threat. "Then I have no choice. How do I know who is lying? My witness or my counsel. There is only one way to resolve this."

They all knew what he was coming to.

"Trial by combat," he said.

204

Fulrich spoke for the counts. "Then let us choose our champion. We will choose the best man among us."

"And the most innocent, I presume," said Chilperic with cynicism.

"Ivar of Orléans," came a voice to the side of the room. The others responded with enthusiasm, knowing Ivar to be one of the best fighters among them, though any of the men present still in their prime could have adequately represented them in combat.

"Who will he fight?" asked Fulrich, still curious as to who had betrayed them.

"I will produce a warrior for him. They will fight at dawn tomorrow. May God decide who speaks the truth."

He turned and exited the room, leaving them with their thoughts. He did not like to lose Ivar, but Fredegund had told him that Ivar had been present at the gathering. Indeed, she had named all those present. Chilperic would not, of course, produce Fredegund as his witness as then she would be known as his spy and she would never again be trusted with information. No, it was better for the court to believe that he still banished her. At least for the present.

But he was pleased with her, and he would soon keep his promise to elevate her status. She would make a very good queen; she was intelligent, resourceful, and unafraid of enemies. She already wielded power among several of the lords who did her bidding. And it rankled him that in order to gain their loyalty she had had to sleep with them. He wanted to possess her fruitful body for himself and as long as she served only in the capacity of spy, he could not keep her to himself. In very quick order he must rid the court of those who thought they could act without his blessing. Then he would make Fredegund queen.

As to thoughts of Galswinth, he had solved that dilemma. He would not openly set her aside because then he would have to return her dowry. But he would be able to turn a blind eye to any accident that befell Galswinth. He would not even have to bloody his own hands.

Quickly the news spread through the court, and when Mosella hurried into the chamber where the ladies were engaged in their needlework, she had to catch her breath before speaking.

"There is to be a trial by combat at dawn," she said, her eyes still wide and her cheeks tinged pink with the excitement of the news.

The women turned to look at her.

"Go on," said Galswinth.

"The counts of the palace were accused of high treason and they have selected their champion.

Judith's temples throbbed. The king knew of the meeting at Ivar's demesne. Mosella's next words proved it.

"Ivar of Orleans will fight for the counts."

Judith dropped her work and stood up, the silken threads and the linen tunic she had been working on falling to the floor. The other women began to talk excitedly.

"At dawn tomorrow," said Mosella.

"Who does he fight?" asked Adelais.

Mosella shook her head. "No one knows. The king has a witness, but he produced no one."

Judith thought she knew who the witness was, but she was not prepared to openly accuse her. Who would Fredegund choose to fight for her? Surely not one of the counts, for none of them would claim disloyalty to the king. And it was possible that none of them knew of her treachery.

And Judith could do nothing. She could not go to the king and tell him what he already knew. She would only be placing herself in danger. She had seen Fredegund and her servants depart. Where else but to return to the palace and inform the king? If they knew that Judith had seen her she would most likely be done away with.

Her hands trembled both for herself and Ivar, but she sat down again. All the women turned to look at her. She tried to moisten her lips. She knew she had to say something.

"My lord Ivar," she began, meeting the inquiring gazes of all the eyes upon her, "is a champion. I'm sure he will acquit himself and the counts with honor."

The women mumbled speculations and began to talk among themselves, but Judith felt she could no longer work. Galswinth met her gaze.

"Please excuse us," said the queen. "I wish to be alone with Judith."

The other women gathered their things and left the chamber, still whispering about who Ivar would fight. When they were gone, Judith set her own work aside and leaned against the back of the couch.

"You know something," said Galswinth, observing her friend.

"Yes," said Judith tonelessly.

"Tell me."

Judith tried to swallow, and seeing her distress Galswinth poured wine and handed the goblet to her.

After taking a sip, Judith continued. "There was a plot to invade Saxony, but not to go against Chilperic, rather to distract him from the business with Sigibert. But they have been found out."

Galswinth sighed. "Then they are guilty of treason."

"No," said Judith more in Ivar's defense than anyone else's. "It cannot be treason to advise the king as to what they think is right."

Galswinth shook her head. "I know Chilperic. If he,

207

himself, did not decide a matter and the counts did, then he will call it treason."

Judith went on. "It was Fredegund who informed him. I saw her leave the gathering."

She told Galswinth what had happened, feeling that now she must make sure Galswinth was on her guard. For Fredegund's actions could mean only one thing, that she wished to elevate herself in the eyes of the king. Judith did not want to hurt Galswinth's feelings, but it seemed that the queen was already prepared.

"I know," she said. "I have seen the way he looks at her when she passes in his vision and he thinks I do not see. Chilperic has little respect for me, I'm afraid," said Galswinth. "I'm afraid I disappointed him."

Judith trembled. "Surely you can regain his favors."

But Galswinth shook her head. "We are not cut of the same cloth. I have not produced new life within me. I think he will send me to a convent if I do not produce a child soon. He does not even come to my bed very frequently. I am not ignorant. I know where he goes instead."

Judith felt the dagger penetrate her own heart. But she could see that Galswinth did not love Chilperic and so the infidelity hurt her pride rather than her heart. Judith left the couch and went to sit on the hassock near Galswinth's chair.

"We cannot let Fredegund become a recognized concubine."

Galswinth looked at her friend as if she were an innocent child. "And how are we to prevent it?"

For the first time Judith thought in terms that those more experienced in palace intrigue would naturally consider. It was a surprise to think that she, who was raised in a convent, would contemplate taking another life. But her fear of Fredegund and her belief that she meant Galswinth harm drove her to place the matter above all other considerations. But of course she immediately restrained her thoughts. She could not place her own soul in such danger. She slumped her shoulders.

"I do not know. But I will think of something."

Galswinth touched her shoulder. "Do not think of me, my friend. Your protector fights in the morning; you must pray for his life to be spared."

"Yes, that is true."

She clasped Galswinth's hand for a moment and they looked deeply into each other's eyes.

"Go now," said Galswinth. "I wish to be alone."

Judith did not think she meant it, but Galswinth was giving her the opportunity to go. She stood, gave Galswinth one last look and left the chamber.

Her impulse was to go to Ivar, but he would not want to see her now, she was sure. He would be preparing himself for the coming confrontation. Tonight she would succor him in the only way she knew how. But she was no good to him in the light of day.

Instead, she went out to the animal compound and sought out Kahluli. The cat was growing. Already she was twice as big as when Ivar's father had given it to her. A lump rose in her throat. Supposing Ivar did not win the challenge tomorrow. The little cat would be all she had left to remind her of him.

But she mustn't think that. She took the cheetah from her cage, making sure the collar and chain were fastened. In a firm voice she ordered her to sit, pushing her rump to the ground as she had dozens of times. When Kahluli obeyed, she placed meat in front of her as a reward.

"Kahluli is good," she said. "Kahluli is good."

Judith saw Ivar in the distance, but did not approach him. He emerged from the blacksmith's shed, carrying his throwing axe, the blade of which gleamed as if it had just been sharpened. Later when she saw him riding out of the compound, his horse at a walk, she surmised that he was going to view the field on which he would fight tomorrow.

A chill passed along her spine as she watched him, but she turned away, telling herself that Ivar could take care of himself. Pewter clouds came from the west, and the air felt heavy. A vague foreboding accompanied her for the rest of the day. The palace was abuzz with speculation as to who Ivar would fight. Certain warriors were ruled out, those who had stood with Ivar claiming they were not guilty. Who then, would Fredegund produce as her champion? Judith had seen no one who seemed as strong or as brave as Ivar, and she began to sense that her premonition had nothing to do with tomorrow's challenge, but that something else loomed which would threaten them all.

She paced about the palace nervously, supped with Galswinth and sat in the chapel, unable to pray or meditate. Still, the fires, the incense, and the twinkling gems that adorned the cross and holy vessels on the altar helped soothe her. She wished Father Gregory were here to talk to and she considered writing to him. But what would she say? By the time he got her missive, the outcome of tomorrow's confrontation would already be known.

When the moon passed its zenith, she returned to the women's chamber where as she suspected a short but muscular slave with no hair on his chest waited to take her to Ivar. She quickly sprinkled rosewater over her neck and shoulders and followed the slave to Ivar's quarters. Judith entered the room where he was sprawled, fully dressed on the fur rugs atop his large bed.

"See to the fire," Ivar ordered the slave, "and then leave

us."

The slave threw another log on the fire, poked it with an iron, then exited the room.

Judith stood at the foot of the bed looking at her lover. He lounged against the cushions, his mantle still fastened but splaying about him as if he had just come in. She knelt at the foot of the bed and began to unlace the leather boots that came almost to his knees. After she had pulled off the boots, Ivar unfastened his mantle and pulled off his leather shirt. Then he beckoned for her to sit beside him. He drew her back against his chest and they gazed into the fire.

"You smell like roses," he said, sniffing the lobe of her ear and her throat.

"Oh, Ivar," she finally said, hugging the strong arms that encircled her waist. "You may be killed tomorrow."

"Ha. I doubt it."

She was relieved that he seemed so sure. "But it is a trial by combat."

"God will be on the side of right," he said.

"But . . ." His comment confused her, since the counts were lying about their conspiracy to go against Chilperic if he did not want to join them in their campaign in Saxony.

Ivar understood her question and answered it. "Whoever Fredegund picks to fight me will undoubtedly be guilty of a great many other crimes. The best man will win."

She could hear in his voice that he was certain it would be he. "I am glad then," she said.

He shifted her in his arms. "And if I die? What of you, my pet?" he asked in a teasing voice.

The unease that had haunted her earlier that day returned. "Do not say that, my lord."

Her expression was grim. She was afraid for him and

yet not afraid, but she could not voice her thoughts.

He kissed her and then helped her remove her clothing so they could lose themselves in the sensations and fulfillment of desire. Ivar's lovemaking was even more urgent as if he, too, sensed a coming danger that might separate them. He seemed to want to taste every last part of her so that he might remember it when he went to Valhalla, which equated to the Christian heaven in Ivar's mind.

Judith tried to drown herself in their passion, and later as she lay snuggled against his strong back amid the fur rugs, she tried to push the threat of nagging evil from the corner of her mind where it lurked. She prayed then. After tomorrow, she would try to face the coming dangers with fortitude, but first, Ivar must live. He must beat his opponent tomorrow and prove to God and to Chilperic that he stood for right.

Chapter Fourteen

Dawn saw Ivar standing on a slight rise of ground, wind ruffling his shoulder-length blond hair, his arms crossed, feet spread a slight distance in front of his pile of weapons. A shirt of mail covered his leather tunic, and the gems on his wide metal-studded belt gleamed like the morning dew. Muscles in arms and legs flexed as he waited.

His round leather-covered wooden shield rested against a boulder that protruded from the ground. His insignia emblazoned the center of the shield in bronze, the edges of which were reinforced with a rim of bronze. Against the shield rested a bronze-emblazoned scabbard. It, too, was shaped from strips of wood, covered with leather and lined with greased sheepskin to protect the sword blade from rust.

The sword hilt was fashioned from silver, the cross guard richly scrolled in gilded bronze. Beside the sword lay the throwing axe with its wicked blade and carved wooden handle and the deadly scramasax, the heavy, double-edged dagger hidden in a wooden scabbard, the cloisonné motif masking its power. Only the curved hilt lay ready to fly into the owner's hand.

Standing with the onlookers, Judith fingered her talisman for luck, her numb state telling her that she was about to witness a fight to the death.

Now the opponent marched onto the field and a murmur went through the crowd. The man was well known in Neustrian circles, none other than Count Beppolenus, a gallant fighter who had raised a valiant army to fight for Chilperic against Brittany. He was a tall, strong man ten years Ivar's senior, but more experienced. The crowd murmured as dark eyes took them all in. It had been some time since Beppolenus had been seen at court. But Germanus's money had brought him today to fight for the accuser. Now he was in Fredegund's league, having agreed to champion her.

He carried similar arms to Ivar's onto the field. Then both men slowly fastened weapons to their belts, each taking the other's measure. Ivar's eyes blazed across the distance, gleaming eyes, blue as the cloudless sky above his head. Judith watched as Ivar picked up his helmet of bronze and placed it on his head, strapping it next to the cheek guards. The wind touched the hair that hung below the helmet, and when he rose and faced the other man who was still thirty meters away, he seemed bigger, stronger, almost like a god. He lifted the metal-studded baldric over his head so that it crossed his chest. From it now hung his sword.

And when he drew his sword from the scabbard, it sang. The blade came out, the point tapping the metal mouthband of the scabbard, and the ring carried to the ears of the crowd gathered to watch the trial.

Chilperic raised a hand and faced the court. He called in a lordly voice. "Two champions meet here on this day to settle the matter of the counts of the palace and the king of Neustria. With God as witness, innocence will be proclaimed. Wrong shall be avenged. He who is guilty of treason will be hung. But he who proves in the eyes of God and these witnesses his fidelity to the king shall walk with grace."

He paused and turned to eye the crowd in that unique way he had of letting his gaze rest on every pair of eyes there, as if he were speaking to that individual alone out of all the crowd. Then he turned back to face the warriors.

"To the death," he bellowed.

The warriors approached each other, swords drawn. Ivar looked into his opponent's face, his sword raised as in a salute. Then with a roar from their throats they fell on each other. The swords clashed and met with the leather, bronze and the wood of the shields. They withdrew and thrust again, and again. They circled, and as Beppolenus drew his sword arm back a longer distance than his opponent, Ivar's sword hewed at his sword arm. His blade slid off Beppolenus's and sliced his arm. The wound did not stop him, but blood spewed from the arm.

Ivar jumped away just as Beppolenus's sword sliced the air by his neck, but he nimbly retained his footing and squatted, thrusting up and under Beppolenus's shield. With a grunt, Beppolenus backed away and then charged again, falling on Ivar so that arms, shields, swords were tangled in the press. Then Beppolenus ran his sword blade along Ivar's arm, gaining the advantage and forcing the sword out of his hand. The sword landed on the ground, but the scramasax flashed from its scabbard and thrust in between Beppolenus and his shield and a great howl followed the wound under his arm where the mail left him uncovered. Ivar sprang away.

Beppolenus's other arm flew up to hold off Ivar, and he dropped the sword grasping his own scramasax for the close fighting. He got to his feet. The champions were well matched and though blood flowed, shields and deft moves protected their most vital parts. Then they came apart, but wasting no time they fell on each other again.

With every blow Judith absorbed the power of the thrusts herself as she stood next to Galswinth, who was seated in a carved wooden chair, squeezing the back of the chair until her hands bled from the splinters.

The warriors parried and thrust, sometimes backing off, picking up the swords again. Metal clanged on helmets, the rims of the shields. Metal met metal as the swords crossed each other. And then Beppolenus's response was slow enough that Ivar sliced through to his opponent's hip. But Beppolenus retaliated with a cut to Ivar's leg. A grunt was all he emitted.

Judith turned, thinking she could not stand it any longer, but the desire to know if her lover lived or died was strong, and she faced the battle once again. The two men had separated, and Ivar was on his knees, but now he reached for his throwing axe, and Judith held her breath as his arm swung over his head and his hand let loose. The terrible axe flew across the distance as swift as Beppolenus raised his shield to meet it, but his arm had been weakened and the axe grazed off the rim of the shield and fell against the cheek guard, not without leaving behind a slit in the skin of his neck.

The crowd gasped, for such a cut could be fatal. Beppolenus staggered, but he did not fall. Ivar, too, was bleeding from several wounds and took the opportunity to rekindle his strength.

Out came Beppolenus's throwing axe, but his throw was heavy and the axe hit the ground where Ivar stepped to the side. Both men were worn from the blows, but they staggered to their feet. With a shout Ivar rushed his opponent, sword outstretched. Beppolenus lifted a spear to descend on him, but Ivar was too quick. With the hilt of his sword he knocked the shield aside, then the tip caught Beppolenus beneath the chin and continued through his throat. With a gurgling sound, Beppolenus walked backward as blood spewed from his throat. Then he spun and fell to the ground, dead.

Ivar lowered both sword and shield and stared at his opponent, his own blood running down his tunic and legs, matting his hair under the helmet. For an instant no one breathed. Then Epoald walked to the field, knelt and rolled Beppolenus over. Staring eyes followed the soul that had taken flight upon the instant of death.

Epoald stood and faced the king and queen. "Count Beppolenus is dead, my lord. Count Ivar lives. Let the accusations be dismissed."

Chilperic nodded his head and raised his hand. "So be it."

The crowd cheered and took to the field. Judith sank to her knees next to Galswinth. Then the nobles picked up Ivar and carried him on their shoulders, cheering their champion.

"The counts are vindicated," said Galswinth. "And Ivar is safe."

Judith caught a glimpse of the menace in Fredegund's eyes as they stared at her fallen hero. The venom in her eyes reached to Ivar as he was carried from the field amid adulation. Then she turned her stony stare to the queen and to Judith kneeling before her. In that moment Judith felt her hate and felt the threat that emanated from her. She was still the king's spy, no doubt. But God had been on the side of her enemies.

In spite of the outcome of the trial by combat, Chilperic did not banish Fredegund from court. He took to sleeping with her regularly and no longer visited Galswinth's bed. He was only in the queen's presence on public occasions, preferring Fredegund's pleasures and allowing himself to be persuaded by her reasoning. He did not think she lied about the affair of the counts of the palace, there was simply nothing more he could do.

Fredegund now dressed in finery befitting a concubine. She went where she pleased in the palace and openly snubbed the queen. No longer did she act as serving woman. Chilperic had not proclaimed her his royal mistress, but everyone knew it was so. And her daughter Rigunth was courted by several nobles, thinking that the king would most likely dower her since her mother was in unofficial favor.

But it was the ambassador from King Sigibert who rode in with a small escort at top speed that changed all their lives. Count Marcus Petronius came with an urgent message for King Chilperic. He had ridden with little rest for three days, for the Austrasian court was at Metz. Before that he had led an army against the Saxons who had crossed the Rhine.

Arriving in the courtyard of the villa, Marcus and his guard dismounted. Stable boys ran to take the horses. Others passing across the courtyard stopped to speak to the Austrasians. When it became known that the ambassador was here, Epoald came out to stand on the steps to greet him.

Marcus halted when he saw Epoald and, sweeping aside his traveling cloak, he bowed. "I come from the court of King Sigibert bearing urgent news for King Chilperic."

Though the shadows under his eyes showed that he had had little sleep, determination showed in his face. Mud had spattered the hem of his cloak, his leather shoes, and his leggings. But his aristocratic bearing and the command in his voice revealed the importance of his office.

"In the name of the king, you are welcome," said Epoald, his eyes sweeping Count Petronius cautiously. "The king is in counsel but I will inform him of your arrival since your appearance bears witness to a matter of great importance. There was no messenger to announce a

218

formal deputation from Austrasia, thus no formal welcome was prepared."

"There was not time," said Marcus.

Then he reached into a pouch fastened to his belt and withdrew a scroll. On it was Sigibert's seal. He handed the scroll to Epoald.

"If you will give this to your king, I am sure he will want to see me at once."

The gold flecks in his eyes flashed in the sun, and though he spoke with the deference due the king's right arm, his own breeding gave him a superior command of tone, and the importance of his mission made him impatient. However, he would have to wait for the formality upon which he knew the mayor of the palace would insist.

Epoald took the scroll and gestured toward the doors. "Follow me. I will see that you are accommodated so that you can prepare yourself for your meeting with the king. And your men will receive adequate quarters."

Marcus glanced over his shoulder at his stouthearted vassals, men of courage who had also fought in the recent campaign with the Saxons and who held personal bonds of loyalty to Marcus.

The delegation followed Epoald into the palace and along the shadowy corridors to an inner garden. Epoald sent slaves scurrying ahead of them to prepare quarters where the men could refresh themselves. He showed Marcus his chamber and then nodded, the missive for Chilperic in his hand.

"I will hand this to the king directly."

"Do that," Marcus said. "I will be ready to see him in a half hour."

Servants followed with saddlebags containing everything Marcus needed to make a presentable appearance. For traveling over the roads, he did not wear his gold-embroidered tunic or jeweled girdle. But after washing from the ewer and bowl of water placed at his disposal, a servant helped him into a change of clothing. With his short-cropped copper hair brushed clean, and the travel grime washed from his extremities, his noble bearing was even more apparent. When Epoald came to fetch him, he was ready.

As the two men walked along the arched passage to the royal chamber, Frankish nobles stepped aside and stared at them as they passed. Even those who did not know Marcus recognized by his dress that he had come from one of the royal courts. A group of ladies to the queen paused in their conversation, and he glanced over them. A recollection of the girl he had spoken to at Chilperic's marriage came briefly to mind. But he did not see her, and the thought left his mind quickly.

Chilperic was seated on a chair of gilded bronze set with jewels. Some of his nobles were seated on the steps of the dais, others stood in groups. All stopped talking as Epoald opened the doors and announced, "Count Marcus Petronius, Ambassador from King Sigibert of Austrasia."

Marcus swept his deep blue mantle aside and bowed low.

"Come forward, Count Petronius," said Chilperic. "I have read this missive from my brother concerning the Saxons who have invaded your lands. Tell me what my brother wishes."

Marcus rose and met Chilperic's gaze. His sharp brown eyes also took in the nobles who stood around the chamber, for these men were Chilperic's advisors and needed to hear what he had to say.

"My lord," he said, addressing the king. "It is true, the Saxons have laid waste as far as the city of Liège. Not only have they raided from the sea on the shores of both our kingdoms for the last two summers, but now they have determined to reclaim some of the land taken from them when Clovis consolidated Gaul under his rule eighty years ago.

"As warriors the Saxons are fierce, and they still live like tribes, not content to clear more of their own land, but preferring the already cultivated lands we have fought to tame. They are more interested in plunder than in conquest, but even if they should retreat they will leave our land desecrated, our women raped and dead, our children taken slaves or killed. Even now they scatter through the villas between Liège and the Rhine, seizing booty and wreaking great destruction.

"And there are more of them. Pushed from behind by Slavic tribes who live on the edge of the Baltic Sea, the Saxons think it easier to cross our borders and ravage our lands. Already a threat along the shores of the sea to the north of both our lands, they threaten to cripple our kingdom unless they are stopped. Not satisfied with the border they agreed to in our treaty with them, they have already pushed as far as the Rhine and only with great effort have our own armies stopped them there. But not for long, I am afraid."

"I see," said Chilperic, rubbing his chin. "And how is this my problem? True, the Saxon pirates on our coasts are a menace, and my nobles," he cast a sidelong glance, "have a great desire to retaliate." He spoke with irony of the matter just settled. "But are my brother's armies so weak that he cannot hold back the Saxon threat? Why does he come to me?"

Marcus was ready for Chilperic's goading. "My lord, King Sigibert did not think you would relish having the Saxons for neighbors."

The lords in the hall shifted weight and vocalized their thoughts; this was the very issue for which they had all nearly been executed for treason. But Chilperic held up a hand. If he were to fight the Saxons, he would decide in his own time.

Marcus took advantage of the discussion to press the point. "Certainly you are aware of the consequences. A united front will break the Saxon aggressions once and for all. Push them back across their marches, and a share in any booty acquired from them."

Chilperic grunted. "Hardly booty worth raising an army for. Their metals are no better than ours, and the huts they live in are not worth looting."

"Surely my lord, King, you will not sit by and let the Saxons encroach on Frankish land no matter which kingdom," said Germanus. Mutters of agreement followed.

"True," said Chilperic, who had decided he had made his point long enough. "My counsel had already advised me on this matter. You may tell Sigibert that I do not wish to have Saxons for neighbors. We can have our armies ready to march in three weeks' time."

Chilperic rose from the dais and walked the side of the room where a map of Gaul had been drawn on a large sheet of parchment. He picked up an ivory pointer and stabbed the map. "We will cross into my brother's territory here and rendezvous here," he said.

Marcus memorized the spots. It would be important for the populace of the towns through which Chilperic's army would pass to know that they came as allies and not as foes.

"Very well," said Marcus. "Then it would be wise to spend time now on strategy. I am empowered by King Sigibert to relay to you what his generals have gleaned about Saxon movements and see if your generals agree."

The nobles had gathered around the table and all listened to what Marcus outlined. They saw that Sigibert's ambassador well understood the best way to rout the Saxons and as they listened to what he outlined they were

222

mostly in agreement. Marcus traced the Saxons' depredations, recalling in his mind the slaughter he himself had witnessed. Though his own army had fought valiantly, they were outnumbered. For every Saxon felled, another came behind to replace him, until the field was left strewn with bodies and shields.

"The outcome was a draw," said Marcus to the men gathered about him as he spoke of the battle he had just fought. "The numbers dead on both sides were legion. But our information is that the Saxons will regroup and attack our weakest points here and here." His finger indicated vulnerable spots on the map where the Rhine spread out in a wide delta.

"Any farther south and the hills form an impenetrable barrier."

Ivar, whose wounds were healing, stared at the map, seeing not lines and dots nor fingers pointing with an ivory stick, but men, his army formed for battle and the line of Saxons they would confront.

"Why do they muster their forces here?" he asked Marcus. "Why not follow the rivers into Burgundy and maraud there as well?" It was best to outthink the enemy and to consider all moves he might possibly make.

"If it is booty they want," answered Marcus, "then the cities of Austrasia hold more attraction for them. But your point is well taken, Count Ivar. For King Guntram has also agreed to send forces to encounter the Saxons."

"Then we shall have a grand army," said Fulrich. "Fit and ready to meet any contingent of those ruthless pagans."

With the plans conceded, the nobles gave way to boisterous enthusiasm.

A banquet was given for the Austrasian embassage and

to celebrate the joining of forces for the coming campaign. The nobles were in high spirits, for they were to get their fight at last. In the women's quarters Judith prepared for the banquet, then went to join Galswinth who was arrayed in all her queenly finery. Except that her pallor gave away her misgivings. Even before she and her ladies entered the banqueting hall, she seemed to know that she would not be the most radiant woman there.

The nobles converged at the long banquet tables and it was not until Chilperic led Galswinth in and they sat in their chairs at the high table that Judith saw Marcus. She blinked in remembrance, her mind reeling back to their meeting at the wedding feast.

He was dressed in a cream-colored tunic with gold-embroidered trim at the edges of the sleeves and borders. A dark blue mantle was fastened over his right shoulder with a large cloisonné pin of red, blue, and green pieces of ivory. But it was his face and bearing that she noticed most. She remembered the tanned complexion; he was darker than the blond Franks she had been living with these many months, and his hair was cropped closer, curled around his ears in a copper color that reflected his dark, alert eyes. She wondered suddenly if he remembered her.

Then her attention was drawn to Fredegund who entered the hall. Eyes turned to her for a moment and the hubbub subsided. She put on a close-lipped smile and turned to the high table, bowing to the king and queen. But her action gave the lie to her haughty demeanor. She turned from the head table and walked to the bottom of one of the banqueting tables. Count Germanus poured her wine.

Judith felt the serpent crawl up her spine. She could almost read everyone's thoughts so clear were they as they all gazed at the voluptuous, richly clad and jeweled Fredegund. No longer kitchen slave, this was the king's mistress. When Judith glanced up at Galswinth, seated by her husband, her dark eyes looked like glass, staring at the crowd before her, but seeing no one.

And then the platters of food were brought in and the nobles and ladies fell to. From time to time, Judith glanced toward the high table and noticed Marcus engaged in conversation with Epoald or with Chilperic. At another table Marcus's delegation had their heads lowered in talk with many of the counts of the palace, Ivar among them. The talk that flowed along with the wine was of the coming campaign.

Judith also had a clear view of Fredegund and did not mistake the smugness of her expression. The fear that lay in Judith's breast seemed to grow as the feasting became louder and more excessive. Though she drank a full goblet of wine, she could not bring herself to participate in the celebratory mood. The other women flirted with the men, some of whom rose from their seats to come and grasp the women, hoisting them onto their laps and slathering their affections over them. In many ways the Franks were still the barbarians their forefathers had been no matter how much they thought they had taken from Rome.

Judith rose and slipped out of the hall. Her green linen mantle was enough cover for the cool spring night and she drank in the air along the balcony that overlooked the courtyard below. How many times had she left feasts such as this one and walked in the night air to seek . . . what?

"A woman of the mist, I see."

His words startled her and she turned to see Marcus Petronius also standing by the scrolled balcony railing but farther down the arcaded passage than she was. There was a fine mist and so his figure appeared hazy from this distance as hers must have appeared to him.

"You startled me," she said as both moved. Then she relaxed her limbs. She still could not tell if he were merely being polite or if he remembered their similar encounter on the portico of the palace when Galswinth celebrated her wedding to Chilperic.

But in a moment he registered her features and a smile lit his lips. Here was the woman he had wondered about. For he did indeed recall their talk that day he had been in Neustria before. A very different mission, that from this.

"And are you now more accustomed to life in the Neustrian court than that of the abbey?" he asked, his gaze taking in green mantle, white tunic, silver girdle, and gold necklaces. He particularly noticed the engraved symbol of the talisman she wore between the folds of her breasts.

Seeing his gaze drop to the talisman, she self-consciously fingered it. "I'm not sure life at a Merovingian court is something one can easily become accustomed to," she said candidly.

He understood the irony. Though she was not Gallo-Roman, her upbringing in the abbey had instilled in her a gentler, more cultured bearing than many of the Franks she must have to rub shoulders with.

Perhaps it was Gallo-Roman adaptability or a feeling of superiority over their conquerors that had enabled them to come to terms with the Franks who had overthrown Roman domination. It was the Gallo-Romans who already had skills of office so that not only the Catholic church, but the administrative structure still existed here like the ghost of the Roman empire.

And looking at Judith, Marcus sensed that she was more akin to his people than to the Franks she served. About her own tribe, the Visigoths, he knew very little, never having crossed the Pyrenees into Gothic Spain.

"Something seems to worry you." he said, seeing the trouble on her brow. "Do you fear the coming confrontation with the Saxons?"

She frowned. "I . . . do not know the dangers that lie ahead on the battlefield, but I fear . . . something."

His natural instinct to protect a lovely woman in distress rose up in his breast. "And what is that?" He spoke in a low voice as if already understanding that whatever it was, she did not want it overheard by the wrong ears.

She looked into the brown eyes, the gold flecks she remembered from before now seeming tinged with silver, more like pieces of the moonbeams that tried to penetrate the soft mist.

"Did you notice the handsome blond woman dressed in the lavender and gold tunic who bowed so formally to the king and queen when she entered the hall?"

There had been many people in the hall, but Marcus thought he remembered of whom Judith spoke. "I believe so. Yes, I remember now."

Judith turned and faced outward, placing her hands on the stone railing. "She is the king's mistress."

Dark eyebrows shot up. "This is indeed a piece of information to be reckoned with. Chilperic swore in his marriage agreement to put aside all concubines and former wives."

Judith knew that whatever she said to Marcus would reach King Sigibert's ears. And Sigibert was married to Galswinth's sister, Brunhild. But even so, she felt helpless. What could Sigibert do about Fredegund? Especially now that he was about to unite with Chilperic in war.

"He has not formally declared Fredegund his mistress, but everyone knows she is. He seldom visits Galswinth's bed, and she has not conceived."

Marcus appreciated the gravity of the situation. But in the next moment he sighed in exasperation. Domestic business of the kings was no business of his.

"Why does she not return to her father's kingdom?" he asked impatiently.

"Perhaps she will have to. But she knows that Chilperic will never let her dowry go with her if she goes voluntarily. She will face disgrace."

"Chilperic sought to emulate his brother in acquiring an educated and virtuous queen," Marcus grumbled sourly. "It seems to have done him little good."

Judith took a deep breath. "Perhaps she could travel to be with her sister. Perhaps she would be safer there."

Marcus's brow furrowed further. He did not wish to take the responsibility of bringing one queen to visit the other.

"I would like nothing more than to oblige your queen," he said smoothly. "But such a move might set Chilperic against his brother and start them fighting again. It has taken all my negotiating skills to get them to join together to repel the Saxons. Domestic crises must wait."

Judith tried to swallow the hurt that she felt at his considering the queen's plight too petty to deal with. She lifted her chin and said, "I would not want to endanger the alliance."

There seeming to be no more they could say on the subject and no more advice Marcus was willing to offer, Judith's thoughts turned to the coming campaign.

"And will you lead an army against the Saxons as well?" she asked him.

"I already have," he said, grasping the railing with his hands and leaning against it. "They are a force to be reckoned with."

"But surely the combined forces of the Franks will outnumber them?"

He shook his head. "I do not know. No one knows how large their forces are. A few have volunteered to go ahead of the armies to spy on them and ascertain their positions and their numbers. Six men, two from each of the kingdoms. Your Count Lupus and Count Ivar have volunteered for the mission."

Judith drew breath, her eyes rounded. "Ivar? He said nothing."

Marcus turned his head to study her. Her half-open lips and widened eyes gave her away. His eyebrows lifted slowly. "You know him?"

She stumbled in her words, embarrassment filling her, and she fingered the talisman and looked away. "Yes," she said.

Marcus turned and leaned on one elbow. With the other hand he took the round, flat medallion with the engraved symbol from her hand and examined the fine workmanship.

"This?" he asked, the intention in his voice making her look at him.

She nodded, but said nothing, then looked down. The blood pumped through her veins and she felt a warm flush creep over her face.

Marcus held the talisman in his hand for a long moment, rubbing the side of it with his thumb, watching the warmth creep over her face. So, she had found a protector in this court after all. He noticed the rise and fall of her breasts, her rapid breathing and the flutter of her lashes on downcast eyes. Then slowly he replaced the talisman against her breast. He could not say that he blamed her. Still, the revelation that she was not an innocent anymore made him look at her with new eyes. Fresh from the convent this Count Ivar had taken her. How had that felt?

Marcus straightened and moved away imperceptibly. Another man claimed this girl who he had been talking to so casually. The irony struck him and only now did he realize fully how he had perceived her. Her culture and her fine intellect and conversation made him see her as a woman of his equal.

"Hmm," he grunted in expostulation, more to himself than to her. Then he sought words to cover his feelings. "This Count Ivar must be a brave man with many war honors."

Judith, too, struggled for words. "Yes . . . I believe he is . . . He just proved himself in a trial by combat against an accusation that the counts of the palace plotted treason against the king."

"Ah," said Marcus. "I see. Then he must be a man to be reckoned with."

Judith still had not gotten her own emotions under control. She felt tongue-tied talking about Ivar, embarrassed, as if Marcus could see her innermost secrets. And yet she also felt angry for losing her composure. Was she not proud of Ivar, grateful that he was her protector? Did she not worry for him when he went into battle even though she had seen with her own eyes how he could acquit himself?

And yet looking at the tall, broad-shouldered, refined Marcus Petronius standing beside her she was filled with confusion. When she had met him those many months ago, she had thought that she would like such a man for a friend. For she, too, recognized in him qualities of something she could not put words to.

His intellect was fine, his gestures noble. She struggled against the truth of what she felt, that he rang a chord in her heart, a chord of identity and recognition. She had rued that he had not stayed at the Neustrian court, and after tonight he would not stay this time either, and she did not like the regret she felt about his leaving.

As if both were too uncomfortable to stand still, they began to walk along the colonnaded balcony, away from the banqueting hall. Oil lamps in stone sconces sputtered against the mist. Some had burned out.

"I believe Chilperic plans to move Galswinth to Poitiers

230

before he leaves on the campaign. He must wish to get the queen and her entourage as far from the skirmishes as possible."

"Poitiers? I had no idea," said Judith.

Then he remembered that was where she had lived at the abbey. He gave her a half smile. "Perhaps you will have the opportunity to pay your respects to the nuns who kept you."

Judith sighed. "Yes. I would like to see them."

She wondered though if there would be any comfort in it. And she felt miffed that Marcus had so easily dismissed her suggestion to take Galswinth to her sister.

When they stopped walking near the passage that would take her to the women's chambers, she hugged herself beneath her mantle.

"I must go," she said. It seemed pointless to speak to him any longer.

And yet they stood looking at each other, dissatisfaction with the moment tantamount in both their minds. Finally Marcus pulled back his lips in his most ambassadorlike expression, swept his mantle aside and bowed to her.

"I am sorry I cannot render you the service you ask of me," he said. And then he rose, his eyes penetrating hers. "But perhaps there will be an opportunity for me to serve your queen at another time."

She gave a little movement of the chin. Then he turned, the mantle flowing behind him as he strode back the way they had come, the mist swallowing him before he turned the corner, out of view.

Chapter Fifteen

The counts returned to their cantons to raise their armies. Most had no trouble, for the men who were beholden to them rallied to fight. Most were fighting men who had seen other campaigns with their lords and had some sense of unity. Along the way they picked up other farmers, tenants, proprietors, and paupers alike. Even those who murmured discontent dared not refuse. Franks and native Gallo-Romans marched under the nobles who tried to organize them into a fighting army.

From every corner of Neustria the armies converged toward the rendezvous points where they entered Austrasia. Many of the rabble had to be forcefully kept from pillaging and looting along the way. They had fought the Austrasians so many times it was hard to get through thick skulls that they were now allies.

Now that the weather was warmer, the rivers ran full from spring rains. The armies trampled through forests and fields, avoiding cities where it would be harder to keep the men under control. Within the appointed time, they gathered on the heath east of the walled town of Liège, near where the river Meuse turned east to flow toward the North Sea. Each count and his followers found a place within the encampment where there was time to sharpen weapons and polish blades with fleece lanolin. A motley lot they appeared to be. Only the wealthier possessed shirts of mail, helmets, body armor, and horses. The rest came with spears, throwing axes, sword or dagger. And most would fight bare-chested and on foot.

When the two armies were gathered, the two kings met with their generals. Chilperic pushed aside the canvas flap of his brother's royal tent and strode in. Sigibert sat in a carved chair behind a table on which was a map similar to the one on which the Neustrians had plotted out their strategy.

"So, brother," said Chilperic. "We have done as you wished. I have brought every able-bodied man with me to repel the Saxon menace. I hope it is as your ambassador says. That the Saxons themselves have been hording gold from their raids and that we will not only repel them but break their ranks so our men can earn their booty."

Sigibert stood, his long hair falling over shoulders covered in rings of mail sewn to sturdy shirts, for both kings were dressed as were their generals in the field. Only his gem-encrusted belt and inlaid armor showed that he was king. He had similar features to Chilperic though his eyes were darker and his look more direct.

"Do not fear, brother," answered the Austrasian sovereign. "With our three armies, we shall take care of the Saxons once and for all."

"Ah yes, where is our brother, Guntram?" asked Chilperic, looking around as if he really expected to find him there.

"He has sent word. Already several of his generals are encamped."

Chilperic and Sigibert sat, while the rest of their generals remained standing.

"Very well then," said Chilperic. "Tell me your strategy."

Sigibert accepted a goblet of wine handed him by his steward who likewise poured one for Chilperic.

"The Saxons have been trying to lodge themselves between the Rhine and the Meuse. But their movements are hard to pin down. Now that you are here we can send the scouts. No doubt they will give us a more accurate report than the hearsay that travels from mouth to mouth along the roads where gossip goes faster than a courier on horseback."

"My scouts are ready."

"As are mine and Guntram's, though our dear brother has lagged behind in Dijon. He sent his best general, as it is not his practice to lead his armies into battle."

"As we both know. Very well. My scouts are Count Ivar and Count Lupus. Both men have proven themselves for cunning and courage."

Ivar stepped forward as did Lupus. Then two men stepped out from the ranks of Austrasian nobles standing against the canvas walls of the tent.

"Good," said Sigibert, signaling for more wine. "Then they will be a good match for my two."

He gestured at the two warriors who crossed their arms across their chests. Sigibert's scouts were tall, and like Ivar had long fair hair and moustaches. Muscles bulged from their short-sleeved, fur-vested tunics, and polished weapons were slung from their belts.

"Are they rested?" asked Chilperic.

"They are. And their saddle pouches are full of provisions."

"Then after my men get a few hours sleep, they shall start for the Saxon marches."

"Agreed," said Sigibert.

A contingent of guards were left to escort the queen

and her retinue to Poitiers. They kept on the old Roman roads, which were in good enough repair to travel on. Here and there the surface paving blocks or cobbles had eroded through, in which case the chariot in which Galswinth and Judith rode lurched forward. Curses followed during which the escort ordered the strong slaves who traveled with them to extricate the wheel.

They passed by thick forests, but any brigands who lurked there were dissuaded from attacking the train, so large and so well armed was the guard. They spent the nights at monasteries and abbeys as well as the villas of wealthy Gallo-Romans who were prepared to entertain royalty.

At Tours, they were welcomed by Judith's friend, Father Gregory, who was now thirty-three years old. His background, family connections, and education had prepared him to move up to a high position in the church when the time was right. And during the years he had served as deacon, he had received training invaluable to his career. One day, he hoped to become bishop.

Now he hastened up the steps of the royal villa where the queen and her retinue were ensconced. There were fewer men about, most having gone with Chilperic for the campaign to the northeast. But he gave his name to Epoald, who he recognized. The short, stocky mayor of the palace bowed, and servants opened the doors to a chamber where Gregory was to wait for the queen.

Gregory waited in the sunny, whitewashed room with mosaic floor. A further door opened onto a garden, and the scent of lilacs and roses drifted in. In a few moments Galswinth entered, flanked by Judith and Clothild.

"Father Gregory," she said. "How nice to see you again."

Gregory turned and bowed low.

"Thank you, my lady. I sincerely hope that if I can

serve you in any way while you are at Tours, you will not hesitate to ask."

"I am always glad to have the opportunity for such spiritual solace as those like yourself can offer. I will take advantage of asking you to hear my confession."

"Of course." He bowed his head with dignity. "I will hear your confession at your convenience."

"Good. And my companion, Judith, has been looking forward to renewing her acquaintance with you, Father Gregory."

Judith moved forward and knelt to be blessed. Then she smiled at Gregory as he assisted her to her feet.

Galswinth knew that Judith wanted a word alone with Gregory and she now came forward again. "Perhaps you would like a private word with my companion. My ladies and I will visit your church tomorrow, bringing with us offerings to see to its sustenance and to your good works."

"You are very generous, madam."

Galswinth left, followed by Clothild, leaving Judith with Gregory, who she felt was an old friend, though they had only met twice. Something in their natures made them seem like kindred spirits in spite of his clerical trappings.

"It is good to see you again, my dear," said Gregory.

A servant entered and offered them goblets of wine. Gregory took his and sipped it while Judith took hers. "You look healthy and if I might be so bold, not unduly anxious. The last time I spoke to you, you were not feeling easy. Tell me. Has that changed at all?"

She met his sharp gaze, certain that he would miss nothing. "Many things have occurred," she said, lowering her voice and walking with him to where they could seat themselves on a sofa. "I still feel that all does not bode well. But now the king and the counts have gone to meet the Saxons while we are on our way to Poitiers."

"Hmmm," said Gregory. "And Fredegund? Does she accompany the queen's entourage?" he asked, not meeting her gaze.

"No," said Judith. "At the moment she is a camp follower. She is now the king's mistress though he has not declared it publicly."

"I see," said Gregory with a frown. Of course he could not tell Judith about his discussion with Fredegund, but he wanted to let her know that he had at least tried to intervene. One way was to speak of things Fredegund had *not* said.

"When I saw her," he said, knowing Judith would get the point, "she did not mention it."

Judith pressed her lips together and then said, "No, I suppose she wouldn't. She is gaining power though. She spied on the counts at a meeting and then I'm sure she told the king what the counts planned. He accused them, but in a trial by combat they were proven innocent."

"Ah. Then perhaps she lied," he said. Wanting to say something comforting, he offered consolation. "At least she is not with you now. Is" — he trod delicately — "Is the queen troubled by her husband's infidelity?"

Judith shook her head. "She never loved the king. It is not so much the infidelity that troubles her. She has never been happy here. I believe she wishes to return to Spain, but she is afraid to go because Chilperic would keep her dowry, and her father would be angry."

Gregory placed the wine goblet on a round marble table beside him. "That is too bad. Dear me. I do hope I can lift the queen's spirits. Perhaps if she becomes involved in good works, it will take her mind off her domestic crisis. I will certainly chastise both the king and his mistress for their sin."

Judith held doubts that they would listen. But a priest could say anything he wanted to the king. There seemed nothing Gregory could really do, but she enjoyed the comfort of being in his presence nevertheless.

"Is your position here full of very much responsibility?" she asked.

"Oh, dear, yes. It is a large sea to minister to. Luckily, we have been well endowed and so do not lack for funds to carry on. And we have enriched some of our churches with newly discovered saints' relics. But we are most fortunate. Many wealthy widows assist in helping the poor. And one must attend many councils." He half smiled. "And try to keep the Merovingian kings from squabbling among themselves."

"At the moment they are allies," said Judith.

"Yes," he said, raising and lowering his brows. "And that worries me. No sooner than they seem to form an alliance than they turn on each other. I wait with bated breath for news that one has betrayed the other and attacked his brother's city. Then the church shall have to step in. Either that or offer asylum to the one who comes running." He sighed, rubbing his temples with long fingers. "These are indeed troubled times."

"Yes," said Judith. "And you, yourself. Are you still writing your history?"

The mention of his literary work brought a light to Gregory's eyes. "I do seem to have accumulated a pile of manuscript sheets. I have gone rather hurriedly over Clovis's generation and come to the present. I feel there is so much to record that I must get it down."

Judith smiled; talk about literary work was her favorite topic. "Good. Just think. When I am old, perhaps I can read your history and remember some of the things you are writing about." Then her smile dimmed. "Provided of course that things turn out well and that I would want to remember them."

Gregory patted her hand and rose to take his leave.

"We must hope they do. Now, you must keep me informed on everything that happens at court."

"I will write to you, if you really want me to."

"Yes, please do. And," he coughed into his folded hand, "if the king's mistress returns from the king's camp, let me know that, too."

"All right."

It made her feel good that he cared about the matter and she would do her best to keep him informed. Perhaps Gregory could rain down God's wrath on Fredegund for her crimes.

She laughed. "Can you work miracles?" she asked, repeating the question she had asked him when they had first met at Chilperic's wedding.

Gregory smiled, lines forming along the side of his cheeks. He accepted her teasing, remembering their early conversation on the subject. "I'll see what I can do."

Fredegund waited in the darkness of the forest, unbetrayed by the two horns of the new moon that pointed away from the sun's path. Though the slaves she had brought along for protection waited in a clearing within shouting distance, she had placed them where they could not see who she met or hear her conversation. Confident not only in what she was about to offer the spies she was going to meet, a swift brush of her girdle with her hand assured her that her special sheath knife with poison encrusted in the engraved tooling would defend her if the need arose. However, she did not expect it to arise.

A crush of branches warned her, and then out of the dark woods there they stood. Two brawny men, tunics of leather covered with breastplates of gilded scales. Belts of leather surrounded their hips to which their weapons were attached. Over their shoulders hung chains of polished iron, from which were suspended wooden scabbard and bronze sword hilt. Cloaks made from skins hung from their shoulders.

She stepped away from the tree where she had been sheltered so they could see her. "There's no hunter's moon this night." She gave the code that had been agreed upon.

"By this moon next we will be over the mountain," one of the men answered.

The words were right, but was the plan? Knowing that she might be placing herself in danger in spite of all her precautions, she nevertheless faced them boldly. They were large men and fierce looking. They could snap her spine in an instant, more quickly than she could call out for help. But evidently their leader, Beornred, had received her message and was tempted by her plan.

"Do you have the gold?" she asked, for though she did not care about the money, she knew the Saxons would be suspicious if she were to offer them such information without pay.

The larger man nodded. "Yes. Where is your information?"

"Show me the gold."

He grunted but untied a small satchel from his waist and tossed it to the ground so that she could hear the clink of gold coins. "There," he said.

"All right." She stepped closer. "The queen and her entourage are in Tours. In two days' time they will take the road to Poitiers. Your best chance of waylaying them will be north of Poitiers where you can wait in trees that line the river Vienne. She travels with many slaves, some women and a guard of forty warriors. But they won't suspect an ambush, thinking that your forces are gathering to the northeast. Do not wait until they reach the city, which is fortified, but take them on the plain."

The man nodded slowly as if absorbing the information. "We will be ready. We will have our boats waiting on the coast. The country is flat to the sea, our horses fast."

Then he exchanged glances with his companion who also nodded. The first man looked at her and at the gold. For a moment, she thought he might make a move to take it back. She stiffened. She would not take her eyes off him until they were gone.

He said nothing more but gestured toward her with his bearded chin. Then he and his companion turned and disappeared into the woods, remarkably silent for two so large and so encumbered with arms.

The camps of the Frankish soldiers worried the Saxon leader Beornred and his council of chiefs. Unused to pitched battles, the Saxons preferred quick invasions and plundering to a decisive clash. Whereas the Franks had learned from the Romans for whom they had guarded the territory until the day there were so many native Frankish generals in the Roman army it was easy to take it over from within.

And so in his own camp Beornred squatted beside his fire, considering what to do. Every day more Franks seemed to swell the camp on this side of the Meuse.

"Let us strike now while they are not yet ready," said Godafred, one of Beornred's chief advisors.

Beornred grunted. "We cannot surprise them. With the woods at their back and the river on their flank, they will see us coming across the plain. There might be a better way."

"What?" demanded another chief named Woolgar.

Beornred frowned, struggling with the thought, for strategy was not much of a Saxon ability. They owed the success of their raiding to swift, merciless strikes that terrorized the citizens of small enclaves whose armies for one reason or the other were off somewhere else.

"We might lure them to us."

"How?" asked Woolgar.

"By retreating. Make them follow us. Divide our forces where the river forks. One group taking position on the plain and the other force disappearing into the woody bogs. Then circle around at night through the woods and bogs."

"The bogs are dangerous. And for an entire army?" asked Woolgar.

The other thanes muttered agreement. But Beornred held up a hand. "Our men know the bogs. But the Frankish army will get caught in the mire behind us and get sucked down of their own accord. The rest will make easy targets when the sun rises. And we will leave a guard behind to prevent their retreat.

The thanes nodded, admiration in their eyes for their leader. It was a sound plan.

In the Frankish camp three miles away, Ivar paced around the fire in his own council with the generals. He and Lupus had returned from their reconnaissance and had informed the Franks of the Saxons' position. Now the two kings were sequestered in Sigibert's tent, talking about the charge they planned for tomorrow. But something about the king's plans bothered Ivar, and he voiced his thoughts to Lupus and Fulrich, who stood with him gazing out from the firelight onto the long flat plain that stretched before them.

"Many of the Saxons come from just over there," said Ivar, uncrossing his arms and pointing northeast. "They know the territory better than we do. Surely they will use that knowledge to their advantage."

"Our guards are posted to prevent any surprise attack,"

said Fulrich. "And guards in the woods in case they try to slip through that way. On the river they would be seen miles away."

But Ivar shook his head. "If there is no surprise attack, then we must assume they are up to something. If we were the Saxons, we would take advantage of the landscape in some way." He furrowed his brow to consider what he might do in their place.

He wore no leggings now, and the light flickered across powerful muscular legs up which climbed the cross-gartered straps from his sandals. He turned to glance at the camp behind where men polished armor, testing their sharp blades to make sure they would cut deeply at the least touch. He had a black feeling about the coming battle, a feeling neither his offerings to Ardhuina nor his prayers to the Christian God could rid him of. Tomorrow or the next day he would follow his king onto the battlefield and they would either be triumphant or he would die before letting the king fall. For there was no worse disgrace than letting one's king be captured or killed. No German warrior of any tribe ever faced that. Death was preferable.

Normally, Ivar looked forward to battle, for a chance to glorify himself and his king. But tonight he squinted into the darkness, keenly aware of his own mortality.

In the morning the Saxons moved. They were headed toward the Franks with half their force near the forest that stretched south.

"Aha," said Chilperic as if he had read Beornred's mind. "They mean to trick us into following them into the forest. But we will not fall for that ploy. We will stay together, one group lagging behind to prevent their army from attacking us from the rear. No matter what their trickery, they cannot beat us."

The generals around him raised their fists and cheered. "We fight as one to repel the Saxons," commanded Chilperic. "Tell your men not to disperse in confusion. Beornred is a thorn in our side and we have determined to expel him once and for all."

The counts cheered then turned and rode back to their waiting troops to relay instructions. Meanwhile, Chilperic and Sigibert mounted and rode along the lines of soldiers shouting encouragement, letting the men see them, because soldiers would follow more eagerly kings who led the battle themselves. The battle standards, flags bearing St. Martin's blue cloak, rose at the head of the large formation, and the soldiers were aroused to a fever pitch, longing for Saxon blood. Many of them fought on foot, and the generals had arranged the cavalry on both flanks with the wedge of foot soldiers with swords, axes, and spears in the middle.

"We will vanquish the Saxons once and for all," said Sigibert. "We will show them they cannot ignore their tributes. They cannot rape our lands and our women."

The soldiers clashed their weapons together to show their agreement. When the cheers and calls for blood were so loud they could be heard by the Saxons three miles away, Chilperic and Sigibert wheeled their mounts and led the Frankish formation out, a close, disciplined formation, wind in their faces, prepared to pierce the enemy line in a single mass.

The Saxons waited as the line of Franks approached, the long line of the Frankish army a formidable sight, even to the bloodthirsty Saxons. At Beornred's signal his forces split, one force suddenly wheeling and fleeing for the woods, making it look almost as if they were running away.

But Chilperic was not fooled. Ivar led his army on the

left flank and maintained their line, knowing that to follow into the woods would be suicide. And behind them came a cavalry made up of Germanus's men who would form up and face the woods, protecting Chilperic's main flank.

The Saxons saw the large cohesive force, and the chiefs cursed when the Franks did not follow their decoy into the marshy woods. Some of the Saxon force fled eastward toward a branch of the Rhine where it broke into several long arms that reached for the sea. They ran for their fortifications on the other side of the branch, but Beornred rode along the lines trying to gather the force to meet the onslaught.

Onward came the Franks, trampling across the wide delta. For a moment it looked as if the Saxons would all turn and flee, but now the leading contingent of Franks, led by Chilperic, Sigibert and the counts, spread out across the line of cavalry, charged, and Beornred succeeded in making the Saxons stand and fight. The Franks flung themselves forward thrusting swords and spears in one great shock.

Seeing that the battle was enjoined, some of the fleeing Saxons returned and engaged, and soon the onslaught broke down into hand-to-hand combat, fighting at close quarters. A giant Saxon warrior with silver rings hanging from one ear, his pointed spear held high, bore down on Ivar who let go his throwing axe in time to sever the man's arm to the bone, the spear clashing under the horses' feet as the man howled in pain. Quickly, Ivar grasped the spear he'd held in front of him and used it to deflect the sword of a Saxon who came in behind the fallen man. Beside him a spear dug into the thigh of a thane. Lupus, who had dismounted to fight, drew a bloody knife from a fallen warrior and hurled it at a

245

Saxon brute.

The battle was long and bloody. Hand-to-hand fighting grew fierce. The brook flowing from the fields where they fought swelled with blood. Eventually the better disciplined Franks pushed the Saxons back past their supply wagons toward the Rhine. Pushed toward the river, the fighting grew even more dense, permitting barely enough room for use of weapons. Some of the slain remained upright where they died.

At last evening fell, and darkness made an end to the slaughter. Some eight thousand lay dead on the fields, bodies hewn with sword cuts. The remaining Saxons fled across the branch of the river before they could be taken prisoner, leaving behind supplies. The Franks suffered nearly as many casualties as the Saxons, but they were the victors, and the Saxons were for the moment forced back toward their own kingdom.

Galswinth's train left Tours before they had news of the battle at the Meuse. They traveled confidently, guarded by forty mounted soldiers with another thirty slaves on foot. Winding through the verdant Loire Valley, which had not been trampled by battle in several years, they savored the fresh smell of wheat and tall summer grasses. Scattered farmsteads were the sole tokens of life against a vast horizon.

And so when at dusk they passed near a clump of oak lining the river Vienne they were startled by the host of horned-helmeted warriors that emerged suddenly from the gulch, shouting terrorizing war cries.

Judith, who had been riding in a cart with Clothild, felt her heart stop beating. All she could do was stare at the host that fell on them, gripping the sides of the cart until her fingers lost all blood. She was too stunned to move even when the message of danger traveled slowly from mind to limbs.

The soldiers drew their weapons, but the attacking force had the advantage, for the party, sensing they were near Poitiers had dropped their guard and were surprised. Sword clashed sword. A throwing axe pierced through one Saxon's helmet and Judith saw with her very own eyes the man's skull split in two.

Finally she looked around toward Galswinth's chariot. The queen was nowhere to be seen, and most of the fighting was centered there. The guards had backed up against the queen's chariot to protect her and now, roused to fighting pitch, they were doing a better job of repelling the attackers.

Clothild grasped Judith's shoulders and pulled her out of the cart. "Get under here," she said to Judith, and the two women crouched beneath the cart for a small degree of protection. Judith reached for the dagger at her waist, but before she could pull it from its jeweled scabbard she screamed as a huge hand grasped her under the arm.

She turned to face a huge, bearded Saxon. His studded leather belt, gilded scales and the curved horns rising out of his bronze helmet struck terror into her heart. He picked her up and slung her in front of him on his horse as if she were no more than a sack of grain. She screamed in terror, struggling to reach her dagger as her eyes met Clothild's terrified ones where she crouched under the cart.

Then a Frank and a Saxon came between them, slashing at each other, and the last thing Judith saw before her captor wheeled and rode away was Clothild huddled in a mass screaming behind the fighting warriors. Screams and cries saturated Judith's mind, but soon the bumping of her body against the horse that took to its heels numbed all other awareness except that of more thundering hooves behind them as a group of the Saxons broke off from the fight and lit out to the west.

And then she fainted.

Chapter Sixteen

Falling in and out of consciousness, Judith was carried overland, losing all sense of time. Each time she awoke in a hazy fog, she assumed she was approaching death, only to have her bruises make her keenly aware that indeed she was still alive. Her captors galloped along tracks that led in and out of forests and crossed fields and vineyards with no concern for the damage they did.

They stopped to change horses and Judith was set upon a horse, tied to her seat, the reins held by the man who had dragged her away from the procession. Her dull senses registered that they were not Franks; they were dressed in leather tunics with no ringed mail, and they wore beards and moustaches and carried long spears. When they spoke to each other it was in a guttural dialect she did not understand.

Beyond fear, she did not know where they were taking her or why. She wanted to ask about Galswinth and the rest of the party, but she feared that even if she could speak to her captors they would tell her the rest were all dead. Why then spare her? As they rode through the night, avoiding towns and farmsteads, she half dozed, half fainted in the saddle. But when she smelled the sea air as they neared the coast, her senses revived. She heard the waves washing onto the shore before they reached it, and then saw the torches lighting the beach where a larger contingent of these fearful-looking men, some in weird-horned helmets waited for them.

New terror struck at her as they undid her bonds and lifted her from the steed. She was pushed toward the double-ended ship that rode at anchor in the water some distance out. Fourteen pairs of oars waited in rowlocks on either side of the narrow ship. A mast stood upright near the middle of the ship, and from a raised platform at the stern, another fierce-looking man shouted orders.

They were going to take her to sea! She knew without question that once she set foot in the ship, she would never again see this land. She glanced around frantically, as if there were any possible way to escape. But when she was pushed into a small rowboat her limbs responded. She might as well be dead. Galswinth must be dead, so why not she? She thought briefly of Ivar, fighting the Saxons on the heathlands to the north. Then suddenly she realized who these men were. From their guttural speech, their beards, and their frightening headgear she guessed they must be a Saxon contingent. But what were they doing here? The Frankish armies had marched north to meet them.

New fears consumed her as she wondered if the Frankish armies had been misled. Perhaps they had been tricked into going north, leaving the seacoast wide open for attack. She shivered as she sat in the little boat.

They reached the bigger, seagoing vessel, and she was suddenly hoisted in. A push sent her sprawling across one of the ribs that stretched across the ship and were lashed to the planks on either side.

The oarsmen took their places on small seats affixed to the ribs at each end, and sacks of goods were tossed in. Now she noticed another such ship into which the remaining men climbed and pulled the rowboat after them. The horses were loaded onto a third ship. All proceeded in what looked like chaotic fashion, but the leader of the party continued to bark orders until all was loaded, the anchors drawn in, and the oarsmen began to row away from the shore.

Judith hugged herself as the waves in the bay slapped around them and didn't even realize when she was tossed a cloak, which she clutched around her where she sat. Now torches lit their way, and allowed her to see the curved prow of the ship and the red and blue-striped sail that the sailors unfurled as soon as the wind was at their back. These were Saxon pirates, she realized, and she was their captive.

Where were they going? If they did not plan to kill her, they would surely take her somewhere and either sell her into slavery or use her for their own purposes. Perhaps then they would be merciful enough to toss her into the sea and allow her to drown.

She stared overboard at the dark waters and wondered if she should not take matters into her own hands and leap into the arms of the sea. There could be nothing to live for. And yet she huddled where she sat until the sheer weight of the ordeal overcame her and she spread herself on the curved bottom of the ship, wrapping the cloak around her and drifted into a semblance of sleep.

Cramped and numbed she awoke to the creak of planks. For a long time she lay where she was, cold and damp, until she sensed light on her eyelids. She fluttered her eyes open to see the bright-colored sail puffed out above her, and the oarsmen rested as the wind was pulling the ship. The men slept where they sat, heads on arms resting on the gunwale. She turned a stiff neck and saw the man still standing on the platform at the prow, gazing ahead. The sun caught his fiery red hair and made it seem for a moment as if his entire head was burning until she could sort out hair, beard, and golden helmet.

She shivered again and tried to sit up. She needed to relieve herself, but there was no place to do so, and she would rather die than embarrass herself in front of these animals.

The sun rose higher and the men roused themselves. A scurry of activity followed, and Judith now saw that they were heading toward land again. Where they were she had no idea, except that they sailed at a northeasterly angle to the sun.

They sailed up to the beach of a small island. There they disembarked and Judith was allowed to go into the bushes to take care of bodily needs. A guard waited for her, but it was useless to think of running away. They would simply follow and kill her. And no doubt they had landed at an island infested with pirates like themselves, or else it was uninhabited, in which case she would not survive here.

So when she was ready she marched back to the beach, holding her head erect. Though she trembled when the men looked at her and refused to meet their fierce blue eyes, she did not show them how afraid she was. At any moment she expected one of them to throw her to the ground, use her, and then tear her from limb to limb. Her countless prayers to let death take her from this horrible plight went unanswered, though now she wondered for what reason she was being kept alive.

Here the men seemed not to fear anything; they made a fire and roasted meat, which she was fed, though the tough, flavorless stuff nearly choked her. Still, she found that she was hungry enough to get it down.

Able to see better in the daylight she began to discern details that her numbed mind had not taken in before. The leader of the group was even larger than the rest, with muscles in arms and legs that looked like iron. For these pirates wore no leggings. Their simple leather shoes were cross-gartered to the knee, and their short-sleeved leather tunics came to just above the knee. All wore metal-studded girdles from which throwing axes hung, but no swords were evident. Rather these men carried long spears and small round shields of hide-covered wood.

The leader wore a golden torque about his neck, and the hide of a large beast formed a cloak, which was fastened with a large gold pin at the left shoulder. Her gaze then wandered to the ships, anchored near enough so that the party could quickly leap into them for a hasty getaway if need be.

The sleek lines of the ships were built for speed, and she was fascinated with the detailed carvings of interlacing design on the prow of the ship, rising to a point.

The warm sun and the ocean breeze combined to lull her, but before she could indulge in the luxury of sleep, a muscular pirate seized her arm and propelled her in the direction of the ships. The party broke camp more efficiently in the daylight and set sail. They rounded a point of land and sailed directly east as the sun passed over their shoulders. That night, perhaps because they were in safer waters, they beached the boats and the men spread themselves around and slept on skins.

Judith huddled in her cloak thanking the fates that it wasn't winter, for surely then the north wind would bring icicles to torment her. Again she was left alone and decided that she was being saved for a purpose, perhaps to be presented as a gift to some ruler.

Totally alone, afraid for her life, and certain that everything she had left behind was lost, Judith began to recall scenes from the brief time she had passed on earth. She thought of Mother Radegund and tried to repeat the prayers the noble mother superior had taught her. The prayers soon became poetry recited by Fortunatus, and then she thought of him, wondering how he fared in his role at the abbey. She lay with her head on the ground, trying to listen for the vibrations of war that surely came from the lands where Ivar fought with Chilperic. She remembered Ivar's naked body and the pleasures he had shown her. But that thought made her tremble for surely unless she was killed, these Saxons would give her to a man to use in the same way. Except that the idea of being mauled by one of the abhorent Saxons made her skin crawl.

When morning came and she was again aroused, she felt she had not slept at all, rather wandered in some nebulous land between earth and heaven. Now as the Saxons broke their fast and handed her dried meat, she began to listen to their words more closely and from their gestures found that she could make out some of what they said, more from intention than actual words.

She climbed into the ship without assistance and took her place. A fog began to cover them, and now Judith feared the helmsman would steer them into one of the rocks that protruded dangerously near their course every so often. The rough water made the ship roll and pitch, and she knew they had left the more gentle waters of the bays behind them and were traveling in the treacherous North Sea.

She heard fish leap out of the water to their sides and then dive back in, but the pirates did not make any attempt to stop and fish, rather the oarsmen bent their backs to the task of keeping the ship moving on its course, for the brightly colored sail was furled limply against the mast.

Eventually Judith dozed; when she came alert again, she heard the sound of a distant horn being blown from shore to show the pirates their way home. The waters eased and suddenly she felt the hull scrape on a beach. The men cheered, and the fog seemed to blow toward sea. She shrank involuntarily at the crowd of men she saw waiting on the beach. Then there was much talk. The sailors jumped onto the beach. And then she was dragged out also, feeling like a sack of grain.

The man who had acted as leader now gesticulated and spoke in loud tones, evidently relaying their adventures to another man who stared at Judith and nodded. It took all her strength to remain standing, and then she was pushed from behind and led up the beach to lands that were cleared. For the first time she saw buildings of timber and blinked dumbly. It was a settlement of some kind. Still not knowing where she was, she examined the landscape for clues. But though the loamy soil and the sparse trees told her she was on some northern shore, she could only guess at what land she had been brought to.

Some of the pirates accompanied her through an opening in a bulwark of tall stakes carved from the length of trees and fixed next to each other. They got inside the compound where wooden buildings were arranged at angles to each other. The one directly ahead was quite tall with smoke rising from an opening in the center of the pitched roof. Pigs rolled in the dirt and dogs barked at the arrival of the procession. Other men were dressed much as her captors were except that here they wore no helmets. And now she noticed women who stopped their work to stare at her.

She was marched into the large hall, her ears taking in the guttural sounds she had almost grown accustomed to. Still they made no sense to her, and as she began to think she might not be killed immediately, she decided she was going to be made a slave. But how a slave when

255

she did not even understand what her captors asked of her?

Being a slave was nothing new to her. The Franks had captured her in a raid, but she had been a child then and turned over to the nuns at the abbey. She shivered comparing her fortunate upbringing to the circumstances she now found herself in. Here there would be no abbey, for these people were not even Christians.

A man seated at one end of the hall and surrounded by a group of thanes looked up as she approached. The thanes broke off their talk and all turned to stare as she was presented to this man, who by the deference of the others, she presumed to be the chief.

She halted where she was, but the man behind her grunted and pushed her forward, then pushed on her shoulder making her understand that she should kneel. Having little pride left, she did so, keeping her eyes to the floor. Beside the sound of her heart beating against her ribs, she heard the breathing of those present.

Finally, she saw the edge of a colorful tunic approach and to her surprise the female voice who spoke to her spoke a dialect she understood.

"You may rise," the woman said. "Our chief accepts you as a gift. You are not to be harmed if you tell him what you know of the Frankish forces who have invaded our lands."

Judith blinked and looked into the blue eyes of a tall blond woman whose hair was parted in the center and fell in two yellow braids across her breast. Her finespun garment was died yellow-orange, and she wore a wide silver collar at her throat. At her waist was a leather girdle decorated with rich metal ornaments and small chains.

The woman's eyes held an expression that told Judith she understood what she was thinking.

"Yes, I spent time among the Franks and so can speak

the language. I was captured by these people a decade ago and am the wife of one of the warriors."

Being several days among people she could not talk to, Judith found it difficult to find her tongue even now. But she did stand and nod to the woman, then she looked at the chief who leaned forward, studying her.

Suddenly she shivered. Talk she might be able to do, but she could sense what would happen next. She had been given to this man as a gift. He would make her his mistress, and the thought made her skin turn clammy and her stomach churn. The chief grunted, and she looked with wide eyes at the woman who had spoken to her.

"Chief Woolgar wants to know what the Franks intend now that they have pushed our warriors this side of the Rhine. What plans have they for further invasions?"

Her throat dry, Judith tried to think of an answer. She searched frantically in her mind for what she'd heard at the council at Ivar's family estate. Not that she would betray the Franks, but she knew that Woolgar would not believe she knew nothing. He must already know she had traveled with the queen's train. It would do no good to say that women were seldom let in on the men's plans for such things as military tactics and invasions.

"Tribute," she finally managed to get out. "They want tribute from the Saxons."

Woolgar must have understood something of what she said, for before the woman finished translating he roared and pounded his fist on the sturdy arms of his large chair. The blond woman turned to her.

"He says the Saxons have paid enough tribute. Now we pay in blood."

Judith swallowed. She looked at the woman helplessly, not knowing what to say. Further words were exchanged between the chief and the woman translator.

Finally the woman said, "Our chief wants to know who you are. Since you are our hostage perhaps the Franks will negotiate with us."

Judith shook her head, saying, "I am of no value to anyone but my friend the princess Galswinth." Then she found the courage to look into the woman's eyes and ask, "Is she dead?"

The woman asked a hasty question. Mumblings were exchanged. Then the discussion grew louder, and for a moment it appeared that they had forgotten about Judith. Finally, the chief gestured a signal of dismissal and the woman motioned for Judith to come with her. She followed the Saxon woman out of the hall and across the compound. Again heads turned to stare at the newcomer, and so when the woman led Judith into a smaller timber-framed building and shut the door, Judith felt some relief.

"My name is Leagh," she said. "I am Thuringian."

"You spent time among the Franks?" asked Judith.

She nodded. "I ran away, but was captured by the Saxons." She gave a shrug. "It makes little difference."

Judith could not see how Leagh could feel that way if what she had seen so far represented the style of life of the Saxons. Their buildings were primitive, their dress and manners warlike. But from her appearance it did not look like Leagh had been mistreated.

"You will stay here until Woolgar sends for you."

Judith sank onto a mattress that felt as if it were made of horsehair and covered with muslin. But Leagh would waste no time on sympathy.

"Please him and you will be treated well. If you have information to impart, give it freely. Woolgar suffered a great defeat at the hands of your people. He is very angry and longs for revenge. If you help him, your life will be spared. If you anger him . . ." She drew her finger across her throat.

Leagh walked around in front of her and eyed her carefully. "You are young and healthy. If you are willing to work and to please your lord, you have nothing to fear in a Saxon camp. But I will tell you this. Do not try to escape. For you will be caught, and then you will be dragged by the hair from behind a horse over rocky heathland and torn from limb to limb. There are more pleasant ways to die."

Leagh left her to herself in the small hut, and Judith lay back on the bed, a bolster supporting her head. At first all she could think about was resting her weary limbs and in spite of her anxiety she fell into a deep slumber. When she awoke she felt ravenous. When she got up and explored the hut, she found wood for a fire in a stone fireplace but no vessels for cooking and no food.

It was then that she realized she still had the dagger fastened to a belt around the waist of her undertunic, which her overtunic had kept concealed during the long, wet journey here. She unfastened it now and looked around for a place to hide it. For if the Saxons found it they would surely take it away from her. Finding a loose brick in the fireplace, she laid it there and then replaced the brick. Although she knew it would be useless against a thane the size of the Saxons, it was her only defense and she intended to keep it as a last resort.

Leagh returned, over her arm a clean undertunic which she held out to Judith. It was similar in construction to Leagh's and was printed with small blue triangles. Her own garment was torn and dirty and she stripped it off, putting on the fresh, clean-smelling one Leagh gave her. Then Leagh gave her an overtunic fastened at the shoulders with fine gold brooches, allowing the sleeves of the undertunic to show through. Then she surprised

Judith by showing her a chain of gold which she wound into Judith's hair as she braided it. And a bright red mantle was draped from her shoulders, fastened with an ornamental pin carved like a horse's head.

When Leagh was satisfied, the two women again crossed the yard to the hall where it appeared everyone else had gathered. Now two long tables stretched down the sides of the room. Woolgar sat in the center of the table on the north side. But Leagh guided Judith to one of the cross benches at the sides of the room where the women sat. A fire burned in a bricked pit in the center of the room, the smoke being drawn out by the chimney Judith had seen earlier.

Again Judith was filled with a despairing sense of loneliness, for in this hall filled with people there was not one friend. Even Leagh, who seemed to have been assigned to look after her, and who had been handed from one tribe to another, did not seem to have any real warmth for Judith. So she ate the hunk of roast pig and bread she was given and tried to drink the strange liquid called mead, that tasted odd to her tongue, so used to wine was she.

After she had eaten her fill, she longed to return to her little hut, but the feast was far from over. The men at their tables continued to drink to the great god Thor from drinking horns continually refilled with the mead. They ate more meat than she imagined any man could put away, and some left the table and found a seat on the floor against the wooden posts that rose to beams that crossed the ceiling a great distance above them. Before her eyes the Saxon warriors ate and drank to excess and then fell asleep in their mead.

When the men were either too drunk to know what they were doing or snoring on the floor, Leagh touched Judith on the arm and motioned with her head that they should leave. She was only too glad to follow the Thuringian woman out of the hall; to breathe the fresh, moist air was refreshing after the stuffy, sooty hall.

"Wait in the hut," said Leagh, pointing. "Woolgar will come to you later."

For an instant Judith thought she sensed a modicum of sympathy, for Leagh's eyes seemed to soften. But she said no more and she started to leave Judith in the hut. Then she turned back.

"Do not attempt to escape," she repeated her earlier warning. "There is nowhere to go. The sea, the forest, and the hills hem us in. Any people you would meet would only return you to Woolgar, for by your speech you are obviously a foreigner."

Though Judith had not planned to try to escape alone, the words drove her into further despair. Was this where her life would end then? On a peninsula by the cold North Sea, living among heathens who would use and abuse her? She thought of her little dagger, secreted in the fireplace and wondered if she shouldn't use it on herself.

Marcus Petronius walked among the dead on the field where the Saxons lay scattered and lifeless. The Franks had gathered their dead for burial and had bound the wounds of those who could be saved. But the Saxons had fled, leaving their dead to rot. However, Sigibert did not want the disease and smell of seven thousand dead to pollute the Rhine and so ordered them burned.

Marcus supervised the bringing in of spoils, seeing to it that arms, jewelry, and valuables were duly counted and loaded onto carts to be divided among the men as their reward for the fight.

As the sun died on the day after the battle, Marcus turned away from the carnage to return to Sigibert's tent. As he approached, a contingent of horsemen descended from a hill to the west. From the speed of their horses, he guessed that they bore important news. They converged on the tent just as he pushed back the flap to enter.

Inside, Sigibert sat at a table and Chilperic paced the canvas floor discussing whether or not to follow the Saxons and destroy their lands.

"Messengers from Poitiers, my lords," announced a soldier behind Marcus.

"Bring them," said Chilperic with a frown.

The group of messengers entered and one Frankish soldier stepped forward.

"The royal train was attacked by Saxon pirates," he said. "Our guard beat them off, and the queen is safe at Poitiers. One hostage was taken and five of our men died. No horses were stolen."

Chilperic grunted. "What hostage?"

"The lady Judith who was companion to the queen."

Marcus stared at the messengers. The lady Judith? The one he had spoken to on two occasions when he had found himself at the Neustrian court? He paid closer attention as the messenger relayed what had occurred.

"They were waylaid on the road to Poitiers. Farmers saw them ride away to the west, undoubtedly to the sea."

"No one gave chase?" asked Chilperic.

The messenger shook his head. "Every able-bodied man was here fighting the Saxons, and the guard thought it their duty to protect the queen."

"So it was."

Marcus noticed the lack of enthusiasm in Chilperic's voice about the queen's safety. He seemed more interested in the fact that the Saxon pirates got away. The king shrugged.

"By now they will be home. As you say the queen is safe and the guard did their duty. How many Saxons did they kill at the point of skirmish?"

"Three."

"Then they shall not be reprimanded for not giving chase. But I want to be sure there's no nest of pirates left on the coast."

"Part of the contingent who saw the queen safely to Poitiers is scouting the neighborhood now to make sure."

"Very well. You may go."

It seemed to be the end of the report. When the messengers had gone Marcus gave his report to Sigibert.

"The Saxon dead have been tossed in a heap with wood set round for burning."

"Then we want to be on the march before the fire is lit," said Chilperic. "Already the stench is great."

"Then you do not plan to cross into Saxon lands and finish them off, brother?" said Sigibert.

"I do not," said Chilperic. "Our job is done. Would you have me fight all your battles for you?"

"I do not. But the Saxon's hoard gold. I only thought your men would want a chance at their share," said Sigibert.

"And why are you suddenly being so generous?" inquired Chilperic.

Sigibert spread his hands. Marcus decided to use his negotiating skills to prevent the argument from growing and tried to intervene.

"Perhaps King Chilperic is right," said Marcus to his king. "His job is done here. His men want to return to their homes and farms, while our men, aggravated by the Saxon raids of their own homes and lands want a chance for revenge. Let us take our own force into Saxony to hunt down the pagan warriors and teach them a lesson."

Sigibert shrugged. "Good advice as usual, Marcus Petronius. I did not want my brother to think me unfair."

Marcus's keen sense of understanding picked up something in his speech to lead him to believe there was more to it than he was saying. The Merovingian kin, never friendly for more than a few weeks at a time never failed to seek ways to better themselves at the expense of the others. Surely Sigibert had something up his sleeve in inviting Chilperic to continue the campaign. But it was not really Marcus's concern at the moment.

"Marcus, assemble the counts," ordered Sigibert. "Now that the Neustrians plan to go home, we will need to plan our strategy."

Marcus bowed and left the tent, then he sent word to the counts who were busy reassembling their forces and ascertaining who among them were dead and who were still able to march. That done, he went to his own tent to find his junior officers and ask for a report on his own men. When he pushed back the tent and then sank down onto the camp stool beside his bed, his thoughts turned to the lady Judith, now a slave of the Saxons. He frowned. Already an idea was forming. Chilperic did not appear to plan to do anything about it. Evidently she was nothing to him, even if she was a friend of Queen Galswinth's. He remembered the name of her protector, Count Ivar. Oughtn't the man be informed? He had not seen Count Ivar since the battle. Perhaps he was one of the wounded.

Marcus rose and poured himself a cup of wine from a flask that had arrived with supply wagons. He took a swig and thought again of Judith. Recalling the green-gold eyes, the dark brows, the golden complexion, and the thick sandy hair that made a man want to crush it in his fingers, he knew what he would do if he were her protector. To allow those Saxon brutes to maul her would be unthinkable. He tossed back the rest of the wine, then strode out of the tent and set out to find Count Ivar.

Chapter Seventeen

The only thing that kept Judith from being raped by the warriors in the camp was that she was marked for Woolgar, and no man would defile the chief's woman. And so she lay huddled in her blankets for most of the night waiting for the big leader to awaken from his mead-induced stupor and come and use her. But as the gray herald of dawn began to lighten the sky, he still had not come, and Judith finally fell asleep.

A few hours later the smell of smoke and sunlight streaming in the small window of her hut awakened her. She went out to the compound and was directed to a stream where she could take care of her needs. When she returned to the main compound a group of horsemen rode in and dismounted, then thundered into the hall. Moments later a cry of alarm went out.

"The Franks are coming this way, burning the land as they come. We must prepare to fight!"

Suddenly the whole village seemed to be awake. Women screamed and shouted. Wagons were rolled out, and goods loaded onto them. Horses were saddled, oxen harnessed to the wagons. Men spilled out of the hall where they had been rudely awakened after last night's revelry. Now they armed themselves, and shouted for their horses. It was a scene of mass confusion.

Judith thought of the orderly way in which the Franks prepared for war. She cowered against her hut, everyone ignoring her. The Franks were coming this way? Which army? But they would not know she was here. Still, it was some small hope.

She went into the hut and removed the brick hiding her dagger, which she quickly put on. She was looking around for anything else that could be used as a weapon when the door crashed open and a huge thane stood there. She backed against the wall in terror as he crossed the room uttering sounds she did not understand, though his meaning was clear. She was to go with him. She started to reach for her dagger, but the size of his drawn knife stopped her. He grasped her shoulder and sent her flying toward the door, the point of his knife pricking her back to goad her.

In the yard, she was picked up and tossed into a wagon with sacks of grain, the thane grasping her hands and forcing them behind her back until she screamed in pain. She had no choice but to wriggle into a more tolerable position while he lashed her wrists together. Then the wagon trundled out of the gate following other such carts and vehicles, while all around them the warriors, who by now were mounted with their helmets and shields, shouted war cries and prayers to Thor, raising their spears in the air.

Then it seemed the entire community was on the move, leaving the compound behind. Whether they were fleeing the advance of the Franks or riding into battle was impossible to tell. But they seemed to take to a course that led along a track by the river. Judith's bones seemed to knock each other as the cart jostled along. Only the grain sacks kept her from falling out. She tried to move to a position where she could unbind her hands, but it seemed impossible.

Then she saw a paralyzing sight. From the crest of the hill away from which they were fleeing, a line of horsemen appeared, stretched, it seemed, as far as the eye could see. A shout went up, and the Saxon warriors wheeled their horses and prepared to fight while the carts with women and children continued the way they were headed. Judith struggled harder. She had to get free.

The dust from hooves grew thick and she could feel and hear rather than see the two forces come together in a clash of metal and cries. The impact of two bodies of men and arms was so strong it carried even to where her cart still rumbled along beside the river. And then came the anguished cries of wounded men.

The dust cleared enough that she could see one flank of Frankish horsemen circle around and enclose the Saxons. As the tail of the flank made its circle, she cried out for help. Miraculously, several of the horsemen heard her cry and being behind the main force of Saxons, they turned in her direction. She hoisted herself up on one of the grain sacks to better be seen and shouted again and again as the Franks came on. The figure in the lead began to look familiar in his shirt of mail and flashing armor.

The driver of the cart shouted and turned around to knock her down, but by that time the Frankish horsemen were abreast and a quick thrust of the sword knocked the driver off the seat. To her astonishment Judith stared at Count Marcus Petronius from the Austrasian court.

"Cut the ropes that bind my wrists," Judith shouted as she rolled onto a grain sack. A dagger slit the bonds, and then Marcus helped her up.

"Get on the back of my horse," he ordered, and she slithered from the wagon to the back of the horse, her tunic loose enough to allow her to straddle the beast and hang onto Marcus for dear life. Then he turned his horse. A few of the Saxons now noticed their flight and broke off from the fray to chase them, but the men who accompanied Marcus turned to fight them off.

267

Judith heard the scrape of metal and the grunts of the fallen as Marcus's horse dug its heels into the dirt and flew away. She dared not look back. She shut her eyes and clung to Marcus, her arms pressing against the mail shirt, but not caring if she were scratched or bruised so thankful was she to be escaping the Saxons.

"Hang on," he shouted over his shoulder.

Opening her eyes she saw that they had to go around the main skirmish, and there was the danger that more Saxons would give chase. Onward they galloped, the thunder of horses' hooves ahead and behind, and the rattle of swords everywhere.

One Saxon warrior broke from the rest and rode toward them, his arm upraised, an evil grimace on his face. With horror Judith watched the throwing axe fly from his hand, its blade headed directly toward them. But Marcus transferred his shield from his left to his right hand and lifting it, met the axe, which thudded against the shield and fell harmlessly to the ground.

Judith's lungs nearly burst from being held, and she finally expelled a breath. Then they were away from the vortex of fighting and speeding up a rise, Marcus's horse galloping across the heath in a streak. The other men stayed behind to finish off the remaining Saxons.

They took the rise and continued across a long plain for some distance, Judith pinned to Marcus's back. Then when he judged that they were safely away, he slowed the horse from its flat out run to a gentler gait, finally to a trot and then to a walk. The horse was winded and Marcus let it walk some distance to even its breath. Finally, he guided the horse to a boulder and reined in so that Judith could slide off easily.

She slid off and leaned against the large rock, gasping for breath, while Marcus dismounted, patting his horse on the flank.

"Good girl," he said, acknowledging the horse for a job well done.

Then he turned to Judith, who was still catching her breath. "Are you all right?"

He reached out to touch her arm where the sleeve of her tunic was torn. She winced from a scrape she had acquired on the splintery wagon.

"Let me see," said Marcus. "Are you wounded?"

"It is nothing. A few scratches."

Her chest still heaved and her words came in phrases. "How did you know? . . . The Saxons . . . brought me here . . . Galswinth. Did they kill her?"

Marcus extracted a wineskin from his saddle and untied the mouth. "Drink this," he said. "It will give you strength."

She did as she was told, letting the liquid wet her parched throat. "Thank you," she said.

Marcus took a swig of wine himself, then looked back in the direction from which they'd come. But seeing no one chasing them, he decided the Saxons were by now well in hand.

"We outnumbered them," he said. "We vanquished their main force at the Meuse, but King Sigibert wanted to teach them a lesson. And so our forces decimated their lands and burned Woolgar's camp. Perhaps now they will understand what will happen to their people if they continue their raids on our lands."

He turned back to face her. "Your queen is safe. The guard fought off the pirates who abducted you."

She heaved a great sigh, attempting to stand. "You speak as if you knew I was here."

He lifted a dark eyebrow. "I did know."

Her eyes widened and her heart began to return to its normal beat. She blinked at him. "How did you know?"

"King Chilperic got word of the abduction at

our camp."

She frowned. "But you fight for King Sigibert. And the men with you were not soldiers I had seen before."

"No," said Marcus. "King Chilperic has returned to Neustria, taking his share of Saxon booty. But Sigibert wanted to advance further and make sure the Saxons were pushed across the Rhine for good."

Her mind took in the facts. Marcus glanced again at the horizon, distracted by the skirmish that had taken place and anxious to make sure all had gone well. Now he faced her again.

"We must find a place to meet the returning forces and follow them to camp. Sigibert will march again this way once Woolgar's village has been burned to the ground."

Judith thought of the women and children with the Saxons. "What about the innocents among them? When your forces attacked, women and children followed the band of warriors."

Marcus looked grim. "Sigibert may take some prisoners. But I doubt many will be left."

Her heart contracted as she thought of poor Leagh. Marcus took the bridle and led his horse a little way. Judith followed. There were still many unanswered questions. She went over what Marcus had said about having word after the Saxons had attacked the royal train to Poitiers.

"Why . . ." she began but did not know how to finish.

His voice was gentler as he responded to her half-formed question. "Yes?"

She raised her chin to look at him. "Why did you come and not . . ." Her mouth felt dry. "Not Chilperic's men, if you knew I was at Woolgar's camp."

Marcus looked away from her, and she saw his jaw tighten. He seemed not to want to look her in the eyes. "I know what you are asking," he said slowly.

She waited. Marcus finally looked at her. "Count Ivar is dead," he said. "An enemy spear pierced through the rings of mail. Someone saw a Saxon warrior strike him in the thigh. It must have weakened him and he fell, unable to defend himself. He must have died quickly. In any case, he died nobly, protecting his king. It would have been the way he wanted to die. I am sorry. He was a brave warrior."

He reached out to steady her by grasping her arm as she took in what he had said. *Ivar was dead.*

For a moment she simply stared dumbly at him, unbelieving. She could hardly grasp the fact that the man she saw fight to the death with the fiercest opponent the day of the trial by combat had been struck down by a Saxon heathen.

She felt her knees buckle, and Marcus reached around her to hold her up. She leaned against him, grasping his shoulders with her hands.

"I can't believe it," she whispered, her heart twisting inside of her.

Then from the east a blur of horsemen approached. Marcus stiffened and then spoke. "Quickly, into the saddle."

He cupped his hands to give her a step up, and she obeyed. Then he hoisted himself up behind her, and wrapping his arms around her, grasped the reins. He urged his horse forward. From this distance they could not make out whether it was Franks or Saxons approaching.

"We must be ready to fly," he said in her ear, "in case for some unthinkable reason, the enemy prevailed and those are they. Though I do not see how that can have happened."

He rode his horse at a walk in a circle toward the oncoming horsemen, then turned at an angle to them, so that if need be, they could light out over the plain in a fast getaway. But Marcus's eyes were keener than hers, and she heard him breathe in relief.

"We have prevailed. See the standards flying in the wind."

And then she saw it, the flags of St. Martin's blue cloak, waving from the long pole carried by the standard bearers. Marcus urged his horse to a trot, and rode to meet the men coming this way. Judith saw from the emblem in gold on his leather shield which one was the king. He was surrounded by the standard bearers.

The Franks halted and Marcus rode up to the king. "I rescued the hostage," he said to the king, who looked Judith up and down.

"I see. So this is the woman who is friend to my sister-in-law," said Sigibert.

Judith found her voice. "I am that, my lord. My name is Judith."

He chuckled. "Well then, we've done a good day's work. Decimated a Saxon camp and rescued a lady." He saluted to Marcus. "My compliments, Count Petronius."

"I will see that she is returned to her people," said Marcus.

She did not miss the ironic smile in Sigibert's eyes. "She must be our guest for as long as she likes first," he said.

"Thank you, my lord," said Judith.

Then Marcus turned and they rode in line with the rest of the men, some hundreds of them coming along behind at a greater distance. She did not speak, rather she concentrated on grasping the raised part of the saddle where she sat, staring at the wide delta with bogs on either side, which they avoided. As the horse jostled along, guided by Marcus's firm arms, which were wrapped around her, she tried to form some semblance of thought. Ivar was dead. Gone, his body buried on this dreary plain. She tried to think of Galswinth, who was safe at Poitiers. In her heart she reached out to try to touch the spirits of her other friends at Poitiers, but felt she did not succeed.

When they arrived at the main body of the camp, Marcus took her to his tent, which was comfortably furnished as was fitting for his rank. His servant met them and held the horse while they dismounted. She slid down into his arms, then he guided her to the tent.

"You will be at least as comfortable here as at the Saxon camp, I hope," he said. But his attempt at humor did not lighten even his own heart.

As he looked at the dirt-stained face and the ripped clothing of the lovely woman standing before his tent, he felt his own heart twist. Her eyes were wide with disbelief and shock, and he wanted to comfort her, knowing her uncertainty. Even though he had felt the sting of jealousy when he had first learned that she had a protector, now he felt only compassion. It was not easy to lose a lover in battle. She would need to give vent to her grief.

Judith entered the tent and stared about her at the simple camp furniture, seeing little. Then she sank onto the camp stool and stared at the edge of the table on which was spread some parchment sheets, a wax writing tablet, and stylus.

Her hand went to the talisman she had kept around her neck and finally the grief welled up inside her. Tears slid down her cheek as she clutched the talisman and thought of Ivar. Then she stood. The military camp was too crowded and noisy. She needed to be alone. She walked outside, not sure where she was going, but she went past the soldiers huddled in groups, stumbling here and there until she saw a copse of trees some distance away. She pushed her way through servants and around supply carts until she found the main gate of the camp.

273

There the guard stopped her. "Whose woman are you?"

She lifted her head. "My protector, Count Ivar, was killed in the battle with the Saxons. Count Marcus Petronius brought me here."

The man glared down at her and for a moment it looked like a battle of wills. Then she said, "I want to be alone." She pointed. "Over there, in those trees."

The guard exchanged glances with his companion, who shrugged. Then he removed the spear he had thrust in her way. "Very well," he said. "There are no Saxons left to harm you."

And the two soldiers laughed loudly as she scurried around them. The camp had been built near a shallow stream, and she found her way to it. Wide flat stones led across, and she took them, escaping to the other side. Here the shade of spreading oaks offered solitude, and Judith wandered among them, touching their bark.

She grieved for a man she hardly knew, yet a man who had shared intimacy with her, who had given her strength and shown her a way of life in the Merovingian court. She let go a sob and leaned into the bark of an old oak tree.

"Ivar," she whispered, and the trees dipped with a breeze as if his spirit responded.

She sank to the base of the tree and remembered him. Removing the talisman and its chain from her neck, she held it in her palm and thought about the times she had spent with him, flying the falcons, training the cheetah, riding in the forests and finding shrines to the old gods, and making love. For a moment she communed with Ivar's spirit, and then she knew suddenly what he had known the day of the battle at the Meuse. He had known that he would die that day.

She knew it as surely as if he were there telling her so.

"You knew, didn't you?" she whispered.

A crow cawed in the branches above her and flapped its wings as if in answer.

Then she thought of the first time she had seen him, when he had saved her from the boar and thought how her fate had been entwined with his. So brief had been their time together. They had not really had time to experience all of life. It was rather more as if they had been thrown together for mutual survival in a whirling vortex of danger and uncertainty. But she had clung to him, and she knew that she had also given him solace, relief from the hardships of a man's world and perhaps bolstered his courage to fight his battles.

"Did I serve you well, my lord?" she whispered to the breeze, clutching the talisman harder as the tears slid down her cheeks. She bent her knees and wrapped her arms around them, sobbing into the folds of her tunic as the afternoon sun stretched long shadows across the plain before her.

After a while, when her grief had spent itself, she rose and walked a little way into the woods. Long fingers of setting sun stretched through the woods like a golden pathway, and for a moment she could almost see Ivar's spirit walking through the woods he so loved. She felt the talisman she still carried in her hand and raised it to her heart.

"Farewell, my lord," she whispered. "Walk with grace in the next life."

Then she raised her arm and held the talisman high in the air where the sun caught it and turned it to gold fire. She would keep it forever, but it would also belong to the gods of the forest, just as Ivar would. She stood, the streaks of gold flying from her hand in the forest.

And it was thus that Marcus found her.

Chapter Eighteen

She heard the footfall and turned slowly, the streaks fading as the sun died in the woods. Marcus gazed at her, relieved to have found her. For a moment they stared at each other.

"I did not know where you had gone," he said a little gruffly in order to cover his own feelings of concern. "The guards were foolish to let you wander about alone."

"I wanted to be alone," she said.

Relieved that she was unharmed, Marcus relaxed slightly, glancing at the peaceful glade, which had been unscathed by marching armies.

"I understand."

She did not move toward him, so he took some steps in her direction. The urge to comfort her was strong, but he withheld any gesture of solace. She seemed so determined to be self-sufficient. The straightness of her spine, the lift of her chin, even her dry eyes told him she did not want to share her grief, though he could see the red rims and knew she had been crying.

Twisted emotions coursed through him. She was not his responsibility. He was too busy to take on the care of a ward. He would have to see her safely back to her queen, if that was where she wanted to go. And yet as he gazed at the soft folds of her tunic as it drifted, still in shreds, around her, at the face that tears had washed, at the defiant yet compassionate spirit he sensed in her, he felt drawn toward her.

She was desirable, but he had always been aware of that. When he had first set eyes on her at Chilperic's wedding he had felt the pull of sensuality that her face and figure had aroused in him. But she was not his to touch, and so he had forgotten her. Now, alone in the forest, with a battle behind him, her own sense of loneliness and her solitary fortitude reawakened his senses.

But a woman in his camp was a complication he had not planned for and had not time for. The Saxons were beaten for the moment but there was still much work to be done. Already he heard his king's grumblings about King Guntram's lack of support in the campaign, and Marcus feared that the Austrasian forces would no sooner march toward home than Sigibert would decide to revenge the slight he felt Guntram had paid him by not coming to his aid. And so his mind was busy contemplating what he would have to do next to avoid senseless battle.

Marcus was not afraid of killing for a just cause. And certainly the Saxons' marauding of Merovingian lands was worth a reprisal, but the endless squabbles between the Merovingian kings was senseless, and he hated wasteful wars and worked to prevent them with the skills of negotiation and law he had inherited from his ancestors.

Judith herself perceived the difficulty she posed for Marcus. She pressed her lips together, then walked toward him.

"I haven't thanked you for rescuing me from the Saxons," she said with embarrassment. "I was lucky you heard my screams."

Marcus gave her a half smile. "It was my pleasure. I

wouldn't have let the Saxons have the satisfaction of keeping you."

She answered his smile with a bittersweet one of her own. Marcus Petronius had a bravado that reminded her of Ivar, and yet he was very much his own man.

He looked at the sylvan glade, knowing she had come here to commune with nature and to say goodbye to the warrior who should by right have come to claim her from the Saxon camp, and he wondered if she had found solace. Then he looked at her with a gentle expression.

"Are you ready to return?"

She nodded, turning from the spot she would always remember. Marcus led the way, and when they reached the stream, he crossed on the flat rocks, then stood on the opposite bank extending a hand to help her across. She felt the strength in the firm grasp, and was reluctant to let it go once she was safely on the other side.

The camp was settling down for the night, soldiers gathered around fires that dotted the camp as night fell. Marcus left her alone in the tent to bathe from a bowl and pitcher of fresh stream water. She unbound her hair and combed it out with her fingers.

When Marcus returned, he served her a cup of wine, and his servant brought them meat and vegetables roasted on skewers and served on a platter. They sat at the table in his tent, a lantern casting a soft glow in the small, intimate space. She didn't realize how hungry she was, and the taste of fresh vegetables was greatly appreciated.

"We will leave tomorrow," said Marcus. "I will see you safely back to the court in Neustria."

"Thank you," she said, lowering her eyes. "I am sorry to be so much trouble."

He set down his cup and let his fingers brush her arm as he leaned forward slightly. "It is no trouble."

She slowly raised her eyes to his and blushed. Hadn't she once regretted that this man, with such a cultured Gallo-Roman past and such a noble bearing, did not reside in Neustria? Now she was alone with him and could have the opportunity to talk to him all she pleased. And he was volunteering to escort her back to Neustria. There was no denying the kindred spirit that sprang between them every time they met, but now in his presence, she felt tongue-tied.

"I . . . shall . . . be anxious to see Galswinth," she managed to say.

"Yes, I'm sure she will be relieved that you are alive." As he said it, he had the absurd notion that he wished Judith would remain with the Austrasian court and not return to Neustria. But he knew she had duties to the queen.

"You are very close to the queen then?" he said.

She nodded. "We were childhood friends in Spain. I never thought to see her again until the day she came through Poitiers on the way to marry King Chilperic."

"Yes, so you told me."

She felt oddly pleased that he remembered. He smiled, the lantern casting a soft glow about his gold-brown eyes. She liked the way his smooth, tanned skin creased about the corners of the eyes and his mouth when he smiled.

Marcus brought his mind back to more serious matters, afraid that if he stared at her vulnerable smile, the inviting folds of tunic across her breast, that he might lose control of himself. He sensed that she might return the feeling, but it was too soon after the death of her lover. She would not appreciate advances on the heels of such an occasion. The thought that she would be in his care all the way back to Poitiers was equally disturbing, and he chided himself for his desire.

Not that he did not have plenty of opportunity to choose a woman from among slaves, nobles, or peasants, it was just that he had difficulty finding one who suited him. The intelligent ones were too old and too full of life's experience to please the senses the way a man his age needed, and the sensual ones were only bodies with too little experience to prove interesting dinner companions. Those women with whom he could share matters other than that of the flesh were more like older sisters, mothers, or nuns, and his physical needs were left to be satisfied among concubines and whores, making him feel like a bull sent out to rut. It was the reason he had put off marriage.

Marcus poured more wine, for instead of taking his mind off the matter, he dwelled upon it. He poured more wine for Judith as well, letting the feelings flow between them.

Judith relaxed in the comfortable atmosphere. Though a part of herself still felt lost and lonely, Marcus was going a good distance to close the wound. She both looked forward and feared her return to Neustria. Without Ivar she felt as if an arm were missing. And she fought back a new surge of grief as she thought how she must now care for the cheetah alone.

Then she blinked. What of Kahluli?

"Is my cheetah still alive?" she asked Marcus.

He lifted his brows slowly. "So it is your cheetah?"

"Yes," she said. "Kahluli was in a cage when we were attacked. Did the Saxons kill her?"

Marcus laughed. "No. One of your guards got the cage doors opened, and the cheetah attacked a Saxon. They succeeded in getting her back in the cage after it was all over because she was still collared to a chain."

The thought made Judith smile sadly. "Then I will see her."

"Yes."

Judith sighed. Galswinth needed her, but she even contemplated spending some time at the Abbey of the Holy Cross, if they would have her. Time to regain the sustenance she needed, time perhaps to decide what to do with her life. For as much as she loved Galswinth, would she grow old in her service? Then what?

Marcus looked at her, seeing the thoughts flicker across her eyes. Then he rose and walked around the table, taking her hand and lifting her up.

"Make yourself comfortable here for the night," he said. "I will sleep outside."

She started to protest, but then pressed her lips together. She could hardly invite him to share the tent with her. So she gave a little nod.

Marcus gathered a bedroll and blanket and prepared to leave while his servant came to clear the table. Then they were left alone again.

"Sleep well," he said to her. "We will break camp early."

"Yes."

He gazed at her for a long moment, and then he raised his hand to her face and did what he had said he would not do. He leaned down and kissed her.

His warm lips found hers, and one arm drifted across her narrow shoulders, and at once his body responded to her softness. But he kept the kiss chaste and comforting.

Judith, already relaxed from the wine, returned the kiss, a fresh set of tears threatening at the contact of Marcus's soft lips, his strong arm holding her lightly. It was a kiss of solace, and she placed her hands on his chest lightly. She did not push him away. Ivar was gone; what did it matter if she took a little comfort from this man who had compassion for her plight?

And then Marcus gently lifted his head before desire gave itself away, and he stepped back.

"Good night," he said, keeping the emotion out of his voice.

"Good night," she said, feeling the emptiness of the air between them. And then he lifted the flap of the tent and was gone.

Judith blew out the lantern, lay down on the canvas bed and drew the blankets around her. His kiss had warmed her, but now she contemplated the future as a confused mass of imagery swirled through her mind.

The next day they rode across the low fertile plain lying between the Rhine River basin and the forest-covered Vosges Mountains, passing the lush vineyards, hopfields, and blossoming fruit trees. Marcus rode in advance of the army, requisitioning last year's dried fruit and arranging payment before turning the soldiers loose to satisfy themselves. The army began to disperse as each count rode off to his canton, his men following. Except for the regular soldiers and guards, the men recruited for the battle at the Meuse were released to return to their homes.

Judith rode in a chariot, enjoying the ripe, moist day. Her eye delighted in the color of the gay red poppy, contrasting with green grasses. At the end of the day's march, they made camp, and after bathing in a stream, she again shared supper with Marcus, this time listening to him tell her of his family and his villa near Verdun.

The following day they crossed the Marne, and now with a smaller force, they kept to the old Roman roads to avoid clashes with robbers in the woods. Judith found she enjoyed the sojurn, many times walking with Marcus and talking, reveling in the joys of spring. They passed many homesteads where industrious peasants were planting their crops, and they took many meals at abbeys whose occupants always enjoyed news from travelers and had plenty of good wine to serve from their vineyards.

By the time they reached Neustria, the court had returned to Tours, and Judith was reunited with her queen with much celebration. While Marcus was made guest of honor at a banquet, Judith was called upon to relate her adventures to round-eyed, excited women who had never seen Saxons until that awful day the pirates fell on the train.

"We thought for sure you were dead or worse," said Clothild, tears coming to her eyes as she recalled reaching out to Judith as the Saxon brute had snatched her away.

"And so did I," said Judith. "And I feared they left you all dead. I knew nothing until Marcus Petronius's men came to my rescue."

Clothild eyed him at the high table with the king and queen. "He is quite the hero." Then she swallowed and placed a hand on Judith's arm. "Though I am sorry about Count Ivar."

Judith lowered her gaze. "And so am I."

"But he died bravely," said Clothild, "and they say he killed many Saxons before he fell from his wounds."

"Yes," said Judith. "He did." Then she added. "He was a good man."

At the other end of the table, Fredegund eyed Judith and Clothild with narrowed eyes. The friend of the queen had returned from the dead, for she had hoped that the bungling Saxons would have at least done what they were supposed to. And the lady Judith looked none the worse for the experience. The Saxons appeared not to have even touched her, outrageous though that seemed to Fredegund, who had spent much gold on assassins who had failed to do their job. For the queen still lived. There she was, graciously entertaining the handsome Austrasian ambassador who had plucked Judith from the Saxons and restored her to the court. Damn him! Damn the three of them!

Fredegund swallowed several large gulps of wine to quell her anger. But all it did was stiffen her resolve. She had had enough of these nobles. Tonight she would take matters into her own hands, if she could find two trustworthy strong slaves who could be bribed with gold. Not that the gold would do them much good. For after they had done what she asked, they themselves would be too dead to spend their newfound fortune.

Her plan in mind, Fredegund slipped out of the hall and went to her chambers, which were private now that she was back in the king's good graces as mistress. First, she went to the writing desk and took out a sheet of parchment. Then she unstopped the bottle of her special ink and dipped a stylus into it. She wrote a message in handwriting that looked enough like Chilperic's to pass for it, if one did not look too closely, for she had studied his writing for some time, thinking she might have need to imitate it.

Then she went out into the hall and found a serving woman. "Here," she said, putting the note along with a piece of gold into the woman's hand. "Give this to the queen as soon as she returns to her bedchamber."

The woman nodded and slipped the gold coin into the folds of her tunic. Then Fredegund returned to her chamber where she unlocked the small wooden chest she had formerly kept hidden in the woods. She took out an envelope of powder and poured its contents into a carafe of wine, then swirled the liquid around so that the powder dissolved. Setting the carafe and two gem-encrusted goblets on a tray, she went to the door and summoned her maid, waiting in the outer room by the fire.

"Go to the stables," she ordered. "Bring the two slaves, Salomen and Apponius here at once."

The woman nodded and slipped silently out the door to do as she was bid. By the time she returned with the brawny slaves who had been captured from the Frisians, Fredegund was arrayed in her chamber, draped across a sofa, her blue tunic complementing breast, hip, and thigh.

"Welcome, my lads," she said when her serving maid had shut the door.

The slaves bowed low. They had done several tasks for the lady Fredegund in the past and had always been well paid.

"How may we serve you, madam?"

Fredegund fingered a long, stout, silken rope which she twirled and wound between her fingers. "You will use this tonight on someone. It will not be hard. But first, enjoy a glass of wine to strengthen you for the task."

She smiled maliciously, enjoying her little ploy. The two slaves took up the goblets and drank down its contents. As slaves, they were seldom given wine, and reached for more.

"That's right, my lads. Enjoy it." She moved her head seductively as if to suggest that there were more pleasures in store for them after they did their job.

"Now," she said, as they stood listening, "Tonight the queen will be in her chamber. I have seen to that. She will be alone, because I will see to it that the king is here." She snapped the silken rope tight between her own two strong hands. "Use this on her throat. Make sure she is dead."

The two men stared at the rope as Fredegund continued to outline her plan. "That door leads to a passage. To the left it goes to the courtyard. At the other end of it is the door to the queen's chamber. You will wait there in the darkness until the king passes through. Once he is here, go to find the queen in her bed. When you are done, leave through the courtyard. No one will see you."

285

The older slave nodded in understanding and extended his hand for the rope. Fredegund gave it to him, smiling into the hardened dark eyes and admiring the muscles in his well-developed chest and arms.

"It will be easy," she whispered. "Her neck is small."

She poured more wine, then sent them into the passage to wait. She left the chamber and returned to the banquet hall where the revelry was now accompanied by lyres, cymbals, panpipes, and timbrels. She had no difficulty wending her way along the tables where men and women mixed in gay companionship.

The queen, whose back was turned, was engaged in conversation with Marcus Petronius, so Fredegund leaned next to Chilperic, placing her hand on the back of his chair in the skillful way she had of giving him a view of her swelling bosom.

"Tonight, my lord," she whispered into his ear. "I promise you new raptures I have discovered from the arts in the faraway east." And she let her tongue trace her lower lip as her eyelids lowered.

Chilperic, his senses filled with wine and rich food responded to the inviting mistress, staring at the gold-braided edge of material that seemed to slip toward the point of a breast that strained against thin silk.

"I will be waiting in my chamber, my lord," she said, rising so that her breast brushed his shoulder.

Chilperic felt the surge in his groin and took another swig of wine. The entertainment was well underway. His eyes followed Fredegund as she left the room. He would go to her as soon as he could get away.

Marcus was enjoying his conversation with the queen, finding in her some of the qualities that Judith had mentioned. He told Galswinth what he could of her sister, who longed to see her, and he promised to relay Galswinth's messages to Brunhild. When he felt he had dominated the queen's time long enough, he made his excuses.

"I must start my journey homeward early tomorrow morning," he said. "And so with your permission I will go to take my rest."

Galswinth smiled in understanding. "I, too, do not take to late-night revelries, but prefer a night's rest and an early rising before the court is about its business."

As he got up, Galswinth gave him her hand and looked solemnly into his eyes. "I can never thank you enough for returning Judith to me," she said.

Marcus looked over to where Judith sat among the other women. "I can see why you treasure her, my lady," he said with feeling.

Then he smiled and bowed low to the queen. As he turned to leave the room, he gazed at Judith. He would at least like to tell her goodbye.

Watching Marcus out of the corner of her eye, she saw him hesitate at the door. He was leaving tomorrow, and she must thank him again for bringing her back to the court. She made her excuses to Clothild and the other women and rose to follow Marcus out.

He waited for her in the courtyard by a fountain, his dark blue cloak blending with the night. He turned when he heard her soft footstep, and watched her glide across the flagstones toward him. When she came to him, he took her hands in his and looked into her eyes.

"And so," he said, "I must leave on the morrow. My duty calls me back."

"I know," she said, "though I wish you could dwell among us longer."

"Do you?"

He felt a rush of emotion and was tempted to take her in his arms again, but he did not want to offend her.

Judith trembled, knowing now that if Marcus stayed

at the court of Neustria much longer, the affection between them might grow. She was no longer afraid of it. She had mourned for Ivar and could no longer remain tied to him. Life marched on, and the living, breathing man before her touched her in a way few other mortals had. But she could not ask Marcus to stay.

For his part, her words encouraged him, and he began to formulate a thought.

"You might come with me," he said suddenly, closing the distance between them.

Judith drew a sharp breath, but she could not speak. "I . . . cannot," she finally said. "It is . . . too soon."

Nevertheless he drew her to him and kissed her forehead. Too soon, yes, he could understand that. But he hated to leave her here.

"What will you do?" he said. "Your protector is gone."

"I shall not need a protector," she said bravely, taking in the scent of him, her cheek on the soft muslin of his silver- and gold-embroidered tunic, his cloak half draped over her shoulder as he held her with one arm.

Then his hand threaded its way beneath her hair to the base of her neck and upward to tilt her head toward him. "How do you know that?" he breathed.

Her eyes half closed, she reminded him of a cat, stretched out in the sun.

"No one will harm me," she said. "I have even greater status now, having escaped the Saxons." Her eyes came open and she favored him with an impish grin.

He smiled at her cleverness. "So you have."

Still, he did not resist lowering his mouth to hers, to a kiss that was new but familiar and moving his lips against hers. She stretched her arms around his neck and returned the kiss, her body betraying the desire for his embrace to grow tighter. Suddenly, the longing she had held suppressed spilled over in the way her breasts pressed against him and the way her mouth parted to receive his tongue, which probed delightedly.

Pleasure rushed through Marcus as he tasted what he had wanted to taste the many days and nights they had traveled together, though he had remained circumspect, glad when they slept at an abbey where there was no chance of visiting her during the night. But here in the garden where sensuousness reigned in the Merovingian court, it was more difficult to hold himself back. He folded her against him and kissed her more ardently now, his hands roaming along her back and the sweet curves of her hips.

"Judith, come with me," he whispered as he bent his head against her ear. "I will make you mine. No other man shall claim you. The court in Austrasia will please you. And you will greatly please them."

She could hardly answer for the beating of her heart and the quickness of her breathing as his hands slid up her sides to cup her firm breasts. His touch was gentle, like music from a lyre, in contrast to the demanding, fierce touch of Ivar. Marcus moved slowly, dropping kisses on her throat and shoulder, pushing her mantle aside. Then he wrapped her in his arms again and held her as she pressed against his firm body.

How tempting was his offer, how much she wanted him. But she, too, was duty bound, surely he could understand that.

"I cannot go . . . yet," she said breathlessly. "Come back for me, one day soon. Perhaps when . . ."

"When what?" he asked between soft, quick, moist kisses that clung to her lips.

She burrowed her head beneath his chin. "When I feel it is safe."

Marcus felt the tremor that went through her. "You still feel danger here?" he asked.

She nodded against him. "I cannot name it, but I know it is here. I cannot leave until it is banished."

Marcus smiled into the night. "My brave one. Duty before pleasure?" And yet he could not help but admire her sense of loyalty and responsibility.

He forced his limbs to cooperate and release her. "Then I must tear myself away before I am lost."

Still, she clung to his hands. "Will I see you again?"

Marcus removed a ring from his finger and pressed it into her hands. "I promise you will."

Then his words turned more serious. "I fear the old rivalry between the two kings will flare. With no one else to fight, they will soon turn on each other. It will be my job to keep them apart. So you see, I will return on official duty in the near future. But send this ring with a fast messenger if you should need me, and I will not wait on duty to bring me to your side."

She blinked back tears and pressed the ring to her breast. "Yes," she said. "Then I will wait patiently."

"Not too patiently, I hope," he said in a more guttural voice and clasped her to him once more.

Then, while he still had a semblance of control over his body, he stepped back, turned, and left her alone in the courtyard, thinking how he would remember her beauty in the moonlight, soft and pliant against the ferns and wide leaves of the garden.

Chapter Nineteen

The cheetah had grown in the weeks Judith had been away, and when she went to visit her in the cage, she moved cautiously, letting Kahluli get her scent as she gave her food, then slowly opened the cage door.

"Kahluli's a good girl," she said in a lively voice. "Kahluli's a good girl. Come here, Kahluli."

The cat came toward her making the puffing, purring noise made by letting air escape from her cheeks through her mouth while vibrating her lips. It was a friendly sound. Then she reached into the cage and secured the chain around her neck.

The cat rolled playfully, her paws in the air. When Judith took her out of the cage to begin their walk, Kahluli moved along easily at her side, and Judith felt relieved. Kahluli had not forgotten her. She worked slowly and carefully. She had to pick up the training where she and Ivar had left it.

Leaving the long chain on the cat, Judith knelt beside her. "Sit," she commanded, pointing to the ground.

Kahluli turned around and looked at Judith in the eye.

"Sit," she commanded again.

This time Kahluli sat and was rewarded with a

piece of meat. While she ate, Judith praised her. Then when she had finished eating, Judith rose slowly and commanded the cat to stay. She walked away, the long chain winding behind her like a snake. She had turned and was about to call Kahluli to come, when a loud scream from the second floor of the palace sent a shiver up her spine. But her eyes did not leave the cheetah. Instead, she tightened the length of chain between herself and Kahluli, not wanting to frighten the cat and have her try to run.

But the cries inside the palace built as several shrieks echoed from the women's quarters and even before the words were intelligible, a paralyzing fear crawled along Judith's spine. But she had to get the cheetah safely in the cage, even though her first impulse was to bolt to the palace to see what was wrong. As soon as she had Kahluli secured in her cage she walked away, not wanting to show fear in the presence of the animal.

Then she set out at a run across the compound. She took the outside stairs to the second-story and slammed into Epoald at the top. He waylaid her, holding her arm.

"It's the queen," he said grimly. "She's dead. Strangled in her bed."

A lead weight seemed to drop in Judith's stomach, and for a moment she could not move. From the gray pallor on Epoald's face she knew there was no mistake. Even so, she whispered, "Are you sure?"

Epoald's grip on her lightened, as he nodded, glancing from left to right as if the murderers might be near.

"Strangled with a rope around her neck." He gestured with a finger around his own throat.

Judith stared at him for another instant, then set off

down the corridor. She had to squeeze past the people crowded into the royal chambers. The women were weeping, the palace physician had just arrived and was bending over the queen. Judith made her way to the bed and stared down at the pale, lifeless body. The arms lay akimbo, the head cocked, the throat purple with marks of a rope that had squeezed the life from her. Mercifully, the physician shut the eyes, which even in death bulged in horror.

Judith sank to her knees, not to pray but because they would not carry her anymore. She clung to the bed as everyone buzzed around her. She stared at Galswinth's body and murmured her name as the horror enveloped her. What her friend had feared since the night of the *Sortes Biblicae* had finally come to pass. But who had wrought this terrible deed?

Then the crowd parted behind her and murmuring stopped as everyone turned to stare at Chilperic who entered the room. When he saw Galswinth, his own face paled. Judith stared up at him and the question that formed in her mind must have laid on everyone's lips. Had he done this thing?

Chilperic staggered, then fell to his knees, his lips trembling. He reached out to touch Galswinth's body, then withdrew his hands, burying his face in them and began to sob. Judith watched his display of emotion, but her stomach twisted. Chilperic had not loved his wife. Was this display of emotion for show only? Or was he touched by her death as he never had been by her life?

Judith rose slowly. One thing she vowed: She would discover who had done this and they would pay. She silently mumbled a prayer then, vowing to do this for her friend. She would not rest until Galswinth's death was avenged.

* * *

Father Gregory conducted the funeral services for the queen with much honor and display. Then a great procession wound its way to the city of Paris, where the body was interred in the church of Saint Germain des Prés. Judith rode numbly with the funeral procession, and stayed at the tomb after the body was interred, feeling lost, more lonely than ever, and confused. It was Father Gregory with whom she could talk, and who began to bring her back to life as they walked one day along the Left Bank of the River Seine past stalls of vendors. Peasants with ox carts rumbled by carting their goods to market. Just ahead was the Roman theater, now falling into disrepair out of lack of use. The newer part of the city spread along the left bank and up the slope of Mount St. Genevieve, though the older buildings and the center of government remained on the Île de la Cité. Gregory had traveled to Paris with the funeral procession because of his close association with the royal family.

"This is a great loss for you, my dear," said Father Gregory.

Judith nodded. For long hours she had kept a vigil by the casket before it was entombed. She grieved for her friend, for her own lost past, for the emptiness, and what she struggled to find words for—the uncertainty of her future and of where she belonged. Now anger took over where grief left off and her words were harsh.

"The murderer must pay."

Gregory sighed as they walked on. "I know. So difficult to establish who is responsible."

"I will find out," said Judith.

He did not miss the determination in her voice.

"And then?"

She looked at him and said nothing, but the vengeance in her eyes was clear.

"My dear," he said. "Vengeance is the Lord's. The murderer must be rooted out and punished as God would want him to be, by the law."

"The law may not be severe enough for those who can escape it," she said, her resentment unmasked.

A small shiver passed up Gregory's spine. "You must not endanger your own soul, Judith, for the sake of revenge." But even as he cautioned her, he suspected he spoke to the air. For revenge was so deeply ingrained in these people that even professed Christians still believed it their right.

Judith said nothing. To her it was clear who the murderers must be. "The murder must have been ordered either by the king or by his mistress Fredegund."

Gregory shook his head. Her words were nothing new to him. "Perhaps. But we must have proof. I will certainly entreat the murderers to confess."

Judith went on. "Of course their hands are clean. They will have hired it done. But the assassins must be sought out."

Gregory spoke gently, trying to assuage the troubled soul before him. "And what of your life, my dear? What will you do now?"

She spoke more sharply than she meant to. "Nothing until Galswinth's murderers pay for their sins." Then she looked meekly at him. "I'm sorry, Father. But I have no life except for Galswinth."

He placed a hand on her arm. "I know how you feel, and your sorrow is great. But you are young and your life lies ahead of you. After your period of mourning, you must think of yourself. Your friend would have wanted it that way."

His soft words brought tears then. Tears for both Galswinth and for Ivar, the only two people in the Neustrian court she had been close to. The other friendships were superficial and would be forgotten as life marched on. But Ivar and Galswinth she would always remember, though for very different reasons.

She walked over to a stone bench by the river and sat down, wiping her eyes. Gregory followed more slowly, giving her time to get a hold of herself. She appreciated the priest's friendship. He was solace in a time of sorrow, and his gentle piety was comforting. She could not expect him to understand her need to discover who had ordered Galswinth's death and see them brought to retribution. But his next words surprised her.

"As the king's spiritual counselor, I feel it my duty to get to the bottom of this matter. I will use my influence to conduct an investigation. Perhaps the guilty party will see fit to confess."

"Yes, Father." Her resolve gained strength. "And I myself will look for any information that will help you."

Gregory nodded and patted her hand. "Then as a team we will try to root out this evil."

Strong words for a priest, she thought. But that was why she liked Gregory. He had a certain worldliness that made his job as spiritual protector easier. He understood what lay in the hearts of men.

There was no funeral for the two Frisians who suddenly died after violent cramping. They were carried into the countryside and buried by their fellow slaves. Simple wooden crosses marked the graves. No one mourned them.

It was no surprise, when a few weeks later, Chilperic married Fredegund in Paris and made her queen. As Judith sat in the incense-filled basilica and watched the showy ritual, the phrase *murderers* kept turning over and over in her heart. She thought Father Gregory's admonishment to the couple to make their confessions and lead a chaste life were wasted.

There was one worthwhile outcome of the wedding celebrations. Marcus was here. He had come as official representative of Sigibert's court, and Judith knew he would remain for a few days. As soon as they set eyes on each other in the formal court, understanding had been exchanged between them. Now she only waited for the official ceremony to be over so that she could speak to him.

They had no difficulty slipping away from the celebrations. They made their way through the excited peasant crowd, who waited as near the wedding feast as they could to pass along gossip and who hoped for gifts from nobles whose celebratory mood often made them generous, then they crossed the bridge to the Left Bank and found an isolated spot. In a grove of poplars on the gentle slope, they could see down to the Île de la Cité and the part of the city that had spilled across to the Left Bank.

Judith wasted no time in telling him of her suspicions. Marcus, who looked even more handsome than before in cream tunic and green mantle, listened grimly.

"And how do you propose to discover the truth, covered as it will be by bribes? Where even is the rope that strangled her?"

He placed his hand gently on Judith's shoulder. "I know you loved Queen Galswinth. But if you remain here where the awful deed was done, the poison that has infected the royal household will infect you as well. You cannot stay here where evil abounds. What good can you do in Fredegund's employ?"

"I have an idea," said Judith, undeterred by Marcus's warning. "When the court retires to the villa at Soissons there will be no one at the palace at Tours. It will be the perfect opportunity to investigate the crime."

Marcus blinked in surprise. "What do you expect to find?"

She looked at him with determination. "I expect to find out how the murderers got into the bedchamber to do the deed. The palaces are built with many passages. We can see how the murderers escaped. No one saw Chilperic go to Fredegund's room the night Galswinth was murdered. And yet that is where he was. How did he get there?"

Marcus let the idea sink in. Then he focused on the word she had let drop. "We?"

She dropped her eyes hastily. "I admit I was hoping you would assist me. For I cannot travel to Tours alone."

Her invitation half amused him, and already his mind began to fabricate an excuse to send to his court to explain the delay in his return. He slipped his arms around her shoulders, his voice dropping to a soft, seductive tone.

"And you, my love? What will you tell that beast Fredegund in order to explain why you are leaving the court?"

Judith began to swoon at the long-awaited touch of this man who she had sorely missed, though she had not wanted to admit it to herself. In answer to his question as he kissed her hair while his fingers trailed upward through it, she said, "I will tell her I have taken a lover."

Marcus smiled as a surge of pleasure raced through his body. With one hand unfastening his mantle for them to lie upon, he lowered her to the ground. "That," he said, "is at least something she can understand."

Marcus's lovemaking was slow, sensuous, each caress and kiss lingering so that the pleasure could be stretched out in the long, balmy afternoon, shaded as they were by leafy boughs in a cleft of hill that protected them from any wandering shepherds. Judith lost herself in the caring and pleasure and in the delights of new experiences that were different from what Ivar had shown her.

On the one hand, she felt pleased that she could respond to Marcus with her own experience making her feel somehow worldly and able to give pleasure as well as to receive it. But her freshness and artlessness stirred Marcus to a depth he had not found before and he used every means at his disposal to show her that he meant for their love to be memorable. As she lay against him later, drinking in the pleasure of his slow breathing beside her, her heart turned over with new hope and bittersweetness. She did not know what the future held, but she clung to the moment with every fiber of her being.

As the day faded, they replaced their clothing and Marcus carefully brushed every leaf from her hair, gazing deeply into her eyes, his heart full of the love he felt for this woman, knowing he would go to any length to please and protect her. Then they walked back to the city slowly, reluctant to let go of the idyll they had left behind in their grassy lovers' lair. But by the time they reached the palace steps, each had carved out an appropriate expression on a face that could have been more plaster than flesh, as if they had done no more than take a walk to the fruit vendor's cart by the Seine or given out alms to the poor. Any hint of the intimacy they had shared was hidden from inquiring eyes.

Epoald eyed them from a balcony above, his own curiosity taking reason a step further. But that was his job, to know what things went on inside and without the palace so that he kept his finger on the heartbeat of the court. Epoald had his own suspicions as to how the late queen had died, but he kept them to himself. But looking at Judith and Count Petronius, he wondered what the girl who had been such a close friend to the late queen would do. She had strength and more determination than one would suspect from her humble, fragile origin. After all, she had survived, if only for a few days, among the Saxons, something most women would not come away from unscarred.

That evening in Fredegund's presence with the other women who now served her, Judith was calm, satiated by love, which helped mask her agitated feelings. When Fredegund asked her to brush out her hair, she took up the brush and began long, placid, soothing strokes on the golden strands.

Fredegund considered Judith. She knew how close Judith had been to Galswinth, and she watched the girl carefully. Deciding that she needed to ascertain what was on Judith's mind she excused the other women.

"Leave us alone," Fredegund said to the other ladies, who were only too glad to do so.

Most of them had been loyal to Galswinth, and were unhappy serving Fredegund. But the Visigothic women had no way to travel back home to Spain. A better alternative was to remain here and find husbands among the court.

Judith, too, was grateful to put her case before Fredegund, which she must do carefully, for she knew the woman's cunning.

When they were alone, Fredegund said. "Your hands are soothing. But I am surprised that you wish to use them to serve me since the late queen died."

Judith was prepared for such a challenge, and laid down the brush, beginning to form Fredegund's hair in a long, soft braid.

"It is true I mourn Queen Galswinth. But you forget, I am a slave," she said with humility. "I came to Galswinth from a convent, and my only alternative would be to return there."

"Ah," said Fredegund, picking up a silver bracelet and trying it on her wrist. "And you do not think yourself suited for the veil?"

"No, my lady." After a moment she continued, her voice lowered. "There is something I wish to ask, however."

"Yes?"

"I do wish some time away from the court. There is a journey I wish to make."

"A journey? And where is that?"

Judith managed an embarrassed blush. "I have taken a new lover."

"Ahhhh." Fredegund gave a half smile, turning her head to examine the girl. "I see you did not waste any time. With your protector Ivar buried on the field, of course you would not wish your gifts to go unappreciated."

Judith ignored the slight sarcasm veiled by Fredegund's conspiratorial knowingness. Instead, she sighed as if helplessly in love, which was not far from the way she felt.

"My lover wishes to take me away. I have explained my duties at court, and my desire to remain here where—" She looked at Fredegund, casting her an expression she hoped the queen would understand. "Here where there is always enough to eat, fine clothing, and the occasional jewel. I hope you understand, my lady, that after being deprived of such luxuries for half my life, it is not easy to think of leaving them."

"I see." Fredegund smiled and Judith thought from the queen's look that she had conveyed the right amount of greed. "So that is why you remain here, to possess the comfort and riches of the court life." She gave a knowing laugh. "Then you are not stupid, after all."

"I should hope not."

Her own heart hammered at the dissemblance, but she felt she had convinced Fredegund, who now smiled broadly and laughed.

"So you want it all, do you? Food, clothing, riches, and a lover. You are clever then. And who is this lover?"

Judith lied again, so that Marcus would not come under suspicion.

"A younger son of a landowner. He fought the Saxons, but he is not a noble. Though he wishes to marry me, I refused."

"You are wise. If you married such a man your beauty would be worn out in a year, and he could not support you in the manner you have learned to enjoy. I can see that you are not foolish enough to put love before survival. Nor do you wish to carry out your affair under the eyes of the court where you might ruin your chances of getting a suitable husband."

She looked at Judith with renewed interest. If the girl spoke truth, then she was cunning. But she must tread carefully. If Judith were too intelligent, she might become a danger to Fredegund as well. Though she was satisfied with Judith's answers, the girl bore watching. Fredegund suspected she had not plumbed the depths of her soul yet. But she waved a hand.

"Very well, you may go off with your lover. But take precautions that you do not bear his child. Or if you do, expose it in the woods so that you are not saddled with it."

Judith struggled to keep her expression neutral. "Thank you, madam. I will not be gone long."

Marcus took his official leave of the court and rode out of Paris with his guard of soldiers. Once across the river, he ordered them to continue without him and give word to Sigibert that he was making further inquiries into the death of Galswinth. This was a matter that Sigibert's queen would very much appreciate and so not begrudge him the time spent in the Neustrian kingdom. Brunhild was angry over Galswinth's death and already urging Sigibert to take revenge. However, Sigibert hesitated, for it could not be proved that Chilperic himself had ordered Galswinth's death. It might be other rivals to the queen instead, and he did not want to march on his brother until he was sure.

Judith left the women's chambers when the tower church bell rang for prime at dawn. Trudulf had seen to it that her horse was saddled. He asked no questions. And so she mounted, her long brown cloak trailing over her and the horse. She took Kahluli with her, secured in a wooden cage covered with canvas on the back of her horse. She left the palace, the horse's hooves clipping softly on the cobblestones of the empty streets until she reached the city gates.

The guard at the bridge was snoring. Then she saw Marcus, waiting on the other side, and she breathed easier.

"You had no trouble getting away?" he asked when she crossed the bridge and they sat on their horses at the beginning of the road that would take them to Tours.

"None," she said, smiling in remembrance of what she had told Fredegund. "As I suspected she queried me as to my presence at court now that Galswinth is dead. I gave her reasons she could understand."

"Oh?"

"Greed. I told her I liked the luxury of the court after my life in the abbey."

"And your absence from court?" he inquired.

She smiled at him. "I told her I had taken a lover."

"Indeed," said Marcus, amusement and admiration mingling. "Then let us be on our way."

They rode at an easy gait through the early morning, alert to any signs of highway brigands. But their horses were swift, Marcus was well armed, and the well-traveled road was not dangerous while the sun was in the sky.

From the basilica tower, Gregory watched them go. He knew their mission and wished them God's speed. He himself would return to Tours, but at a slower pace, and help them with any new information they should uncover. But a count and a lady would have access to places a bishop could not go. He rubbed his hands together in the early morning dew, anxious for their discoveries.

Chapter Twenty

Judith and Marcus made the journey to Tours with no difficulty. She reveled in his company, enjoying riding by his side even when they made no conversation. At night they sought hospitality at either monasteries or inns. When they ate and slept at the holy houses, they were comfortably entertained, Kahluli providing much comment, and they were put in separate chambers to sleep. But when they stayed at an inn, Marcus procured a room for them, where Judith experienced the joy of sleeping beside him through the night. Meanwhile, Kahluli was cared for in the stables for a handsome price and the threat that if the cat went missing the stableman would be killed.

On one such night after they had made love, they could not sleep. Marcus propped himself on his elbow and gazed down at her.

"You must come back with me to Austrasia," he said. "I have waited long to find a woman I wanted to be by my side." He kissed her forehead, then gazed at her seriously. "Marry me, Judith, and leave your Neustrian court behind."

Tears sprang to the corners of her eyes and she lifted her hand to touch his cheek with her fingers. Her Frankish lover never asked her to marry him, and she knew that had he lived, Ivar might have tired of her one day. She also knew that what she was beginning to feel for Marcus was bigger, deeper, more all-encompassing than what she had felt for Ivar, but it was too soon to accept his proposal.

"I would like nothing more than to come with you," she said. "But not until Galswinth's death is avenged."

He grasped her fingers and kissed them. "You cannot bring Galswinth back," he said gently.

She shook her head. "But it is my duty to avenge her death. She would do the same for me."

He knew it was useless to argue that point. Revenge was too much a part of Visigothic and Frankish nature to be argued. He took another avenue.

"I do not trust Fredegund or Chilperic. What if Chilperic takes a liking to you and orders you into his royal bed, hmmm? How can he ignore such beauty in his own household?"

She smiled. "If the king or any other man tried to bed me, I would defend myself with the dagger Galswinth gave me. I shall wear it on my person at all times that you are not with me."

Marcus chuckled at her ferocity.

"And if our two kingdoms go to war, as Queen Brunhild is pressing, it will be dangerous."

"It is not I who shall be in danger. You will be leading your troops into battle, will you not?" she said grimly.

"I shall not die in battle," he said with certainty. Then a glint of conspiracy came into his eye. "I shall live to a very ripe old age."

Then he gazed at her lovingly and caressed her cheek. "I love you, Judith. I do not want you to slip from my fingers."

"Do not worry. If the kingdoms go to war, I shall remain as a spy for you. I can profess loyalty to Fredegund. She does not suspect me because I have made it known to her that I am greedy and wish to remain in the lap of luxury while enjoying the favors of my poverty-stricken lover, whose identity shall remain unknown."

"Clever," he said, dropping kisses on her lips. "Very clever, indeed."

Emotion poured over her as she reached for him, this most noble of men and held him close to her, love and grief mingling in her heart as they kissed and held each other tenderly.

"Do not fear, Marcus," she finally whispered as he nuzzled against her throat. "I will not let you go, my love."

The next day they reached the palace of Tours, which was minimally staffed without the court present. They found a stable boy to take care of their horses, then a serving woman brought them food and drink. When they were finished they went through the palace rooms, careful not to arouse the suspicion of the few servants who were about. They posed as lovers wishing for privacy, and all eyes were averted from their actions.

When evening came, they made their way to the wing where the royal bedchambers were located. Making sure that no one watched them, they pushed open the heavy door to the king's chamber and entered. No fire burned in the brazier, and the only light was from the fading evening outside the round-topped window set into the stone wall above eye level. But they dared not light a torch for fear someone would wonder where the light came from.

"There must be passages from this room to the others," said Judith, excited now that the business of gathering facts was at hand. "We must discover the movements of Fredegund and Chilperic that night," she said.

Both she and Marcus began to explore the walls with their fingers, feeling for loose stones and lifting wall hangings to see what might be concealed from the eye. The door that they were looking for was covered only by a large wall hanging of turquoise, purple, and gold. Once lifted, an iron handle opened the door. Judith peered into the dark passageway.

"We shall need a candle in there," said Marcus and took one from a basket by the bedside. Flint was kept in a niche by the brazier, and they soon had their candle lit, then took it within the passage, leaving the door half open behind them, though Marcus inspected for trick latches that might accidentally lock them in.

"It seems safe enough," he said, leaving a brick to hold the door open.

"Then we can proceed."

They followed the passage, which was wide enough for two people to pass through. The ceiling above them was built to accommodate the king's height. They passed a branch off the passage but chose to stay with what appeared to be the main part of the passage. Soon they came to another door, which Judith pressed inward slowly. It took only a moment to recognize the three rooms as Fredegund's apartments. There was a sitting room where she had entertained, a bedroom, and a dressing room.

"This is where Chilperic installed his mistress," she said. "The outer door faces onto a different wing from where the king and queen's chambers are, so that no one would suspect."

"Then this is how the king came to Fredegund whenever he pleased," speculated Marcus.

"Yes."

For a moment the anger and grief Judith felt over the deed done that night threatened to overcome her, but she got a hold of her feelings. She had to be effective, not a victim of her emotions.

"Come," she said. "We must see where the other branch leads."

They returned to the passage, retracing their steps until they came to where branches veered to the right and left.

Judith tried to orient herself as to which part of the palace they must be in. "Come," she said. "This way first."

As she suspected, the passage led to Galswinth's room where she must have received word that the king would visit her that night. Instead, her murderers came for her. This time Judith buried her head in Marcus's shoulder as his strong arm held her.

"Whoever did the deed must have concealed himself in the passage until Chilperic passed through to Fredegund's rooms," he said grimly. "Then they came here." He said no more, not wanting to further upset Judith.

Grief and rage still mingled, but Judith roused herself. "We have little time," she said, more to remind herself of their mission than to warn Marcus. "We must make use of it."

Marcus shut the passage door firmly and stepped back into Galswinth's chambers.

"The door is hardly visible in the wall," he said.

"Yet she must have known of it, for the king must have used it on occasion."

"Perhaps not," Judith said sadly. "He did not visit her that often, from what she confided to me. And when he did, why not use the main corridors? It would be natural for the king to visit his wife here."

"That's true." Marcus crossed the room to the heavy door with its iron bolt. "This must led to the outer corridors. But of course, she had little time to escape."

Judith nodded solemnly, then sighed. "We must look for the murder weapon."

"It is doubtful we will find it here," said Marcus.

Judith had a thought. "Yes, you are probably right. But we have not examined the rest of the hidden passages. Perhaps they dropped whatever they used there."

Marcus glanced around him at the royal bedchamber, not envying the recent occupant. "Very well."

Taking the candle, they proceeded back into the passage, this time taking the route they had not explored. Though they searched carefully, they found nothing. Coming to what appeared to be a door, they pushed. It gave way, and they found themselves in a covered walkway that led to the courtyard.

"So this is the way her murderers escaped," said Judith.

It was clear to her what had happened, and the desire for revenge was overwhelming. They stood half in the open doorway and half in the covered walkway, and Judith reached back to replace the snuffed-out candle on the small shelf she had noticed behind the door.

"In case we need to come this way again," she said

to Marcus as she placed the candle there. But her finger brushed something and she drew it away, thinking it might be a rodent or insect of some kind.

"What is it?" asked Marcus, coming back to where she stood.

She almost dismissed it, but then she turned around. "Up there," she said. "On that shelf. There is something."

Marcus peered onto the shelf, then reached for the coiled object and brought it down.

"This," he said, knowing at once what it was.

Judith gasped, taking the silken cord Marcus unwound. Neither had to say what was obvious. This was the weapon that had strangled the life from Galswinth.

She stared at it in horror, and yet a certain excitement pervaded her. She looked at Marcus, whose face held compassion and in whose eyes shone fierce determination whenever he was confronted with a crime that demanded justice.

"We must find out who used this," said Judith, her jaw set. "I doubt Chilperic or Fredegund did their own dirty work."

"No," said Marcus. "They will have hired their assassin."

They found the steward who looked after the minimal staff when the mayor of the palace was not in residence. The man, Bosio, looked at the cord and identified it as one used to tie back draperies in the queen's dressing room. Taking the key, he led them back to Galswinth's chambers, which he unlocked from the main corridor. Judith's eyes flew to the hidden door beside the wall hanging, but it was now concealed, for they had shut it firmly behind them.

311

Bosio led them to the dressing room and pointed to the draperies that could be pulled on a rope across the alcove. The right drapery still had its silken cord, and it looked exactly like the one Judith held in her hand.

"Clever," said Judith. "They took the cord from here so the guilt could not be thrown on anyone else."

"I beg your pardon, madam?" said Bosio.

"With this cord," said Marcus, holding it close to the steward's face, "the late queen was murdered. I suggest you cooperate with us in telling us what you know. If you do, your position here will be preserved."

"I know nothing, sir," said the steward, but his face lost color under Marcus's threat.

"Oh, come now," said Marcus. "Gossip among a household staff is the best source for information. I deal in information. Was there nothing unusual the night Queen Galswinth died? Did any of the servants suddenly disappear or grow rich? Who among them saw someone slip into the passage to the east side of the courtyard. Think, man."

The steward's eyes took on an opaque look as if he would rather not confront what they suggested. But Count Petronius was quite persuasive.

"Two slaves died the next morning," he said hurriedly. "You can ask the overseer who lost them."

"What did they die of?" asked Marcus.

Bosio shrugged. "Stomach cramps. By the time the physician got to them, there was nothing he could do except administer a drug to make their pain less. Talk to him."

"I think we will." Marcus looked at Judith. "Where is this court physician?"

"In Paris," she said. "He travels with the court."

"I see," said Marcus. "And the overseer?"

"He is here," said Bosio. "He takes care of the fields belonging to the estate year round."

"Get him," said Marcus.

The overseer was not much help. He was a large, brawny man who worked outdoors most of the time, disciplining the slaves. His greatest complaint was that many of the slaves died or ran away, leaving him short-handed.

"The two Frisians," said Judith as they interviewed the man in a reception room, "they were not ill before they died suddenly?"

"No," said the overseer. "They were strong. I know the type. Give them a chance and they would'a run away. But they did good work while they were alive."

Judith frowned. "Where were they the night before they died?"

He shrugged. "Woman who carried the slops that night said she saw them come back to their hut from the kitchens. Thought maybe they were filching food, so she reported it to me. When I went to find them they were both lyin' in their beds groanin', but I couldn't find any food. They swore they hadn't stolen any. I told 'em their sickness was proof they were lyin'. They must'a ate something in the kitchens that made 'em sick."

"Was anyone else in the household, whether noble or slave, ill from the food that night?" asked Judith.

The overseer gave a visible shiver. "Not ill, lady. But that was the night the queen died. Could be the slaves' dyin' was an omen."

"Yes," said Judith. "An omen of evil deeds."

They dismissed the overseer, and Judith circled the room thoughtfully. Marcus shut the door and turned to her.

"They must have been the ones," she said. "They returned to their hut from the kitchens, which are between the slave quarters and the palace." She shook her head and wrung her hands. "They must have been hired to kill her."

Marcus came to her and placed his hands on her shoulders. "We cannot know that for sure. It might have been a coincidence."

But Judith gave him a hardened look. "Why do you think they died?"

"I don't know. We won't know that until the court arrives here and we can question the physician. Until then there is nothing else we can do."

She turned from him, shaking off his grasp and walking a few steps. "We can question the rest of the household, ask them if they have seen anything."

Marcus moved to her again, letting his hand caress her hair and cheek.

"And so you can, my love. But not tonight. It is late."

"I don't care how late it is," she said, still determined to carry through her plan. "When Father Gregory arrives here, I want to have the facts to place before him. He will help me see that justice is done."

Marcus could not help but admire her determination, but he cautioned her.

"Then let him handle it. His office protects him. But if whoever murdered Galswinth learns of your plans for revenge, I am afraid it will be you who will have the silken cord around your neck."

Marcus pulled her against him. "Can you not see that the menace you fight is powerful, Judith? Your

314

purpose is noble, but dangerous."

She raised her head to meet his challenging eyes. "You would have me leave Neustria. But can't you understand, Marcus, that I cannot? My memories will not let me."

He drank in the green-gold eyes and answered her with a kiss. "We will do what we can then," he said. "Before I must leave."

He did not like to speak of leaving, but he had to make her understand that he would be torn from her side very soon. And he did not want to waste the time they had together.

Judith let him persuade her. They put off questioning any more household staff until morning and spent the evening in each other's arms. They lay propped on their elbows sipping wine on a couch in chambers with doors opened onto a private balcony. They said little, afraid to speak of the future, and when he kissed her a new pain seared her heart for now she knew she had fallen deeply in love with him. She was sorely tempted to leave the court and go with him, but when she thought of Father Gregory's arrival, she knew her duty.

"Let justice be done," she told Marcus. "Then we can be together, and I will have a pure conscience. Galswinth will rest in peace if I can rightly accuse her murderer."

Their night together was far too short, and in the morning, a message arrived for Marcus. She saw him from the balcony, speaking with a rider who looked as if he had ridden all night. Marcus read something from a piece of parchment, then rolled it up, tucking it in his girdle. He walked rapidly back toward the palace, and Judith ran downstairs to meet him.

315

She saw the look on his face as he crossed the tiled floor, and she hurried to grasp his hands. "What is it?"

"It's from Sigibert. I sent word with my vassal, Valois, where I could be found. No one else knows. I'm afraid I must return at once. Brunhild has insisted that the Austrasian warriors avenge her sister's death. She feels that the cities Chilperic bestowed on Galswinth as a wedding gift should now belong to her. Sigibert has sent troops to capture them. This means there will be war."

"Oh no." The threat of the two armies clashing meant that Marcus would be among them. "Surely you can stop them," she said, though she knew in her heart that was not true.

"I doubt it, dearest." He clasped her to his chest. "I will ride quickly and try to talk reason into Sigibert. But I am afraid that the vengeance Brunhild feels will be too great."

"Then you must leave?"

"Come with me," he said desperately.

"I can't," she said, tears forming at the corners of her eyes. "The court will arrive here soon. I must speak to Father Gregory. Perhaps you can get the kings to make an agreement. Then when things settle we can be together again."

"Yes, perhaps."

He looked down at her, knowing that their words were futile, and time was of the essence. He kissed her hard on the mouth, trying to imprint the feel of her body and her lips in his mind so that he could carry them with him all the miles he must go.

"You will wait for me then," he commanded.

She nodded, not daring to speak. She watched him

order the servants to pack his things and ready his horse. Then she stood in the yard to watch as he mounted up, his green cape trailing off his noble shoulders. He raised his hand in a salute, squeezed his horse with his knees, and rode quickly to the gate that now opened before him. Her heart twisted in her chest and she wondered if she had been wrong to stay here. So much uncertainty separated them. She did not think she could stand the death of another lover in battle.

She uttered a little prayer that he not be killed and then returned to the palace, forcing herself to the task of questioning the rest of the servants of the skeleton household staff as to what they might know about the movements of the Frisian slaves the night of Galswinth's death.

The court traveled to Tours. Fredegund rode in the queen's chariot, making regal appearances whenever they passed through towns. But her journey was marred by one thing: Her nubile daughter Rigunthis was attracting undue attention both from the nobles in the royal train and the crowds that greeted them. Now that her mother was queen, Rigunthis had taken on noble airs. Fredegund watched from her seat in the chariot as her daughter chatted with Count Fulrich from her seat on a fine chestnut horse.

Fredegund turned to Chilperic, who rode beside her. "We need to find the girl a husband," she said. "She is getting above herself."

Chilperic was amused at his wife's scrutiny of her daughter. "She has her own mother's ambition, perhaps?"

Fredegund narrowed her eyes. She did not like the way Chilperic watched Rigunthis as she chattered gracefully with the count.

"Marry her to royalty of another kingdom and make a diplomatic tie, my lord," she suggested.

Chilperic laughed. "And get her out of your sight, is that it?" He chuckled at his wife's jealousy. However, he knew it would not do to tease her. "I will give the matter some thought," he said. "Perhaps I should offer her to the Visigoths."

"An excellent idea," said Fredegund. "Send her to Spain."

While the royal procession wound its way to Tours, Judith waited with great anticipation for Father Gregory's return. She spent her time training Kahluli, who had now learned to ride on the back of her horse without the cage. They made an interesting sight, riding in the countryside around Tours and they were remarked by all the townspeople. She followed the instructions Ivar's father had given her on training the animal, praising and feeding her every time she did something correct. A bond had formed between mistress and cheetah, and it helped ease her mind to take Kahluli out riding and to work with her.

She kept the cheetah on a long rope, so that the first time she commanded her to catch a rabbit there was no danger in the cat running away. They rode quietly through the trees, horse, cheetah and girl alert to the sounds of birds and small game. Then a small rabbit hopped across the path and Judith seized the moment.

"Fetch," she cried, and the cheetah bounded off the back of the horse and into the underbrush. Judith waited tensely, listening to the scramble and animal cries. She did not like death, but the rabbit would be eaten by the servants. As soon as Kahluli had made her kill, Judith tugged on the rope and the cat brought the rabbit back, dropping it at her feet.

"Good Kahluli," she said, reaching into her bag for fresh meat to feed her instead of the game. "Kahluli is good."

Then she put the rabbit in a bag, which she tied to her saddle. When Kahluli had finished feeding, she commanded her to leap back on the padded seat on the back of her horse, to which she had become accustomed. The sun had drawn low in the sky by the time they returned to the palace compound. She took care of both animals, then crossed to the palace amid the shadows that preceded dusk.

The animals helped her retain her sanity during the day, but it was the nights that weighed heavily. She tried to spend the evenings writing verses on parchment. Writing could purge the soul, Fortunatus had once told her. And she wondered if the verses she wrote now would be good enough to show him. Such thoughts helped keep her mind occupied until the time her eyelids drooped, and she climbed into her cold, lonely bed.

As soon as she received word that Gregory had returned to the see, she left the palace and made her way through the streets to his house. He welcomed her eagerly and ordered refreshments for her.

"I am glad you are safe and well, my dear," he said. "The royal train is right behind me. My progress was faster of course because they are weighted down with baggage trains and slaves. How have you found your stay here?"

She smiled conspiratorially. "I have found something that will interest you indeed." She opened the canvas bag she had carried with her and pulled out the silken cord they had found in the secret passage. "This."

Gregory lifted his brows and took the strong cord in his hands, turning it over. "And where did this come from?"

Judith leaned forward. "From a ledge behind a door that leads to a secret passage connecting the queen's bedchamber with that of the king's and"—she paused for emphasis—"also to the king's mistress."

Gregory hissed through his teeth. "Interesting indeed."

"The steward showed us where the cord had been attached to draperies in the queen's own dressing room. The murderers must have ripped it from the draperies and used it on her throat."

Gregory dropped the cord on the table between them and rubbed his hands together. "I see. But how can we know who used it?"

She told him about the Frisian slaves who died the same night.

"Are you suggesting that they were the hired assassins and that they, too, were murdered so they wouldn't talk?"

"What else can we surmise?" she asked.

"Unfortunately with the slaves dead, we cannot ascertain who paid them."

"But I think we can," said Judith, saving her prize bit of evidence for last. "The woman who carried slops saw them leave the kitchens area and go to their huts the night they died."

"Then we are getting warm. Still, to whom do we point the finger?"

"It's obvious to me. Fredegund had Galswinth killed so that she might marry Chilperic and become queen."

Gregory gazed at Judith's animated face, saw the determination in her eyes. Still, he spoke cautiously.

"You may be right, my dear. But we cannot indict the present queen without an eyewitness, I am afraid."

"You can do it, Father. You are her spiritual counselor. You must make her confess for the salvation of her soul." Judith gripped the edge of the marble table before her.

Gregory uttered a great sigh. "I wish I could. And I assure you that from the pulpit I will chastise whoever did the awful deed. But I am afraid that you may be sorely disappointed if you expect Fredegund to fall on her knees."

"Why?"

He gestured with his beringed hand. "Because, I am afraid our Queen Fredegund has no conscience."

Chapter Twenty-one

Determined to find more evidence against Frede-gund, Judith kept near the queen, keeping her ears open. On the day Fredegund summoned her daughter for a lecture, Judith contrived to stay in the next chamber, reading a letter she had received from Father Fortunatus, with whom she had exchanged some poetry. The window to the room where she worked was open as well as that of the room where Fredegund and Rigunthis held their exchange, and once the two women raised their voices, she could hear everything.

Fredegund had been trying to talk sense into her daughter's behavior, but the girl was intractable.

"You cannot throw yourself at Count Fulrich like some whore," said Fredegund, losing patience. "Chilperic and I are planning to negotiate a royal marriage for you, perhaps to the king of the Visigoths."

"How nice," said Rigunthis. "But he cannot expect to have me without some experience in matters of love."

"Rigunthis," snapped Fredegund. "How dare you speak that way. Your behavior is already attracting the attention of the court. We cannot present King

Athanagild with a slut for a wife."

Rigunthis wheeled on her mother. "You should talk, Mother, you who slept your way to power."

Fredegund raised her arm and slapped Rigunthis across the face. The girl cried out.

"Don't you talk to me that way," said Fredegund, taking another step closer as if she would do more than slap were she provoked.

Rigunthis held her hand to her burning cheek. "Well, it's true. At least I have noble blood from your first lover, so you can marry me to a king. If it weren't for Chilperic, you'd still be a kitchen slave. I should be the mistress of this palace, since my father's blood runs in my veins."

"May I remind you that I am now the queen of Neustria," said Fredegund through gritted teeth. But Rigunthis would not be stopped.

"And we know how you got there. But then you had to do something about your low birth, didn't you?"

The insult was too much for Fredegund and she seized Rigunthis by the hair, yanking her across the floor. But Rigunthis dug into her mother with her fingernails, and soon the screams and yelps of the women brought others running. The door to the chamber was not bolted, and Judith was one of the first on the scene.

"Please, please," she cried and she threw herself into the rolling, clawing bodies, trying to separate them. "Stop this."

Servants stood, their hands on their faces, watching in horror, afraid to interfere. But Mosella came into the room and Judith sent her a desperate look.

"Help me," she cried, and Mosella grasped Rigunthis, trying to pull her away. Other ladies came into the chamber. Some clasped their hands to their mouths in amusement, but Clothild was not afraid to plow into the fray and helped get Fredegund away from the scratching, kicking girl. Clothild and Mosella dragged Rigunthis away to her chambers, while the servants brought wine to calm Fredegund. Judith waited until the queen was seated, then took her leave.

"If everything is all right, now, Your Majesty, I will leave you," said Judith.

Fredegund eyed her. "I must thank you for coming to my rescue," she said levelly. "One wonders that you were able to get here so quickly."

Judith rose to the accusation that she might have been eavesdropping. "The windows were open, my lady. I heard your screams of distress and came immediately."

Fredegund gave her a haughty look. "Many thanks. My daughter has no manners, I am sorry to say."

"Yes, madam."

Seeing that she was not needed, Judith left the room, pulling the oaken door shut behind her. She had indeed heard more of the argument than Fredegund would have liked her to. Truly Rigunthis was arousing her mother's hatred, and there was no telling what the mother would do to the daughter if she did not behave as she was expected.

The following day Fredegund rode out with the ladies of the court. As Trudulf assisted each lady into the saddle, Fredegund spoke to the assembly from her white mount.

"Why not have the lady Judith bring her cheetah

that can ride behind her on horseback?"

Judith looked up at Fredegund, sensing the challenge. She hesitated only a moment. She did not know what Fredegund had in mind. Perhaps she hoped that the cheetah would turn on its mistress or that it would become unruly and have to be shot. Such was the way the queen thought, and Judith knew it. She did not want to risk Kahluli's life in her presence, but at the same time she could not refuse the challenge. She felt confident enough about Kahluli's ability by now to trust the animal in a crowd of people. She had trained with the cheetah every day and knew that the bond between them was strong. In a crisis, the cat would come to its mistress.

"As you wish, madam," said Judith. "I will fetch her."

Trudulf, standing near, said under his breath, behind her horse where Fredegund could not hear him, "Do you think it safe, my lady?"

"It will be all right," she answered him. "Kahluli is obedient now. But I will be careful."

He lifted his chin and met her gaze with a look that said he did not trust the queen. "Perhaps I can ride in the woods behind you in case you need protection."

"Do as you wish," she said as they examined the saddle and the reins. "But be careful."

Judith led her horse across the stable yard and on toward the hut where Kahluli was kept. The cat got up in her cage when Judith entered. "Hello, Kahluli," she said. "Ready for a ride?"

She opened the cage door and took up the chain that was fixed to the cheetah's collar. Then she walked Kahluli out of the cage.

"Come," she commanded and they walked to the yard where Black Lady waited docilely. The other women waited on their horses on the other side of the yard, interested to watch the performance.

She walked the cheetah first around the yard, then for the benefit of the watchers, she removed the chain from the cat's neck and commanded it to walk beside her. Then she stopped.

"Sit," she commanded. The cheetah sat.

"Come," she said and they began walking again.

Finally Judith mounted and then at her command, Kahluli leapt up on the back of the horse. Judith petted the horse and spoke in a low, soothing voice to the cheetah, then she refastened the chain to the cat's collar, not wanting to take any chances until they were in the woods away from the distractions the palace might offer. She took up the reins and walked the horse to where the others waited.

Fredegund gave her an icy smile. "How amusing." The challenge in her eyes was clear, and it caused a shiver to run along Judith's spine. What was the wily queen up to?

They rode away from the palace, which was on the edge of the city, taking a track through the countryside. The morning was fresh and bright, and were it not for the weighty matters on Judith's mind she would have enjoyed it. They crossed a stream, and then rode along beside it, past cultivated fields where the peasants stopped their work to watch the train go by. When they reached the woods, Fredegund turned to Judith.

"Perhaps you will show us how your cheetah can hunt."

Judith removed the chain from the animal's collar,

talking in the tones that she used to communicate to the cat. Then she urged her horse forward, the other ladies falling in line behind her. The woods were silent except for the thrust of hoof on dirt track. Then Judith sensed the cheetah tense. She saw the pig rooting among the leaves. In an instant she realized this was no wild pig, but rather, one from the neighboring field.

"Stay," she commanded the cheetah, who was poised for the spring that would have killed the farmer's pig. She clapped the chain on Kahluli's collar.

She realized the trap before she saw the farmer himself emerge on the far side of a clearing, carrying bow and arrow. A slingshot hung from his belt. Curious implements for a farmer to carry.

"Stay, stay," Judith continued to command, then spoke in soothing tones. Finally she spoke so that all could hear. "A hunting cheetah does not kill domesticated farm animals," she said, and she turned her horse and walked back the way they had come. When she reached Fredegund, she met her eyes, seeing there the evil intent, the flaming cheeks of the queen.

"Tell your farmer, his pig is safe," she said, the venom stroking her words. "He will not need to murder Kahluli to save his animal."

And she continued on her way, her own heart beating at the close call. Evidently Fredegund had tried to set a trap so that Kahluli would attack the innocent pig. The farmer, searching for his animal would have shot an arrow into Kahluli, killing her.

Judith shivered. Fredegund did not trust her. Marcus's warnings came back to her, and she thought again how she had missed her chance to go with him. He was right. Fredegund was too powerful. She would not allow Judith the chance to avenge Galswinth's death without she, herself, being hanged in the process.

The Austrasian army marched south, Marcus with the other generals at its head. Influenced by Queen Brunhild's ravings, Sigibert would not listen to reason. Nothing less than leveling Chilperic's cities would satisfy the grieving queen who demanded recompense for her sister's death.

Marcus sat with grim determination in his saddle. The dust bit his eyes, the sun caused the sweat to dampen his tunic. He was sick of these senseless wars. Marcus did not lack courage. He had always been brave in battle, rallying his men for a charge, and in peacetimes he had served the Merovingian kings faithfully, but the seed of Gallo-Roman sensibility was strong in him. Stronger, perhaps now that he was well past thirty years of age.

He longed for a civilized life. The memories of his youth on his father's well-run estate were fresh in his mind. Overseeing a large district of productive people, who flourished and prospered under a kind sun nourishing a rich soil brought joy to his heart. And he had always seen himself in the role of civil servant. As count of his district, he would one day dispense justice as his father did now, and make time for a luxurious life shared with a loving family.

But quarreling kings allowed for none of that. Now his army marched on the people of Neustria, who by this time must be preparing themselves for war.

One thing he was determined to do. He must see Judith to safety ahead of the havoc he was sure Sigibert's forces were going to reap. Brunhild herself had ridden before the troops, stirring them to a fevered pitch that would motivate them to loot, rape, pillage, and burn.

When they crossed into Neustrian territory, he planned to send his lieutenant ahead by night with a message for Judith. Valois was to take her to Poitiers where she would be safe with her friends at the Abbey of the Holy Cross, which was far enough removed from the initial scenes of confrontations that Marcus would feel secure knowing she was out of danger. He, himself, would go to her as soon as matters were settled. If they were ever settled, he thought disconsolately. That was the problem with this turbulent land. Ever since the Romans had left, nearly a hundred years ago, Gaul had been subject to these Frankish feuds. Territories changed hands again and again, rendering any structure of government unstable. Change would come eventually, he thought. He foresaw a day when a strong hand would put a stop to the nonsensical feuds. But he knew the current Merovingian rulers, and he did not foresee that day to be in his present lifetime.

Rigunthis followed her mother to the strong room where Fredegund's personal treasures were kept in several large chests. Fredegund smiled her catlike smile at her daughter and opened one of the chests, which gleamed with jewels.

"I have given much thought to what you said about your own noble blood, my dear," said Fredegund, giving a great sigh. "I have too many jewels in any case. Take what you want of these."

Rigunthis approached the case, her eyes gleaming with excitement. She had her own ornaments of course, but seeing the rich treasure all together excited the greed she had inherited from her mother. She kneeled by the side of the chest and Fredegund did likewise. Both reached in and lifted out necklaces, pins, bracelets of gold and silver, all set with exquisite gems.

Fredegund laughed and draped one necklace after another over her daughter's head.

"You must wear this one, and this one . . . and this one."

They scooped up handfuls of jewels, until at last Fredegund sat back, exhausted. "I am tired. Put your own hands in and take whatever you like."

And at that she rose, watching Rigunthis lean forward into the chest. Fredegund raised her arm and seized the lid. With a sudden effort, she slammed the lid of the chest down on her daughter's neck, pressing so hard on the girl's throat that she choked for breath.

Harder, and harder she pressed, forcing the life out of her. And so Rigunthis would have died had it not been for a servant who passed the window and happened to peer in. The maid dropped her basket of acorns and screamed at the top of her voice.

"Help, help. The queen is choking her daughter. Come quickly." And she ran for the guards.

All who stood in the yard heard the girl, and Judith turned from her conversation with Clothild, who hissed through her teeth. "What, again?"

By this time the guards were racing toward the

330

strong room, and by the time Judith and Clothild reached the room, they had dragged Rigunthis out, who was gasping for breath, her eyes seeming to bulge from her face. The queen spied Judith and Clothild and decided to take her spite out on them as they stepped through the door.

"Always butting into my affairs," she snarled.

Rigunthis by now had regained enough breath to howl. "She tried to kill me," she shrieked. "My own mother."

"Slut," yelled Fredegund. "She deserves nothing better. She sleeps with every man who looks at her."

The others did their best to calm the two women, but by the time Judith and Clothild followed Fredegund to her own chambers, no one was safe from the lashings of her tongue. Judith went through the motions of handing her a goblet of wine and of sending the maid for a bath for the queen. Clothild lit incense to sweeten the chambers. But the menace that pervaded the palace would not be assuaged.

Judith struggled to keep her own emotions from her face, and when she was excused from the royal chambers, she wrapped herself in her mantle and went outside. Confusion plagued her. She thought of Father Gregory and wondered if it would be too late to go and see him, feeling sorely in need of someone she could talk to. She was standing alone in the courtyard when Trudulf found her.

He had not made any noise, so when he spoke behind her in a low voice, she gasped and turned.

"Oh, it's you, Trudulf. You startled me."

"I did not mean to," he said. "But I did not want to attract any attention." He pressed a folded piece of parchment into her hand.

"There is a man in the stables who wants to speak to you. As proof, he told me to give you this."

Judith unfolded the parchment. She recognized the signature. Marcus. It was from Marcus. She scanned the message, then looked up at Trudulf.

"Where is this messenger?"

"He still waits in the stables. He said it was important that he not be seen."

"Tell him I will come there immediately. You go ahead, and I will follow."

Trudulf nodded and slipped away. Judith pressed the parchment note to her breast and glanced around. It did not appear they had been seen. Then she walked slowly across the courtyard to the stables, trying not to betray her beating heart to any who watched her. Then she slipped into the shadows of the stables and made her way along the stalls.

By a partition near the other end Trudulf waited with Valois, and Judith hurried up to him.

"Valois," she said on a breath. "I cannot believe you are here."

The young, dark-headed vassal smiled, aware of the fondness that existed between this woman and his master. "Count Petronius sends his good wishes," he said. "But he is concerned for your welfare. I have words to convey to you privately."

Judith glanced at Trudulf. "You can trust Trudulf. He is a friend."

But Trudulf raised a hand. "I will wait outside, should you need me, my lady." And he left them in privacy. Valois moved closer, his words urgent, but low.

"There is imminent danger, my lady. King Sigibert is bringing a large force to lay waste to this kingdom

332

to extract vengeance for Galswinth's death. Count Petronius fears for your life. Even now the army approaches, and word will carry to King Chilperic very soon. By dawn, he may have received word and will mount his army. I am to take you to the Abbey of the Holy Cross, where you will be out of danger."

Judith glanced out of doors, as if able to see the approaching armies. "And Count Petronius?" she asked.

"He rides at the head of the army with the king."

"Then I must wait for him."

"You cannot, my lady. It will be too dangerous. King Sigibert has given his men permission to rape and pillage."

She knew that Valois's words were true, but she could not bear the thought of going in the other direction if Marcus were coming this way. For a moment she stood facing Valois, their viewpoints at odds. Trudulf's steps sounded outside, and he entered the darkened stable.

"Forgive me for interrupting," he said.

"It is all right," said Judith. "Valois wants me to go with him. Apparently there is to be an attack."

She knew that Trudulf would help her, and that he would not betray them. He himself had become disillusioned with the rulers of the kingdom and might want this chance to fly himself.

"If you are to travel," he said, "it will be best to take fresh horses out of the compound before the guards lock the gates, and I can leave by the west gate now without attracting attention. I can return on foot and take you to the woods where Valois can wait with the horses."

She closed her eyes and took a deep breath. "I suppose you are right." She looked at Trudulf. "Come with us. A party of three will be safer on the roads."

It did not take Trudulf long to decide. "If you wish me to accompany you, I will."

"We go to Poitiers, to the Abbey of the Holy Cross."

He nodded his head. "I have heard of the Mother Superior Radegund. I would be most happy to serve her."

"Good, then I shall come here when you hear the bells for compline. I must get a message to Father Gregory. Can you take it to him?"

Trudulf nodded. "Most certainly."

"Tell him where I am going. And that he is to tell Count Petronius to send for me there."

Trudulf nodded, then he turned to Valois. "Let us take three fresh horses and leave now before the guards secure the palace grounds. We have not long."

Judith left the men to see to the horses and went through the stables. At the other end, she slowly left the stables and walked normally across the compound as if she had just been to see her own horse. Then she remembered Kahluli. She would have to take her, for Fredegund would kill the cheetah if it were left behind.

She hurried into the palace and went to the women's chambers. She could not make preparations that others would notice and so resolved to take nothing she could not fit in a small pouch that would fit around her waist, the pendant that Galswinth had given her and her dagger.

Then she sat down with the other women to spin wool while they gossiped. Evening was drawing on when they heard a great commotion and went to the balcony to look down into the central yard where soldiers had just ridden in. For a moment Judith's breath caught, for she feared that Valois had been discovered. But he was not with them.

Several of the soldiers shouted and exchanged words with others of the king's vassals and there was general confusion as orders were shouted and servants began to run about. Clothild leaned over the balcony and shouted to Count Germanus.

"Germanus, what's happened?"

He called up to the ladies peering over the carved railing. "The Austrasian army approaches. They have already seized Rouen and march toward Orléans. King Sigibert calls for war."

"War . . ." was repeated by all the female lips except Judith, who stood with her lips pressed tightly. If they took Orléans, Tours would be next. But now that the alarm was raised, perhaps they could get away more easily in the confusion of armies being called up. Another problem presented itself, however. The women were excited and some hurried to help the men prepare for their departure. If the palace did not settle down to sleep tonight, she would be seen as she left.

Fredegund came out to the balcony to stand regally looking down at the courtyard where Chilperic now appeared with Epoald.

"Men," the king called, and the furor died down to listen to his words. "My brother marches into our lands aiming to destroy. We must prepare to defend ourselves. Arm yourselves for battle, send out the word to your armies. We must march to Orléans, which is ours by right. My brother's army is committing rape and plunder and must be taught a lesson.

335

By committing these atrocities, he is no longer my brother but has become treasonous to my own eyes. We go to teach the Austrasians a lesson."

A great cheer went up in the courtyard which was echoed throughout the compound. Now everyone scurried about. Judith hurried back to her chambers, gathering the things she wanted to take with her while everyone else's attention was engaged elsewhere. But as she was fastening her dagger to the chain about her waist, she felt a presence behind her and straightened her head slowly. Then she turned.

Fredegund's cold blue eyes pierced hers. She raised a questioning eyebrow at the sheath in Judith's hands. But Judith found words quickly.

"If we are to be attacked by Austrasians who rape women, it is best to be armed, is it not?" she said.

Fredegund moved closer, reached out a hand to admire the sheath and the hilt of the small dagger. Judith handed it to her, but kept herself alert to any move the queen might make. Fredegund drew the dagger from its sheath and held it in her hand. The blade gleamed.

"A fine weapon. Where did you get it?" she asked.

"It was a gift."

"Hmmm. Such fine craftsmanship must come from someone who can afford such gifts. Surely this is not from your peasant lover."

"No," Judith said quickly.

"Ah," said Fredegund. "From someone wealthy then. . . . Very wealthy."

The last words were full of accusation and Judith looked quickly into Fredegund's suspicious eyes, her own eyes widening as she read the meaning.

She swallowed. She did not want to say the gift

was from Galswinth, but she had to say something to allay Fredegund's suspicions that it was from Chilperic himself. She reached for the dagger. Fredegund narrowed her eyes, but she handed it back.

"It was from Ivar," said Judith. "He had taken it as spoils from a raid on the Visigoths. I admired its workmanship, so he gave it to me."

"Ah," said Fredegund. "I see."

Her eyes slid over Judith making her feel as if the skin of a freshly killed beast were being draped over her shoulders. "Then by all means it will protect you."

Judith kept her eyes off the pouch that rested on the seat in front of her writing desk, willing Fredegund not to look there. The queen walked to the door that led to the balcony, her back to Judith but her voice carrying to her.

"They come to avenge Galswinth's death. Queen Brunhild is behind this. But she shall be taught that she cannot plunder our lands if I, myself have to ride at the head of the army." Then she strode out of the room.

Judith took a deep breath. There was no time to lose. Darkness descended over the palace grounds and torches were lit to help the preparations in the yard and stables below. Judith opened the small case that held her jewels and scooped them out. Some she put in the pouch that tied to her waist. She wrapped others in cloth, tying it securely to put into the bags strapped across the horse. Then she took out her riding cloak, turned it inside out and draped it across her arm.

If anyone stopped her, she could say she was worried that the excitement would alarm the cheetah, and was going to her cage to see about her. No one would want to accompany her, for the exotic cat was still viewed with awe. Most of the household thought it was magic that helped Judith control the dangerous cat and kept their distance. And perhaps it was, for she still kept Ivar's talisman around her neck, which was supposed to enable her to talk to animals.

She went along to the hut where Kahluli was kept. Inside, she found her pacing in her cage and knelt down to soothe her.

"We are going on a journey, my little wild one. You will protect us as we travel."

Then she opened the cage, took up the chain that was fastened on Kahluli's collar and led her out. She donned her cloak, and prepared to enter the yard. The animal huts were far enough from the main palace that she hoped she would not be noticed. Of course with Kahluli she was an oddity, and everyone knew who she was. There was no time to put the cheetah on a cart and harness a horse to it. Kahluli would have to walk.

She led the cheetah around the compound, keeping as far away from the palace proper as possible. The cat gave her no trouble, and as she had hoped, the bond that had formed between them kept the animal close to her when faced with the hurried activities of servants and stablemen hurrying to see the counts off to rouse their armies. They came to the west gate, which was open because of all the traffic leaving the yard. No one stopped her as she walked out after Count Germanus and his entourage had passed through. As soon as she was outside the palace walls, she turned along a path that led toward the woods. Out of the torchlight, there was less chance of being seen, but progress was slower.

She was not sure if she found the correct spot where she was to meet Trudulf at the edge of the woods until she heard his soft whistle. Kahluli turned, swinging her tail at the sound, but Judith murmured low, reassuring her.

Then Trudulf appeared, his brown cloak about his shoulders blending in with the dark woods.

Chapter Twenty-two

Trudulf led her down a track some distance to where Valois waited with the horses, deep in the woods.

When he saw them, Valois said, "So this is the hunting cheetah I have heard about. Is it wise to bring the animal? We will be traveling fast."

"Kahluli will be a help rather than a hindrance," said Judith in defense. "I will be responsible for her."

Valois looked doubtful, but they put Judith's jewels into bags attached to the saddles and mounted the horses, Kahluli springing on behind Judith, the chain on the cat's collar secure.

They kept to the track through the woods, and Judith was surprised at Valois's sense of direction. Or perhaps he had marked the path and remembered the way. But they came out not far from the main road leading south from Tours. Even from where they watched the road, they could see the many torches and traveling parties. It would not be safe to go that way. Trudulf or Judith might be recognized and would be questioned as to where they were going. Trudulf had no difficulty with his decision to desert his king. He no longer wanted to serve a ruler who used treachery at every turn.

And so they kept to smaller roads beside cornfields, coming to the river Vienne and staying by its course. They camped beneath the stars in secluded groves, the men taking turns on watch, Judith sleeping in a canvas tent, and Kahluli on a stake outside.

Morning by the river was refreshing and with plenty of water for the animals and themselves, they set out at a brisk pace, seeing no one for some distance. The countryside grew quiet, but when they passed through small villages the news had spread that the Austrasian army was on the march. Already sons and husbands had put down their plows to follow their overlords to battle.

Of course everyone stared at Kahluli, thinking the party were traveling players. In order to better conceal their identity, Trudulf manufactured a story about them having traveled from one district to another to entertain the counts. But no one was willing to house Kahluli in their stable or barn, and so they bought a cage for the cat at a market town, also procuring a cart and a horse to pull it. From then on Kahluli traveled on the cart. When they stayed at an inn at a market town, either Valois or Trudulf slept in the barn with the cheetah, so that if anyone came to steal her, the noise would wake him.

Now that they were so far south, Trudulf and Valois judged it safe enough to travel on good roads, which would accommodate the cart. They had passed the last homestead some time before when drops of rain began to fall out of the sky. They stopped so that Judith could cover the cage with canvas to keep Kahluli from getting wet.

The robbers came out of the woods and descended upon them almost before they saw them. In an instant yells and pounding hooves turned into the clash of metal as Valois and Trudulf quickly drew their swords. There were five men in dirty tunics with cloths over their faces except for eye holes and a place to breathe. The expressionless masks made them the more frightening, and Judith cowered behind the cage for only a second before she sprang to action. One of the men got off his horse, but before he could reach her, she had flung the canvas in his face, and in the instant it took for him to push the material aside, she grabbed the key that would unlock the cage.

Kahluli let out a piercing yowl, which made the brigands' heads turn. The moment was enough to give Trudulf an advantage, and he threw his dagger into the nearest assailant's throat. With a gurgle, the man fell off his horse.

But the man nearest Judith recovered himself. "Think ye're smart, girlie. Well, we'll see about that."

And he reached her before she could get the key in the iron lock on the cage door.

"No," she screamed as the fighting went on behind her. Valois had disarmed his opponent and turned to meet the sword thrust of the man on his flank.

Judith's attacker grabbed her wrist and twisted it behind her. But with her other hand she reached for her dagger, unsheathing it. When he turned her around to toss her to the ground, her dagger found its home in his side and he gave a cry, bending in the middle.

Quickly she scrambled to her feet, reached the key and turned it in the lock. The cage door was open and Kahluli sprang out over her head to land, claws extended on the man who had straightened and was coming at Judith again. The man's cries as the cheetah tore flesh from his face were so great the remaining two men turned their heads to see.

"Attack," Judith called. "Attack."

And Kahluli crouched on the bloody pulp of the man who had tried to assault Judith. Then she sprang at the robber whose sword was raised above Valois's head. The sword clashed to the road and the cheetah's weight took him over backward. The other robber who was on the ground sprinted to his horse, and the one remaining mounted man turned as his friend mounted. They dug their heels into the horse's sides and fled down the road before the animal had a chance to dig into their flesh.

"Come, Kahluli," commanded Judith, her stomach turning at the sight of what her claws had done to the man on the ground. "Here, girl." Then she hurried to her horse to take out the fresh meat she always carried as a reward.

The cheetah came obediently, tail sweeping, jaws dripping with blood. Judith was still catching her breath as she stared at the carnage. Two men were dead, the third wounded, his face pale, for his mask had come untied in the fight. His eyes bulged as he stared at the cheetah that obeyed the girl.

"Witch," he cried, pointing to her. But Trudulf poked his sword in the man's chest and ordered him to lie on the ground, his hands above his head.

While Judith fed Kahluli, Trudulf and Valois tied their prisoner. She praised Kahluli for the attack, and after they had all caught their breath, Trudulf came over to her, touching her shoulder.

"Are you hurt?" he asked.

She shook her head as she returned the cheetah to her cage.

She examined his face and hands.

"Only a few cuts." He grinned, expelling a breath. "Very impressive. I think that is the first time I've fought side by side with an exotic cat."

Judith smiled in relief. "She has earned her place among us then?" She remembered the doubt the other two had had about bringing her along.

"You did not tell us she was adept at handling brigands," said Valois with a smile.

"Not much left of these two," said Trudulf. "We'll bury them here and deliver this one to the next town."

"Why not hang him here?" asked Valois. "We don't have a horse for him to ride."

Trudulf laughed. "He can walk beside the cart and meditate upon his sins."

And so they used their axes to dig shallow graves to toss the two robbers into after going through their pouches. They had not many valuables, only a few coins and weapons, which they confiscated. Then they put them in the earth.

"When the rains come they'll be washed up for the vultures to pick on," said Valois.

"We've done our duty," said Trudulf. "Let's go."

And so the odd procession set out. The rain had stopped so the canvas cover was left off Kahluli's cage, and the cat paced back and forth, grimacing from time to time at the terrorized man who stumbled alongside, his hands tied behind him, muttering prayers.

Judith felt odd as the city of Poitiers at last came into view on the swelling plain. Several vine-covered towers were visible above the city walls. She remembered so clearly the day she walked on the wall with Fortunatus, staring out at the plain they now crossed, wishing for nothing more than to marry and make a home for some industrious farmer. How much her life had changed since then.

She blinked in the sun that warmed her face as they began to follow the river toward its convergence with the Boivre. The poplars along the bank rustled their leaves as if in greeting, a flock of geese passed over-head, and the breeze touched her hair. A barge glided beside them, filled with sacks of goods a farmer was taking to town. Other smaller boats rowed past, and they began to sense the commerce of the prosperous town.

Closer now and red slate roofs set at random angles peaked over the walls. Peasants working in the fields near the road stopped their work and came to gawk at the little procession of travelers, prisoner, and spotted cat. By the time they reached the city gates, their arrival was expected and townspeople had gathered to welcome them. Kahluli's cage was securely locked now, so that she would not escape. The mayor of the city came out to the road to meet them, and they drew to a halt in a town square.

"What have we here?" said the pudgy man, whose medallion of office hung around his neck.

"A prisoner, sir," said Trudulf from his horse. "We were set upon by brigands some distance back. Two died, and we buried them. The other two fled for their lives and are probably somewhere hereabouts. You can have our prisoner, sir. It was too inconvenient for us to hang him on the spot."

"I see," said the mayor, coming closer and peering at the cat. "You travel with an unusual pet."

"Not a pet," said Valois. "She is a huntress and saved our lives, killing the two who would have abused the lady who travels with us and would have taken our belongings."

"Hmmm," said the mayor as the townspeople crowded around them, pointing. He turned to the prisoner.

"So this man was one of the attackers?"

All three nodded.

"Here is the evidence." And Trudulf handed the mayor the mask with the eyes and nose holes.

The mayor held it up, placed it in front of his face and leered at the prisoner. Then he lowered it. "And what have you to say for yourself?"

But all the man could do was mumble, his teeth chattering. "The . . . devil," he finally got out, gesturing with his head toward the cheetah.

The mayor laughed and turned to the people watching. "Is he guilty?" he asked the crowd.

"Guilty!" the crowd shouted. "Hang him."

Some men standing near the prisoner untied him from the cart and shoved him along with them as the roar of the crowd rose in anticipation. The mayor followed, laughing, and Judith's party watched them.

"That's the end of him," said Trudulf.

Judith felt sick of so much violence and turned her face away. "Let us go on our way. I do not wish to witness death again today."

As they continued through the narrow flagstone-paved streets, they were the center of attention. Merchants and housewives came out of doors to watch them pass. How well she remembered traveling these streets in Galswinth's cart so many months ago, and the thought brought a tightness to her chest.

They turned toward the abbey, approaching the gates that lay within the city. Valois dismounted and gave the gatekeeper their names and their business.

"The abbess and the mother superior will remember the lady Judith who travels with us."

The gatekeeper, a peasant in workshirt and loose trousers, eyed the cage with the strange animal in it. But he went off to deliver the message. In no time, he returned and unlocked the large lock, then swung the heavy iron gates inward.

"Go straight into the yard. The abbess says she'll meet you herself."

They rode in and went along the short drive to the green quadrangle that Judith remembered so well. She need not have feared her reception, for Agnes herself came out of the cloister walk and flew across the lawn toward them.

"Judith, I can't believe my eyes, it's you."

Judith dismounted, moved forward and clasped the hands that Agnes held toward her. "It is me. Oh, Sister Agnes, how good it is to see you, too."

Agnes let go her hands and hugged her, making Judith smile.

"We read your letters with such great interest, and then we got word from Count Marcus Petronius to expect you. But we did not expect you so soon."

"Allow me to introduce my friends. This is Trudulf," she said, "lately King Chilperic's count of the stables, but he has left his position in hopes he can be of service to you here?"

Agnes's hand flew to her breast. "Oh, I see." Then she extended her hand. "I am pleased to meet you."

Trudulf bowed.

"And this is Valois, Count Petronius's vassal."

Agnes's brows raised just slightly under the line of her wimple. "Ah, so you work for the honorable count. I am very pleased that you have brought Judith to us."

She glanced again at Judith. "But why did Count Petronius choose the Abbey of the Holy Cross to receive your party?"

"There is going to be war between Chilperic and Sigibert." Her face colored slightly. "He feared for my safety, I am afraid. I had spoken to him of the abbey, and he thought it safest to put me out of harm's way." A slight anxiousness crept into her last words,

347

and Agnes's own eyes brightened.

"I see," she said, and from her look Judith perceived that she saw indeed.

"Please," Agnes addressed them all. "Bring your horses this way, our stable boys will take care of them. Then I will show you where to refresh yourselves. After you have rested we will serve you a hearty dinner."

"You are too kind, Sister Agnes. I do not really want to put the abbey to any trouble on my account, especially after what I. . . ." She broke off in embarrassment.

But Agnes patted her hand. "Nonsense, my dear. Father Fortunatus is quite anxious to visit with you as is Mother Radegund. Neither holds anything against you. Indeed, your adventure rather fascinated us all. And I am sorry about the late Queen Galswinth."

"Thank you. It is my regret that her murderer has not been punished."

"Vengeance is the Lord's," said Agnes, surprised at the harsh tone in Judith's voice.

"May it be swift," she replied.

The party gathered for a meal in a private banquet room in the refectory building. The conversation was lively, for Father Fortunatus, still a worldly man in spite of his priestly garb, was anxious for news from Trudulf and Valois. Sister Agnes laughed gaily and chattered with Judith, who thought she perceived a degree of happiness in the abbess that had been lacking before. Mother Radegund presided graciously and serenely, and as usual, the two nuns took only bread and broth, while the guests were served meats in sumptuous cream sauces, succulent fruits and cheeses and plenty of wine. Fortunatus did not abstain from the richer foods, though his portions were moderate.

Judith left most of the conversation to the men, finding it hard to discuss her life at court without mentioning Ivar or Marcus Petronius. She did speak of her investigations into Galswinth's death and how Gregory of Tours had helped her.

"He is an astute man," said Fortunatus. "If anyone can extract a confession from the guilty it will be he."

They questioned her about the unusual cheetah, and she told them it was a gift from Count Gararic, though she did not dwell on the relationship. She told about visiting the estate during a council, and how she was entertained.

"A trader had brought Kahluli from Africa, and left it with Gararic. When he learned I was fond of animals, he thought I should have her and showed me how to train her, for she was very young."

"Animals that young can become quite loyal to their owners," Fortunatus observed. "And you say she saved you from brigands on the road here?"

"Yes," answered Trudulf. "Luckily Judith got to her cage and opened it. At once the cat sprang."

The two nuns crossed themselves, but Fortunatus nodded with interest. "You were fortunate then."

Judith changed the subject, not wanting to linger on the attack. "And how have things been at the abbey?" she inquired.

"Very well," answered Agnes. "Our tenants have had a good year. Our coffers overflow, and we have had many guests such as yourselves. Truly we are blessed."

"Yes," said Fortunatus. "We are fortunate to reside in this corner of the kingdom, where there has been relatively little squabbling between kings."

"And yet," said Agnes, "our Judith was plucked from the road not far from here by Saxon pirates." She gave a little shiver. "You must have a guardian angel, Judith, to have survived so many dangers unhurt."

Judith shook her head, remembering that incident. "I thought I would be killed. Every day I was left alive was like a dream."

Seeing that she was willing to talk about her time among the Saxons, the company pressed her for more, and she told them what she could remember.

"I was given to their chief and taken to my hut to wait for him. Luckily the Saxons love to drink, and the men drank so much that night that liquor was their mistress and not I. In the morning the Franks raided the village, and I was saved." Her eyes brightened as she remembered Marcus riding toward her.

"That was when Count Petronius rescued me," she finished in some embarrassment.

Sister Agnes's eyes were round, her cheeks pink, and she leaned forward as if listening to a poet recite a romantic saga. "Then what happened?"

"He took me to their camp. It was some time before I properly recovered." She shook her head, afraid tears would come to her eyes. "Many good men died that day."

Recounting it all made her think of Ivar, though his image had already grown dim in her mind. She remembered him now rather as a good friend who had shown her what life could hold and then had left her on the hazardous road to make her way alone.

"And Count Petronious brought you back to the court safe and sound."

She nodded. "It was just after that Galswinth died."

There was a moment of silence while each present remembered the dead. Then Fortunatus moved in his high-backed chair.

"And you have continued your studies. I can see

from your writing that your talent has developed."

She cast him an appreciative glance. "It has come in useful, and I did not want to get out of the practice of reading and writing. I used to read to Galswinth, and later to Fredegund."

Fortunatus frowned. "I remember this Fredegund. An ambitious woman. I think Gregory is right. She has an evil streak in her and will destroy many who get in her path."

"She tried to murder her own daughter," said Judith. "Slammed the lid of the treasure chest on her neck and nearly suffocated the girl."

"It is a good thing you left the court, my dear," said Fortunatus. "One day you would find yourself her next victim."

Judith pressed her lips together. She had not let go of her promise to avenge Galswinth's death, and if she were to do that she would have to return to Fredegund's court. But just how, she did not yet know.

That night they all attended vespers, and afterward Sister Agnes strolled through the garden with Judith, seeming to want more time with female company alone. Evening had stolen by, but it was not too dark for Sister Agnes to point out the flower beds and the roses. But like a young girl starved for gossip, Agnes continued their earlier conversation about Judith's adventures.

"This Count Petronius must be very concerned for your welfare to send you to us on the eve of war," she commented.

Judith sighed. "I am lucky," she said. "He did not want to return me to Chilperic's court after rescuing me from the Saxons. He asked me to marry him."

Agnes stopped, gasped, put a hand on Judith's arm. "How wonderful. Marriage is a blessed union."

But Judith had to shake her head, and they continued down the path. "I wanted to go with him, but I could not. I was not satisfied with Galswinth's murderer going unnamed."

"I understand. It was too soon."

"Yes."

"And where is Marcus Petronius now?"

Judith lifted her head, breathing in the scent of the flowers. "Leading an army in the campaign against King Chilperic." She shook her head. "War is such a waste."

"Indeed." Agnes sighed. "Useless killing and slaughter. Oh, Judith, I am so glad you came here. We have missed you so."

Judith smiled, letting her eyes take in the garden that darkness began to shroud. "The roses have climbed much farther up those trellises," she said.

"Father Fortunatus likes to take care of the roses himself," said Sister Agnes.

There was something in her voice that made Judith stop and look at her. "They are very well cared for," she said.

Agnes dropped her eyes and Judith curved her lips in a smile of curiosity. How she wanted to speak of things with Agnes that were not proper for an abbess to know of. And yet, Judith sensed that she did know of them, though just how much, she could not tell. She remembered following Agnes and Fortunatus to the woods and stealing a look at their private time together. Her own later knowledge of love had made her wonder if Agnes and Fortunatus continued such walks, or if his holy office now forbade it. But she knew she dared not approach the subject directly. At the same time she sensed in Agnes a desire to talk and share.

"I see the abbey prospers under Father Fortunatus's

hand," she said.

Agnes smiled, a mixture of serenity and personal warmth. "Yes. Mother Radegund was right. There are many matters that needed the attention of a man. I fear that as abbess, I am not a very strong administrator."

"Then I am glad things have worked out well for you." She was not able to probe matters further, for Fortunatus himself appeared on the path.

"Ah, Sister Agnes and my lady Judith. Having a pleasant evening walk, I see."

Judith did not miss Agnes's look of surprise, as if she had been about to say something Fortunatus should not hear.

"It is indeed pleasant, Father," said Judith. "We were just reminiscing. And Sister Agnes was telling me what a good job you are doing since you took holy orders."

He spread his hands wide. "Undeserved praise I am sure. My life here continues to be blessed with many riches."

Agnes glanced at him quickly, then away. "Would you like to have a look from the wall? The moonlight can make the plain a most lovely view."

Judith was about to accept when she had another thought. Perhaps Agnes and Fortunatus were used to strolling together on the wall themselves at this time of night. She tried to discipline her thoughts. Perhaps she was reading too much into the surreptitious looks exchanged between them and the warmth that might be the result of a deep friendship. Who was to say? But was it not possible that in this lush country that produced such a boon of harvest, the flesh quickened to the stimulation of tart wines, ripe fruits, gentle breezes, and a canopy of stars on a summer night?

Holy orders proscribed the intimacies that warm relationships led to. But as Judith watched the two robust and sensitive individuals standing before her, she thought it would be a great loss were they not to share what she knew could be shared between a man and a woman. Before her thoughts became any more wayward she excused herself.

"I believe I will retire and read by candlelight before I shut my eyes in sleep," she said. "I cannot thank you enough for entertaining us so royally. We must see what we can do for you in exchange tomorrow. Idleness does not sit well with Trudulf or myself."

Agnes smiled. "If it is true that Trudulf wants to remain with us, he will be very useful with the horses. We have a horse that is lame. Prayers have done nothing. Perhaps Trudulf has the gift of healing lame hooves."

Judith returned her smile. "Perhaps indeed. I will speak to him of it."

She left them on the path. But when she reached the hewn stone corner of the gardener's hut, she risked a glance backward as she turned the corner. Fortunatus and Agnes were standing very near each other, smiles upon their faces.

Chapter Twenty-three

Fredegund rode victoriously among her troops, for they had succeeded in recapturing Orléans and were pouring into the city on the heels of Sigibert's retreat. Much to Chilperic's displeasure, she had rallied the troops and ridden with the charge at the far right where she could cheer the men on but remain protected by the soldiers of the flank.

The city held out for a day, then capitulated, helped from the inside by citizens who were ready to betray Sigibert for a price. Now to the cheers of Chilperic's troops, the counts who had led them and the king and queen entered the city triumphantly. There were not many citizens left to lean out of their windows to watch. Most had fled at the approach of the army, fearing the town would be burned and the women raped.

Bodies still littered the streets and were quickly relieved of weapons. Soldiers entered homes and stores, taking their share of the loot, and as evening fell, the revelry was in full sway. The nobles ensconced themselves in the mayor's house, while the soldiers billeted themselves in timber-framed houses, whether or not the occupants remained.

The mayor, who really did not care which of the feuding kings ruled his province, wished only for peace and stability. But he had a great agility when it came to politics. When he had learned that several of the town's administrators were planning to help Chilperic reclaim it, he made sure that if Sigibert prevailed he could show how he had resisted the traitors, but if Chilperic took the day, he would show how he had supported the revolt from within.

Fredegund swelled with newfound power, finding that the counts listened to her now, as her advice was as strategically sound if not more so than Chilperic's. Eventually the armies grew tired of fighting and the remaining cities in question were divided between the feuding kingdoms. Everyone was for the moment satisfied. Fredegund decided on a royal tour of the kingdom and outlined her plans to a tired Chilperic in their chambers one balmy evening.

"Our subjects must see their new queen," she said, pacing back and forth while Chilperic lounged on a sofa, eating from a tray of grapes. "The counts know me and respect me, but I need the loyalty of our people as well. They have heard of their new queen, but now they must see her."

"Most of them did not get to see the last queen," said Chilperic.

Fredegund faced him, hand on hip, her golden hair splaying across her shoulders. "And a good thing they did not. She was weak. You need a powerful consort beside you, my king, if you are to mold this kingdom into something resembling unity."

Chilperic was aware of his wife's cunning and did not disagree. So he shrugged.

"If you want a royal tour, then you shall have it. Perhaps you are right. There are a few unruly counts and bishops it will not hurt to impress with our sovereignty."

And so it was that Chilperic and Fredegund and

their entourage traveled about Neustria that month consolidating relationships with their counts, seeing to tributes due from border tribes, fortifying boundaries and settling administrative difficulties in various parts of their kingdom. At last they approached Poitiers, where Judith watched their train from the city walls with Fortunatus.

They had been standing in the late afternoon sun for some time with an excellent view of the plain over which the royal train curved. How like the first time Judith awaited a royal party, and though it had been almost a year ago, it seemed like yesterday.

Fortunatus squinted into the distance, while at the same time sniffing a rose he held in his hands. He was aware of what Judith must be feeling at this juncture, and he tried to find appropriate words. After all, he was supposed to be her spiritual counselor. And since she had returned to the abbey, they soon found out they shared more than before. Judith had traveled some of the same roads Fortunatus had traveled. Experience and like interest in literature had made them good friends more than priest and parishioner.

"Soon they will be here," said Fortunatus. "I shall have to call on them. I have not seen Chilperic and Fredegund since I retired as court poet and took on holy garb. But you, my dear, need not let them know you are here."

"I don't know," she said slowly. "There are reasons I would like to see Fredegund."

She narrowed her eyes and Fortunatus turned and leaned against the stone wall, still twirling the rose beneath his chin.

"You have not forgiven her for Galswinth's death."

"No."

He sighed. "There is very little you can do about it,"

he said gently. "Though I do understand how you feel."

"Do you?" she said. Then she glanced at him through thick lashes. "I'm sorry, Father. I do not mean to be disrespectful."

"It's all right, child. Queen Fredegund is something to be dealt with. But until she herself sees her own flaws, there is nothing the rest of us can do for her."

"You speak as a spiritual counselor. But there is the law. She could be punished."

He shook his head, turning to look again at the royal train snaking its way toward them.

"Do not fool yourself. Even your silken cord is not enough evidence to pin the murder on her. She will have covered her crimes. She has gained too much power, I am afraid. You would only endanger your own life were you to embroil yourself in it again."

Judith did not answer, but continued to stare at the plain. The last weeks at the abbey had been something she needed, though she did not know it when she had first arrived here. The abbey walls shut out the tribulations and violence of the world and allowed one to heal both inwardly and outwardly. She had spent long hours talking to Agnes and Fortunatus, working in the gardens and in the scriptorium, finding physical tasks an outlet for confused emotions and the fatigue of life at court.

At the same time, she had had time to meditate on all that had happened to her since she had left here. The spiritual retreat had been greatly needed. How wise of Marcus to have sent her here.

Dear Marcus. He wrote faithfully from his duties with King Sigibert, and though the letters were often delayed, they arrived. All filled her with sweet delight and longing. And yet Marcus, too, seemed patient with her need to rest, to think, to consider her life. He spoke of love, of a future by her side, and yet he did not press her, as if he, too, had some plans that he wanted to put into action before he could take the step of marriage and life away from court.

And so both spent long hours writing to each other, and Judith enclosed some of her poetry in her letters to Marcus. Other poetry she shared with Fortunatus, who was pleased with his protégée. She knew in her heart that Marcus would come for her when the time was right and when she was ready to go. That time might have been sooner rather than later had it not been for Chilperic's approach to the city. As Fortunatus said, she herself did not have to make her presence known. But given the chance to speak to Fredegund once more, she began to see how she would use it.

Her own plan followed perfectly after all. When the court rested at Poitiers, Fortunatus went to call on the king and queen, who, of course, remembered him from his days as court poet. He entered their august presence garbed in the robes of his holy office, his hair now tonsured, a satin stole flowing gracefully across his shoulders and down his cream-colored robe. Rubies and garnets still flashed from rings on his fingers, and a heavy gold cross, set with ivory and sapphire hung from a gold chain about his neck.

The guards who escorted him stood aside as he approached the dais upon which Chilperic and Fredegund sat. He strode forward, smiling congenially and then bowed.

"You are welcome, Fortunatus," said Chilperic extending a hand to raise him up. "Don't lower yourself. Now that you have taken holy vows, surely you are our spiritual superior."

Fortunatus nodded humbly, gesturing gracefully with the beringed hands. "My lord and lady. I am God's representative on earth, it is true, but I am still your subject. You treated me well when I was in your court."

"Ah, Fortunatus," said Fredegund. "Still the honeyed tongue. What the court lost, the church has gained. I only hope your talents are appreciated in that sphere."

Chilperic rose and stepped down. "Do you partake of wine?"

"Of course," said Fortunatus.

"Then let us drink to your health while you tell us of your conversion and your duties at the Abbey of the Holy Cross."

"Most certainly."

They toasted and drank, then Chilperic led Fortunatus to a couch where they sat comfortably. Fredegund took a seat in an ivory chair across from them.

"My duties are many and varied, and I am quite happy. No more dusty roads traveling here and there. I am needed to oversee the estates of the abbey and to advise Mother Superior on many matters, especially financial ones."

"How is my aunt Radegund?" said Chilperic. "I shall look forward to seeing her."

"She is well, though she keeps to herself more and more. She spends much time in solitary now. She was never one to contemplate this world."

"A pity," said Chilperic. "Though I respect her wishes. She was a fine woman and a very good queen."

Fortunatus reflected for a moment on the difference between the self-effacing, charitable queen Radegund and the haughty one sitting across from him now, but he said nothing.

"If we must be deprived of your court poetry," said

Fredegund, "then surely we will be treated to one of your sermons. We shall attend your church to hear you, if you will have us."

Fortunatus's lips curved in a pleased smile. "God's house is open to the most high as well as the most lowly. Before him all are equal. I shall be honored to have the king and queen attend my humble service as will be the nuns at the abbey."

Fredegund smiled her catlike smile, her own bejeweled hands twisting through a necklace of beads on her chest.

"Then we will come."

The sun streamed in the windows of the church at the Abbey of the Holy Cross, crowded with the entourage of King Chilperic and Queen Fredegund who had come to hear Father Fortunatus preach. The hymns were sung, some of Fortunatus's own composing, the liturgy and responses intoned, and now all sat down to hear the sermon.

Fortunatus climbed the curved steps and stood at the lectern, looking at his flock of nuns and the royal visitors, complacence on their faces. That complacence would not last, thought Fortunatus, as he rested one arm on the lectern and leaned forward, addressing not a congregation, but every individual singly.

"Earth is a prison, and we are slaves," he thundered at them. "The way to spiritual freedom lies in knowledge. Knowledge that you are spiritual beings, not one with the flesh you inhabit. We identify too strongly with the human body and along with that identification comes a desire to control other humans. Think you that by making a slave of another, you gain superiority? No!"

He shot out a finger and stabbed it into the heart of the gathering, all of whom were stunned at his forceful beginning. They had become used to Fortunatus's colorful and poetic sermons meditating on all there was to be thankful for, peppered as they usually were with literary allusions and beautiful images. This raving was unlike him.

"Some among you have sinned. Who has not? For we are not perfect beings. We err even in our desire to do good. But it is those among us who desire not to do good but to do evil who I challenge today. Come forth and confess your evil, your lust for power."

On the last word his eyes settled on Fredegund, who met his stare, her own eyes large, her skin prickling under her linen mantle. As Fortunatus continued on his harangue it was clear what he was about, and she began to grind her teeth. He continued for some time exhorting those who had sinned to examine their hearts. His milky-blue eyes roamed about the church. For a time he turned to softer allusions, speaking of the glories that accompanied true spiritual knowledge, of the spiritual freedom that awaited seekers of truth, admonishing those who were concerned for the comfort of fleshly bodies only.

"You are not your bodies," he continued. "You are spirits. Who is it that decides to move the body? Who is it that looks at the images in your mind? Who, that reaps treachery on yourself in exchange for treachery done?"

Then he leaned both hands on the lectern and looked straight at Fredegund.

"Yea, I say, there are even murderers among us."

A gasp floated through the congregation, and at that moment a lark flew in the open door at the back of the church. One of the nuns pointed to it, then all eyes turned as the lark flew about. Hands went to mouths and chests as the lark began to fly from one oil lamp to the other. As it passed, the lamps were extinguished.

"A sign," said Sister Agnes, who sat at the front of the choir. "A sign," echoed the other nuns.

Fredegund was on her feet, facing Fortunatus, who stared her down. It might have been only the two of them, for all they paid attention to the rest of those who watched with eyes bulged and hearts beating like the wings of the lark.

"Repent," shouted Fortunatus. "Repent before you are excommunicated."

Judith held her breath as she watched from her place. But Fredegund stood, her back stiff as the lark continued to circle, extinguishing the lamps. Then she turned, grasping her mantle in her hand and walked quickly down the aisle, her expression black, her head held high and haughty.

Judith swallowed and glanced again at Fortunatus who still leaned over the lectern, following Fredegund with his eyes. After she had left the church, he slowly pulled himself up and drew a deep breath, which he expelled through his nostrils.

"Repent," he said, this time more softly. "So that your sins do not rest heavily on your heart alone. Confess your sins to those you have sinned against. For know that man is basically good and wants to be free of his sin. And if one you love confesses his sins to you, accept them, wrap them in a bundle, and throw them over your shoulder. Wipe the slate clean and start anew in all goodness."

When the service concluded, Judith followed the others out. But she no longer hid from Fredegund. If the queen saw her and asked what she was doing at the abbey, she was ready to explain.

Fredegund went to the stables and demanded her horse. She was so angry at Fortunatus, she did not recognize Trudulf, who was surprised by her sudden appearance on Sunday when everyone else was in church or preparing for the midday meal. But he saddled and bridled her horse without saying anything.

It was not until she sat on her bay steed, looking down on him in the shadows of the stables that he felt her gaze resting longer than it needed to.

"Don't I know you?" she said.

Trudulf took a step backward and met her gaze. "I formerly worked in your stables, madam."

Her horse stamped a foot impatiently. "And what are you doing here?"

"I have decided to serve the holy mother Radegund. I felt a need to be in a place of solace."

Fredegund smirked. "In a house of nuns?"

Trudulf withstood the barb and let go the horse's bridle. Fredegund chuckled.

"Enjoy your holy house," she said. "Far be it from me to recall you to duty at court. Others serve as well."

And dismissing the man from her mind she gouged her horse's side with her heel and rode out, leaving by the side gate to the countryside and flicking her horse into a run to give vent to her anger at Fortunatus for condemning her from the pulpit.

Judith did not see Fredegund leave, and so after the midday meal, she, too, went to the stables to take Black Lady for a ride. Trudulf told her of his meeting with the queen.

"She was in an evil mood," he said as he pulled the straps beneath Black Lady's belly.

"That is because Fortunatus accused her in church of murder."

Trudulf straightened, his eyebrows arched. "Did he now?"

"A lark flew in and extinguished all the lamps. Everyone took it as a sign, and she left the church."

"Then she is guilty," he said thoughtfully.

"I knew she was," said Judith as Trudulf led Black Lady to the mounting block so she could seat herself in the sidesaddle.

Then Trudulf went to fetch his own horse. "I will ride with you," he said. "If you run into Fredegund in the woods, I would fear what she might do."

Judith smiled. "She could hardly harm me in broad daylight."

Trudulf eyed her. "I would not be so sure of that."

But Judith did not protest the company. It was a fine day. The wheat was ripe and golden in the fields, awaiting harvest. The abbey was sleepy, and they rode out the gate, taking a path that led close to the brook where birds flew low over the silver water.

They exercised their horses where the land was gently rolling, then they stopped to rest, hobbling the horses where they could graze on the rich grass. Judith and Trudulf walked into the shade of the woods, examining the trees for wild berries. And so they came to a peaceful clearing and decided to sit in the shade and rest, their backs against a large rock outcropping.

But they were not alone. A pool of water was fed from the brook on the other side of the rock, and voices carried to where Judith and Trudulf sat.

"Listen," whispered Judith. "Do you hear someone?"

Both listened intently for some moments and then Trudulf frowned at Judith. Leaning closer, so their own voices were covered he said softly, "I do hear voices. They might be brigands. Let us go before we are discovered."

But the voices came, sharper now, and feet rustled in leaves by the pool. Trudulf and Judith were hidden by the rock and by overhanging boughs, but Judith grasped his arm and lifted a finger to her lips. If they moved now, they would be discovered. But there was another reason for her stillness. The voice speaking on the other side of the rock was none other than Fredegund's, and she did little to keep her voice from carrying to where Trudulf and Judith huddled, so still they did not even breathe.

"Here is the dagger you must use," said Fredegund. "The poison is encrusted in the incised figures that are engraved from end to end of the blade. Keep it safe until you are in Sigibert's tent, and then do the deed. Your families will be well cared for in the event you do not escape. Here is half your payment in advance. When I hear that King Sigibert is dead, the other half will go to your homes. Do you understand?"

There was a chink as coins were tossed from hand to hand, and Judith and Trudulf stared at each other. They had just heard Fredegund's latest plot to kill King Sigibert. If they were discovered, she would have them killed first.

"We leave at once," came a gruff voice, one of the assassins.

Fortunately the pool separated them from where Fredegund and her hirelings stood, and when they heard the rustle of footsteps in the leaves, they perceived that the others were going away. Still, Judith and Trudulf remained silent for some time to make sure the others were gone. Finally, Trudulf leaned carefully around the rock. Then he sat back with a sigh.

"They are gone, the other way, thank goodness. But we must hurry to the horses and get out of here in case they circle around and suspect we have heard."

They got to their feet and hastened back through the trees to where they had hobbled the horses. Looking quickly about, but not seeing anyone, they freed the horses' feet and mounted up, then they rode along the path the way they had come. When they approached the city once more, Judith pulled beside Trudulf.

"It is clear what we must do," she said, still glancing about to see where Fredegund might appear again. "We must get word to Marcus. He will stop them. One of us must go."

Trudulf shook his head. "If I go, it will arouse suspicion. Fredegund has already confronted me in the stables. I persuaded her I felt the call to serve a religious house. If I suddenly leave, she will suspect something. And you cannot go. It would be too dangerous. We must send someone."

"But who?"

"I will find a messenger who can ride fast. It's too bad we did not get a look at the assassins so he will know who to look for. But do not worry. I know where to find my man."

Judith returned to the abbey, but Trudulf went off to town. As soon as she emerged from the stables and headed across the quadrangle, she encountered Fredegund. The woman appeared unexpectedly from the cloister walk, two female companions with her that Judith did not know.

"So, this is where you have got off to. I thought I spied you in the church this morning. I suppose you, too, have felt a call to serve this religious order?"

Judith stopped, knowing full well what Fredegund's slur referred to, but she did not rise to the bait.

"How nice to see you, my lady," said Judith in all humility. "As you may know, I was raised in this abbey,

367

and when the wars broke out, I decided it would be safest here."

"With your lover?" queried Fredegund.

Judith managed a quick smile. "He thought it best. He . . . went to fight with the army."

"I see," said Fredegund, more acrimonious now.

For a moment they faced each other, and Judith sensed the battle of wills. But she exuded what charm she could muster.

"I have missed my friends at court. I hope the queen and king are in the best of health."

"We have our health," answered Fredegund. "And as to your friends, they seem to have run off with prospective husbands, from what I can gather. Perhaps it is well that I am rid of the lot of you."

Judith warmed, but hoped that her reference meant that Mosella and Clothild had left the court for greener pastures.

"Then I wish them well," she said, not to be cowed by the goading queen.

"You would," said Fredegund, and with a toss of the head, she moved on.

Only as Judith crossed the quadrangle, did she allow herself to tremble. She felt as if Fredegund saw right through her and knew she had been listening to her meeting with the assassins. But that was impossible. By now Trudulf would have sent his messenger on his way. There was little else she could do.

Several hours later, one of the nuns spotted a horse walking toward the town. Tied to its back was what appeared to be a man. Concern was at once roused and townspeople and nuns alike went out to the road. Horrified news spread quickly. The man was dead, his throat slit.

Judith was with Kahluli when she heard the news.

She quickly put the cheetah back in her cage and rushed to the gates where the man was being brought in. She nearly collided with Trudulf as the body was untied and laid out. The blood had dried on his clothes, and Judith felt nausea threaten. Then she froze. She felt rather than heard Trudulf's words.

"It's him," he said, then slid his gaze sideways to Judith.

It took only a moment for her to grasp the meaning. Then she seized his arm.

"Quickly," she said. "Meet me in the stables."

Trudulf's messenger had been caught. His death was obviously a signal. There was not a moment to lose. Judith fled to her quarters and gathered a few things, fastening them to her girdle, then as calmly as she could, she walked to the stable where Trudulf was busy preparing the horses.

"She knows," hissed Judith, moving close to him.

Even then they both kept their eyes trained on shadowy corners of the stables, waiting for thugs to jump out at them.

"She knows a messenger was sent," said Trudulf. "She might not know who sent him."

"We can't take that chance," said Judith.

At last she was ready to flee. Her solitary reflections had come to an end. Fredegund was an all-powerful menace in her life and in the lives of many, and Judith knew at last that it was best to remove herself as far as possible from the evil queen's influence.

Valois had already returned to the Austrasian kingdom. Trudulf and Judith would have to travel on their own. She went to fetch Kahluli, who would now ride on Black Lady's back without a cage, only the chain fastened to her collar.

"Quickly, Kahluli," whispered Judith as she removed

the cheetah from the cage. "Be a good girl, now."

With the chain secured, the cat came as docilely as a domesticated pet, which Judith would never be fooled into thinking she was.

When she returned to the stables, Trudulf had everything ready. Judith stopped then, realizing they were fleeing without telling anyone of their departure.

"I must say goodbye to Sister Agnes," she said suddenly. "If we simply disappear, everyone will look for us, and that will draw Fredegund's attention."

"Be quick then. There is no time to lose." He tied his weapons onto the saddle.

She left Kahluli in Trudulf's care and ran back to the cloister walk, casting about for where Sister Agnes would be. At this hour she might be in her study, going over accounts, and Judith headed that way.

Her luck was with her, for Sister Anna said the abbess was in and led Judith in. Sister Agnes looked up from her ledgers and put down her quill pen.

"Judith. What brings you here?"

Judith moved closer to the large desk. "I must leave," she said in a low voice. "At once."

Agnes rose and came around the desk. "Why, pray tell."

"Trudulf sent a messenger to King Sigibert warning him that Fredegund intends to have him assassinated. The messenger turned up dead, his throat slit, a sign that he was found out. If Fredegund finds out who sent the messenger, Trudulf and I are no longer safe. We must ride tonight."

Agnes was stunned, but she grasped the significance of the matter and embraced Judith.

"Farewell then. Travel safely. I will inform Mother Radegund and Father Fortunatus. I will see that no one at the abbey answers any inquiries from the palace

370

as to your whereabouts. There are times when silence is the greatest good."

She folded her hands righteously. Judith squeezed those hands. "Thank you, Sister. Thank you for everything."

They took time for one more hug, then Judith turned and hurried out. By the time she reached the stables, twilight had fallen, aiding them to leave unobtrusively by the gates to the fields. Finally, Judith sat upon Black Lady, Kahluli perched behind. Trudulf looked at her from his mount, which also carried bags of food and supplies.

"Are you ready then?"

"Yes," she said.

And they walked their horses out of the stables and behind the abbey outbuildings. The gatekeeper let them out, unconcerned with the reasons for their leaving, and they took a path that skirted the fields and did not join up to the main road for some distance.

Chapter Twenty-four

Trudulf knew the route his unlucky messenger had taken, and so they avoided going that way. They kept to tracks through the woods and cut across fields. They talked little, rode steadily, and did not stop the first night until it was too dark to see. Then they slept in a barn at an out of the way farmstead, where they paid for their lodging, though it took some persuasion to explain that Kahluli would not kill any of the livestock if she were well fed with raw meat and she was kept on her chain.

They were up and on their way before dawn, and rode persistently the second day. The hours passed with little thought, and Judith's body was so sore, it was all she could do to concentrate on staying mounted and staying alert to Kahluli's moods. Their route was circuitous enough that they avoided being followed, but Trudulf was not fool enough to relax his guard. Once Fredegund discovered they had left Poitiers, she would no doubt suspect where they might have gone, and their lives would be forfeited if they were careless. They cut through the countryside and into Burgundy, where Sigibert's army was encamped.

They came out of the woods on a rise where a peasant was leading his cow by a long rope. He stopped to stare at them, and Judith reined in, realizing he would be frightened to see a spotted cat on the rump of her horse.

"Good day," said Trudulf. "We are travelers and mean no harm. Have you news of the Austrasian army?"

"Encamped over that next rise, they are," answered the farmer. "If that's where yer headed, you'll run into 'em. Taken over these parts they have. Spread out over that valley yonder."

"Many thanks."

And they spurred on, bounding through the grass. At last they stood on the top of a hill and paused to look at the sight of an army encamped. Tents were arranged in a semblance of order behind a deep trench dug around the camp. There seemed to be much activity and movement around the tent over which flew the king's banners. The central gate to the camp was left without a trench but with a gate of peeled logs.

They hastened down the hill. When they approached the gate, the guard came out to question them.

"We've come from Neustria," said Trudulf. "With an urgent message for Count Marcus Petronius."

"From Neustria, ay?" He scratched his chin. "And what are your names?"

"Tell Count Petronius the lady Judith has arrived and former Count of the Stables Trudulf of Chalon."

It turned out there was no need of an announcement. At that moment a group of riders was seen at the top of the hill from which they had just come, but farther to the west. Leading the group was a rider on a white horse. It took Judith only a moment to see that Marcus looked down on them. At once her heartbeat quickened. Even from this distance she saw his noble bearing, the sun glinting on his copper hair, and she felt as if she saw his eyes and read his face.

"We're too late," she breathed. The knowledge was

quick, certain, transmitted across the distance between Marcus and herself. Then she spoke out loud to Trudulf.

"We've come too late," she said. "The king is dead."

Trudulf spoke down to the guard, who also watched Marcus's approach.

"You there. We have knowledge of assassins. Is King Sigibert alive or dead?"

"Dead," said the guard. "Two men snuck into the camp while the king slept and did their nasty business. One was caught, the other escaped. That patrol went after them."

"Too late," said Judith again, stunned at the news.

Trudulf cursed. For all their hard riding, the assassins had beat them.

"I should have come myself instead of sending a messenger," he said, getting down from his horse. He held Kahluli's chain while Judith dismounted.

"Don't blame yourself," she said, touching his shoulder. "If you had gone, you would be dead by now."

"Perhaps not, and King Sigibert would be alive."

"It is fruitless to think so."

They turned at the sound of Marcus's voice, for he had ridden up, his eyes bright. He got off his horse and strode toward them.

"We caught the other assassin," he said, "and hung him."

The three of them looked at each other. Finally Marcus took a step closer.

"It's over. But I am surprised to see you here."

Now that she was in Marcus's presence and the hard riding and anxiety of being followed was behind her, she started to shake. She could not think of words to say, but Marcus put an arm around her, seeing her start to crumble.

"Come, both of you into my tent and tell me what you know."

After being given water for sponge baths and clean clothes to put on, the new arrivals were offered a meal of fruit, bread, meat, and wine. When they had sated themselves, Trudulf and Judith told Marcus what had happened.

"It is a black day, indeed," Marcus commented. "Sigibert is dead. There will be a royal funeral, and Brunhild will rule as queen of Austrasia now."

The food and wine seeped through Judith's limbs, and though the mood was a tragic one, all she wanted to do was sleep. Marcus spread rugs on his camp bed for her and led her to it.

"You look as if you could use some rest," he said, brushing her hair off her brow. "You did your best, my brave one."

And he dropped a kiss on her forehead. A look of love passed over his eyes, but since they were not alone, Marcus said no more, but lowered her to the bed.

"Trudulf can come with me to inform the other leaders. Then we will prepare to remove Sigibert's body to the church of Saint Médard at Soissons."

While the camp bustled around the tent, Judith fell into a badly needed slumber. It was evening when she awoke. She sat up as Marcus entered the tent, and the look of heavy responsibility on his brow relaxed when he saw her.

"Feeling better?"

He crossed the small space and sat on the edge of the camp bed. She raised herself on her elbow and smiled sleepily.

"Much better. How long did I sleep?"

"Several hours."

Then his arms slid under her waist, he lifted her to a

375

sitting position and she fell gladly against him. For a moment they said nothing, just held each other. Then he kissed her temple.

"You are with me at last," he whispered.

She nodded, then met his kiss, long, lovingly, and tender. Alone at last, the blood began to flow and their embrace deepened. Marcus lowered her to the bed and began long awaited for caresses. But when his hand slid under her tunic, she shyly protested.

"What if someone comes in?" she whispered.

"No one will enter," he said. "I have a guard posted outside."

She protested no longer, but met his embrace with all of her own desire. In moments their clothing was shed and as darkness fell about them, they lay together, reveling in something they had both needed for a very long time. No words were spoken, but love and desire blossomed as they found themselves at last where they were meant to be, in each other's arms.

After the fulfillment of their passion, Marcus held her against him, her side nestled into his chest, her hand on his side, feeling his even breathing and the feathering his breath caused her hair.

"Let us walk outside," Marcus said after a while. "The evening air will feel refreshing."

They rose, dressed, then walked through the camp to the gate. Marcus addressed the guard.

"We will be walking on the hill."

"Do you wish to have an escort?" asked the guard.

"No," said Marcus. "We will be within earshot of the camp and I feel there is no danger."

He led her up the track, and with the campfires of the army dotting the plain behind them, they walked up the hill, breathing in the fresh night air.

For a long time nothing was said, and when they

reached the top Judith turned and looked over the plain, past the firelight, into the distance, seeing many things, seeing the past and seeing the future somehow vaguely.

"Have you healed your heart and mind yet?" Marcus asked.

She looked at him, understanding something of what he meant. "If you mean have I gotten over Galswinth's death, I am not sure how to answer. I know I cannot bring her back. What happened was her own fate; in the end I could not change it."

Marcus put an arm loosely around her shoulders. "Wise words. What a person pulls into himself in this life is his own doing. Help though we try, we cannot always change what a person has written for himself."

"Yes," she said, nestling closer to Marcus. "I think I see that now. My own life has had many interesting twists, has it not?"

All of a sudden her throat caught and she thought again of the people she had known and loved so well, and then she felt the love and security emanating from Marcus, who stood beside her. He turned her slowly in his arms.

"Are you ready to begin anew then?" he asked gently, almost afraid she would not answer as he wished, so used was he to her stubborn refusals.

She shut her eyes. "I know that I am not as powerful as Queen Fredegund, and though I do not understand why, she cannot be stopped." She opened her eyes and sighed. "She will never admit to the death of Galswinth. Father Gregory was right. She has no conscience."

Marcus slid his hands up to her shoulders. "Come with me. I am tired of this land and I know where a kinder civilization lies. I have served my king, and now he, too, is dead. Would it not be better to begin our lives anew in Byzantium?"

"Byzantium?" The name evoked a faraway place, one she had heard little of.

"What is left of the remnants of Rome is there. Three generations of Frankish kings have corrupted the Roman Peace that once blessed Gaul," said Marcus. "We will never rest here, because Fredegund will not forget."

Looking into Marcus's stern eyes, she knew it was true. Fredegund would never let them rest. Perhaps it was time to make a break with the past. Leave what there was here behind.

"But your family?" she asked. "Your lands."

"My cousins will take care of them. I have spent several months arranging it. If the day comes when the Frankish kingdom learns to live in peace, we can return. But I do not know if that day will come in our present lifetime."

Emotion overwhelmed her. She knew she would go with him this time. Then behind Marcus a bright star blazed in the sky. It shone brilliantly, then arched through the black night, shooting through the other diamondlike points of light.

Judith creased her brow. "Which way is Byzantium?"

"From here?"

"Yes," she nodded. "From here."

Marcus turned, looked at the night sky and got his bearings. Then he pointed in the direction the star had fallen.

"That way," he said.

Judith's heart filled with certainty and she smiled at him.

"Then we shall go there," she said at last.

Epilogue

Bishop Gregory held up the oil lamp and drew it along the line of bound volumes of parchment that rested on a shelf in his library. Many years had passed since he had begun this work, and he mumbled to himself as he looked at the titles painted in gold leaf on the leather-covered boards sewn around the pages that made up each volume. When he came to the one he wanted, he smiled to himself and set down the lamp.

Pulling the heavy tome off the shelf, he carried it to his writing desk, his step a little slower, and his shoulders a little more hunched than they used to be. He lowered the heavy volume to the top of the desk, which was slanted to better see the pages he scribbled upon when he got the chance. Though his duties over the years had increased, he had never forgotten his history. He was devoted to it. This particular volume he remembered, told of the rise of Queen Fredegund and the death of King Sigibert. That was a long time ago now.

He moved the lamp closer and squinted at the pages as he opened the book. Yes, here was one of the few joyous parts he had recorded. After the lady Judith had been reunited with Count Marcus Petronius, they had sewn jewels and coins into the lining of plain cloaks and at night, the wind billowing their cloaks behind them, they had ridden south and east to Marseilles, where they boarded a ship.

They knew that if captured by the Vandals, who ruled the southern shores of the Mediterranean from their kingdoms in Africa, they would be sold as slaves. But they had accepted the risk. Gregory envisioned them watching for pirates from the deck of the ship, every moment together even more precious.

But they had come to no harm. And a year later, he received a letter from them. They had sailed into the gleaming port of Constantinople with its resplendent domes, where they were welcomed at the Byzantine court and began a new life.

As for Fredegund, she had taken lovers, murdered, battled, and ruled into a ripe old age and was buried with honors. She had not been punished for her sins in this life, but Gregory knew that darkness and misery would rule her next life. Her feud with Brunhild had torn the Merovingian kingdoms apart until at last Brunhild had been tied by the hair, one arm and one leg to a horse and had been killed by its hooves as it galloped.

Gregory let the pages fall shut, and pushed the volume away. He sighed and bent forward, taking up his stylus. Not much time left. He knew that his life was coming to a close. He dipped the stylus into the ink jar and scratched out:

I have written this work to keep alive the memory of those dead and gone, to bring them to the notice of future generations. My style is not very polished, and I have had to devote much of my space to the quarrels between the wicked and the righteous.

He paused and thought of what this age of change might mean to future generations. And with the acorns still unripe on the oak trees outside his window, Gregory laid down his pen.

The End

The End

Author's Note

The Dark Ages (roughly the time between the last Roman emperor in the west, deposed in 476 A.D., and William the Conqueror's invasion of England in 1066 A.D.) is fast becoming rich ground for researchers and novelists alike.

Of all the barbarian tribes, the Franks most emulated the Romans. The reign of the Merovingian dynasty, which spans the time between the retreat of Rome from Europe and the rise of Charlemagne, is a curious mixture of savagery, cunning, and a democratic spirit.

The ancestor of the Merovingians was a minor chieftain, Merovech, whose band of warriors fought with other German tribes against Attila the Hun. Attila lost interest in Gaul, and Merovech's little band inherited the battle-scarred land.

Two generations later, Merovech's grandson, Clovis, managed to unify the squabbling Frankish tribes into a kingdom with one leader. His history is one of brutal conquest and, at his wife's request, conversion to Christianity. Throughout all this conflict, some of the old Gallo-Roman families managed to keep their estates, for Clovis left Roman administrative systems in place.

The Merovingians had a habit of dividing the land among all the sons upon the death of the father, so the map of Gaul changed with each succeeding generation. This policy gave rise to much dispute, further brutality, and battle.

No less ambitious and ruthless were Chilperic's infamous queen, Fredegund, and his brother Sigibert's queen, Brunhild. Both women outlived and outfought their husbands, riding at the head of armies, their feud lasting for thirty years.

Fortunately, we have two eyewitnesses. Gregory of Tours recorded the history of his times, and his writings have survived. Venantius Fortunatus began life as a court poet. He then settled down, took holy vows, and lived out his life as priest at the Abbey of the Holy Cross. His writings, too, illuminate the times — with the births, deaths, and marriages of kings and queens in early years and later with the flowers, fruits, and presents given and received, and with the taste of food prepared for him by the nuns of the Holy Cross.

The Merovingian tendency toward licentiousness and debauchery finally weakened the line. Meanwhile, the mayor of the palace, an office that was handed down from father to son in the house of Pepin, became the power behind the throne. During the latter century of the Merovingian dynasty, it was the mayors of the palace who actually ruled the kingdom. By that time, the long-haired Merovingian kings were trotted out only as figureheads, for the descendants of Clovis still held the loyalty of the people.

Finally in 753 A.D., Pepin usurped the throne, and the Carolingian dynasty came to power. The future Charlemagne was then eight years old.